RAMSHACKLE

Raegan of Ruin Book Three

A. L. Rook

PLAYLIST

BRN - Aviva
Jet Black Heart - Arrows to Athens
Bulletproof [feat. XYLO] - The Score
Panic Room - Au/Ra
Numb Without You - The Maine
human - Christina Perri
You Are The Reason - Calum Scott
How Villains Are Made - Madalen Duke
My Name Is.. - Once Monsters
On My Own - Ashes Remain
Rescue Me - Alesso
Stronger (feat. Kesha) - Sam Feldt
Hallelujah (I'm Not Dead) - Citizen Soldier
Champions - Kurt Hugo Schneider
Warrior - Atreyu
Finish Line - SATV Music
Follow You - Imagine Dragons
Little Do You Know - Alex & Sierra
Don't You Know - Jaymes Young
Iris - Goo Goo Dolls
Animals - Maroon 5
Just Pretend - Bad Omens
Don't Threaten Me With a Good Time - Panic! At The Disco
Can't Stop Me - State of Mine
Monster - Willyecho
Clarity [feat. Foxes] - Zedd
Love You Still - Tyler Shaw
Say You Won't Let Go - James Arthur
Slow - The Diviners
Supahuman - Michael Hodges

Listen on Spotify

TABLE OF CONTENTS

Chapter One

Kellan

Lightning slams into me before I can reach Raegan, electricity binding my muscles so I'm a prisoner in my body. The sharp, stinging pain that strikes indiscriminately is nothing compared to the sight of my girl's hand in Gordon's as they walk toward a portal that leads to fuck-knows-where.

Move, goddammit!

I draw on a desperate attempt to somehow break free of this bastard's gift long enough to get to her. But it's like all communication between my brain and body has been severed, and I'm forced to watch the son of a bitch who hurt Raegan smirk gleefully as he takes her from me.

From us.

Get your filthy fucking hand off her! I'm furious that I can't open my jaw to say anything. If I could at least get something out, I might be able to buy us more time. Or convince Raegan to take down Sparky and then we can all fight Gordon and the portal girl.

The pain isn't enough to draw my gift out, though I have no fucking idea if it repels electricity or not even if I did have it active. I'm not burning and nothing's broken skin, which means my scales are useless right now.

Raegan steps in front of the portal, and I scream at her internally. *Don't go. Don't leave. Fight, beautiful!*

She turns and looks at me.

Hope blooms in my chest until I notice her expression.

No...

Her sad, but determined look is shared with the others as she gazes past me before it softens at the end. She blinks and takes the final step, disappearing before my eyes.

RAEGAN!

Heat scorches through my veins, burning me from the inside. My body quakes, fighting off the lightning's hold. She's not gone yet. The portal's still open, and I can still bring her back to this side.

My boot scratches against the sand.

"Holt, did that guy move?" The girl who conjured the portal points at me.

Sparky frowns. He curls his fingers on his raised hand, and a new rush of electricity swarms through me, sinking in deeper until my heart and lungs stall.

"Make sure you don't kill him or Gordon will be upset with you," the girl quips, but this time, it's more of an echo as my mental alarm bells are ringing that I'm about to be done for and there's shit-all I can do about it.

It feels like minutes pass, but it must be mere seconds before the lightning ends abruptly and I drop to the hard and rocky beach face-first. Air fills my lungs, and I choke and gasp on it in my rush to breathe again while my heart's trying to find its rhythm.

My muscles twitch and jump involuntarily, still working through the remnants of electricity until it finally peters out.

I dig my fingers into the sand, fisting a handful of it as I catch my breath.

The portal. It's gone.

She's gone.

I shove to my feet, swaying to the side and then staggering forward to where it was.

"Kellan," Aiden calls out from behind me, but I can't even consider doing anything else until I've checked that spot. Maybe she left a clue behind like Jack had at the firehouse.

The area reveals nothing. No lingering *something* in the air, no trace of anything in the sand.

A growing ache in my chest pulsates with every thump of my heart.

Though I don't know how it's still beating when it feels like it's been ripped out, leaving me hollow and incomplete.

"Dane!"

I follow Vera's voice reluctantly as she pounces on him with a hug. Dane doesn't react immediately. It takes a second for whatever is on his mind to be put on hold before he hesitantly raises his arms and then wraps them slowly around his sister.

"Vera," he breathes, his voice muffled by her shoulder as they hold each other.

I ball my hands into fists. I take a step toward them, ready to unleash my anger on her—

"Kell!" Aiden demands sharply, and I snap my head around to follow his voice.

He and Reid are kneeling in front of someone in the shed.

Oh, shit.

Jackson.

I turn and run.

Aiden peers at the blood on his hand. "He needs a healer. Pick him up and we'll all head back."

"What are you going to do about Raegan?" Reid inquires, his stoic tone edged with something more.

It's suspicious as hell, and I narrow my eyes at him. "Get her back, of course. What's it matter to you?"

"She was the reason you'd asked for my help in coming here. If you're still going after her, then I'll continue to assist you until you get her back." His blue eyes slide to Dane and Vera's mini reunion, his expression darkening before returning his gaze to Aiden. "And Vera?"

I carefully slide my arms under Jackson, cursing at the wetness I feel, and lift him as Aiden replies, "She's coming with us."

"To the bunker?" Reid presses.

"No. Back to the firehouse."

I can't read his face very well, but I can almost feel the relief from him at Aiden's answer. He'd said something about Vera at the library, hadn't he? I can't remember now, but it doesn't matter because the point is moot. We can't put the Guild in danger by bringing Vera to it.

Aiden faces the open doorway. "Dane! We're leaving. Now."

Dane grabs Vera's hand, pulling her behind him as they jog into the shed.

We crowd around each other, making sure everyone has a point of contact with someone before Reid's gift activates. The moment our feet land in Old Red from Reid's teleportation gift, it's chaos.

"Get him on his bed and strip him. Reid, bring Cassandra here. Dane, stay with Vera in the living room."

The firehouse is still a mess from the attack. We didn't waste time fixing anything after putting the fire out. We'd called Reid down here immediately so we could follow them with the clue Jackson left us once he flew away with Raegan and Thorne.

Jack is motionless in my arms. He hasn't moved once since we got to the island, where he was unconscious in the shed behind Raegan. I do as Aiden ordered and carry him to his room to set him on his bed. Snatching a pair of scissors, I roughly cut up the middle of his hoodie. It's a pain in the ass because of all the knives he has stored there, so I keep angling the scissors to go around them until I reach the end.

Carefully, I extract his arms from the sleeves and roll him out of it without cutting him further. Not that a few small nicks would mean anything at this point.

He's *covered* in blood.

No one would notice by looking at him. There's blood spattered and smeared on his face, but otherwise, his dark clothing hides the rest. I only know because I could feel it as soon as I touched his saturated hoodie.

I shove his black shirt up under his arms to check for injuries on his chest and hold my breath. Nothing but some bruising.

I roll him over.

Fuck...

"How bad is it?" Aiden questions, entering the room.

I don't answer, letting him see for himself when he stands next to me and peers at the deep gash from Jackson's right shoulder to his left hip bone. There are other deep cuts around it too, but they're nothing in comparison.

His breathing is so shallow that I don't see his body rising and falling. I check for his pulse.

"Well?" Aiden demands.

I bite back a growl at his impatience. As pissed as I am at Jack, I don't want to lose him either. "It's there, but it's slow. Where the fuck are they?"

"I'm here!" Cassandra shouts breathlessly, running into the room and pushing past us to kneel beside the bed.

I take a step to the side to give her more room to work while still enabling me to see what's going to happen. She shakes her hands out like she's removing any anxious energy and then places her hands on either side of Jackson's back. She doesn't look squeamish or uncomfortable with all the blood, which is one of the reasons she's such a great healer for the Guild. Cassandra takes her job seriously, even if she can be overly flirtatious. I'd trust no one else to fix my brother.

She hums under her breath, eyes closed.

"His hoodie is soaked with blood. Does he need more?" I'll rob a hospital if I have to. Anything to let me *do something* other than standing here like a useless idiot.

Frowning, she shakes her head. "He's lost blood, but not too much. It must be someone else's, too. I can get this patched up and then he'll need at least a week's bed rest to recover fully."

Aiden and I exchange a look over her. We both know if he wakes up and Raegan isn't here, there's nothing and no one who will be able to stop him from going after her. "We'll need to sedate him," he tells me, echoing my thoughts.

I nod and cross my arms over my chest. "Just tell me what you need me to do."

"Go keep an eye on Vera. I'd rather she not be alone with Dane longer than necessary in case she tries something. I'll make some phone calls about getting the supplies we'll need for Jack."

Great.

Cassandra's gift is already working to close the large wound.

Outside, Reid leans against the wall next to the door, his arms crossed like some silent soldier waiting for his next order from Aiden. I'm not sure yet if I buy it. He wants a spot in the Guild, so it could be why he's trying so hard to be helpful, but I also think he's hiding something. Not that I care at this point if his gift is what helps us get Raegan back faster. I walk past him to the main living area.

Anything that had been on a wall or an exposed surface is strewn across the floor. Papers, shattered glass, knives from the block in the kitchen. There are some drawers and cabinets that had blown open from Thorne's wind and are now empty. I focus on the overturned table, where Raegan had accepted Jack's hand and walked away from us.

From *me*.

I snarl and lift the table back to its legs, proceeding to pluck the glass shards stuck in the tabletop. I know that wasn't what she was doing. Just like I know her going with Gordon was her trying to save us. It shouldn't have gotten to that point. We're supposed to save *her*. Not the other way around. She's been through enough, and now she's doing it all over again.

I'll find you and drag your ass back here, beautiful. That's a fucking promise.

"—live in a place like this? What a dump!"

In the living area, Vera's sitting on the bend of the long U-shaped couch. Her brother is a few feet away on the long side. Within reaching distance, but not right next to her like I thought he would be.

Dane runs his fingers through his hair and sighs. "We were attacked right before we went to the island. We haven't had time to clean up yet," he explains tiredly.

"I wasn't talking about the trash on the floor. Why are you living in a *firehouse*? The brick is ugly, and it looks like you're living in the eighties. Don't you have your own place, Dane? Or do you really still live with your friends like some frat boy?"

I grind my molars at every word out of her mouth. Clenching my fists, I glare at her.

Dane's voice begins in an appeasing tone, but I'm not having it. I storm up behind the couch on the opposite side of them.

"You don't like it? Then get the fuck out. Just tell me where Raegan is before the ugly door hits your bitchy ass on the way out."

Vera's mouth gapes open like this is the first time anyone's ever called her out on her attitude before. Well, tough shit. She wants back into the family, she's gonna have a rude awakening of the crap she can't get away with anymore. She turns to her brother with a melodramatic sulk. "Do you really want me to leave?"

"No—" Dane starts, but she cuts him off.

"Are your friends going to treat me like this the whole time? I haven't done anything to them."

Dane sighs again, loudly, scrubbing his hands over his face a couple times and then back through his hair as if he can wipe away all the stress and emotions he's caught up in. I can tell he's conflicted. He should be happy—no, *thrilled*—to have his sister back. This is everything he's ever wanted. And yet, he looks miserable already.

"Kell, just...lay off for now."

I frown, my hands fisting and loosening repeatedly, before I finally choose to let it go. Not for *her*. But because I can see that Dane's dealing with his own issues right now and doesn't need me complicating them.

Vera smiles at me. "I hope we can become good friends again, too, Kellan. We were once a long time ago, so I don't see why we can't be like that again. You still like cars?"

Nope. I can't do this. Not when my girl is stuck somewhere, forced to do whatever fucking shit Gordon did in the past. Turning to the kitchen, I rummage through the cabinets until I find whatever liquor bottle isn't currently on the floor. I grab the first one and spin the top until it flies off, then bring it to my lips.

I haven't had a drink since that night Raegan and I snuck out to dance. Or our mini dance party here at Old Red. And then, since she just came back into our lives before that. The smooth burn of whatever I'd grabbed, Aiden's bourbon, I think, is like reuniting with a long-lost friend. I know I shouldn't go right back to this the second she's gone, but I'm having a weak moment.

Sue me.

Aiden walks in as I'm downing my second long drink. I raise a brow, daring him to say something. Instead, he huffs and checks his phone. "Cassandra and Reid went back to the bunker to sleep, but they'll return in the morning to check on him. Let's go sit in the living room. I want to know where everything stands with Vera. As of right now, she's not to leave the firehouse." He keeps his voice to a soft murmur, so the conversation stays between the two of us.

I flick my eyes over to the couch and catch Vera watching us closely.

Fantastic.

We've let a rat in the house.

"Jack's going to murder her when he wakes up," I mock, even though we both know I'm not entirely joking.

He doesn't even argue it. "We have a week to get this figured out before we have to deal with that."

My hand tightens on the neck of the glass bottle. "You mean we're getting her back before he wakes up, right? Tell me there's a fucking plan to get her back, Aiden."

Aiden looks at his phone again, ticking me off that whatever he's waiting for is more important than this conversation, and then he checks in on Vera and Dane. He shakes his head when we see Vera still eyeing us, then strides into the living area to sit on the seat across from her.

That head shake better mean 'not now' and not 'no'.

I growl and take another drawn out swig of alcohol, then follow him. I sit between Dane and Aiden on the couch, although there's still plenty of room between us.

I stretch into the corner where there are some throw pillows to lean against, then spread my legs out in front of me to get comfortable.

"It's been a long time, Vera," Aiden begins smoothly.

She smiles softly and reaches over to put a hand on Dane's knee, then gives her brother a sorrowful look. "I wish I could have told you that I was still alive sooner. But at least we're finally together again now, right?"

Dane stares at her hand on his knee. He doesn't move to take it, but he doesn't pull away either. "Why couldn't you?" His expression becomes serious when he lifts his face to look at her again. "Who's been controlling you, Vera?"

Her body flinches the barest amount. She retracts her hand from him and laces her fingers in her lap. "No one. Even if I wanted to reach out to you, you ran away. I didn't know where you were until I saw you on the roof that night," she states matter-of-factly with a small shrug.

Aiden crosses his leg over his knee and links his hands together on top of it. His phone is resting in his lap, screen up, so should a text or call come in, he can look at it right away. I consider snatching the device from him to find out what he's up to. If Vera wasn't here with us, I would. I'll just have to confront him about it when she's not around. Whenever the fuck that will be, since she's going to be staying here with us, and I have a strong feeling Aiden's going to make me her babysitter.

"We're jumping ahead a bit. I want to know what happened from the beginning. When did you start working for GE and with Gordon?" he asks calmly as if we have all the time in the world to chat about her last six-plus years and Raegan isn't behind enemy lines.

I take another drink.

Vera raises her eyebrows and looks around at us. "You mean she didn't tell you?" She looks genuinely surprised, then contemplative before she answers. "It was just after I turned sixteen. Gordon was helping me train my gift. He would tell me about all the great things they planned to do. How they were training us up to be like super-heroes from the comics, fighting bad guys and all that. I mean, who wouldn't want to join that?"

I lean forward and slam the bottle down on the coffee table with a caustic laugh. "And you believed that bullshit?"

"Kell—" Aiden tries to stop me, but fuck. That.

"You think they're *heroes*?" I spit out. I jump to my feet and take a step closer. "They murdered my family! My little sister! Just to kidnap and try to brainwash me like they did you. They're not saving anyone. They're power-hungry maniacs obsessed with controlling anyone with a gift to use as a weapon to get what they want."

"Kell! *Kellan!*" Aiden's hand touches my arm, snapping my focus on Vera to swing around to him. "I know you're upset, but you need to calm down."

I breathe heavily, my chest heaving.

"If you can't calm down, go walk it off," he adds.

I almost do. I would. But I want to hear what she has to say about it. What else she's been doing the last six years for GE, and if she plans to change. If there's even a chance that she'll see reason to make Raegan's sacrifice worthwhile, or if she's well and truly gone.

I drop back to the couch and snag the bottle to drink some more.

Aiden waits another second to make sure I'm not going to start something up again before he finally sits as well. He turns his attention to Vera, who's now staring at me like she thinks I'm going to attack her.

Which isn't off the table completely. Only my respect for Aiden—and Dane—keeps me from trying to shake some sense into her.

"What do you have to say to that?" Aiden prompts her when she doesn't say anything. He's acting like some fucking counselor trying to get a patient to open up rather than interrogating the enemy. It pisses me off how it contrasts with his efforts to get information from Raegan. But then, he always acts erratically when she's involved.

Vera looks uncomfortably at Dane and then at her hands. "I don't know why that happened, but I do know we don't do that now. Most kids aren't even taken from their families anymore. Parents are willingly dropping their kids off to get help because they don't understand what's happening. The ones we kidnap are just saving the parents the trouble they'd go through when they did realize their child was different. It's better for everyone."

Oh, so it's *we* don't do that? And she's making us sound diseased. That we need *help*.

Fuck, I need to drink more to keep my mouth shut or I'm really going to lose it. I do exactly that, chugging the bottle until I can't breathe and then a few more gulps after that. I'm going to be completely trashed tonight, but I don't think I can stay here with her otherwise.

Aiden moves on to the next topic. "You said that Raegan killed you, but you're still here. Can you explain that?"

"I *was* dead, but they brought me back before it was too late." Vera shifts in her seat. "Can we, maybe, hold off on the interrogation for a bit? I'm really tired." She stands, and both Dane and Aiden follow suit.

"Of course," Aiden answers. "We'll need to figure out the sleeping arrangement since the other rooms need to be fixed up before anyone can stay in them. Dane, I can get you the supplies tomorrow for whichever room is in the best shape."

She tilts her head to the side and holds a finger up to her chin. "Where did Raegan sleep? I can just sleep in there."

"No." All three of us blurt out in unison.

Her forehead creases in confusion, but Dane is the first to speak up. "You can sleep in my room. It won't take me more than a day or two to fix up one of the other rooms. I can sleep on the couch for a couple of nights."

"But..." I know what she's going to say. That Raegan's not using it. Or she's not coming back. And I'll grab and choke her if she tries to say any of those words in front of me.

Thankfully for her, Aiden intervenes. "Good. That's settled. I'm sure you understand that while you're here, we expect that you'll stay inside and won't try sneaking out."

Her face drops with disappointment. "Am I your prisoner, then?"

She should be. If Raegan is GE's prisoner, then Vera is ours until we get my girl back. Unless GE couldn't care less about Vera anymore and she's an empty bargaining chip. I refuse to believe that's true, though. She's already brainwashed and has a useful gift at their disposal. It's only a matter of time before they'll want her back.

"Of course not," Aiden counters smoothly. A lie. "But the purpose of you coming back with us was to spend time with your brother, was it not? So, catch up." He steps around the couch and holds his arm out. "I'll show you to Dane's room and the women's bathroom so you can get settled."

He leads her to the dorm hallway, and as Dane moves to follow, I grab his arm. "Take my room."

Dane frowns. "Where are you going to sleep?"

"The couch." If I even sleep tonight. The best I can hope for is a complete blackout.

He nods and starts to walk away but pauses and looks over his shoulder. "We'll get her back, Kell."

"Yeah," I mutter sarcastically. "We're doing a bang-up job of that so far."

"It's the first night. We'll figure out a plan in the morning once we've gotten some rest."

I raise an eyebrow at him. "Oh, yeah? With your sister around? You gonna let her go so we can get Raegan back?" His lips flatten, and I bark out a laugh. "That's what I thought. Go, rest easy now that you've got your sister back, Rapunzel."

He looks ready to say something in return but shakes his head and walks away instead. I don't care if I'm being an asshole. The solution is easy. Find a way to get in contact with one of them and say we want to trade Vera back for Raegan. It wasn't a deal I agreed to, anyway.

Even as I tell myself that's all it would take, my gut tells me it won't be as simple as that. Gordon got what he wanted, and I doubt he'd be willing to give her up easily.

If we want her back, we'll have to fight.

Chapter Two

RAEGAN

I JOLT AWAKE, SITTING upright and gasping for air. A twinge of pain stabs the back of my neck, and I reach for it subconsciously, rubbing the area as I wrack my memories for what was real and what was just a dream.

I remember being on the island with Jackson and escaping through the window. Gordon found us, and then...

My eyes sweep around an unfamiliar room. It's plain and basic, as any bedroom can be. It has white walls and a hardwood floor with a massive rug covering most of it. There's a single upright dresser, an attached bathroom, and the simple twin bed I'm in.

And nothing else.

It's reminiscent of the room I'd once shared with other girls back on the island, but just my small corner's worth of furniture.

What's strikingly different is the glass wall on the side opposite the bed. The only privacy I'll have is my time in the bathroom. I shove the blankets down and drop my feet over the edge of the bed until they touch the scratchy rug. I move around the room, inspecting it for cameras or anything else I may have missed in my cursory glance.

The bathroom is tiny. It barely fits the toilet, sink, and a standing shower that's only three feet across. I know my elbows are going to hit the walls while trying to wash my hair, but I'll take the private bathroom. It could be worse.

I do a double-take in the mirror when I see myself. My hair tie came loose in my sleep, leaving my hair disheveled. Blood smears my face and neck, and when I look at my arms, the left one has dried blood cracking off like a dead second skin.

My chest tightens, and I can't breathe.

Jack.

Is he okay? Did they get him back to Cassandra in time? Will I ever see him again? Or the others?

I shake my head and slap my hands to my cheeks to stop that train of thought. I have to believe that they're all okay. I'll do my best here so they can get Vera back and keep working to take down GE. I'll just have to stay strong until they get to that point. I can help them from the inside.

The initial pain in my neck looks like an injection site where Gordon probably had me sedated as soon as we stepped through the portal. I can't remember a single thing after walking through it. The rest of my neck is aching from the collar still around my neck.

My fingers poke and prod at the skin underneath, testing its soreness from a combination of its uncomfortable fit and being shocked in it.

This thing better be waterproof, because I need to wash this blood off me. I turn on the sink faucet and test a drop of water on it, waiting for a shock. Then I touch my wet hand to it slowly, again waiting for pain to follow, but nothing happens. Once I'm thoroughly satisfied that it is, in fact, waterproof, I return to the room and check the dresser for a change of clothes.

My options are a black workout outfit with the GE logo or a gray workout outfit with the GE logo.

Wonderful.

I grab the black and bring it with me into the bathroom, where I get to work on cleaning my hair and body of the previous day.

I roughly towel dry my hair and return to the room to inspect the glass wall and the only other door. I rap my knuckles against the glass, but the sound is muted. Tempered glass? Now I *really* feel like a pet trapped in a cage. I try the door for shits and giggles, but of course, it's locked from the outside with no keyhole for me to attempt picking it.

Sighing, I step back from the door and then jump when I see someone standing on the other side of the glass.

"Shit!" I curse, slapping my hand against my chest to keep my heart from bursting out of it. Recognizing them, I take a step back, my next curse spilled on a breathless exhale. "Fuck."

There's a good reason why I didn't recognize him at first. Because while the major characteristics are there, they're also...not quite right. His skin is ashen in color, no longer a solid peach that made him appear...well, human. He has dark, sunken eyes.

His ears don't sit right on the sides of his head, which is made all the more obvious because of his short hair that does nothing to hide it. And there's a thick white scar wrapped around his neck where Jackson sawed it in two.

"Thorne?"

He sneers at me, revealing perfect teeth behind bloodless lips. "This is your fault, you stupid bitch. I should have just killed you when I had the chance. Now, *look at me*!" he roars, banging his fist against the glass.

I startle. A zombie is yelling at me. What's more terrifying than that? "Um...I see you. Why aren't you dead?"

Thorne's fist slides down the glass while his one good eye glares at me with pure malice. "I'll never die until he's done with me. Even if all that's left are my bones. I should do the same to you." He pauses as the words leave his lips, his expression turning thoughtful. "Yes, that's exactly what I'll do." His mouth stretches to a wild smile that has dread dropping in my gut like a sack of rocks.

"I'll kill you, make him bring you back to life as another of his puppets, and then Jackson will do anything that's asked of him to keep you alive. Well, you know. As alive as I am," he amends.

I swallow, trying to ignore the blatant threat to my life and focusing on gathering information. "So, this guy's a necromancer? Is that how Vera's alive?"

He rubs his chin. "Not like in the movies. He traps a person's soul in their body before it leaves, which preserves the body in its current state. A healer heals the body as well as they can, but as you can see, you can only be put back together so many times before it starts...losing its life."

That sounds horrifying. And I also have no plans to join him and Vera in that experience. I keep him talking, hoping to buy enough time that someone else will walk by and I can flag them down to get Gordon. I know he wouldn't agree to this plan at least. He wants me only obeying him and no one else. His own personal weapon.

It speaks volumes about my predicament that I'm counting on him to keep me from joining the league of undead soldiers.

"How was Jack supposed to help with that? If your body is...you know..." I don't want to piss him off by saying any of the words that come to mind, so I just nod at him and let him fill it in for himself.

Thorne keeps his eyes trained on me as he starts to walk along the glass to the door.

"Royce manipulates and controls souls. Which means he could move my soul into a better body. Kill them without causing much harm to the body itself, pluck out that soul and stuff mine in. I've already picked out the body as well. I just need Jackson's help to set the plan in motion."

I make a mental note of the name and everything he's telling me, but then I see him entering numbers into a keypad next to the door and realize my time's almost up. There are two beeps in rapid succession, and when the door doesn't open, I assume it means he guessed the wrong code. He tries again. More double beeps.

I move further back, but the closest thing to a weapon in this room is the hairbrush in the bathroom that would do fucking nothing against a man as powerful as Thorne.

"Who did you pick out? Maybe I can help instead," I rush out, trying to buy more time.

There's a single, higher note beep, and then a click as the door pops open a crack.

Fuck a duck.

I'm dead. So dead.

The door pushes inward, and he slowly steps inside with a smirk. He closes the door behind himself, and I hear another click that tells me he's locked us both in here. He moves toward me again, and I back up step by step until my ass hits the bed. Then I scramble up and stand on it to get whatever distance I can from him. Even though I know it means *nothing* when he can stop me from breathing or slash me to pieces with air from a distance, it's just not in me to stand still and let it happen.

"You're too weak to take on Royce. I need Jackson to do it, which is why you're worth more to me as his puppet than alive. Incentive for Jackson to fight him." He raises his hand up, and I dive to the bed, rolling off it and trying to avoid his aim. A swift breeze sweeps behind me, telling me how close I'd come to being hit. He laughs mockingly while trying to track my movements with his hand. "Stand still, girl. I'm trying to do Jackson a favor and keep your body intact for this death, which is more than he's done for me. If you keep moving, I'll have to slice you up and let you bleed out."

"What do you think you're doing?!" Gordon demands angrily from the other side of the glass.

Thorne scowls. But he doesn't drop his hand. He raises it instead, and my gut tells me he's going to try for a kill in a single blow.

I run to the dresser and shove it forward so I can use it as a shield, then duck to make myself as small as possible. The dresser shatters to pieces around me, knocking into my back and shoving me face-first into the wall. My head hits it hard enough that I black out for a second, then wake to find myself lying on the floor.

"Call your puppet, Royce. He's not to harm my pet now or ever, do you hear me?" Gordon's voice echoes from somewhere in the room.

I grab my head and groan as it pounds relentlessly, drawing myself up so I can see what's happening. I blink a few times through the pain as Thorne storms out of the open door. If I wasn't in so much pain, I might try to make a break for it.

No, wait. I can't do that. I swore to stay. Breaking that promise could mean he goes after the guys and brings Vera back here. She's another person who will try to kill me as soon as an opportunity presents itself.

"Such a waste," Gordon chides as he walks over to me. He kneels and grabs my chin, jerking my face up and tilting it this way and that. "I'll have a healer come down to fix you up. I'm not losing a day of training because of that imbecile. You're weak enough as it is when you're not injured." He tosses me away as he stands to make another call.

I pass out on the floor before the phone starts ringing.

When I wake up next, the headache has disappeared and I feel as I did before Thorne arrived—better, actually, because the pain in my neck has also vanished.

Gordon stands over me with his arms crossed and foot tapping impatiently. "I don't have all day, pet. Open your eyes and get out of bed. We're already almost an hour behind schedule."

I push myself out of bed and move to stand, hoping Gordon will step back to give me some room, but no, of course not. I brush against him when getting back on my feet and feel nauseated at him starting this so soon.

He takes my arm above my elbow, pinching it between his thumb and fingers while directing me out of the room. "Your tour is going to be briefer than originally planned, but you'll have the opportunity to explore later. For now, I'll give you the basics of how to get around or the different areas we'll be working in so you know where to go."

Cringing, I try to tug away under the guise of getting more comfortable, and I'm surprised when he releases me. "I don't understand."

Gordon stops walking, and I stumble in my effort to do the same. His hard brown eyes travel from my feet to my face. "Don't tell me your brain's gone stupid while you've been away as well. I'm not sure I've met anyone more worthless than you, pet. If not for your gift, that is. It's a shame that *you* were born with it."

My jaw tightens at the jabs he effortlessly throws my way. I've worked a lot on my self-confidence since the last time he had me. I realize it still may not be enough when a twinge of pain slides its way into my psyche. *Worthless.* I hate that fucking word.

"Since you are here *willingly*, I see no reason to keep you locked up. We both know if you try to run or fight back, Vera will come immediately home, and I'll send hunters to track down and kill those five boys who were with you."

Five? Oh, shit. Reid was there. *Good job, Rae. Another innocent in danger because of you.*

I nod to show him that I understand. This was what I had offered, and I won't put everyone else in danger by not upholding my end of the deal. Dane needs this time to try to win Vera back. *Try* being the keyword. I don't have much confidence it will work, but at least she's not here. And the others can focus on GE the way they were before I came along to distract them.

"Good. The fifth through tenth floors are off-limits. First through fourth is where you'll find food, the indoor pool and recreation area, the gym, the library, or anything else you might need. The eleventh floor is for medical, and the twelfth floor is where we'll do any indoor training. The thirteenth floor and up are primarily sleeping quarters, plus some mini apartments and such. Your room is on the thirteenth floor, and as of right now, you're our only guest on the island. It's new, so others will eventually join us, but for now, it's just staff and you."

I nod again, even though I'm trying to wrap my head around how big this building is. We head down in an elevator to the first floor, walk through a lobby and then through the wide front doors that have a perfect view of the beach. We're on a hill, but I can see trails that lead down on either side to get to the water.

Gordon leads us in that direction, and I pause to look back and up at the building we just left.

It's...massive. Like a luxury hotel propped on a cliff on its own private island. I count at least twenty stories but lose track when the windows start to blend together.

"Keep up!"

I spin and jog to catch up. "When can I take this collar off?" I ask him, touching it as it chafes my neck.

"Mm...yes. A formality for when you're not with me. The staff was uncomfortable with you being here unless you would be wearing it." The staff? Why would they think I'd attack them over Gordon? Probably guessing my confusion, he shakes his head and continues, "The last time you were on an island, you broke it with your gift. Not just the manor, but the island, too, eventually crumbled to sand at the bottom of the ocean."

Oh.

Fuck.

I knew about the manor and had seen some cracks in the ground, but I didn't realize...

"Figures you're too dumb to realize the full potential of your gift. I want to see more of that while we're training. *Without*"—he looks at me pointedly—"destroying this island, of course."

My palms sweat at the memory of what caused me to lose complete control of my gift back then. I want to snipe at him because he was the reason it had happened in the first place, but I can't bring myself to say the words. Even thinking about them makes me sick to my stomach. *Then don't rape me again.*

The last thing I want to do is remind him of it. While I agreed to train and do what he wants as his weapon, I *won't* let him touch me again.

"Just play nice, do as you're told, and I think this time, you'll have such a good experience that you won't ever consider leaving me again. I'll give you everything you need to be happy so long as you make *me* happy, pet."

My stomach twists and binds at the possible implications of what he might ask of me, and I'm forced to wonder if I'll make it out this time with my life or my sanity.

The tour concludes in a clearing about half a mile behind the main building. There's scrub and other low island bushes and trees surrounding it, with nothing but sand in the middle. That, and a huge mound of concrete that's the size of three monster trucks.

"This is where we'll meet every day to train. You'll be here first thing in the morning as soon as the sun is up. If you choose to eat beforehand, that's up to you, but be sure you aren't late. I'd skip breakfast in the beginning until your body starts getting used to these warm-ups." Gordon's seated off to the side in a tall chair with a wide umbrella over the surrounding area. Mini fans hang off the poles on the underside of the umbrella to give him an additional breeze.

"We'll be training from sunup to sundown every day, with a break for lunch. After that, you can do whatever you please, so long as you're up in time for training the next morning."

I stare at the pile before me with apprehension. This was how he started training me last time. No wonder he's saying I can do whatever I want on the island after training. I'll barely be able to drag myself back up the hill to the lobby after this, let alone wander or do anything else. At least he removed the collar when we got here. I rub absently at the temporary freedom on my neck, but I'm more relieved to feel the connection to my gift again.

"Your body seems to have forgotten how to use your gift, or you're still fighting it. You're going to get rid of this entire pile, and then I'll let you off for the rest of the day. How long that takes is going to be up to you." He leans forward, gripping the tablet in his hand. "You've grown weak, pet. It's time to break you down and build you back up again. Just like muscle fibers must be torn for your body to adapt and get stronger, the same is true for your gift." He punches something on his tablet screen. "Begin."

I call to my gift, reaching into that place deep down and spreading it up and then to my hands. The burn is worse in this heat, but I clench my teeth and push through it. I haven't even started yet, and I know I won't be allowed to eat or sleep until this is done. If I can somehow power through, then maybe I can make it and still have time to rest.

It doesn't help that he has yet to let me eat since waking up here, so my body's fuel is already low, leaving me at a disadvantage.

I get to work grabbing each piece of cement and thrusting my gift into it one at a time.

I'm only five minutes in, and it feels like I'm going to be sick. My hands are on fire, my stomach is growling fiercely, and I'm unsteady on my feet. When I pause to see what progress I've made, I can't see it. Have I even made a dent?

I keep going until my body switches to autopilot. I'm numb to the pain now, just going through the motions and trying to stay conscious.

Until I'm not anymore.

Sand pelts me in the face, and I sputter awake, choking out the grit that went up my nose and into my mouth as I try to brush it away from my eyes.

"Pathetic." He grabs my hair at the roots, twisting it back and yanking hard so I'm forced to look up, eliciting a cry from my lips when the pain snaps me completely awake.

Gordon's scowling at me. "You need to do better than this. Consider today your orientation and practice run. If you fail me like this tomorrow, Holt will shock you awake every time you pass out until you finish the job." He shoves my face down into the sand and then clicks the collar back around my neck.

Footsteps peter away, but I don't bother raising my head to confirm that he's leaving. I know he's done with me today, and it's better for me to keep my head down until he's out of sight than look at him where he could misinterpret it as some act of defiance.

I move my forehead onto my arm and take a shuddering inhale. It's like my entire body has been sliced open and filled with sand. Heavy. Burning.

You can do this, I tell myself, even as my body screams otherwise. This is just day one, and I've already seen how it gets worse.

But I survived before.

And I'll do it again.

Chapter Three

JACKSON

I CAN ALMOST FEEL myself rising into consciousness out of oblivion. My last memories play before me like on a movie screen, and I watch it with rapt attention.

The island.

Thorne.

Escaping with Raegan.

My little one.

My mind is conscious, but it's taking longer for it to connect with my body. I urge it awake, seeking any sign of my physical body so that I can move enough to fully rouse myself.

There's a painful twisting in my chest as I think about where my little one is and what she's dealing with at this very moment while I'm not there for her.

Finally, I'm able to drag my eyelids open. My entire body feels heavy and sluggish. And it *aches*. I should expect pain after the fight with Thorne. Far more actually, but my aches seem to be more related to stiffness all over rather than centralized on my back.

Above me is a white ceiling. I turn my head to the side, noting the pillow beneath it, to find Aiden sitting in a chair, watching me. He's wearing a suit, as usual, but the shirt's unbuttoned and rumpled. The rest of him doesn't sound any alarms until I see the exhaustion written in the furrow of his brow and the tiredness of his eyes.

"Before you say or do anything, I need you to make our conversation here private," he murmurs.

My gaze slides to the door of my room, where Kellan is leaning against it with his arms crossed over his chest. His expression is shadowed and tight, and when I try to make eye contact, he dodges it by turning his head.

I force myself upright, shucking the blankets that are surprisingly still on me—instead of tangled around me like usual—and turning my back against the wall so I can see them clearly. My fingers twitch when I realize I'm in nothing but boxers and I don't have my knives within reach.

"Where is she?"

The fact that they're both here and she isn't is telling enough.

"If you want that answer, then do as I ask first. Then I'll tell you everything."

I do it without further prompting and give him a firm nod. I'm ordinarily quite patient. I can wait forever for something to be just right before I make my move. But with her? I've never felt the crawling need burrowed under my skin to *move* before. To find her. To hold her. To fuck her until there's no doubt in my mind that she's with me and she's safe.

Aiden clears his throat. "Gordon has her."

I don't react. Not outwardly, at least. I expected it was bad. And I could lose myself to the rage, or I can save it, store it up for Gordon or anyone else who stands in my way. If there's anyone to blame for losing her, it's me.

I got her involved in my plan with Thorne. I let her stubbornness win in coming to the island when she should have stayed behind. I wasn't strong enough to protect her after fighting only one man.

I know it.

And they know it, too.

Aiden looks determined over something, but it's Kellan who's glaring at me to make sure I'm clearly cued in on his opinion of how this all happened.

"Where?" I ask, even knowing it's too hopeful to expect that they'll have figured out her location and are here to come up with a plan to get her back.

He shakes his head. "We don't know. We went back to the island for any clues, but there was nothing left by the time we got there."

"How long have I been out?"

"About a week. We sedated you. It was the only way to let your back heal fully."

"A week," I repeat slowly. "He's had her a week." And they still don't have a single clue to her whereabouts. A lot can happen in one week. Especially with someone who I suspect is the reason why she doesn't see herself clearly anymore.

She told me she wanted vengeance. Was that for what happened with Vera and Dane, or something for herself?

I clench and unclench my hands in my lap. Where could she be? I killed everyone tied to GE in this city already, so I'll have to spread my radius until I find someone who will know. Someone must know Gordon's name and his location or contact information.

"He wouldn't have her at all if you didn't play villain and deliver her to the enemy!" Kellan snarls, stepping away from the door and closer to me.

Aiden sighs. "He's not wrong. You swore you could be trusted to protect Raegan, and now, we've lost her."

Kell growls at him now. "Don't say it like that! She's not lost." He shoves his finger at the door. "That bitch knows exactly where she is, and she's smug as shit about it."

I glance to the door and back to Kellan. "Who?" I demand. If someone knows where she is, there is nothing, and I mean *nothing*, I won't do to get that information from them.

Aiden's eyes narrow at me. "No. That's not an option." I raise an eyebrow in his direction. So *he* thinks. There isn't a single person I've interrogated who didn't tell me what I wanted to know for the information they had. This one will be no different. "Vera is here."

Well.

I'm not surprised often, but I wasn't expecting that.

She may have started out in our group, but I was never close with her. There was always something about her that annoyed me. From the brief time I saw her on the roof of the warehouse, it looks like her irritating attitude has been amplified, and whatever good that had been in her is now twisted. Her life means nothing to me against Raegan's.

No one's does.

"You can't hurt her. Any harm comes to her, and Gordon will take it out on Raegan," Aiden adds, bringing my attention back to him. "She traded herself for Vera and our lives. As long as Vera stays with us, then Raegan won't try to escape. And if she does, then he can take Vera back and will most likely punish Raegan by going after us."

He can come after us all he likes. Even better, because then I have a simple trail that will lead me right to him.

I cock my head to the side, studying Aiden and wondering why he's here. He has to know that I'm not going to sit back and wait. "Why are you both here?"

"The only way we're going to get her back is by working together. I need to know that you'll work with us and not run off on your own like last time," Aiden answers. "Vera can't find out that we're all looking for her. I'm sure she's still communicating with GE, and they have to believe that we're happy enough with Vera to leave Raegan alone."

Kellan snorts from where he's standing.

Aiden continues, "If too many of us are missing or keep going in and out, she'll notice. I leave enough as it is for the Guild, so I can't go as far as I'd like, and Kellan has to stay here to keep an eye on Vera with Dane."

Which leaves me to be able to go wherever. "What does Dane think of all this? That he may have to return Vera once we bring Raegan home?"

Kellan shifts, and I catch him rolling his eyes. "Rapunzel wants to have his cake and eat it, too. He's all in on this plan, but he wants us to trap Vera once we find and get Raegan so she doesn't leave."

Aiden nods. "Dane will help try to narrow down locations and people with ties to GE. Once you're out there, keep us updated on what you find out so we can dig deeper and point you to people with possible information. Keep your cell phone and this credit card on you. Eat and sleep so you're not useless when we do find her location because we'll be moving immediately using Reid." He passes a card over to me, which I flip between my fingers. "And Jack…" He pauses until our eyes lock. "This isn't a solo mission. We'll find her faster if we work together. It's already hard for some of us to trust you after what you did."

"You pretended to be evil way too well," Kell chimes in, and I smirk at him.

I never said I'd been pretending.

But I like this plan, and believe it or not, I've learned my lesson about going solo.

For now.

I hop off the bed, using a push of air to help me to my feet and start pulling on clothes and loading them with my knives.

"You're going now?" Aiden asks. "You've just woken up and should rest a bit longer."

I tug the gaiter over my head to settle around my neck. "I've rested long enough."

"Then at least grab something to eat on your way out so I don't find you passed out from hunger in the drive later."

I smirk at Aiden. "Anything else?"

They shake their heads, and I nod, releasing the sound bubble I'd buffered us in and opening the door to walk out. I can already hear Vera's bothersome voice in the living room groaning about something, but I don't care enough to focus on the words. I'm planning on stopping in the kitchen, but once I've entered the main room, I can't not hear Vera.

"Ugh! I can't just sit around here forever, Dane! This place is *boring*. Is this how you live your life? Just sitting around here all day?

I want to go out!"

Smirking, I lock my cold blue eyes on the woman who's standing between me and Raegan before I speak. "I'll take you out," I offer chillingly.

Vera's head whips around, and her eyes widen when she sees me. "Oh, you're—"

"—awake," Aiden finishes for her as he walks past me and into the living room so he's between us. As if that makes any difference to me. I'm sure she was going for *alive* and disappointed in that. "And, not funny," he shoots my way.

I shrug because I wasn't trying to be.

I meant it.

"Well, great. But I want Dane to take me out so we can spend time together doing fun things."

"You guys fixed up your room together. You can work on the others. Watch movies. Play video games," Aiden offers her.

She scoffs. "Video games? What am I, twelve?"

Her attitude is grating. I'm surprised Kellan hasn't done anything yet, but then I see him leaning back against the kitchen cabinets with a bottle of liquor in his hand, as far away from her as possible while still within eyesight.

I call on my gift, on the power I finally obtained to match Thorne's, and thrust it at Vera. The wind shoves her up and against the wall, her head inches from the ceiling and her body pinned where she can't do anything but listen.

"Jack!" Dane shouts, turning to look at his sister, who is trying to fight me. She can't, but I let her try, anyway.

Aiden's dark gaze swings my way, silently asking me what I'm doing.

I can feel Kellan's presence at my back, but he doesn't move to attack me. His dislike of Vera is strong enough that he'll wait to see what I plan to do first.

She struggles like a fish at the end of a line. "I just need your attention. Then I'll let you go."

"You *psycho*! Put me down! Dane!" she screeches. Before Dane can say anything, I begin my piece. If I'm going to be out hunting, it means that this is the only real interaction I'll have with her before my little one comes home. And I have a message for her.

"Where is Raegan?" I ask calmly, still smiling. I can tell it freaks her out—as it does so many others—when I look so collected while I have their life in my hands.

Even though she can't know we're *all* looking for Raegan, I'm enough of a wild card that she won't think the others are connected at all. And one person looking in a big world for another doesn't seem like much for her to worry about.

"I. Don't. Know," she spits out. I don't believe her. Maybe she doesn't know where she is right now, but I'm sure she has a short list of guesses. It would be so much easier if I tortured it out of her. I can do it without lasting damage. "But even if I did know, I wouldn't tell you. You were too busy being asleep, so you missed the part where she *chose* to leave you all so that I could be reunited with Dane. What do you think she'd do if she found out it was all for nothing because you dragged her back? Do you really think that's what she wants?"

I know what she wants better than anyone.

She doesn't want to be anywhere near Gordon or GE, especially not under the terms she agreed to. I don't like that my little one isn't fighting back right now. She isn't trying to escape. How can she hold on to who she is if she has to fight against her instincts?

"The deal between you isn't my problem." Besides, she broke a promise to me that came first. "I'd like you to know that when I get her back, and I will, I am going to find out every mark or transgression made against her. And I will personally mete out the same on you to match. So, you'd better hope that Raegan is being treated well. Or else wake up and fight GE to get her back yourself. It's your call."

Her face pales and another drop of rage falls into the pool I'm cultivating. She knows something about what's happening with Raegan, and it isn't good.

Dane storms over to me. "I won't let you do that."

I raise a brow in a mock challenge. "She did this *for you*," I remind him. Raegan sacrificed herself to give Dane this time with Vera, and all it looks like is a waste of time. "If she's being tortured or hurt wherever she is just for you to sit and listen to your sister complain, then you'll be lucky if I don't do the same to you."

His jaw clenches, but he doesn't argue. Hmm, interesting. Is he feeling guilt over Raegan being gone? Is he wondering what she's going through for him to have his sister back?

I drop Vera while my eyes are still locked with Dane's, letting gravity yank her down to crash on the floor. Dane rushes over to her and tries to help her up, but she swats her arm.

"If Raegan is Gordon's prisoner, then you're ours. Remember that the next time you think to complain about being bored, because I can always give you far worse things to do."

She looks around the room for a friendly face. Even Dane's is tight, like he doesn't completely disagree with some of what I said.

Vera turns and speed-walks out of the room, slamming a door in the dorm hallway.

Aiden sighs and runs a hand over his head. "So much for subtlety."

"Fuck subtlety," Kellan chimes in behind me. "Now, let's get our girl back."

Chapter Four

RAEGAN

I LOSE TRACK OF the days when all it seems I do is use my gift, get shocked awake, and use my gift again with brief intervals of eating food and taking a shower while sitting on my ass.

If I want to look for a silver lining in anything, it's that the lightning from the sky is not as painful as it looks. Sure, it feels like tiny needles stabbing me from head to toe until my entire body is a ball of pain and I can't move after it stops. But that's where it ends. There's no lingering aftereffects other than the temporary paralysis. No visible wounds or deeper damage.

It sucks, but only in the moment.

I can handle that.

What I can't handle is how Gordon is apparently set to wear me to the point of exhaustion each and every day.

He has some predetermined goal in his mind of where he wants me to be or what he wants me to accomplish by the end of a day. If I meet that goal, he'll ask Holt to carry me back to my room. If I don't, he'll leave me in the training circle to crawl back myself.

One night, I couldn't make it up the hill, and I passed out there, too tired to move or so much as breathe.

The next day, without any dinner or breakfast, was the worst in all my time here so far.

I've promised myself to never let that happen again. Even if it takes me hours to crawl back to the mansion to get some food, I have to do it.

I'm back in the training circle at the end of the day, working on a new trick I've learned. I can already see the improvement in my stamina and the decreased time to activate my gift, but this one is...well, the possible applications of it will be terrifying, but I try not to think too hard about it.

I'm trying to convince myself that I'm just in a training boot camp. That my life isn't in danger, Gordon isn't going to use me as his weapon like he'd planned before, and I'll eventually be going home and I'll be stronger for it.

It's the only thing keeping me going at this point. That, and the fact that I have no other choice.

My hands press into the concrete slab at the same moment I've called on my gift so that the response is almost instant as soon as I make contact. Instead of throwing everything I have into that single piece, I focus my gift into a steady stream, holding half of it back and directing it to reach out to everything that this slab touches. Cracks appear in the current slab and stretch outward, dancing out to every connecting piece of concrete until I've reached the entire pile.

And then I use the full power of my gift, and everything I've already connected to crumbles to dust.

The pile that took me days to destroy in my early time here is now gone in the span of minutes.

Gordon scribbles notes on his tablet. I don't know why I look to him for any sort of positive feedback, so I know if I'll be crawling back tonight or catching the Holt-Express, but I do anyway. He finishes his notes and then looks at me. "Too slow. That took three minutes and forty-nine seconds. You need to stop thinking about the steps in your head and just do it. Go to the next pile and do it again. We'll keep going tonight until you're at least under three minutes."

I release a shaky breath.

Then I move to the next mound and get back to work.

I must make it under three minutes by the time the sun goes down, because Holt has me cradled in his arms and is walking me up the hill to deliver me to my room. I hate that I actually look forward to this. It has nothing to do with the brute who's carrying me and everything to do with the fact that my arms and legs are jelly and I couldn't bear weight on anything if I wanted to.

I've tried talking to Holt before. Maybe to gain an ally or get him to see things from my side. But the guy's an absolute, stone-cold dick. I think he gets off on shocking me and then insults me for the fact that I have to be carried after my training sessions.

I'd like to see him do what I have over and over again and *not* collapse into a heap afterward.

I wait until I'm back in my cage and Holt leaves before I grab the alarm clock I'd requested and set an alarm for an hour from now. I'll give myself one hour to get some energy back. Then I'll eat and go searching for clues of my past.

If I wait until I have a night where I'm not too tired, I think I'll never get there. I need to just do it. If I'm on an island with Gordon, odds are that my file will be around here somewhere, too. And that just might have information about my parents.

First, sleep. Then, answers.

The library is on the third floor at the very end of the right wing, but it takes up almost two-thirds of this side. After a quick meal in the dining hall, I ask the staff for its location and then muster up enough energy to make it there.

There are books of all kinds here. Fiction and non-fiction alike. I'm wondering who all these books are for and why they have so many of them on such a small island, when I'm reminded of something Gordon told me earlier.

New "guests" would be arriving this week. And this place is nothing, if not a larger version, of what I'd experienced on the island growing up. An overwhelming building with all the entertainment and activities one could think of within your reach. It's hard to think of this place as a prison when it's made to seem like a paradise.

I frown at that stark reminder and keep walking beyond the aisles of bookcases organized by genre until I reach the back of the library. There's a sign for the restroom right in the middle, but I see other doors further down one side and wander to those.

The words on the glass window read *Records Room*.

Perfect.

I try the handle and the door *opens*. A mistake, or do they really not care if anyone snoops around in here?

Or there's nothing important stored inside.

The room is a simple rectangle with filing cabinets lining the three walls and making up aisles down the middle.

Of course, none of them are labeled with anything as simple as letters of the alphabet. They each have numbers on them that are five digits long and mean absolutely nothing to me. So, I start with the cabinet closest to me and start flicking through files for a name or picture that looks familiar.

I'm sure I'm in here for hours by the time I make it through a single row with nothing to show for it. Well, not nothing. My legs are shaking with weariness, and I know I'm not going to be able to stay awake much longer. I'll have to pick up where I leave off tomorrow and keep going.

Even though that's what I tell myself, I still open the next drawer and start checking each file.

I freeze, my fingers pincered open on a file when I see a picture of a girl who looks startlingly like me. Her eyes are a bit bigger, her smile less jaded than mine, and her nose and ears aren't quite the same, but there's no mistaking the resemblance.

I yank the folder from the drawer and flip to the first page.

Merina Laivins.

Discovered by Gifted Enterprise when she was seventeen and a senior in high school. She destroyed a parking garage while at the mall with her friends. Two of her three friends died, and the third wound up in a coma.

I stare horrified at the newspaper article about the parking garage that's nothing but rubble in the image.

The next pages look more like medical records once she's under GE's care. There are psych notes discussing her progress in controlling her gift and her desire to do anything GE asks. She doesn't want to return to her old life out of shame and guilt for what happened over a misunderstanding.

Her gift was apparently explosions emitted from her body and a high level of heat resistance. She was a walking bomb who could detonate and then walk away without a scratch on her. The heat and energy radiating from her immediately after she went off kept any harm from coming to her like a protective shield until it eventually faded.

More medical records go over her vitals repeatedly, which I swiftly page through until I get back to a training report of her progress.

> *Training Note 985:*
> *Subject unable to continue beyond two hours of training today. She reports increased tiredness.*

> *Training Note 988:*
> *Training session canceled today due to subject's tiredness and mild nausea. It is my recommendation that a slowed training schedule be implemented over the next few months to prioritize the subject's health. She has shown greater control over her gift*

and at this point is no longer considered a threat to GE.

Medical Note:
1. Viability scan completed. Fetus has normal heart rhythm and measures at 9 weeks.
2. Reviewed care plan with the patient, including diet changes and supplements to take. Training limitations will be put in place for the safety of the patient and fetus.
3. Kitchen staff will be provided a list of approved meals and snacks.
4. Science department will be provided recurring status notes of current limitations.
5. Supplements were provided to the patient today.
6. The president was updated per his request and will be copied on all future notes.

I stare at the proof of her pregnancy with me on the island. The rest of her pregnancy is uneventful, and I skip past all the doctor visits and unremarkable training notes until I find one that mentions my birth.

September 26th
Raegan Laivins. 6 pounds 8 ounces. 20 inches.
Born to Merina Laivins and Charles Whitmore.

I take note of my father's name. There was no mention of him in any of the earlier notes, but maybe I'll see his name more after this.

Training Note 1270:
Subject is continuing to refuse completing tasks in her training. She is proving uncooperative, unwilling to use her gift, and I am unable to re-assess her threat level and current control over her gift at this time. Recommending psych eval for feedback on motivating the subject before I'm forced to retire the subject in the current program.

Medical Note:
Following a thorough interview and discussion with the patient, I have determined that the birth of the patient's daughter has changed her goals and they no longer align with the company. The patient wishes to go back to a regular life to raise her daughter and has asked the company for assistance to return to her home country with a fake identity. I advised that this is not an option for her, especially now that her threat level cannot be confirmed after so much time out of training. Any willingness the patient has at this point will hinge solely on her daughter. Strongly advise an alternate training program or separation from the child.

I keep scanning through the next pages, but they're all the same. No progress.
Training has stalled.

Unfocused on anything beyond her daughter, so they try separating them. This only makes her worse.

A news article falls from the stack. I bend and pick it up.

Terrorist bombs office building downtown

At 3:17 pm, on Wednesday, October 3rd, a bomb was detonated in the lobby of the Gifted International building. The explosion caused the five-story building to collapse, trapping victims inside. There have been over twenty reported fatalities so far. Rescue teams are still searching for survivors.

The terrorist was identified as Merina Laivins, a woman in her early twenties who had gone missing seven years ago during an investigation of a similar explosion at a mall parking garage. Her body has been recovered from the rubble.

I grip the papers and slide down the filing cabinet until my butt hits the floor.

She couldn't have died from her own explosion. The notes on her gift were clear that her gift protected her during it.

Someone killed her.

There's a final report at the end, with a note that her daughter, Raegan, was taken to the States by Merina, and her whereabouts are unknown.

I close the file and hold it against my chest. She risked her life to get me free. I'm sure of it. She got me to Grams and then went somewhere that would get their attention and used her gift as a distraction. Grams must have known what was going on because I spent my early childhood in Alaska, as far away from the islands as she could get without having to leave the country.

She wasn't a terrorist.

She was a human being who made a mistake, and GE swooped in to take advantage of her. And then she risked her life to save her innocent daughter before she could be caught up by them, too.

"I hear you were poking around the Records Room last night." Gordon's words trip my concentration, and my gift destroys only half the mound at once rather than all of it. He tsks loudly at my failure.

I stumble over to the rest of it, falling onto my knees and practically leaning against the concrete to keep myself upright as I try again.

I thought I woke up with more energy today. Or more...something, after learning about my mother last night. But Gordon's session still wears me into the ground. I don't have anything left in me to raise a finger, let alone talk back if I wanted to.

"Useless! What if you're being attacked while using your gift? Do you think anyone is going to stop and wait for you to get your head on straight? How could you let some simple words mess you up so easily?"

I grit my teeth and concentrate on controlling my gift while unsuccessfully trying to block him out.

"Holt!"

Wait. No, he wouldn't.

Who am I kidding? Of course, he would.

Holt's lightning hits me without further warning, grabbing me with a burning fist that rakes across my skin and pounds into my muscles, seizing them in a vise.

"Even if you can't move, your gift can. Finish the job!" Gordon snaps. He sounds closer now, like he's moved from his seat to get a closer view of my punishment.

I try to home in on my gift, but the pain is overwhelming my thoughts until it's all I can think about. Pain. Pain.

It stops abruptly. My body is still frozen in place, my muscles locked exactly as they were as my body twitches from the residual energy zapping through me.

Gordon grabs my hair while I'm still paralyzed and yanks it backward until I can see him sneering over me. I can't move or even scream at the rough move that feels even worse while my body is over-sensitized. "Are you even listening to me, or is your head so full of thoughts of your mother that I need to clear it for you? *She* at least had better control over her gift and would have been a true asset had it not been so wasted. You pale in comparison."

He shoves me forward into the concrete, and because my reflexes aren't back yet, I can't stop my nose from smashing into it. Hot blood pours down my face and throat, choking me. My fingers twitch around the concrete as feeling and control slowly returns. I cling to it to keep myself upright as my head swims from exhaustion and pain.

"Now, I'll give you a head start before Holt strikes you again. Don't let my kindness go to waste."

I reach for my gift and send it into the piece I'm holding on to and keep pushing it farther and farther out. It feels like I'm shooting fresh lava through my veins, and I scream, forcing myself through it to try to get it done quickly enough, but then the lightning finds me again.

My mouth stays open in a silent scream as I'm burning from both the inside and out, but I shove through the pain and keep feeding my gift more and more until I unleash everything I have left.

The cement pile bursts and then falls into rubble and ash, and my body collapses with it, no longer there to hold me up.

I feel empty.

Numb.

Like the end of an ice cream bucket scraped clean.

I don't even feel when Holt's attack ends. Only that one minute, I'm lying on the ground, lost in a haze of fiery pain, and the next, I'm being carried.

I expect to arrive in my room, like usual, but when my eyes crack open after he sets me down, I have no idea where he took me. It's dark, wherever this is, with no lights in the ceiling and no windows. The only source of light in the room is the blue glow emanating from a white pod that I'm leaning against to keep me upright. It's taller than me at my sitting height, so I can't see what's inside, and then there's a curved lid sprung open above it.

Something gets shoved into my ears, and then Holt lifts me again.

I try to speak, but only air escapes past my lips. I suck them into my mouth to moisten them and taste dried blood.

I'm lowered down in water within the pod. I couldn't even feel it when my body touched it. It's just warm enough that it feels like sinking into a cloud.

I have a moment where I wonder if Holt plans to drown me. If this is why I've been brought here, but it passes as soon as I think it.

Holt is Gordon's dog. He wouldn't spend all this time on me just to kill me like this.

Holt keeps moving around me, strapping me in, I think, because I'm suddenly floating on my back, half submerged in the water, as something helps keep me perfectly afloat. I go to touch my nose, to feel if it broke or just burst a blood vessel, but my hand doesn't budge.

Neither does the other one.

My eyes snap to Holt, and his lips move, but I can't hear anything.

Then, he closes the lid, and I'm trapped in darkness.

My heart pounds, which is now the only thing freely able to move after I test every other body part. Even my head is restricted. I'm stuck in this position, floating half in and half out of water, in pitch-black silence.

I close my eyes and take a deep breath.

This isn't so bad if I stop worrying about how vulnerable I am right now.

I continue with calming breaths as I begin to drift in and out of consciousness. It feels like my mind is floating in space, cocooned in a cloud. I have no body. Just my mind. And it feels freeing. Weightless.

I drift off for a bit and then Gordon's voice is suddenly clear as day in my head.

"You're a monster. A danger to everyone around you."

My eyes fly open, but there's still nothing and no one to see. I'm alone here.

"It would be better for you to be alone."

I remember Holt sticking something in my ears. I thought it had been to keep the water out, but it must also have some sort of

Bluetooth or recording in it of Gordon's voice.

Shut up, my mind tells him.

"How many people have to be hurt before you realize that you're too dangerous to be around them? That girl you chased after? Vera? Those boys you think who still care about you? They don't, you know."

My chest tightens at his words.

They do! Well, maybe not all of them. But Kellan and Jackson care about me. And Dane...we just started working things out.

"All they ever wanted was to make their family whole again. And now they have that. They've forgotten all about you now that Vera is with them. They don't need *you anymore."*

That's...not true.

But...I was the one who broke our family. I'm the one who betrayed them. Now that they have her again...are they happier? Are they better off?

"No one needs you. Not your dead mother. Not your friends who only get hurt by being near you. No one."

The water swallows any tears from my eyes before they get a chance to fall.

Stop.

"I've been checking up on them to make sure they are holding up their end of our bargain. They're living happily in some firehouse. No one is looking for you. No one even cares that you're gone. They have everything they've ever wanted."

*Please...*I plead as if he could somehow hear my thoughts. *No more.*

"But I *need you, pet. I'm the* only *person who wants you. I can make you into something great, if you'll only let me in. Give yourself to me completely, and you'll want for nothing. Just obey my every wish, make*

sure to please me, and do whatever I command, and I will take care of you. You'll find great rewards waiting for you. You won't ever feel forgotten or left behind again. And together, we'll save the world."

I fist my hands and try to tug on my restraints, to ground myself with pain or pressure to remind me of where I am. He's lying. I know he is. It's what he does: lie, cheat, and manipulate.

But it doesn't stop the sliver of doubt that slips in. It doesn't stop me from wondering if they are all happy now that I'm gone. Now that I'm not there to cause stress within the group or mess up Aiden's plans. Now that they have Vera again. They wouldn't risk getting me back if it meant losing her again.

He even knows about the firehouse. How could he be lying if he knows that?

Fuck, stop it!

I'm trapped in my mind, with nothing but Gordon's voice to keep me company for what feels like an eternity.

Chapter Five

AIDEN

No one cares to stay up late or hang around while Vera's here. As soon as she gets bored enough to turn in, we quickly retire to our rooms to have some privacy.

Aside from Kellan, who gets drunk as a skunk each night and passes out on the couch. It's one of the reasons I'm sure Vera decides to go to her own room shortly after dinner. He takes up a good portion of the couch on the long side, sprawling out, and half the time winds up snoring obnoxiously so you couldn't carry a conversation in the same room if you wanted to.

He's suspiciously quiet after her door closes, and I have to wonder if he's faking his drunken state for the very reason of annoying her.

I check my phone for the hundredth time, waiting for a call from Jackson to tell me what information he extracted from our next target on the list. Or news from Cibrina. Evie. Silas. Fabian. *Anyone* I've recruited to track her down. When my notifications are still clear, I sigh and stand from the dining table. There's no point in me staying out here anyway where Vera could overhear our conversation.

After I found a piece of a radio in my Aston Martin before leaving for the bunker one morning, I haven't left the firehouse since. If Cibrina needs me for anything, she'll have to call or send Reid directly to my room so no one even knows I'm gone.

I'm ninety percent certain it was a tracker.

Vera may be trying to play the sweet, misunderstood sister since Jackson threatened her, but we've all seen what she's really like. None of us are fooled. At least, I hope Dane isn't. He's been talking with her more, and it *seems* like they're getting along. I'll have to follow up with him to see what that means and make sure his stance hasn't changed.

If it has, we'll adjust, but not in a way that would compromise the mission of getting Raegan back.

I can't get her out of my head.

Not the pain in her voice nor the words she'd shredded me with before she was taken.

I didn't get a chance to talk to her alone after that, not that I have any idea what I'm going to say yet to fix all I've done.

All I can see when I close my eyes at night is the fear on her face when she'd seen Gordon during the attack on the Guild. And then the sinister smile Gordon wore when she'd promised herself to him in order to save us.

It makes me sick.

I almost walk away from Kellan but stop and turn back to reach over the couch and pick up his liquor bottle. I bring it to my nose and take a short whiff.

Nothing.

The label says vodka, so it would be easy for him to swap it out for water. A smile tugs at my lips now that I have confirmation.

Setting the bottle down, I stroll out of the main room and stop a few steps into the hallway. I wait for noise to indicate if Dane or Vera are still awake. It's past midnight.

Passing my own room, I stop in front of Raegan's and open the door. I'm careful to close it softly behind me. This is a routine I've adopted over the last several weeks that has become a compulsion more than anything. Even if I try to go to my room and sleep, I toss and turn until, inevitably, I wind up in here, anyway.

It starts with me walking around the tiny room, which takes a matter of steps, my fingers grazing over books, clothing, and any random things she had in her room. At first, I would find something new to look at; another piece of her that I missed before that I can learn about now. What she's reading. What sorts of clothes she wears when she's not in her vengeful assassin getup.

But it's barely a week before I've seen it all.

And none of the items really tell me more about her. Not in the way I'd hoped they would. She's an enigma. A mystery that she guards as if her life depends on it. As if, by sharing her secrets, she believes this world, or perhaps just her world, will end with it.

Then, as with all other times, I find myself at her bed. Her sheets are always a mess, because she can't be bothered to ever make it. I'd considered making it for her one night but couldn't do it. It looks like she just rolled out of bed and will be back soon. It doesn't make her being gone look so...permanent.

I kneel by the side of her bed, leaning over it and clenching the sheets in my hands. Her vanilla scent is still there, but it's faded so much that I have to try hard to find it. Once it disappears completely, I don't know what I'll do.

I thought I could let her go again if I had to. I'd done it once before, so why not?

I'd done my damnedest to push her away before it was too late. I threatened her. Insulted her. Yelled at her.

But none of it mattered.

She's done something to me this time that makes her impossible to forget. She's like a disease that's invaded my soul. And even if someone were to hand me the cure, I'd want no part of it.

She's the fire in my blood. The driving beat of my heart.

I don't let myself imagine what she's going through right now. Anything I picture sets my teeth on edge and pushes me to walk out the door and start doing as Jackson is right now until I find her. Fortunately, I'm not as impulsive as he and Kellan are. I can't let emotions rule the decisions we make when time is of the essence.

I tell myself that whatever happens, we'll figure it out. I can't stress over what I don't know yet.

I suck in another lungful of her diminishing scent and whisper her name like a promise on my lips. I push myself up from the sheets, stroking them, and then stand. I *will* make it all work out. We just have to get her back first.

The doorknob creaks, and I move to stand behind the door. It opens slowly as whoever is intruding peeks around to make sure it's clear. Everywhere except where I've hidden.

Vera lets the door fall closed behind her without bothering to shut it all the way or even look. She starts pulling open drawers and moving things aside, then sweeping through the items on the floor or on the dresser surface.

"Yes!" she whispers excitedly as her hand closes around something in one of the drawers. She lifts it out, and it's none other than the gift-muting cuffs that I'd last used on Raegan. But how...?

It clicks. The congressman. She'd been at the warehouse when he'd used the original cuff on Raegan. Was she the one who had given it to him?

I wait to see what she plans to do next, but then my phone rings in my pocket and gives me up. She twirls around as I pull the phone out to see if it's Jackson.

It's not.

Why Elias is calling me at this time of night is a question for later. I hit the side button to mute his call.

"What are you doing?! You scared me!" Vera hisses to keep from waking anyone else.

I sidestep in front of the door before she can think to escape through it with the cuffs. "I should be asking you that, although I think I know the answer." I nod to indicate the cuffs in her hands and then hold my palm out. "I'll have those back now."

She frowns and clutches them tighter. "These don't belong to you."

"No, they belong to Raegan after she acquired them from the late congressman."

I'm already working my gift, twisting and reshaping the metal on my arm, around my neck and chest, with my thoughts alone, until it's a living, moving thing that joins together to form the image I'm impressing on it in my mind. I haven't found a limit when it comes to what I can do with my gift. So long as I can think it, touch it, and have enough metal for it, I can do it.

It moves to my hand, settling the handle in my grip and pointing the tip of the sword at Vera's neck. I have a second twin sword in my other hand that I use to pluck the cuffs from her grasp.

She gasps at the first sword, too distracted by it to notice the second when I relieve her of the cuffs. I catch them against the pommel of the second sword with a few fingers.

Vera raises her hands in submission. I've been careful of what technology she has access to, particularly since finding that chip in my car, but even with limited access, I wouldn't be surprised for her to have an ace up her sleeve.

I don't drop the first sword yet. "I'm curious. What did you plan to do with them?"

"Nothing bad," she says with a small shrug, trying to play innocent now that she's been caught. "A piece of my brother's in there. I thought it was only right for me to give it back to him."

My brows raise. "Oh? That's all? So, if I tell you that he's already said he wants nothing to do with them, you'd be fine letting them stay with their current owner?"

"Their current owner isn't here anymore. What use does she have for them?"

"What other use would *you* have for them?"

Vera sighs loudly. "Fine. Whatever. Are you going to let me go? I don't appreciate you pointing that thing at me."

I'm not sure of anyone who does, but I choose to keep that to myself. Once the sword is lowered, I step out of the way so she can leave. She does like her ass is on fire.

It feels like we're running out of time.

Like there's a clock looming over us the longer we take to find Raegan, and Vera keeps sneaking around with whatever she's been up to. She hasn't left the firehouse. Of that, I'm positive. But has she found a way to communicate with GE still? Is she just trying to find the rest of the Guild members, or does she have some other goal for being here?

For someone who is still sided with Gifted Enterprise, she didn't put up much of a fight leaving them.

My phone rings again, and I pull it out just enough to view the caller ID. Elias. He's not usually so persistent, or such a late caller, so I exit Raegan's room, locking and closing the door behind me, before stalking all the way to the locker room. I answer before the last ring.

"Adams?"

"Yes, Thorton, I'm here. What's so urgent?"

"I can't reach Raegan on her phone. Get her for me."

The smile on my face is nothing short of malevolent at the implication that I'm some messenger dog who will do his bidding. "You can give your message to me."

There's silence on the other end.

"Why can't I reach her?" he asks slowly, and I can practically hear the cogs in his head turning. "What happened?"

My immediate reaction is to lie to him. This is family business. But I remember the way Raegan defended him and how Elias seems to care about her. While he isn't my favorite person in the world, he's also not a terrible ally to have around.

"GE has her."

Silence.

Again, it's Elias processing this information. "...Are you trying to get her back?"

I tighten my grip on the phone. "Of course we are."

He sighs in relief. As if he actually thought—no, *assumed*—that we would let them have her. We, the ones who are actively fighting against GE rather than him, would let them take Raegan, whom we've known most of our childhoods. Yes, we've been back and forth since seeing her again, but it's only *because* we all care about her so much that we fight.

"I've found Portia, but...things are complicated. I'm not able to make it back for a while still." There's a darkness to his tone that's not usually present, even with me, that I file for later. Most likely it's related to Portia's returned memories that prompted her to run away a few months ago.

"I wasn't expecting you to. This is our problem, and we're handling it."

"Well, if you need anything; money, planes, boats...anything, let me know, and you'll have it."

Now it's my turn to pause. I've always wondered but pushed it aside. "What's your interest in her?"

"What do you mean?"

"Raegan. Why do you care so much about her? You barely know her."

He's quiet, and then there's beeping in my ear. I check the screen to see Jackson's name. The call I've been waiting all night for.

"Never mind," I say tersely. "I've got to take this call. I'll give Raegan your message about Portia once we have her back safely."

I hang up on him before I hear his response so I can answer Jack. "What've you got?"

"A list of coordinates," his scratchy voice comes through the speaker. I can tell he hasn't slept. I doubt he's eaten much, either. But we've already gone weeks chasing down leads that dry up faster than rain in a desert.

We're getting desperate, and this lead is the closest we've come to any answers.

"How many?" Hope swells in my chest, but I anchor it down before it can take off.

"Three."

Three. Three possible locations where she could be. Or where she might not be and we'll be back at square one. But the guy Jackson just *interviewed* has a science background where he disappeared for a stretch of years before he suddenly returned with a lot of money and a higher position in the GE ranks.

"Let me get the others."

Striding to the living room, I knock Kellan's foot down and pat his face to make him wake quietly. Normally, I'd just push him off the couch, but the last thing I need is to make a loud enough noise to bring Vera out of her room.

Hopefully, she's so embarrassed from being caught that she won't poke her head out for anything else tonight.

Kell groans, and I slap my hand over his mouth.

"Quiet," I warn, leaning forward so he can clearly see me. He licks my hand, and I huff my irritation before wiping it on my pants. Disgusting.

He grins and sits up.

"Come on," I snap, then head to Dane's room. At last, it clicks with him that something's up, and he follows as we sneak inside. "Wake him up."

I flick on the light and then switch my phone on speaker so that Jack can hear us better, but I lower the volume so he's not too loud after Kell's gotten Dane up. He sits up against the headboard, rubbing his eyes.

Kellan leans against the door to guard it and keep an ear out for an unwanted visitor. Thankfully, Vera's room is two rooms down, so as long as we keep our voices down, she won't hear anything.

I use my gift to unlock the bottom drawer of Dane's dresser and pull out his laptop, which we'd stored for safekeeping there. I hand it to Dane, and he starts logging in without further direction.

"Alright, Jack. We're all here. Do you have the coordinates handy?"

"Got 'em," he replies evenly. The sound in the background has quieted. I can't say if that means the lead is just passed out, better gagged, or dead, but I don't care. If Jack pulled all the information this man has out of him, then there's no more use for him. I've grown callous in the weeks we've been hunting for information. The fewer people who know what we're up to, the better. So, for once, I'm not opposed to Jackson killing and disposing of them to keep our secret safe.

Dane nods at me when he's ready on the computer.

"Give us the first one."

Jackson reads it out twice so we can double-check that it's correct. He then goes through the other two in the same way.

"They're all tiny islands in or around Key West," Dane reports once they're all in. His head pops up over the screen to look at me. "Did we find her?"

"We won't know definitively until we get there. There's always the chance that she's being kept somewhere else, but the lead Jack's with was supposedly involved as a scientist on the islands like Gordon. He likely still has open communication with him and should know where he is." I glance at the phone. "Jack, how long would it take for you to get back here? *Without* running yourself ragged? We need you able to fight when you get here, not worn out."

"Two days," he answers evenly.

"Then take three. Clean up where you're at, find somewhere to eat and sleep, and then start heading back. We'll leave as soon as you're here, so long as you don't look dead on your feet." Next, I turn to Dane. "You know what this means."

His lips thin, and his expression turns serious. "Vera."

I nod in agreement. "Vera."

"What do you want me to do?"

I expect him to fight for her. To tell me that she's changed or they've come to some understanding over the last several weeks. But there's nothing aside from determination etched on his face. Whatever he's thinking, I can count on him to do this. We won't miss this opportunity to find and bring Raegan home.

"We'll use the locker room. I'll start putting together what I need tomorrow, and then the day after, you'll need to get her there. Try and see if you can get any information on Raegan from her. It can't hurt at that point. I know she's hiding things from us. If she can somehow narrow down the islands, that would be the best outcome. If not, we'll trap her there until we come back with Raegan. Then we'll figure out what to do from there."

Dane tilts his head forward in understanding, his expression solemn.

"Need anything from me?" Kellan asks from behind me.

"Keep acting the way you have been and stay a distraction so she doesn't notice when I'm not around as much."

"My pleasure."

I turn to look back at the phone, even though I'm speaking to all of us. "Three days."

And then we would bring her home.

We're coming.

CHAPTER SIX

RAEGAN

I'M LOSING MY MIND.

I can't say the exact moment when the shift started to happen, but weeks of physical exhaustion, of working myself to my breaking point each day, followed by Gordon's voice in my head for hours each night, will apparently wear me down no matter how much I try to fight it.

I feel like I'm still me, albeit a hollow, tired version. But I've been catching myself repeating some of Gordon's words to myself every now and again. Once I realize what I've done, I quickly argue it and try to convince myself why it isn't true. It makes me wonder if there are times I say the words and don't catch it, just letting them live in my mind and believing them.

And then I wonder if arguing with myself makes me a crazy person.

Ever since the water tank was added to my routine, I've tried to counterbalance it every night in bed before I let myself go to sleep.

I think of Jackson. I'll stare at the tattoo on my forearm, touching it to remind myself that it's real. That his love for me was real. He took on an entire city of corrupt GE members on his own for me. We promised each other there would be no sacrifices. I'm sure he's furious with me right now. I repeat the words tattooed on my arm over and over again as a reminder to myself of why I can't give in.

I think of Kellan. Of his promises to me and how he swore he would never let me go again. I picture the look on his face when he told me not to go with Jack. How much pain was there when I went with him anyway, leaving him behind. And then doing it again through the portal while Holt had him trapped.

I think of Aiden. Of what happened in the locker room and how that somehow felt like the most honest, *real* moment between the two of us. And then how his face dropped when I lied to him that it didn't mean anything to me. I was hurt and angry, but I hear you see things more clearly when looking back. Something was happening between us, but I ruined it before it had a chance to unfold.

I think of Dane. I hope he's able to sway Vera back to their side so they can be happy together again. I hope she reads his notebook. We had just worked out peace between us, and I wanted to earn his trust back. Did this do it?

And, of course, I remember Elias and Portia. I swore an oath to destroy GE so she can return home.

I run through these memories every night before falling asleep, hoping they'll be enough for me to keep my head and my heart away from Gordon.

But after weeks on end with no improvement in sight, I'm worried that I'm losing this battle.

The guests that Gordon spoke of finally showed up a few weeks ago. It's a chance for allies against GE. Or even just *someone* to talk to who isn't Gordon, Holt, or myself.

One morning, the dining hall that had been an eerie, echoing room by myself, was filled with two dozen others. The ages ranged from children to pre-teens, with the oldest-looking one probably a decade younger than me.

It reminds me of my younger years with the guys on the island. Back in our earlier days when the school and training seemed like something fun and cool. There's no sign of fear or anger riding them as they chatter excitedly amongst themselves.

At least, there was no fear until they noticed I had walked in the room.

Trying to sit or talk with any of them was pointless after the third table got up and left. A clear buffer of tables surrounded whichever table I sat at. They whispered behind my back or shot looks of fear my way if I so much as looked at them.

She's dangerous.

I couldn't hear what they said but could feel it nonetheless.

Fucking Gordon.

So, even with a room full of people now at breakfast, I still sit alone in my own table-sized bubble weeks later. I tried at first to eavesdrop and learn what I could, maybe see if I could work my way into a conversation or someone's favor. But when all those attempts failed miserably, I stopped trying.

I stab my fork into the scrambled eggs and start in on my plate. If nothing else, I like the buzz of chatter around me when I eat now rather than the awkward silence I'd had to deal with before. I can almost pretend I'm not alone during meal times, even though these people may as well be back in the States for how close they are to me.

A plate appears on my table a few seats down, and I stop eating to look up. I'm half-expecting it to be Holt, coming to insult me to warm me up for Gordon this morning.

A little girl sits there without a word. Her blonde hair is straight with mild waves, and there's a headband pushing the hair back from her face. She's wearing a purple dress that looks more like dress-up than everyday wear.

She finally looks at me with her big blue eyes. "Are you a bad guy?"

I swallow the egg still in my mouth. "I'm sorry?"

The girl shrugs and starts picking at her plate. "It's what everyone's saying. That you're bad and scary and to stay away from you. But I've been watching you, and you haven't done anything scary. So, I think they're wrong and wanted to come and see. Do you think you're a bad guy?"

Talk about a loaded question. But I remind myself that she's just a little kid and to keep it simple. Do I think, at my core, I'm a bad person? "No. I don't."

She smiles at me and nods. "Me neither."

"What's your name?" I ask, returning to my eggs while she devours her pancakes.

"Mallory. What's yours?"

"Raegan. How old are you, Mallory?"

"Six," she answers with her mouth stuffed.

I nod and take another bite of my eggs. "Do you know why you're here?" I keep my voice calm and mildly curious. I have no idea if she experienced any trauma before coming here or if she's oblivious to it all.

Mallory chugs some orange juice and then sets it firmly back on the table with a loud knock. "Yeah. My parents said there's something wrong with me. I think I'm sick. So, they sent me to these doctors who said they'll make me better. And then I can go home."

I bite my tongue. Sick. And her parents *willingly* dropped her off with strangers and let them take her thousands of miles away?

Were the parents tricked or did they know that they'd never see their daughter again?

"Why do you think you're sick?"

She looks around the room and then leans forward across the table to whisper conspiratorially. I mimic her to hear the apparent secret. "Sometimes, when I get really excited or upset, my eyes change color. Or my hair."

I sit back in my seat and subconsciously rub at the collar around my neck. It's been wearing my skin raw while in the water tank and after, so I catch myself bleeding every now and again. At this rate, I'll have a scar around my neck.

"That sounds pretty cool, though."

Mallory's eyes widen, and then she curls a bit into herself.

"Don't you think?" I prompt her when she doesn't answer.

She nods shyly, and I smile.

Her parents probably freaked over it and told her it was wrong, so she never got to enjoy her gift. Of all the gifts I've seen, her parents should be counted as lucky that hers is starting so small and doesn't do any actual damage.

"Well, I need to head out for training, but maybe I'll see you again at lunch?"

Mallory looks up and smiles at me. "Sure."

I return her smile and stand while picking up my things.

At least I've made one friend here. She's no fighter, but maybe she can help keep my mind grounded.

My mouth turns down into a frown when I walk into the indoor training room we've been using the last week and I see other people in there. I was already in a bit of a mood after Mallory was a no-show for lunch today. We've been sitting with each other for over a week now, and it's the first time she hasn't come. That's already worrisome, but now, seeing strangers in the room?

Gordon smiles at me when he sees me arrive.

Another red flag.

Holt flanks him, his arms crossed over his chest and face flat.

The other people are three males, all wearing regular clothes, bound and gagged in chairs in the middle of the room. I don't recognize any of them if they are some of the other *guests* on the island, but I guess I wouldn't really unless they were Mallory.

"You're progressing well, pet. It's time we switch up our training. Pick one of the three and use your gift. See if you can focus it on a specific body part." Gordon pulls up his stopwatch in his hand and presses some of the side buttons. "Hurry up and stand in front of the one you're going to start with."

My blood chills at his words. No. Not again. "No," I tell him, my hands clenching to stop the tremor of what I know will be coming next. "I'm not killing or torturing people for you again. That wasn't part of the deal."

His face contorts with rage. "No? *No?*" He closes the distance between us and roughly pinches my face with one hand. "How mouthy you've become, pet. Shall I put your mouth to better use again like I had to last time? It was always shoddy work, but I'll make the sacrifice to re-teach you the lesson of the only thing your mouth is good for. And *talking back* isn't it."

I'm shaking from the memories, tears pricking the corners of my eyes, but I don't look away from him. "Do what you want with me, Gordon. But I'm not killing anyone again. Not for you."

He buries a fist in my gut, shoving any oxygen out as I keel over for what his grip on my face allows. Then he throws me the rest of the way to the ground. His boot presses down on the side of my face so I'm pinned between it and the cold, lacquered wood floor.

"You'll do whatever I tell you to, pet. *That* was the deal. I don't want to hear another thing out of your mouth unless it's 'Yes, sir'." The pressure intensifies, and I gasp, squeezing my eyes shut at the pain. "I need to know that you'll follow any and every order I give you without hesitation. This is just a *test*, pet. And one you will not fail me on."

His foot disappears, and I curl in on myself, protecting my gut and trying to recapture the oxygen I lost.

"Bring her in," Gordon orders someone.

I hear a door opening and closing and then two sets of steps approaching us. It's easy to tell which set of steps belongs to Holt.

They're heavy and loud. The other set is far quieter.

"You think I didn't notice you getting friendly with someone else?" My heart lodges in my throat. I force myself to look up off the floor at who Holt brought in, hoping that I'm wrong. "Did you really think you could do anything here that I wouldn't find out about?" Gordon laughs cruelly right as I look up at Mallory's tear-streaked face.

He aims his gun at her, and she screams and thrashes in Holt's grip. "Noooo! Let me go! Please! I'll do anything! *Please*!"

Her cries hit me in the gut, twisting until I'm sick to my stomach.

"Get up," he barks at me.

I do what he asks. If it was me, I could refuse. But I can't risk her life.

Once I'm on my feet, he reaches over with his free hand to use the ring on one finger that releases the lock on my collar. Then he yanks it off. "Now, go kill them."

I would think that Gordon couldn't shock me anymore, but once again, I'm reminded of what a monster he is. "But you said—"

"What did I say about talking back?" he snaps. "You lost your chance at just working on your gift. Now, you're going to prove to me that you can follow orders and kill all three of them simply because I am telling you to."

I start to shake my head, and then a gunshot fires, and my heart leaps from my chest. "No!" I look over to Mallory, where she's collapsed on the ground, and run to her. "Mallory!" I lift her in my lap, searching her body for the bullet to see where she was hit. My hands keep checking for any sign of blood, but when there is none, I glance up and see Holt smirking at me.

"What's the matter with you?!" I scream up at him.

"She fainted," he answers, his annoying lips still curled like this is all an entertaining show for him to watch.

I give Mallory another once-over to be sure that he isn't lying before Gordon decides I've had enough time to learn that he must have purposefully missed to scare the shit out of me.

"That was a warning shot. You now have"—he thumbs a button on the stopwatch—"one minute to kill all three of them before I kill the girl."

A minute?!

Is it fair to kill three people for the loss of one?

But it's a little girl. She still has her whole life ahead of her. I *know* her. Her hopes. Her dreams. About her parents and her pet dog. How she hates math and history, but loves science.

"Fifty. Forty-nine," Gordon calls out when I'm still frozen in my spot. He walks up to us, aiming the gun at her head while still counting down.

Fuck.

I have no idea who these people are or why Gordon has them, but I can't let Mallory die because of me. Because she took the chance to be my friend when everyone else was too scared to even look my way. She's the final piece of my sanity, keeping me from giving in. If I lose her, I'll have no one to keep me grounded and remind me of who I am.

I'm sure Gordon knows this. Maybe he's hoping I'll fail so he can kill that last part of me with her death.

I almost forgot that I was never meant to be a hero. I've always been a villain.

"Thirty-two. Thirty-one."

I set her down gently and then run over to the others. Turning on my gift is barely a second's thought now as its invisible flames burn and lick down my arms at the ready. I grab two at a time. I do it from the front so I can see them. So I can remember what I did and try to etch their faces into my memory if I can ever find out who they were one day.

They scream in my grasp, but all I can hear is Gordon's countdown continuing behind me and telling me that I'm running out of time. I push my gift deeper into the person in the middle, shoving it beyond them and into the floor until it climbs up the chair of the third person and starts eating away at them from their feet and legs. My gift works its way all the way up before I bring it to full power.

I step back when I know they're all gone. "Well done," Gordon commends from behind me. "But..."

I turn frantically. Did I not make it in time? Gordon's lip curls when he sees the tears on my face, but I look past him to Mallory on the floor.

There's another gunshot, and then a scream tears from my throat at the blinding, white-hot pain in my knee. I crumple to the floor in an instant as the pain ricochets throughout my body.

Holt comes up from behind me, and my collar is snapped back in place.

"That's for your insolence. We'll end training here for today. Holt, take her back to her room. If she behaves, we'll have a healer look at her knee."

I'm faintly aware of being lifted into the brute's arms before the pain becomes too much, and I lose consciousness.

Chapter Seven

DANE

"Hey, you."

I blink out of my thoughts and look up to see my sister has joined me in the living room. She looks exactly like the girl I remember. Older, but still Vera. She even smiles at me like she used to. In the way that says she enjoys spending time with me.

I can't wrap my head around the different person I see when the others are around. When it's just me and her, I can almost pretend that things are...normal. That she's really back and we're just catching up on all of the lost time together.

And then she'll have random outbursts that completely throw me for a loop. She'll pout or say nasty things that aren't like my sister at all.

All I'm left to wonder is, which one is real? I know which one was real back when we were kids, but now? Is she putting on a show of what she remembers we acted like? Or am I bringing out the actual Vera, and the GE influence slips out when I'm not around or when something triggers her?

"I thought you were picking out a movie for us to watch." Her more golden brown than green hazel eyes flick to the case of movies I'm standing in front of.

I look back at them. "Oh. Right." We agreed to watch a movie since she was tired of watching shows on TV or playing video games. I'm surprised we haven't tried watching movies together earlier, but then I remember that she usually lost interest in them halfway through and we'd never finish them in the past.

That, and it feels more like a me and Raegan thing.

Which is dumb. You can't hoard something like movies for only one person.

...is what I tell myself, but that doesn't explain why I've been staring at the movies without really *looking* at them all this time. Something in me doesn't want to pick. It wants her to grow impatient and decide on something else.

"Oh, what about this one?" Vera tugs on a movie, and my jaw tenses involuntarily when I see which one it is.

"Not that one," I bite out, grabbing it and shoving it back onto the shelf.

"Wow, not a *Jumanji* fan? You didn't need to take my hand off, though, geez. Let's do a horror movie, then. *Saw*?" she asks rather than pulling it out this time.

I remember Raegan curled up against me as she watched through parted fingers.

"No."

Vera huffs but doesn't push it. The difference in attitude she gives me compared to the others is glaring, but I let it go. I'm her brother. Of course, she's going to treat me differently. "Fine. *Napoleon Dynamite*."

I can tell she's jumping genres to try and figure out what mood I'm in, but that movie brings me back to all the inside jokes I'd had with Rae over the movie on the island. I dressed up as Napoleon and she dressed up as Debbie for fun one time, and the look on Aiden's face had been *priceless*. A forever memory.

"No."

"Well, then you pick one. You can't just say no to all of them."

Can't I? Every movie reminds me that Raegan isn't here. That she sacrificed everything for me and Vera. What are they doing to her right now while I'm chatting over movie choices with my sister?

Why didn't she fight harder against them? Why give in so easily? Because of us? Because of Vera?

Because of me?

I should have stopped her. Kell and Aiden were stuck in that asshole's lightning, but he'd left Reid and me alone when we didn't move. If I was fast enough, could I have grabbed her?

I didn't try hard enough. This is my fault. She did this because of her promise to me to get me reunited with Vera.

The sad part of all this is that I can't even focus on Vera since Raegan's been gone. I can't stop thinking about what I should have done differently. And stressing out over whatever the fuck that Gordon guy is doing with her.

I'm not saying I'm giving up on my sister or I don't want to try. I do. I will fix this. But I can't concentrate on that until Raegan is back. I can't abandon her like we did the last time.

"Dane!" Vera snaps impatiently, breaking me out of my thoughts again.

Right. Movie. I scan over them. It should be easy to find a movie that came out after we were on the island that I didn't see with her before, but we were doing a crazy job of playing catch up in the days before everything went to shit.

My eyes catch on a title that we haven't watched yet and I grab it. No memories come to mind when I look at it, even though it's an older movie, but maybe I didn't discover it until after the island. "Got one."

"Ugh. Finally. Put it on and make some popcorn or something." She flounces over to the couch and plops onto it without offering to help with any of it. Raegan would at least make the popcorn and drinks or grab some candies to snack on for us while I was getting it set up.

I frown at the direction of my thoughts and stick the movie in. It's some dumb comedy that I can't really remember, so maybe it'll be enough to distract me for a bit. Once the movie is on the home screen, I hit play to get it started and then work to put together the popcorn and soda for each of us.

After that's done, I sit back on the couch and stick my foot up on the table where it's most comfortable, then dig in to my bowl of popcorn. I gave Vera her own so we don't have to share or bicker about who's eating more than the other.

It's not even ten minutes into the movie when it clicks.

Fuck.

We did see this before. But it was so fucking *terrible* that we cringed the entire time. Jokes that fell flat or were just scream-into-your-pillow awkward.

Why the fuck did I buy this movie?

Then a scene happens and I remember Raegan rolling on the floor cry-laughing because of just how dumb it was.

I look over at Vera. She's facing the screen, but it's clear that her head is anywhere except the movie. Her half-lidded eyes tell me that she's either bored or going to fall asleep. Either of which is a high probability for her.

For this movie, I can't entirely blame her. I just...miss Raegan's reactions. She was never a quiet watcher. I'd be forced to tell her to shut up half the time so I could hear what was happening *while* she asked me what was happening. She'd curl up into me for scary movies. Or push at me and laugh out loud when something was funny to make sure I didn't miss it.

Shit.

Fuck.

I scrub my fingers through my hair, forgetting that I have popcorn butter all over them, and now my hair is likely worse than a bird's nest. But I can't do it. Not without thinking about her.

"Hey, Dane?" Vera scoots closer to me and takes the hand in my hair in hers. I look at our hands between us and then at her. "I'm really happy that we've been able to spend this time together. Aren't you?"

"Uh, yeah. I mean. Of course, I am." I try to smile at her. I *am* happy that she's here. Even if I have no fucking clue what to do with fixing whatever GE did to her, at least she's here, and she's safe. She's not with *them*.

Like Raegan is now.

"Good. I know we still don't...agree...on everything, but that's okay, right? Families don't have to agree on everything all the time."

I blink at her in confusion. I hope she's not actually implying what I think she is. Because I will *never* be okay with her working for GE. She can't expect that I'd let her go back to that and we would just...hang out after.

She takes my not answering as agreement or at least as not an argument and continues, "But I do think, if you would give it a chance, you could find a home with GE like I did. You could help a lot of people with your gift."

I pull my hand from hers as anger boils in my gut. Abso-fuck-ing-lutely not.

I stand and turn to leave. She read my notebook. *The whole thing*, she said. So how could she think I would ever join them after what happened to us on the island? After what happened to her?

I consider the possibility that she didn't actually read it, but that makes me pissed off in an entirely different way.

"Dane, wait!" She runs after me just as my phone dings in my pocket.

I lift it enough to catch the preview of the text on my screen and then slide it back.

Aiden: Now.

About time.

I pivot away from the dorm hallway and past the training room to the door that leads to the truck bays. I slam the push door open and keep going. She's still chasing me.

Good.

I make it into the locker room, and when I hear the door catch before it closes and then opens again, I whirl around to face her.

"If you want to make peace, then help us bring Raegan home."

Vera stops in her tracks, her eyes wide with surprise before her face falls.

"We've been looking for her this entire time. We're not leaving her behind again, and she *will* be coming back here. If you would just tell us where—"

"*Why?*" she asks, her voice pained. "What about the deal? Does she mean more to you than me?"

"I never agreed to that deal! That was a bullshit deal, and you know it! If you cared a single fuck about me, you would stay whether Raegan was here or not. She didn't mean to hurt you, and you're here now. She was just trying to *save me*. Why were you letting them experiment on me so much, huh, Vera? Would you kill me for them?"

"Of course not!" she exclaims. "I love you, Dane! I've missed you so much, and I just want to have my brother again. Please. Don't do this!"

I close the distance between us and grab her arms. "You can have me, Ver. Right here. Don't go just because Raegan is here."

"It's not that simple!"

"Then explain it to me. What hold does GE have on you? If your goal is helping others, then you can do that without them."

Vera pushes at my chest and spins her back to me, breaking my hold. "It's too late," she whispers, almost like she's saying it to herself.

Frowning, I reach for her shoulder. "What's too late?"

"To get what either of us wants." Vera gives me an almost pitying look over her shoulder. "All I wanted was my brother back. I wanted to spend time with you. Tease you. Laugh with you. I miss having you in my corner. I could do anything, because I knew that no matter what, you'd have my back. I could count on you." She draws a long breath. "But you're not even really here with me. Because you won't stop thinking about *her*."

Guilt sits on my chest, and I know I'm giving it away.

She nods at what she sees there and continues, her voice soft. "Would you let her go if I told you the truth about her and Gordon?"

My breathing slows.

"What are you talking about?" I ask, my voice a breathless whisper.

She rolls and bites her lip, sliding her gaze away from mine like she can't look me in the eye for what comes next. My heart pounds louder in my chest. "She's not who you think she is. After she killed me, Gordon took her in as his *pet*. He trained her to kill for him. To...service him as his personal whore. She did anything he asked of her...until he took her virginity and she destroyed the island. But under the condition of her deal with Gordon this time, I'm sure he's already remade her into his obedient pet by now. She won't be the girl you remember."

I feel like I've been punched in the gut as my brain stumbles over everything she's revealed.

The mansion falling apart. The ground shaking and cracking. We thought it had been an earthquake.

And it was because...and we just left her there...

My stomach clenches as the revelations and signs race through my mind.

Her reaction to Gordon at the Guild.

My unwillingness to see it for what it really was.

And she gave herself back to that. To *him*.

For me.

Vera tucks her hair behind her ear. "I'm sorry, Dane. I don't think you'll get her back even if you do find her. It's safer for you to keep your distance from her now."

I swallow the sharp acidity back down, gripping her shoulder harder and forcing her to turn around to face me. "Where is she?! Which island? I know you know where Gordon goes. Where would he take her?"

She shakes her head and presses her lips together.

"Tell me!"

"I won't! You need to stay away from her!"

"How can you say that? She was like a sister to you on the island. Don't you care about what she's been through at all?"

"What *she's* been through?!" Vera rips her shoulder from my grip. "What about what I've been through, Dane? She ruined *my* life. I hate her. She's taking you from me and lied to you about GE being bad! There is no future with us living in this firehouse like our past didn't happen. Like we aren't as special as we are. If you want to be together again, come with me to GE and we can use our gifts for *good*."

I reel back. Ruined her life? The one with GE she's trying so hard to get me to join? And does this mean I've accomplished nothing in her time here? She's just as determined to go back to GE as she was the first night here.

Everything Rae is going through...for what?

"I don't have time for this. Raegan needs me."

I shove past her to the door. I'm not getting anything more out of her that'll be useful to us. I have to save Rae and do all I can for her while I still have the chance to.

I try not to think about how it may be too late for my sister.

Aiden's waiting for me outside the door and grabs the handle before Vera can try to follow. He melds the handle and lock into the wall until there is no door anymore. Then bars come down over the window in the door and the high windows around the rest of the room. She's in a metal cage now, where she'll wait for our judgment when we get back.

Vera reaches for the door, and her face snaps up to us when she realizes what we've done. "Let me out! You can't keep me in here!" She bangs on the window, but the bars are still there to keep her from using it to escape. And there's nothing left of the metal door except more of the same wall.

I spin on my heel and storm back to the main building when Aiden grabs my arm. "Wait, Dane." I stop to look at him. His face is drawn and tight, but his dark brown eyes look obsidian now. Black with a strange light to them that promises nothing good.

So, he heard then.

"You can't tell the others. Not yet."

"Why?" They deserve to know. We all do, now that Aiden and I know. I get why she didn't want to say anything to us, but I wish...no, I've already asked too much of her. I just wish we could go back and fix things. I wish we could have stopped them before they happened.

But wishes for changing the past are a waste of time now. We need to be getting her back. Then I can worry about making it all up to her.

"I want them focused on getting her back. *Not* on revenge. If we can get Gordon while we're there, then even better. But our priority is bringing her back and...whatever that involves."

Right. She could be brainwashed. Broken.

FUCK.

"Fine. After we have her back. Is everyone ready?"

"Jackson just got in before I texted you. I was going to give him an hour to rest, but I'll get him up."

I nod, relieved. Because every hour, every *minute*, counts right now. And we need to get her back from that son of a bitch before it's too late.

Two months, she's been with him. Please. Don't take her from me, too.

Chapter Eight

RAEGAN

"Time to go to work, pet," Gordon says from behind me. His hand strokes down my hair.

Disgust churns in my gut at his touch before it quickly dissipates behind the barrier of emotionlessness I've built to keep myself sane. Numb.

He removes the collar from my neck and I move forward to do as he instructed without a word.

Holt is here in the training room with us, guarding Mallory as the constant threat that's dangled in front of me whenever Gordon requires me to do something he thinks I may push back on. She looks at me like I'm the monster that lurks under her bed, leaning into Holt for his protection. I ignore them both, following Gordon's direction on autopilot while my mind tucks itself away to the safe place I've been using to get through my latest sessions.

I think about all the help Elias has given me. His unwavering faith and trust in me that still feels undeserved.

I remember eating Chinese food with Portia as we shared our stories without holding back, and she continued to stand by me as the greatest friend I could ask for. Or the way her smile lights up any room she's in, immediately uplifting the mood.

Mostly, I go back to my time at Old Red with the guys.

"I have always loved you, and there is nowhere you can go where I won't follow..."

"You don't get to run from me, beautiful...I'm yours whether you want me or not..."

"You don't know how long I've been wanting to do that..."

"I choose to believe in you, because that's what I should have done from the start..."

My right knee buckles, and I crash to the unforgiving wood floor on my hands and knees. The pain snaps me back to reality. I grit my teeth through the sharp, stabbing agony that momentarily blinds me.

After Gordon shot my knee, it apparently shattered the bone there. He told the healers to let it heal wrong. Now it hurts to run or walk on for too long.

I use it as a timer lately of how long I've been training for that day. Reaching this point means I'm almost finished.

"—wrap up this pet project of yours before he makes me do it for you. The president is not pleased that you picked this up again," an unfamiliar, dreary voice says slowly with mild disinterest.

Gordon's standing at the open doorway to the training room, but the person who's talking is still in the hallway, obstructed from view.

"He's the one who approved it. I'm just finishing what I started,"

Gordon counters, annoyed.

"That was quite a long time ago. There are expiration dates on such things," the other man replies, then breathes a long, tired sigh. "I like you, Gordon. I understand your desire all too well, and it's why I've asked the president to give you this second chance before he intervenes. But if you don't show results in the next month, even his patience will have waned."

"After all I've given him—"

"—ah-ah! Careful with what you're about to say. I sympathize with you, but that is all. My loyalty lies irrevocably with our president."

Gordon's knuckles pale as the tablet shakes in his grip. "Why are you here, Royce? To threaten me?"

The other man's name makes me pause mid-motion in my current task. I know that name. Where have I heard it before?

Royce.

Thorne.

The necromancer.

"Of course not. I send my puppets for such things," Royce calmly explains. "I'm here for a fresh soul. Perhaps two or three, even, and I heard that you've been collecting some as of late."

Gordon's frown deepens. "I thought Thorne left."

"This information comes from a different source. You should know by now our president has his eyes everywhere." There's a pause before he continues, "So? Is the one in there finished? That young girl would do nicely as well if she's next."

Don't react.

I force my body to continue exerting my gift without missing a beat, my eyes staring at what I'm doing even though my mind is deep in their conversation. I can feel the moment Gordon's gaze swings my way, checking for a response to what Royce said about Mallory.

It isn't until I hear Gordon speak again that I finally expel the breath I'd been holding. "How fresh do you need them? And are you looking for any particular gift?"

"Within the week would be best. The gift does not matter. I'll be sending Thorne back to that city where his *Guild* is, so he can sniff them out. The president is eager to learn more about what sorts of gifts and members are part of it and how he can use them. Since my puppet created it, he'll have a better idea of where to look or who may be a part of it."

Gordon scoffs. "Your puppet keeps a secret that big from you, and that's all the president has to say about it?"

Royce makes a clucking noise. "Yes, well, that's been rectified. It's time-consuming to go through a puppet's head, but I've made the exception with Thorne due to this connection. That aside, his body is beyond a healer's repair at this point and I need those souls to freshen it up some."

"There are a few in the disposal room in the basement. Have your pick."

"Wonderful. I'll get out of your way, then. Good day."

Gordon watches past the door as footsteps recede down the hall-way in pronounced, steady clicks that remind me of a ticking clock.

Tik. Tok. Tik. Tok.

I can't stay here any longer. Not if Thorne's going back to root out the Guild. The others think he's dead and they won't see him coming. Thorne wants Jackson alive to help him, and I'll bet he plans to use Aiden and the others' lives against him to get what he wants.

But the only way I can escape is if I kill Gordon and the threat he made against the guys with him.

Chapter Nine

JACKSON

The boat tips and sways over the rolling waves of the ocean. It's quiet. Only the motor of the fishing vessel and the water slapping the sides can be heard around us.

No one's said a word since we landed at the southernmost tip of Key West.

Hope is a dangerous feeling that's burrowed its way into each of us. The scientist could have outdated information. I'm confident he didn't lie about what he did have, but it's been some time since he was last involved in this area of GE. The probability that Raegan will be on one of these three islands is slim.

Aiden, who would normally be the voice of reason, hasn't said anything to dissuade our hope that we've finally found her.

I try to be realistic as well most times, but I can't afford for this information to be wrong.

The two months she's been with GE is already unacceptable. If she's not there…

I can't go back. If I have to kill everyone, island by island until I find her, then that's what I'll do.

I close my eyes and lean against the side of the boat, tugging my hood down to further shadow my face even though it's the middle of the night. The moment I let my eyes rest for more than a second, sleep immediately tries to pull me under. The rocking motion combined with the sound of water work to lull my mind.

I've hardly slept in the last two months, letting my body take only what it needed when I had nothing better to do but wait for my next target to arrive. Otherwise, sleep has been an inconvenience I can't afford to give too much time right now.

I'll sleep for days once I have my little one safe in my arms, where she belongs.

"Are you sure you're up for this?" Aiden questions from above me.

I crack an eye open to peer at him. His expression is tight. I noticed it had been that way since he came back with Dane after locking Vera up and then demanding that we leave right away.

I hadn't bothered questioning it since he had been the one forcing me to rest in the first place. If he changed his mind and wanted to leave sooner, then I wouldn't interfere. I could find out what made him alter his plan later. Getting Raegan is all that matters right now.

I smirk. "We're getting her back," I assure him, because I know exactly what he's thinking right now. That I'm too exhausted to be of any use to them. That I'll slip up and we'll miss this chance. He would rather bench me on the sidelines and do this without me than risk mistakes.

He's just as desperate for her to come home as the rest of us.

But he doesn't need to worry about me.

I know once I see her, that everything will come into focus, no matter how tired I am.

Aiden watches me for another second, then nods and returns to Reid's side at the wheel. Kellan's pacing at the bow in what little room there is to do so, and Dane's sitting on the bench opposite me, his hands fisted on his thighs, foot bouncing.

I close my eyes once more to take advantage of what downtime remains.

"We're close to the first island," Reid reports sometime later. His words break through the fog of sleep I'd been wrapped in, and I lift my head to check our surroundings.

The moon's barely a sliver of light tonight, and even the stars are dark from cloud cover. I can make out a dark shadow off Dane's side of the boat in the distance that could be land, but we're still too far from it for me to be sure.

"Kill the motor. Jack, you're up," Aiden commands.

Dropping a hand over the side, I draw air in a rush at the back of the boat. A sailboat would have been our best option, but this was the first and simplest one at the docks.

Once we're close enough, Kellan tosses the anchor over the side. Dane digs into his pocket and holds out something. "Take this and snap it around the first Ethernet cable you find."

I nod and pocket the tiny piece of technology. He flips open his laptop, and Aiden steps between us.

"Here's your comms." He hands me an earpiece. "Tell us what's going on and if you think she's here. Remember, we're not moving in until we know she's on the island. We have three to check, so let's not waste time if she's not here."

The earpiece fits snugly in my ear before I press the tiny button to turn it on. There's a small beep, and then I hear an echo of Aiden's voice. "Reid. Are you ready?"

The probationary Guild member steps forward with a nod. "Ready." Reid frowns when he looks at the growing smirk on my face, but he's smart enough not to comment. He and I don't know each other well yet, so this mini team up will be interesting. He's been working with Aiden and the others while I've been off hunting, and he's apparently won Aiden's trust during that time.

If he doesn't get in my way, I don't care if he'll be joining me.

"Grab my shoulder. And don't let go before I tell you to," Reid reminds me, his tone stoic. I'm curious for a second about what he thinks we're going to do, and then I realize that I don't care so long as he doesn't try to betray us.

Placing my hand on his shoulder, my other readies a handful of throwing knives.

This is it.

I'm getting her back.

The rage I've been holding back slips through my veins like sweet venom, filling me up in a rush of adrenaline that sets my heart racing. A warm buzz settles beneath my skin. A violent dance of energy that demands to be released.

The air thins, and then the world tilts off-balance before my feet land on firm sand. My body takes longer to catch up to where I'm standing, but I use my gift to steady myself and stay upright.

Reid's eyebrows pop up as he looks at me. "Most people fall down."

I don't bother responding. He'll learn soon enough that I'm

hardly ever put into the category of "most people."

"Hey! You!" someone shouts further down the beach.

"Shit. What are we going to—Hello?" Reid calls out, but I'm already airborne. The guy has his focus on Reid now, so it gives me the perfect opportunity to send my knives at him from above.

The first one catches in his throat, cutting off any further sound, and it's followed by another two to the chest. He drops to the ground, and I land in a crouch next to him.

"What was that?" Dane's voice sounds from the earpiece.

"Nothing," I answer calmly.

Reid strides over as I tug the blades free. His gaze travels from the dead security guard to me. "It's handled," he answers into his own comms.

"What's handled?" Dane angrily whispers.

"Quiet, Dane," Aiden cuts in. "If they said they're fine, then they're fine. We shouldn't distract them."

I ignore them and point my finger at the dead guy while looking at Reid. "Take his key card."

Thankfully, he doesn't waste time arguing or demanding more information. He works quickly to divest the guard of his card, flashlight, and taser gun, then faces me when he's ready.

My hand raises, sending air beneath the dead body, and then I push him out over the ocean far enough that he won't come rolling in overnight.

Reid grunts but keeps his thoughts to himself.

We make it to the nearest building, where I dispose of another guard at the door. Reid scans the tag from the first guard to open the door while I send the second security guard out to sea with the first.

The room we enter is dark, with random blinking green and red lights. Reid clicks on the flashlight to reveal an office. With computers.

Good.

I pull out the clip Dane had given me and search for the cable he needs in the nearest computer. Once it snaps on, I speak to the others on the boat. "Got you a computer."

"Fuck, yes," Dane murmurs. The comms fill with the sound of his typing as he breaks into their network.

With that task complete, Reid and I separate to clear the rest of the building. There's no one inside, so we move on to the next one.

This one has a few more guards posted and security cameras every twenty feet. "Cameras," I share in a raised whisper.

"Got it," Dane confirms.

Reid shifts next to me on the roof of the first building. "What's the plan?"

"Kill them," I answer easily.

"We're further from the beach, and there are more of them. How are you going to bring them there without wasting time?"

"I'm not." I wave my hand at the bushes and scrub surrounding the building. "Hide them in there."

He scowls. "I'm not here as your lackey. I can fight, too."

Tilting my head, I regard him warily. "Mm. Why are you here, then?"

"What? I'm here to get you on and off the island faster without you wasting your gift."

Not necessary, but it made Aiden feel better.

"No. Why are you helping us? What do you want?"

"Jack," Aiden warns through the comms. "Now's not the time for that. You can ask him whatever you want after we've gotten Raegan home."

Reid and I stare silently at one another.

"Cameras are on a loop and I've blocked their radios. You're clear," Dane reports.

My lips twist up in a smirk now that time's run out for Reid to answer. He's hiding something. That much is certain.

I nudge him off the roof, letting him fall by gravity first before I catch him just above the ground. He curses at me, but I'm already airborne and attacking the guards in rapid succession. I drop in front of one of them, finishing the kill with the slash of a knife.

The rest of the guards rush at me, and I use my gift to enhance my speed. My strength. To send my fist flying with a force strong enough to break bone. My body is fast and light enough that fighting more than one assailant at a time is more like a coordinated dance between me and them.

I could send my knives at them like the others, but I need the outlet for some of my frustration. I've bottled it up for so long that I'm spiraling in it. My fists and knives attack mercilessly, and I revel in their pain and bloodshed.

This is what happens when you take her from me. When you touch what belongs to *me*.

The last guard hits the sand.

I survey the area once again to make sure there are no others, then stop on Reid. His lips are pressed into a hard line as he takes in the bodies lying around me. Then his blue gaze finds mine. "I'm not dragging every single one of these away. You're helping."

I chuckle softly. Fair point.

He drags three away by the time I have the rest hidden in the scrub, and then I wave my hand with a breeze to cover any lingering signs of blood in the sand. We'll hopefully be long gone with Raegan by the time anyone on these islands wakes up to see anything, but there could always be more guards or the stray scientist working late at night.

Reid flashes the badge at the door to let us in. This time, the room looks more like a hotel lobby, with counters and computers on one side and a large living area on the other. We share a look. If she's going to be somewhere sleeping, this is most likely it.

"We haven't found anything about Raegan in their computers yet. Have you seen anything?" Aiden asks.

I hum. "Not sure yet."

The first floor has all common areas. A kitchen, cafeteria, library, and offices. We head up the floors, scanning for bedrooms until we finally make it to a floor that has them. It's easy to tell them apart from the others considering the hallway wall is see-through like glass.

"We found the prisoners," Reid murmurs behind me to the others on the boat, no doubt.

He swipes the guard's card through the keypad beside the door of the nearest room. A low, double beep and red light respond. His brow furrows. "We need a scientist's badge."

I focus on the face of the sleeping person in each room, using my gift to let me hop more swiftly from room to room.

"Where are you going?" Reid whispers harshly. "Aren't we going to free them?"

"They're not her."

"So, you're just going to leave them here?" he pushes.

I glance over my shoulder at him. He's still stopped in front of the first room down the hallway.

Aiden speaks up while I continue checking through the rooms. "You told me you have a limitation with how many people you can transport over large distances, Reid. The mission was about getting Raegan out safely. We'll have to come back another time for the rest."

I don't check again to see if Reid's decided to keep following me or not. A pile of blonde hair in one room stops me in my tracks. Everything else about the person is covered, and the room is bare of any clues about who's inside.

Little one.

I buffer the surrounding air to keep sound inside, then stab my knife into the wall. It's not glass, or it would have broken within a couple of strikes, but it slowly begins to crack with the force of the wind strengthening my swing. Again. And again.

My arm tires from the motion, but a hole finally appears among the cracks and I'm able to break it large enough for me to squeeze through.

Bending over the sleeping figure, I stroke the blonde hair from the girl's face.

It's not her.

CHAPTER TEN

RAEGAN

MOST OF THE BUILDING'S inhabitants retire to their rooms around ten o'clock, but I wait until midnight before moving from my bed. I slip the knife I stole from dinner out from under my pillow and change into the black GE uniform to blend in more easily if anyone is still up and about. I don't bother with shoes. I trust my feet to be softer on the floor than the heavy boots I wear for training.

When I open the door from my room, I'm careful to keep the latch from making a sound. My door hasn't been locked since the first day. Gordon was testing my resolve in the bargain I made at first, and now he's cocky in his control over me.

I can't really argue that, considering I've been doing everything he's asked without hesitation for the last...I'm not sure how long. A week? Two?

Time stopped meaning anything to me a long time ago. I couldn't even guess how long I've been here. It feels like a year, but again, I can't trust my sense of time anymore.

I cast a quick glance back into my room through the glass wall, checking that the clothes under my bedspread look like a body is in there. Satisfied, I hurry quietly down the hall to the stairwell.

I could take the elevator, but I don't like the unknown of the doors opening and finding someone on the other side. Or how it could alert staff that another person is awake and wait to see who it is.

So the stairs it is.

Which, if I'm being honest, is a terrible idea.

I've only been to Gordon's room twice to bring him something when he was too lazy to get it for himself, and it's on the twentieth floor.

I'm on the thirteenth.

That sucks already. But with my shattered and poorly healed knee? I'll be lucky if I can drag myself to his room once I make it there.

Deep breath. One step at a time.

I'm finally getting rid of the man who has tormented me for most of my life.

I'm taking back my freedom.

I'm going to see them again.

Aiden. Kellan. Jackson. Dane.

I grip the railing and begin. Even though my heart is racing and adrenaline is pushing me to get this done and over with, I pace myself. I don't actually want to be crawling to his room by the end of this, so it does me no good to wear myself out too early.

Half-way up, I take a break.

My knee is throbbing and has been shooting sharp stabs of pain the last few flights, so I decide now is as good a time as any to rest.

I sprawl out on the landing to catch my breath. Every noise sends my heart into overdrive, and panic grips my lungs. I have to talk myself out of it each time, finally deciding that there must be plumbing running along one of these walls and I'm just reacting every time someone uses the toilet or washes their hands.

No one here willingly takes the stairs. Only an insane person would take the stairs when there are two sets of elevators per wing. I think I may be partially insane at this point with how fucked my head is, so the reasoning still stands.

After the pain in my knee begins to subside, I take a deep breath, suck it up, and keep moving.

Onward and upward.

I take another break, albeit a shorter one, once I reach the floor I need behind the door. Even with the pause, my knee is not having it anymore. No amount of sitting or lying down is helping it this time. So, when I decide it's not going to improve and I may as well get this over with, I stand and limp into the hallway.

Gordon's room, or suite, is at the end of the hallway in the corner unit. I move quietly inside, once again thanking his arrogance that he wouldn't need to lock his door. Even on the island growing up, the only locked doors were the ones in the labs or certain offices. They felt no need to fear the children because the children all *wanted* to be there.

Or so they thought.

Gritting my teeth against the pain in my knee, I take another step toward freedom.

It may not be freedom from GE or this island, but the only one that really matters to me right now is my freedom of self. I can only get that back with Gordon's death, and then after that, I have no clue what I plan to do.

I can imagine Aiden's voice chastising me for not being prepared with a plan.

I have never been great with thinking things entirely through. Some of what I think Aiden tried to tell me a bunch of times, but I refused to listen.

Pushing thoughts of him and the others from my mind, I try to focus solely on my task. Most of the suite is open, and I can see all the rooms without barriers and a doorway in the back. I hobble through the rooms carefully. I have to avoid a bunch of furniture in the dark, which isn't easy, but at least all of the windows in his corner suite allow for more moonlight, and I can see the basic shadows of shapes to avoid.

My gaze catches on a map sprawled across a table with penned markings by Gordon. Taking the extra seconds, I memorize what I see before moving on.

I peek through the opening into the bedroom. There's a shape in the bed moving up and down slowly. No sign of a light to say he's still up.

Perfect.

The clock on his bedside table shows just after two in the morning. It took me over two hours to get from my room to his. That doesn't bode well for my escape, but maybe I can find something in his room to help me off this island.

I creep closer to the bed. My hand is raised with the knife at the ready. He gives the slightest motion aside from breathing, and I'm stabbing him immediately. I move into position over him, staring at his prone form as he sleeps peacefully.

How can a man so evil sleep so well? How can he look like just an ordinary man when he sleeps after all the things he's done? After all the things he's made others do for him?

My hand shakes as I look at him.

Do it.

Do it.

Fuck, why am I hesitating?

I think of Mallory. Of the words he's whispered to me on repeat for what feels like half of my life. I'm alone. Worthless. He's the only one who sees anything in me. The only one who says I can matter.

The shaking intensifies. I'm not sure if my body is having a full-on seizure standing here as I have a mental breakdown about what I'm going to do.

I think I'm hyperventilating, which only throws me further into a panic as I struggle to get some form of bodily function under control. I bring my other hand to join the first on the knife as if having two hands on it might help me drive it downward.

This man...he's *ruined* me. Taken everything from me. Broken me and remolded me into what he wanted. He deserves to die.

Now!

His eyes fly open, and my arms swing down.

The knife buries itself in the mattress after it passes right through him.

Fuck. He used his gift.

Fear crawls up my spine and down my limbs like paralyzing webs.

"You *bitch!*" Gordon snarls. A foot kicks me in the face and knocks me to the ground. I try to lift the knife, to swing at him again more in defense than anything else, and he grabs my wrist and yanks the blade from my hands. His leg swings and hits me in the gut without holding back. I gasp and choke, but he keeps kicking me repeatedly while cursing and calling me slurs. His attacks don't discriminate as he pummels me from my torso up to my head.

I raise my arms around my head to protect it, and he stomps those as well until I hear a grotesque *crack*.

My arms drop, and my body surrenders.

 I wake to pain.

Pain that's so sharp and cutting that a scream is ripped from my lips before my brain clicks online that I'm awake again.

It lances across my back and burns in the wake of whatever just happened. Before I can register that the pain is from something striking my back, I feel another one slicing into it from another angle. But it crosses over the first, and the gargled shriek that leaves my body isn't human.

Whatever is doing this stops after those two, and I force my eyes open to take stock of what hell I'm waking up to.

Gordon stands in front of me and watches me critically as I fully come to. I'm a bit higher than him for some reason, but a quick turn of my head shows that I'm strapped to some sort of massive X. There's no headrest or anything for my head to do other than hang down and look at Gordon.

"I'm so very disappointed, pet. You were doing so well, and now this." He shakes his head.

Another strike lashes across my back, and I can only imagine it as a whip of some kind. I cry out again on reflex. There's nothing I can do to hold it in when the pain is this bad. The rest of me already feels like something's not right, and my wrist hanging from one of the restraints is completely numb.

He steps closer to me and strokes the side of my face. "I know what this is, though. You were so close to being completely mine. I'm sure this is your stubborn self trying for a last-ditch effort to fight me." Gordon shakes his head and clicks his tongue. "It's a wasted effort. You *are* my pet now. Accept that, and we can finally move forward. And then you'll know peace and happiness again."

A part of me reacts to the promise of peace. Of that numbness I'd felt before in not wasting energy on feelings and just doing what I was told.

But the rest of me, the *real* me, bucks and fights against every word he speaks.

I collect the blood in my mouth and hock it in his face.

His fist slams into my jaw, and I'm lights out.

Something warm presses into my temple, and I'm drawn back to looking at Gordon's stupid mug. A man steps back from me and moves to the corner, his head bowed and hands folded in front of him.

"Heal her back so it scars. I want another reminder to my pet of what happens when I'm disobeyed or unhappy."

The man scurries to do as he says, and I can feel the healing warmth on my back. But it's not enough. Just when my back is starting to feel better, he pulls away, and I can still feel the ache there from a wound that's not fully healed.

"Good. Now, lash her again. I want five more before I'll be satisfied," he orders to someone else behind me.

I grit my teeth before the first one lands, screaming but trying to keep it to myself even as the tears pouring down my face show Gordon how much pain I'm in.

He begins to talk again. I really wish he wouldn't. Why can't he just let me be punished in silence? But he never does. He always has to use his words to drive home his punishment in ways that no healer could ever fix.

"Oh, I should probably tell you while I have your attention. That little girl you saved? Or, thought you saved, I should say."

Another lash with the whip.

"Did you really think that girl sought you out when everyone was afraid of you? That she stood up and decided to be your friend one morning?"

My teeth grind together, but I don't say anything. He chuckles and continues, "Well, it was her assignment to talk to you. To *befriend* you. She was absolutely terrified of you when I asked her to do it, but she did it. I needed..."

Another lash.

"...an insurance policy, you see. For you to care about someone enough that I could threaten them when you refused me. I knew you might be difficult when we switched to training your gift with people, so I had to put her in place before then."

Something in me snaps. Breaks. My head drops. I can't even manage the effort to keep it up to glare at him, but he lifts my face so he doesn't miss out on whatever expression I'm wearing now. Defeat? Anguish?

Gordon smiles. "So no, my pet. You never had any friends. No one cares about you. No one but me. That girl could care less what you do so long as you stay far away from her. You probably should have let her die back then, but I can't very well blame you when she did such a good job with her sweet and innocent act."

The last strike of the whip flares with pain like the others, but I don't scream. I don't feel it. I feel *nothing*. And just like nothing and a nobody, I close my eyes and find that place in my head where I can float and feel nothing at all.

Chapter Eleven

AIDEN

"We're not going home until she's with us," Dane declares to the rest of the boat. "I don't care if she's not on this last island. There are more islands around we can check."

It's a sentiment we all agree on, but once again, someone here has to keep reality in check and manage the risks. The midnight sky is already lighter than it was before. It's dark and starless, but the hint of blue tells me our time is running out.

"We have less than two hours before sunrise. If any staff get up before then, that further limits our window," I remind him.

Dane slams his laptop shut and jumps to his feet. He was able to download plenty of files from the server we'd hacked, but none of them made any mention of Raegan. We'll look through the information once we're back at the bunker, but all that matters right now is her.

"Who cares? We're already here! What if she's just another island away? What if she's being—" he cuts off when my eyes snap to his. He starts again, slower and more controlled. "It's been too long. He's had her for two months. What if she's..." His Adam's apple juts out sharply. "What if she's like Vera?"

I scan the rest of the boat for reactions first. We haven't told the others what we found out from Vera about Raegan and Gordon yet, and now is still not the time for that truth to be revealed. Kellan's not paying us any attention as he stares out past the bow of the boat, his concentration fixated on the ocean beyond us where the next island will soon be visible.

Reid is at the wheel. He's focused on the direction of the boat, but I wouldn't be surprised if he's listening in. He has been quiet since we left the first island and the prisoners there behind. I understand why he's upset, but he knew why we were coming here. We can't just teleport them to Florida and leave them there, and he can't make that many long trips with so many people to the bunker before he runs out of energy.

We'll have to return for them later.

I doubt these islands will have anyone or anything left on them by tomorrow once the staff wakes up and finds the dead guards.

It's the situation we're stuck with, and I'll give him time to come to terms with it. As long as he doesn't go rogue and leave us behind with a hero complex. Based on what I've seen from him so far, he doesn't seem like the type. Unless Tinsley is involved, he hasn't cared about anything other than helping us find Raegan. His sudden concern for the other prisoners is unexpected and something I'll have to investigate more after this is done.

As for Jackson...

According to Reid, he'd lost it on the last island and killed everyone. Thankfully, there were no prisoners. I have no idea if he would have harmed them had they been on the island, so I'm grateful I didn't have to find out.

He shut off his comms and left Reid behind. I can only assume he went to the last island himself, so I called Reid back to the boat so we could meet him there together.

Plus, I can't guarantee that Reid wouldn't be in danger with Jackson in his current state if he got in his way.

"We'll get her back. Just as strong and rebellious as always," I reassure him, even if the same worry plagues my thoughts. She lasted a year with Gordon on the island and came back a fighter. I can't let myself imagine that it would be any different after two more months.

But she didn't escape him unscathed the first time, did she?

I'd seen evidence of it when I knocked her out on the island, but I'd been so wrapped up in thoughts of betrayal and my own pain that I didn't understand what I'd seen. I never considered the blood on her legs as anything more than an injury from the collapsing building. The fear on her face wasn't because she'd seen me as an enemy who caught her while she was vulnerable. It was because of *him*.

And I let her fall right back into his grasp.

Let her be okay. I won't mess it up this time.

Dane drops into his seat, leaning on his knees and scraping his fingers through his hair.

"I see it!" Kellan yells at the front.

Finally.

There's a beep in my ear telling me that someone joined or left the comms channel.

Jack's voice is cold and dark. "She's here."

Dane's head pops up with a sharp intake of air. "You have her?"

A man screams in our ears. There's a thud, and then Jackson murmurs threateningly, "Where else would she be since her room's empty?"

Kellan storms over to Reid and grabs his shoulder. "Get us over there!"

Reid rolls his shoulder away from his grasp, but Kell's grip doesn't allow him to free himself. "We're not close enough yet," Reid rumbles. "I have to see the beach before I can bring us there."

"Quiet!" I snap at them when Jackson's victim answers him.

"—not usually allowed out at this time. Wait! Wait! The clearing about half a mile from the back of the building. If Gordon has her out early, then that's where she'll be."

"She's not outside. Try again," Jackson coolly replies.

The man whimpers and sniffs. "The—the training room, then. Or the basement. I don't know!"

"Where?"

"Training rooms are on the twelfth floor. You have to take the stairs to get to the basement. Please—please don't kill me, too."

"What's in the basement?"

"Ahh! Fuck, *nngh*!" he cries. "It's programming! The programming rooms!"

Programming.

Dane's wide eyes meet mine.

The motor dies on the boat and Reid turns. "I see the beach. We can go from here."

Kellan throws the anchor overboard and then clasps his hand on

Reid's arm. Dane leaps forward to grab his forearm, and I take the opposite shoulder.

We're gone in an instant.

The world shifts on its axis, and then my feet are planted on the sand with my face aiming toward them. I step my foot forward to catch myself, giving my body the seconds it needs to re-discover balance. Dane and Kellan both topple to the ground.

"If she's in programming, we need to hurry," Reid says before the rest of us have recovered from the jump through space.

"What the fuck is programming?" Kellan snarls while pushing himself to his feet.

Reid's jaw ticks. It's the first sign of real emotion I've seen out of him thus far. "Each room has a different method for brainwashing. I've seen people completely changed after one session in their pro-gramming rooms."

The man with Jackson screams through the earpiece, but it's cut short. And then it's quiet.

"I've already cleared the way inside. Meet me there," Jack mur-murs with dangerous calm.

Dane's arms shake with tension from his fists. "Rae…"

"Let's go," I snap and break into a run, trusting Jackson that the outside is clear of GE workers and we'll make it without a problem. The others stay close behind.

Reid snaps a badge off one of the many exposed, dead security guards near the door. He pushes between us to unlock it, and then we rush inside.

The room is dark, save for safety lighting along the walls. It's enough for us to see that it's empty. Hopefully, it's a sign that the rest of the building is still fast asleep. But we don't have much longer to count on that.

Moving further inside, Kellan smacks my arm and points to a sign on the opposite wall for elevators and stairs to the right. I nod, and we all move together to the stairwell door. None of us care about making a sound once we're inside, our feet pounding on the hard steps that echo through the many stories above us.

Kell crashes through the door first, bursting into a lit hallway that extends on either side of us. All the doors are solid without windows. The painted cement walls fill the space in between them, so there's no way for us to know which rooms are occupied.

"Split up. Kellan, you take the left with Reid. Dane and I will take the right." I don't wait for the others to move before I sprint to the first door. I grasp the door handle, feeling for the metal mechanism inside. The lock is triggered by the badges or a pin code, but that means nothing to my gift. I change the shape of the tumblers, making it smaller and shifting the metal elsewhere until the door opens without anything to hold it shut.

A single chair sits in the middle of the room. There are weapons and metal instruments hanging on the far wall and laid upon the counter against it. But no one's inside.

The next room has a pod in the middle of the room with nothing else.

A *crack* sounds behind door number three.

I rush to that one, grabbing the metal handle and yanking it from the door as a small sword. The door falls open without the latch, and I witness a whip slice across the back of someone tied frontward to a standing X. No, not a whip. It's a woman's length of hair that she's controlling to shape into a whip.

"No..." Dane breathes beside me. He's staring at the figure strung up in front of the woman.

Her long blonde hair is pushed over the front of her shoulders. Whatever she was wearing is torn to expose her bloody back. A quick glimpse at her face seizes my lungs.

"Rae!" he shouts and lunges into the room.

I curse and chase after him.

The woman with whip-like hair spins around. Her hair splits and combines to form multiple whips that fly at us. I grab Dane and throw him behind me. The metal at my wrist and up my arm merges together and drops to my hand, reforming into a second sword that I use to slash and cut the hair.

Dane runs around me to her front. "Rae! Raegan, wake up! It's me! It's Dane!"

An unfamiliar voice chuckles on the other side of the room, but Raegan and the X block my view of them and Dane.

"Grab him!" the voice demands.

Son of a bitch!

I pivot, readying to dash to Dane, when the woman with the hair shrieks, "Got you!" Her hair wraps around my wrists and yanks me off my feet.

Dane gives a battle cry. "*Gordon*! I'm going to fucking kill you!"

Fuck.

"Dane!" I yell.

The other voice laughs, and I hear a thump and grunt from Dane.

Kellan roars into the room like a bull.

My swords slice through the hair that annoyingly keeps growing back. I land on one knee, then throw myself at her. She sends more hair, this time honed to points. I sharpen the blades and swing them one after another, spinning in a circle to keep cutting through the hair until I reach her. The blade of my sword catches her collarbone and drags down to her hip.

She screams and falls to the floor.

Another cry rings out through the room, drawing my attention back to the door where Jackson has entered. Past the hair woman is a man I hadn't seen yet, now also dead on the ground.

"More are on their way!" Reid shouts from the doorway.

I hurry to the door to see what we're up against and curse viciously. Did Gordon call them somehow? Two dozen people, at least, and there's a high likelihood they all have gifts like the hair girl. Kellan and Jack face off against Gordon. Dane's trying to cut Raegan free with the shuriken blade Jack had used to kill the unknown man.

We're not going to get out of here if we stay to fight them all. Neither Jack nor Kell is landing a blow on Gordon, which means he's just stalling them until the others show. His grin is wide as he lets them fruitlessly try to harm him.

"Get ready to take us home," I tell Reid before joining Dane. I transfigure my smaller sword into a perfectly sharpened knife and slice through the leather binding at Raegan's ankle. "Kellan!"

I'm prepared to call for him again since he's in the middle of a fight, but he must see what we're doing and stands behind Raegan in an instant. His hands settle against her upper back and her thighs as I cut through another strap.

"No!" Gordon bellows. Jackson dives between him and us, throwing everything he has at the evil scientist to see what might stick.

I bend down to free the second ankle and then start on her wrists.

Gordon yelps as if one of Jack's weapons struck him, but I'm too preoccupied with making sure Kellan has Raegan in his arms to look.

"Reid! Jack!" I grab Kellan and search for Reid. He's being blocked by the same man who'd struck us all with lightning and kept us from Raegan the last time.

Come on, Reid!

He teleports in front of me, and I put my other hand on his arm. Dane does the same, with his opposite hand on Raegan.

"Jack! Now!" He looks our way but doesn't move to join us immediately. *Don't do it, Jack. Getting her home is more important than him.*

His gaze falls on Raegan, and I breathe a sigh of relief. He flies to Reid with his hand out.

Something flashes above us, and I look up at a sight I've seen once before.

Lightning.

Then, the world disappears.

Reid transports us to the quarantine wing in front of his and Tinsley's room. Tinsley pops out of their room when she sees us and smiles. "Hey, you're back! Reid! Come 'ere. I wanna show you something."

Somehow, we all manage to make the jump without crashing to the ground. Jackson and I hold Kellan to ensure he doesn't drop or fall on Raegan. Once he's stable, I pull my phone out and dial Cassandra. "Kell, get her on the bed in the next room," I tell him as it rings.

"In a minute, Tins," Reid says softly. He looks from Raegan in Kellan's arms to me, and I know he's waiting to make sure I don't still need him for something. He's been beyond helpful in the last couple of months. He follows directions well, and if there's something he doesn't want to do or like, he's straightforward and honest about it. I let him and Tinsley out of their room to wander the bunker and meet everyone, though they're still considered probationary members.

While the other three move into the next room, I start following until I hear Cassandra's voice.

"Hello?"

"Where are you? I need you in the quarantine wing at the bunker."

"I'm out on a job. How fast do you need me?"

Two minutes ago. I should have had her on standby just in case, but I never imagined...

"Now. As fast as possible. How far out are you?"

She curses. "I'm on the other side of town. Is it Raegan? Did you get her back?"

Cassandra is one of a handful at the Guild who knows about Raegan being captured by GE. I've had more than just Jack and Dane working on finding her for the last two months.

I slam the side of my fist into the wall. "It might depend on how long it takes you to get here," I admit, my smooth tone sharpening in frustration.

"I'll get her." Reid steps forward, and I look over my arm at him. He's clearly exhausted from all the jumps he's had to do in such a short time over long distances. I had planned on using the boat and a plane to get back, but Raegan's life is hanging in the balance.

There was no choice.

"Cassandra, tell Reid exactly where you are. He's going to pick you up." I pass the phone to Reid so she can give him clear directions.

He gives it back to me with a nod. "We'll be right back." I blink, and he's gone.

My phone gets shoved away, and I practically run into the room where the others are. Kellan's pacing the floor, pulling his hair back like he's going to tie it again and again. Jackson's sitting on one side of the bed, trying to pick the lock on the collar around Raegan's neck, while Dane is sitting on a chair on the other side, holding her hand between his.

Kell stops when he sees me, pinning me with his blue-green eyes. "Where is she?"

"On a job. Reid will bring her, so it won't be much longer." I move to the bed and nudge Jackson. "Let me." He leans to the side, and I pinch the collar between my thumb and forefinger.

"It blocks her gift," he states, which explains the power I feel thrumming between my fingers.

It doesn't stop me from using mine on it, though, so the collar carefully splits apart on one side and curls away from her skin. Once it's clear of her, I step back with it in my hand. On her neck, there's a dark pink line with some red spots where it rubbed her skin raw.

Jackson strokes the hair from her face, and fresh anger spews in my chest when I see the bruise on her cheek and jaw. It's a tiny fraction of everything I see. Like the bleeding welts on her back crossed over older scars that they never bothered to heal. The blood dribbling out of her nose and mouth concerns me the most. Is it from what caused the bruise, or does she have internal bleeding?

Kellan releases a wordless roar and punches the wall. "She's taking too long!"

Reid and Cassandra pop into the room at that second. "I'm here! Where—Oh, shit." She rushes to the bed where Raegan's lying on her stomach with her head to the side.

I hand Reid the now-mangled collar. "One last thing. Drop this in the ocean or somewhere far from here. I don't know if there's a tracker in it. Then go rest." He nods and takes it. "And Reid?" He pauses to look at me. "Thank you."

Reid's blue eyes slide to Raegan on the bed and then back to me. "Let me know if there's anything else you need for her." Then he's gone.

I move to the foot of the bed to watch Cassandra. Her hands are carefully placed on Raegan's sides emitting a soft, warm light. She must hear my footsteps because she turns to look up at me with her bottom lip pinched between her teeth. Her green-gold eyes seem to glow brighter while her gift is active, but it's the lines of worry on her brow that grab my attention.

"What is it?"

"I can't heal it all." Dane and Kellan both jump forward, but I cut them a slashing look so she can finish. "I'll focus on the most urgent areas tonight, but I'll need to come back over the next few days to slowly heal the rest."

"What's wrong?"

She chews her lip again. "Her body's already exhausted. If I push it to heal itself too much, too fast, she...her body could give out. It would be too much. And it takes time for her body to get the rest it already needs, let alone the healing sleep. I have to do this slowly for her safety."

"Do it."

She nods and focuses back on Raegan, closing her eyes and directing her gift to where it needs her healing the most.

Kellan's watching with arms shaking, fists tight, looking ready to murder the next person he sees.

Dane and I haven't even told him what we learned from Vera yet.

"Get out of here and cool off," I tell him.

He glares at me. "I'm not going anywhere."

"Well, you're not fighting anyone in this room. So either leave and vent your anger out elsewhere, or calm down."

Dane decides to volunteer as tribute when he speaks up to snark at Kell. "There shouldn't be any anger in a healing room."

I grab Kellan's arm to physically get his attention away from Dane and whatever mess might have happened there. "Don't start anything, Kell. If Cassandra gets distracted in her healing because of you two fighting, I'm banning you both from this room until she's fully healed."

He yanks his arm away. "I wasn't going to start anything."

I seriously doubt that, but he thankfully just shoots Dane a glare and the middle finger and then goes back to pacing.

Dane wasn't wrong, but he knew saying anything to Kellan would only piss him off more. I check back in with Jackson to see if he's been watching the spectacle between us, but his focus is completely owned by Raegan and her healing. If anger isn't allowed in a sick room, then Jackson is no exception. Even though he looks calm sitting there and watching, I know he's just as angry as Kellan. He just knows how to hide it better.

"There," Cassandra finally says. She sits up and pulls her hands away. "I've stopped the internal bleeding, healed her broken ribs and her concussion, as well as any other internal injuries. That's all her body will handle for the next day or two."

"She's still burning up," Jack comments almost mildly, his hand resting over Raegan's forehead.

"I heal injuries, not sicknesses. This is just her body's response from...well, everything. Since the internal damage has mostly been taken care of, it should start getting better soon. You can help her sweat it out, too, or see if you can get her to take some medicine."

"Will she wake up now?" I ask, my eyes glued to her barely moving form on the bed. I have to really focus to see the movement of her back that shows she's breathing.

Cassandra spins around to answer me next with a shrug. "Honestly? I doubt it. I'll come by to check on her tomorrow to see if she's up for more or if it will need to be the next day. But with how tired her body is from...before and now the healing, I wouldn't expect her to wake up until it's done."

"What were all of her injuries?" Jack asks next.

My gaze jumps to Dane, whose jaw tightens, but he doesn't say anything. Neither of us has forgotten Jackson's promise to Vera. And I'm not entirely sure if I disagree with Jackson either after what she told us and how she acted about it. Especially after seeing Raegan like this.

Cassandra catches the mood shift in the room, her eyes darting between each of us before she nervously grabs the sheets of the bed at her side. "Um...aside from what I just healed, she has a broken wrist, wounds on her back, significant bruising all over her body, the neck injury, and..."

"And?" I press.

"Her knee...something's wrong with it, but I'm not sure what yet. I won't be able to tell until the rest is healed." She takes a shaky breath, combing her fingers through her hair. "What's making this so much harder is her body's strength. It's like she's already been worn down to her limit, so she doesn't have enough to give to heal a lot at a time. I could have done more if she'd been in better condition before...whatever happened."

She nods to some internal comment and then continues, her voice strengthening, "Get her a brace for her left wrist and find some aloe to coat her back with. Try not to move her too much, but make sure she's comfortable. I'd probably get her hooked up to an IV as well for administering any medications and keeping her body hydrated while she's out."

"Thank you, Cassandra."

She stands and offers me a comforting smile. "I'll be back tomorrow, but call me if anything happens. I'll make sure to stay nearby until she's healed up."

I nod, putting a pin in the request I'll ask of her later once Raegan's finished healing from the worst of it, and wait for her to leave before looking back at the rest of the room. "Kellan, come with me to get the supplies. Then you and I have another errand to run."

He joins me on the brief trip to the medical wing. We could have brought Raegan to this area for care, but the beds here are only separated by curtains for short-term care. I prefer having her in the privacy and comfort of one of the quarantine rooms, where it's also more heavily defensible should anyone find us here.

Not that I'm expecting they will, but I'd rather be ready for that possibility.

They are *never* getting her back again.

And even if they try, I'll make sure she'll never be lost to us.

We deliver the supplies, doing everything Cassandra instructed until she seems settled and Dane is liberally applying the aloe to her back. Jackson's now perched on top of the backrest of the sofa chair, his boots planted on the arms, as he watches Raegan like a hawk in his nest.

"Kellan and I are going to check on Vera and Old Red. We'll have to figure out a rotation between watching Vera and Raegan and sleep, but I can bring some clothes here from the firehouse for each of us." We'll have to figure out what we're doing with Vera now that we have Raegan back. It would be easier to bring her to the bunker and lock her next door, but there's too much technology here for her to access. We have to keep her at Old Red. Which means splitting us up into two groups.

I don't like it.

"I don't know if there was a tracker in that collar or if it was here long enough for them to have caught the signal, but in case they try to portal in and take her again, make sure you're ready. We'll hopefully be back within the hour to come up with our game plan moving forward."

Jackson nods, his eyes still zeroed in on her. "If they come, I'm ready."

If they do show up, it's up to Jackson to keep both Raegan and Dane safe. I'm not sure I trust that Jack will protect Dane as well as Raegan, but I need Kellan with me at Old Red if we need to move Vera. It's a risk, but I don't plan on being gone long.

"Good. Let's go, Kell."

Chapter Twelve

KELLAN

The sofa and pillows have been gutted and the dining room table and chairs are broken. All the plates and dishware are shattered on the counter and ground throughout the kitchen and even to the living room, like they were purposefully thrown. The food is either out and spoiled or torn apart in the pantry, so we're walking on a combination of ceramic, glass, and food crumbs.

The dorm rooms have beds flipped over and drawers left open, but there wasn't much to begin with other than clothes, which were left strewn on every available surface.

I scowl as we take in the mess and damage. It feels like I *just* cleaned this place, too.

We don't bother checking the locker room for Vera. Clearly, she escaped, and now GE knows about this place. "Are we ever going to have one place we live where we don't have to pack up and leave months later?" I growl.

This is the *third* time we've been forced to leave our temporary home in the last six months.

"The Tower is our home. Once GE is taken care of, we can go back there," Aiden replies while tossing things aside in his search for something.

Of course, he would say that. Aiden helped design the Loft into exactly what he wanted. It has high views of the city, custom space for each of us, and it was the most secure location until Vera came back. But there are only four bedrooms. If we're going to convince Raegan to stay, she can't feel like she doesn't have her own space.

Old Red is more relaxed, and it has room to expand our living space.

Tossing a piece of dresser into the mess of Dane's room, I scoff. "It *was* our home. But not hers. She will always see that as ours. But this place...we all shared it together. I think she liked it here."

Aiden pushes more of Dane's dresser aside. Someone had smashed it to pieces to get to the locked drawer on the bottom, but Dane had his laptop with him. That drawer should have been empty.

"We don't even know if Raegan will want to live with us after this. I can't plan for anything until she wakes up," he says distractedly, and I frown.

"And you would let her go without a fight?"

Aiden stops. His eyes close as he huffs out a breath, then he turns his face to mine. "No."

Good. That's all I need to know.

Satisfied we're on the same page, I finally squat and poke at the wreckage on the floor. "What are you looking for?"

"The cuffs."

"Cuffs? Wait, the ones you used on Raegan?"

"They're gone. Vera tried stealing them while she was here, so I moved them and locked them away here."

"Guess she found what she was looking for, then."

Aiden shakes his head and exhales roughly. "I should have taken them with us." He pauses for some internal commentary, no doubt, then continues. "Let's check the locker room for anything. Then grab some clothes and supplies and get back to the bunker."

The locker room hasn't changed much. The metal Aiden hid and stored has been taken, though, which means he'll have to source a new stockpile. The door was still closed as before, so someone had to have transported or portaled her out of the room and to the main area of the firehouse, where they set to work on making that mess.

There are no clues as to who else was with her or how they found her.

It's a dead end and a cold trail.

She's gone.

We fill a couple bags with clothing for each of us, including Raegan, and then drive back to the bunker.

Jackson and Dane haven't moved from where we left them.

"Vera's gone," I announce, dropping the bags on the floor. "Old Red's been trashed again."

"Which means we'll all be staying here now that Old Red has been compromised," Aiden adds.

"She's gone?" Dane repeats, looking at Aiden for confirmation.

"Someone got her out. There's no sign of who or how or where they went. But I'd assume she's with them again," he answers.

Dane's face angles down at the bed, and he closes his eyes. It's hard to tell from here if he's upset that he's lost her again or relieved that she's not there for Jackson to exact his punishment on.

"There aren't any regular rooms available, and I'm sure we'll all want to stay close to her, so we can split between this room and the one next door. Or," Aiden continues when he sees the annoyed look on my face about sharing, "you can go pick out an open bed in the bunk room with the rest of the Guild."

No thanks.

"I'll get an air mattress," I volunteer.

Five days.

Five fucking days of letting her sleep and heal, and she hasn't stirred once.

I stalk to her bedside again, even if it hasn't been more than an hour since I last checked, to press my fingers to her pulse. Her heart beats slow and steady beneath my touch.

"I thought Cassandra said she was healed," Dane grumbles from the other side of the bed.

"She is," Aiden replies dismissively from the air mattress. He took the night shift watch, but instead of going to the other room to sleep, he stayed here. Probably waiting for her to wake up like us. He just hides his impatience better.

Cassandra removed the medical equipment from Raegan yesterday that kept her hydrated and able to stay in bed, so we'd all expected her to wake up soon after that.

Sitting on the edge of the bed, I cross my arms and set my gaze on Jack. He's been an almost permanent fixture on top of the chair, with minor exceptions for the bathroom and food.

"Then she should have woken up by now. It's been almost a whole day since Cassandra was here last," Dane presses.

"What do you think?" I direct to Jackson. He's been quiet for most of this time, save for small conversations we shared when it was my night to watch her. I know there's a lot that he's hiding. He wanted to kill Gordon while we were there. He'd managed to hit him one time right before we left. I'm sure that's on his mind.

"She'll wake up," he answers with so much confidence that I almost believe him.

Almost.

"I agree with Dane. There must be something Cassandra missed," I argue hotly.

Jack's gaze shifts from mine back to her. "She'll wake when she's ready. It's not fair to rush her just to make us feel better."

My teeth snap together. Asshole. That's not how I meant it.

"If you're both so worried, I'll call Cassandra in to check on her." Aiden lifts his phone to his ear. The bastard is just as concerned as us and was probably waiting for an excuse to call her. "Would you mind stopping by Raegan's room to check on her? No. No, she hasn't. Thank you." He stands from the air mattress. "She'll be right in."

We wait in silence until there's a knock at the door. Aiden lets her in, and she strides directly to Raegan's side. I frown when she shoos me out of her way.

Cassandra holds her hands to either side of Raegan's face and closes her eyes. Aiden and I move next to Jack's chair to watch her. Dane leans forward on the bed from the other side as if he thinks he'll see something on Raegan during Cassandra's check.

A minute passes, and Cassandra exhales and leans back. "I don't detect anything new. I've healed as much as I can."

"What does that mean?" Dane rushes out. "What aren't you saying?"

He and Aiden share a secretive look that puts me on edge. What the hell are *they* hiding?

"I healed the fresh scars that were on her back, but the older ones...I can't undo them. The body has already healed itself with scar tissue, so there's technically nothing there. You'd have to..." she hesitates.

"Go on," Aiden orders.

"You would have to cut the tissue from her skin, and then I can tell her body how to heal itself without leaving a scar."

Fuck that.

She nods. Probably agreeing with the shared look of horror on our faces. "Right. It's the same with her knee. Whatever happened to it shattered her kneecap, and then it healed with the bone fragments not put back where they belong. It's difficult because re-breaking her knee doesn't guarantee that all the previous bone fragments will break free, and it can create new ones. It would just make it worse. Unless someone can go in and break each individual piece from where it's healed, I can't fix it."

My chest swells with heat, my limbs quivering with the need to pummel something. No, not something. Some*one*.

That Gordon fucker did this. He destroyed her knee and scarred her back forever.

"Are those injuries what's keeping her from waking up?" Dane asks, his forehead pressed against his hands around one of hers.

Cassandra tucks a bundle of red curls behind her ear. "No, those were already healed as much as they could be by the time she got here. My guess is that her body's still exhausted. Or…"

Aiden's voice is tight. "Or?"

She hesitates, her voice thin when she answers, "She may have suffered so much trauma that she could be in a self-induced coma. She may not *want* to wake up."

Dane's hands tighten over Raegan's. He shoots a panicked look at Cassandra. "Did you find something? Was she—"

"Dane!" Aiden snaps.

What the hell?

"Was she what?" I demand. "What the fuck are you two hiding?"

"Vera told me—" Dane begins, but Aiden interrupts again.

"Cassandra, thank you for your time. Kell, come with me." He strides past me to the door without waiting for a reply. He'd better be planning to fill me in on whatever secret he and Dane have been keeping about Raegan.

We stop in front of the second room we've taken for our own next to Raegan's.

"What's going on?"

Aiden eyes me skeptically. I fist my hands to fight the urge to throttle him for withholding anything about her from me.

"I'd hoped to tell you and Jack after things had calmed down. I would like to at least keep Jackson in the dark for a bit longer if Dane didn't just ruin that." Considering how obvious he'd been about it, I'm sure Jack will be pinning Aiden to a wall later to get the information.

Not my fucking problem.

"What did Vera tell him?"

"She told Dane that Gordon had been...assaulting Raegan the last time they were together."

No shit. Someone had to break her knee, and we witnessed her tied to that post for torture.

"Not just physically," he adds. "Every way possible. Mentally. Emotionally...sexually. The day we left the island and thought it was an earthquake? It was her. Gordon *raped* her."

No...

Everything stops.

My breath.

My heart.

My mind.

All I'm left with is pure, unfiltered rage that scorches through my veins. My chest burns like it's on fire, boiling my blood and demanding action. Without realizing it, I'm moving, and suddenly, my fist slams into a door.

I'm going to kill him. Rip him limb from limb in the most painful way possible. I'll feed him to rabid dogs so he becomes nothing more than dog shit.

"—Ian! Kellan! Snap out of it!" Aiden's voice is distant and faded. Like I'm underwater and he's somewhere shouting in the sky.

But there's nothing left of me other than the rage.

Boom! Boom! Thump! Crash! A girl's scream.

"—going on?" a male voice I recognize, but can't immediately place, demands to my face.

I blink, the red swimming in my vision clearing enough that I begin to make out shapes in front of me. And then a face. A scowl. My hand pinning them to the wall by their throat.

"Kellan, put Reid down!" Aiden snaps. "He has nothing to do

with this."

Reid. *Reid.* Right. I don't want him dead. I want him to—

"Take me to Gordon." My voice is deep and gruff. It startles me enough to take in more of my surroundings. The arm holding Reid up is covered in golden scales.

"If we knew where he was, do you think we'd be sitting around here?" Reid says with a stern face. He doesn't appear afraid or angry. Either he doesn't care I'm holding his life in my hands or else he's damn good at controlling his emotions.

Aiden grips my arm and stares me down. "Don't you think we all want that right now? Do you think you're the only one who's thought of going after him for everything he's done?"

My body still needs an outlet for all that fury. There's so much...

"But this isn't about us. It's about *her.* And what's most important right now is making sure she's okay. When she wakes up, it's not going to be to news that you left her when she may need you most. We have no idea what happened to her these last two months or what she needs. So, you're going to put Reid down, and get your shit together before she wakes up. You're going to be here. For her. You're going to help us make sure that GE doesn't somehow know where we are and portal in to take her again. You are *not* leaving the bunker alone anymore now that I'm sure Gordon has ordered agents to kill us since we broke the deal." Aiden pauses to let that sink in. "Do you understand?"

The adrenaline recedes like a tide going out to sea. It sucks all the energy I have with it, so my arm falls faster than I intend when releasing Reid. He mutters something about getting involved in family shit and pushes past us. Tinsley throws her arms around him and he holds her tight.

"Kellan," Aiden prods when I've taken a few deep breaths and still haven't answered him.

"Yeah. Got it." My hand glides down the length of scales on the other arm. Scales which came out without an injury. I just have no clue how it happened. I've been angry before, but could it have been the degree of it that triggered it? Or something else? It's a puzzle for another time, though.

Glancing at Aiden, I raise an unamused brow. "Pretty mighty of you, telling me what she needs, don't you think? Considering the dick you've been to her."

"I know," he admits, his voice low. But his gaze is unwavering where it meets mine. "I have a lot to make up for."

"Well, I'm glad to hear you finally agree."

"She sacrificed herself for us. For Dane to get Vera back. Of course, I'm not going to brush that off. That, coupled with what Vera told us gives me a pretty good idea of some things she may have been trying to hide."

"You'd better not keep pushing her for details, Aiden, or *I'll*—"

"Save it. I won't push her anymore."

I nod. "Good."

"Good. You're done," Reid interjects. "Now, get out of my room. Also, I need a new door." He gestures to the beat-up door hanging on its last hinge and dented into the wall behind it.

Did I do that?

Aiden shoots me a look, and I shrug.

Whoops.

Chapter Thirteen

RAEGAN

"That's my good pet."

"You're safe now."

"No one else cares about you."

"You can wake up."

"It would be better for you to be alone."

"Please, Rae. Open your eyes."

"No one needs you."

"We all need you. You have to wake up."

"You are nobody."

The words echoing in my head are confusing. Why would Gordon be saying these things? But when I listen harder, there's a second voice. One that I haven't heard in a while, but I'd still recognize anywhere.

And there's something restraining my hand. I jerk it to test its resistance, and it flies back easily. My eyes jolt open to the sight of Dane leaning on his elbows at the edge of the bed, his hands partially open.

His entire face lights up in a smile I haven't seen him wear since we were stupid kids. "You're awake!" I can hear the relief in his tone, but he keeps his voice to a quiet murmur so it doesn't startle me.

I'm still a bit shocked.

By his smile.

By the fact that *Dane*, of all people, is here with me and the one who I think was asking me to wake up.

And the key detail that he's either on the island with me, or I've been rescued. Or else...

"Am I dead?" I ask him in all seriousness.

His smile falls and he reaches for me, but I pull away just enough to avoid his touch that he stops. "No. You're at the bunker. I'm sorry it took so long, but we finally found you and brought you back."

I stroke down my neck without being stopped by the collar, then push myself upright slowly to take stock of my injuries and frown when I don't feel any of them.

I gingerly brush my jaw where Gordon had just punched me. Then slip my hand around to feel my lower back. I'm in some sort of large shirt, so I slide underneath it to feel the skin there. It's not in pain or tender, but I can still feel the rough edges of a scar. Probably more.

My knee aches the same, but other than that and my back, all I feel is an overwhelming heaviness in my body. My mind is awake, if a bit groggy, but my body is still looking for more rest.

"Do you want me to get the others?" Dane asks softly when I don't say anything more.

I feel the sudden urge to pee and shift my legs over the opposite side of the bed from him, looking up to check that the bathroom is still where I remember it. It's dark in the room, with only a single lamp on in the corner to add any light while the shades over the large window to the rest of the bunker are drawn. We're underground, so it's impossible to tell what time it is. Regardless of the time, the last thing I want is everyone in here while I'm just...not sure how to feel yet. About anything.

I throw the blankets off and test my leg strength to try standing. "No," I answer finally. "I just...I need a minute." Or a million.

It's hard to wrap my head around what I went through. And that they came to save me. Why? And what about Vera? How long was I gone for? Does this mean Gordon is going to hunt them down and kill them? Are they all in danger now?

I grit my teeth together and wobble to a stand.

"Here—" Dane starts to move, and I raise my hand to stop him.

"No. I'm fine. I can pee by myself."

Dane backs off, but I can feel his eyes on me the entire slow walk to the bathroom. I'm three quarters of the way there when my bad knee gives out, and I drop.

Strong hands grab and lift me before I hit the ground. "I've got you, little one," a husky voice murmurs in my ear. A cushion of air pushes under my feet, and then I'm cradled in Jackson's arms.

It's dark enough in the room that I can barely make out his outline and that he has his hood pulled up as usual. His hands are gentle but firm in the way they hold me against him. I grip his hoodie and then lean my head into him with eyes closed.

I'm so relieved he's here. He's alive and well, from what I can see so far. I told myself so many times that he couldn't die. He wouldn't.

My hand trembles in its hold on him. I feel the urge to cry, to sob against him as I run my hands over the front of his hoodie to check for myself that he really is here, but the tears don't come. I'm back, but the numbness of it all hasn't worn off yet.

Neither of us speaks for the remainder of the walk to the toilet before he carefully sets me back on my feet. I give him a few seconds to leave now that I'm here, and when he doesn't, my lips turn down. "I've got it from here, Jack."

He flicks the light on, and I cringe away from its brightness. It takes several blinks to acclimate before I can open them enough to look at him again.

Jackson looks the same as before the fight on the island. Black attire from head to toe, in his combat boots, pants, and hoodie. His piercing blue eyes are pinned on me with the force of a thousand stares. It's a stare that sends a shiver running through me, but I don't look away. It doesn't unnerve me like it might others.

It makes me feel alive.

You're worthless.

Important.

No one cares about you.

Irreplaceable.

It gives me strength when my own doesn't seem like enough anymore.

The longer our stare holds, the quieter Gordon's voice in my head becomes. I'd keep it going forever if I could, but my body urgently reminds me of what I'm supposed to be doing, and I regretfully pull my gaze free of his. "Can you give me a minute?"

His lips pull into a smirk that I know spells trouble. He closes the bathroom door.

With him still inside.

He *does* turn to face the door with his back to me, but that does *nothing* to hide the sounds I'm going to make that I am not ready to share with anyone still. If ever.

"Jack…" I start with a sigh, but he just waves his hand to tell me to go on. The very idea of fighting him on it exhausts me.

I have a feeling my shadow is going to be keeping this close to me for a while.

Defeated, I do my business and pretend that he's not in the room with me. I can't imagine him bringing this up to anyone else or even me in the future, so I decide to get over it and move on.

As I'm wrapping up, he keeps his back to me and turns on the shower. The mirror shows what a mess I am, although I'm better than I thought I'd be after the last time I'd been awake. Any blood I'd had on me is gone. But my hair is greasy and flat on my head, telling me how long it's been since I've properly washed.

Jackson's checking the temperature of the shower with his hand when I turn around. "Thanks," I murmur softly. My body is ready to crash again, but I know I'll feel a lot better if I'm clean first.

He reaches over his head and strips his hoodie free, undressing down to boxers. My mouth goes dry as I watch him take his time before me. As I re-catalogue all his black and gray tattoos that mark his chest and arms. The paper crane over his chest that calls to me to run my fingers across it.

He steps closer and reaches for me. I jerk back.

Something dark flickers in his gaze, and I'm afraid I've upset him, but he holds his hand out to me instead. "It's me." He keeps his hand outstretched, palm up between us.

I stare at it.

I'm not afraid of him or what he might do.

I'm ashamed of myself. Of the things I've done again. I nearly lost myself and all of them. He would be so disappointed if he found out.

And I broke our promise to each other.

He should be furious with me. I would be if he'd done the same.

"Raegan."

His voice snaps the present back in focus where I'm still looking at his hand as if I'm waiting for him to take it back at any moment. It doesn't move, though.

It's me.

Jackson.

My hand slowly slides over his. His fingers curl around it, and then he gently tugs me closer to him. He lifts my chin to capture my gaze in his, holding me there as I feel his hands trailing from my thighs up my hips, up my sides. Until my body moves at his silent direction so he can peel the shirt over my head and arms.

Our eye contact is broken for a second, but he's right there again to keep me focused before I can blink. He takes his time to remove my underwear next until I'm completely naked in front of him.

He guides me into the shower, and I follow him like I'm under his spell. I'm as safe as I've ever been when his eyes are on me. I'm brought into the spray while he stands behind it, not avoiding getting himself wet in his boxers but keeping it primarily on me.

Jack lathers up the soap in his hands and starts spreading it over my skin in smooth, deliberate circles. His touch is soft, working it in like a gentle massage. My muscles sing beneath his touch, aching for more, but my mind isn't ready for more than this yet.

When he gets to my hair, turning my back to him and practically leaning against him, my eyes close of their own accord the moment his fingers sink into my scalp.

I'm grateful for the quiet.

He doesn't ask me any questions or even try to talk about stupid things. I don't want to talk. I want time. I want quiet.

He's giving me all of that and taking care of my body so I can focus on my mind, and it's better than anything I could have hoped for. I'm not ready to see the others yet. I would have refused him if he hadn't already been in the room. But now I'm glad he was there and that I'm getting this time to myself, even if I'm not really alone.

It's that thought that breaks the first tear free.

I'm not alone.

I couldn't do it by myself, but I'm not alone anymore. They came for me.

I shudder as the feelings I'd locked away for so long release, and then the tears fall in steady, silent tracks down my face. Jackson can't see, being behind me and focusing on my hair, so I don't bother trying to restrain them. I've done that for so long that it's like a purge of emotion that's welling up inside of me and then bursting free until my body shakes and quivers uncontrollably.

Arms wrap around me from behind, holding me tight as my body convulses through the pain, and my knees buckle. His strength controls our descent to the tile floor as he keeps me with him.

He holds me like that until the tears run dry, even though my body still shakes and wishes for more.

He holds me until I struggle awkwardly to stand, helping me back to my feet, and then continues to do it until I can draw a normal breath.

Only then does he let me go to finish washing my hair.

He doesn't say a word during any of it.

Neither do I.

The shower is turned off after he's finished, and he leads me out to begin drying me off with a towel. There's a set of pajamas on the floor in front of the door that he brings over and helps me into.

Jackson proceeds to finger-comb my hair once I'm dressed, and I can feel the soft air flowing behind me. It's a mere minute or two and my wet hair is dry.

He dresses back in his clothes, drying himself with his gift first before layering himself up again. He leaves his hood down this time so I can see the wild nature of his black hair and have a clear view of his face. He smiles at me when he catches me staring, and I hurriedly look away.

Jack takes my hand in his at his side, interlocking our fingers together, before opening the door and bringing us back into the room.

Dane's head pops up as soon as he hears the door, his face etched with concern as he looks me over. He's still in one of the upholstered sofa chairs next to the bed, but there's a tray in front of him and the bed looks freshly made.

He stands up. "I, uh, told the others you were awake. But I said you weren't ready to see everyone yet and still needed rest." His hand sweeps over the changes on the bed. "Kell came in quick to change out your sheets when I told them you were in the shower. Aiden brought you new clothes and had soup and bread prepared in case you're hungry. Oh, and water. Cassandra said you need to drink a lot of water when you're not sleeping."

I'm speechless.

Why?

Jack nudges me forward, and my clumsy feet finally get me to the bed with his help. He pulls the sheets down for me to climb in while Dane stuffs a pile of pillows behind my back so I can sit up. He sets the tray over my legs and Jackson hop-sails over to the other sofa chair to sit on its back.

I feel like I should say something, but I'm a little stunned at what's happening. Like the current tab in my mind that relates to speech is frozen and spinning in circles.

The smell of soup draws me in, and my stomach growls angrily in response. I pick up the spoon and take the first mouthful. It's potato and bacon. My favorite.

Did Aiden remember that from when we were on the island, or is it just a coincidence?

I dig in like a starved animal. It must have been at least a day or two since they rescued me because I feel like I haven't eaten in days. Shoveling the soup and roll into my mouth keeps that occupied as well, so neither Jack nor Dane try asking me any questions or talking to me.

Having both of their attention while I eat is a bit unnerving, though. Jackson's focus, I expect. But Dane's?

I use the last bite of bread to soak up what's left of the soup along the inside of the bowl. Once I've washed it all down with the cup of water, Dane takes my glass and refills it with a pitcher he has on the side table next to him.

"Thanks," I mumble when he hands it back to me. I take a sip and set the glass back down. I'm clean and fed, and now my body wants to disappear under the covers before anything else can get in the way of that. But I need at least a few answers before I can give in.

I take another look around the room I'm in. It's the same layout as the one Aiden had locked me in, but there's an air mattress set up in the corner. Other than that, I don't see anything to clue me in on why we're here or what happened while I was gone.

"Where's Vera?" I ask first, my voice coming out slow and tentative. Part of our bargain revolved around her being able to stay with Dane while I was gone. Now that I'm back...

Dane's expression darkens to something else. "She's gone," he answers. "We tried locking her up before we rescued you so we could still keep her around, but she escaped."

Escaped. Which means he hadn't been able to get through to her in their time together. She's still a pawn of GE's. I knew it was a long shot that she could be convinced away from them, but Dane deserved that chance to try. "Dane, I'm so sorry—"

"Don't apologize," he cuts in, his hand fisting on the bed and his jaw tense. "I should be the one..." He releases a frustrated breath. "You gave me a chance. And time with her that I never thought I'd have again. It's my fault that I wasn't able to break her out of whatever hold those scumbags have on her. You gave me that time, and I couldn't fucking do it." Dane drops his head. "I'm sorry."

His words trip a memory that gives me pause. Hold on her. Thorne. *Royce.* "Dane, about that..."

He holds my hand. "Don't worry about that right now. What matters is that you're here and you're safe. I'm not going to fight to get her back just to lose you to them, too. No more sacrifices, Rae. It's my turn to look out for you. Whatever I can do...whatever you need...I'll do it. Anything."

I swallow down what I was going to say. I can feel my eyelids getting heavy and my brain beginning to wind down as the food settles and my need for rest begins to take over. Later. I'll tell him later. I offer him a brief nod instead, to which he smiles softly.

"Good. You should get some more sleep. I know we all have questions for each other, but Cassandra said not to bother you right after you wake up." Dane releases my hand and takes the tray away, then begins pulling pillows so I can scoot myself down in the bed.

As I'm shimmying under the covers, the mattress dips. Jackson slides beneath the sheets in a shirt and briefs with a small smile. He wraps his arms around me, holding me to his chest and smelling like crisp autumn air. I grip his shirt, breathing him in like he's the only oxygen I need, letting his calm presence soothe me.

Even though I'm still buzzing with questions, the tiredness wins out within seconds of getting comfortable.

Chapter Fourteen

RAEGAN

Heat, like asphalt on a sunny day, warms my cheek down to my feet. It wraps tightly around me like a heated blanket until even the air I breathe is thick with warmth.

Too tight, I realize, when I attempt to move and fail.

My senses jump into overdrive while I'm gripped with panic at what new torture Gordon has in store for me this time. My eyes flip open to darkness. But when I draw a deep breath, the smell of musk and motor oil soothes the building frenzy.

Kellan.

I'm not with Gordon anymore.

I'm in my room in the bunker where I've been recuperating the last couple of days.

I'm safe.

Now that I know it's a *who* rather than *what* wrapped around me, I shove at him where my hands are trapped between us. "Back up," I tiredly grumble when he still doesn't budge. "Kell, it's too hot. *You're* too hot."

Wait...is he...?

Kellan grunts and shifts, though his arms remain firm in keeping me against what I've now realized is his exposed chest. "Mmm...thank you, beautiful." His deep, baritone voice rumbles above me and vibrates through his chest. "I think it would be a hard toss-up between the two of us on who's the hottest, though. I can't take all the credit."

I roll my eyes and a small smile threatens to break free, but I hold it back to focus on what I've just realized is happening here.

"Why are you in my bed?" I pull my head back as far as I'm able until he gets the hint to loosen his hold enough so I can look at his face. His blue-green eyes twinkle at me with the roguish grin that's so *Kellan*, I can't help the visceral heat that swims through my veins at the sight of it.

"I climbed in to rescue you." I frown in confusion, and he continues, "Trying to wake you up didn't work, and you were thrashing about so much that you were going to hurt yourself. I had to hold you to get you to calm down, and then you looked too comfortable to move."

"Oh," I reply softly, pulling my gaze away from his and back to his chest. It's nothing new for me to get nightmares, though I've never had anyone with me when it happens. I'd been able to keep it private, usually with alcohol and sex, on the nights I shared a bed with someone. It's a vulnerable side to me that I'd hoped to keep to myself.

I gnaw on my lower lip.

Kellan brings my face to his. "What's wrong?" His dark brows are pinched with concern as he studies my expression.

I hurriedly blink away anything he might read. "It's nothing. Thanks for...that." My hands unfurl to push at his chest and bring more space between us. "But I'm fine now, so you can let me go."

His other arm jerks me back against him. "No," he growls. "This is the first time I've been able to hold you since..." Kell tightens his hold again, although this time, it means my face gets closer to his instead of his chest. His countenance turns serious. "I swore to never let you go, and you still ran from me. Twice."

I wince at the reminder. "Kell, it wasn't—"

"I don't need that," he interrupts. "I know why you did it. I know that was your way of trying to protect us. But you forget that I don't need protecting."

I open my mouth to argue but the look he has compels me to snap it shut. He cups the side of my face, stilling the breath in my lungs.

"How many times will I need to chase you until you realize I'm not going anywhere?"

My heart squeezes until I think it'll burst in my chest. I swallow the emotion clogging my throat down, forcing a light smirk onto my lips instead. "Maybe one more time," I tease softly, trying to shift the mood away from getting too serious.

Kellan raises a single brow, but his lips spread open to a wide grin. "Run all you like, beautiful. I enjoy the chase. Just promise me to stay the fuck away from GE from now on."

My smile drops. "You know I can't do that," I huff. "I can't take them down by staying away from them."

His grin sharpens, taking over his face in a dangerous flash of teeth that reminds me more of a feral animal than a human. His hand collars my throat, grasping it enough that I know he can feel the sudden acceleration of my heart rate in response.

I've noticed that three of the four guys in this group have a certain fixation with my throat. Not that I'm complaining.

I love it.

I squirm instinctively in his grip. Not to get away but to put up a small fight to the control he's trying to exert over me.

He responds by squeezing hard enough to have my full attention and my heart galloping with the rush of adrenaline.

"You're never going back to them. I don't care what it takes, but it's never happening again, beautiful. I will fight them to my last fucking breath. It's my fault for not being strong enough last time. But that's all going to change."

The reminder incites a dull burn in my chest. He's right, but not in the way he thinks.

I know now that I won't survive Gordon a third time. Either I'll die fighting, or he'll win and have his obedient pet. I almost lost this time, and it was only because of the guys that I was able to keep fighting him.

Without them, I would have been lost.

Without them, I can't win.

I need them.

My vision swims. Kellan's brow furrows, but before he can say anything, I grab his face and pull it to mine, crashing our lips together.

I kiss him like my life depends on it. Like his kiss is the cure for the ache in my chest and his warmth the balm for my stripped and tattered soul.

I slide my leg between his, shifting until every part of me touches him. I reach between us, searching for his cock. I hum into his lips when I find it hard and bare from any clothes.

Kellan withdraws suddenly. "Are you sure?"

I blink at him, stunned. "What? Why...are you asking me that?"

"Relax." He thrusts his hips, pushing his cock further into my hand. "I know you can feel how much I want you. But I don't know what happened on that island. I don't know if you've had enough time to recover."

Oh.

I breathe out a rush of air, then squeeze his dick and give it a slow pump. He inhales sharply, and his stare hones like a predator readying for the kill. His look makes my heart race. Makes me feel *alive*.

"This *is* part of my recovery," I assure him. "Fuck me, Kellan. Fuck me, so there's no question that I'm back and here with you. That this isn't some dream I made up to pretend I've been rescued. Make my body feel it into tomorrow and the next day, so there's no room for doubt."

I want to feel again. To break through the numbness I've been lost in. I want his heat, his passion, his wild nature to chase away the nightmares that still haunt me.

Kellan's gaze is scorching and savage. "Remember, you asked for this, beautiful." He effortlessly flips me onto my back, straddling me before he descends. His kiss is rough, brutal. It's everything I want and everything I need.

He rips my underwear clean off, and I gasp at the brief pain of its resistance before it snaps, and my body drops back to the bed. His face disappears between my legs. I cry out at the sudden and ruthless fixation. My thighs tense, and I try to shift my hips, but he grabs and pins them to the bed, so I'm forced to take the stimulation that's hitting me too fast, too hard.

Any residual apathy vaporizes. Every scratch of his beard sends a shiver of pleasure vibrating through me. Every feral swipe of his tongue and suction of his mouth has me seeing stars as my muscles clench mercilessly.

"Ahh, Kellan!"

His deep-throated chuckle echoes against my core, and I cry out again.

The pressure builds, lifting me higher and higher as it fills me to the brim and leaves no room for oxygen. I curl my toes and grapple with the sheets while I try to hold on, and then I shatter into a million pieces. Everything falls out of focus except the ecstasy that explodes through me.

"Fuck, you break so beautifully," he says, his voice rough and thick. He drives into me before I've fully come down from my orgasm, pushing me up from my freefall. "We're not finished yet. You're going to come for me again, aren't you, beautiful?"

He sets a terrifying pace, one that grabs my pleasure in a vicious grip and doesn't let go.

I'm completely at his mercy as he uses my body in the way I asked, leaving no question that I'll be feeling this, *him*, long after we're finished.

I wrap my legs around him, racing my hips in time with his as the intense bliss drives me mindless with need. Digging my nails into his arms, I force myself to hold on, to meet him thrust for thrust as my release curls and tightens at the base of my spine.

"That's my girl," he groans.

He bites one of my hands, startling me out of rhythm and making me release him. Kellan moves in that split second, slipping free and then flipping me by my hips until I'm ass-up and face-down. He slams his dick into my cunt with such voracity that my entire body quakes and another moan rips from my throat. My hands are pinned together at my lower back as he drives into me in punishing strokes. "Do you feel me yet, beautiful? Is this how you want it?"

"Yes!"

"Do you still think you're in a dream?"

"No," I gasp.

"Good. Because this is real. You're finally fucking home, and I'm right here. I'm never leaving or letting you go, and I'll fuck you like this as many times as you need to make sure you have no more doubt." His pace intensifies, and my eyes close as the pleasure he's feeding me becomes overwhelming. "Come for me, beautiful. Let go."

I come again, screaming his name as he pounds into me. His dick swells, and he slams in one last time before he joins me, releasing an animalistic roar.

Kellan rolls to his side as I collapse, boneless, to the bed. He immediately tucks me into his side as we each catch our breath.

I close my eyes, basking in the bliss that's buzzing through me. I give myself a few minutes in that glow. To pretend, for that time, I can stay there forever.

And then I return to reality.

"Are my clothes here?" I push from his chest and stand from the bed, then scan the room for any sign of them and freeze. A figure dressed all in black is lying on an air mattress in the corner with his back to us. "How long has Jack been sleeping there?" I hiss.

He laughs and shifts behind me. "A while."

I throw my elbow back at him, which he takes without so much as a grunt, then uses it to yank me against him. "You kissed me first, beautiful." His teeth nip at the crook of my neck, sending a shiver of pleasure down my spine.

"Yeah. When I thought you were the only one in this room with me," I growl, pushing away from him. He lets me go, but crosses his arms and grins at me.

"Which part are you mad about? That you'd prefer to do it behind his back? Or that he could have joined us?"

"What? Neither one of those!"

"Technically, we did do it behind his back."

"You're unbelievable."

"Why thank you, beautiful. I think you are too."

I scrub my hands over my face and sigh. It's already done now and at least Jack appears to be sleeping. What would I have done if he'd been awake?

Kellan reaches under the bed and pulls out a duffle bag. "Jack seems to think you'd be into both of us at once. There any truth in that?" he asks far too casually while dumping the large bag in my arms.

An image of the three of us springs to mind before I can help it. Heat crawls up my neck to my face.

His brow perks up. "Oh? Here I thought he was just blowing hot air."

"I didn't say yes."

"Your face did."

"When did the two of you talk about—You know what? Never mind. I don't want to know." I march to the bathroom with the bag and yank the door shut to Kellan's laughter.

CHAPTER FIFTEEN

RAEGAN

JACKSON IS AWAKE WHEN I emerge, showered and dressed from the bathroom. He's leaning against the wall next to the door like he'd been listening in. At least he didn't stand-watch *in* the bathroom with me this time.

Kellan pushes off the armrest he'd been on across from Jack. "You hungry? We've missed breakfast, but lunch will be ready soon."

"Where are Aiden and Dane?"

I glance to Jack first, who shrugs with a smile, and back to Kellan.

"In his office, probably," he answers, scratching at his beard. "But they can wait. You need to eat."

Tossing the duffle bag on the bed, I start toward the door. "I need to talk to everyone first. I'll eat after." I open the door and stare out into the unfamiliar hallway. "Um…"

Kellan chuckles and wraps his arm around my shoulders. "I've got you, beautiful. It's this way." We turn right, passing other rooms identical to this one, so now I know I'll need help on my way back, too. Jackson smiles at me again when I peek over my shoulder to make sure he's coming along as well.

This catch-up is for everyone. No more secret missions. No more hiding.

The guys came for me. They had my back.

It changes everything.

The least I can do is try to work with them now and see where it gets us.

My knee begins to ache before long, but I grit my teeth and push through it. I don't want Aiden, or any of them, to see this weakness and think that I'm not up for the fight anymore.

But the pain brings back the memory of how I got it, of Gordon and Mallory, and I bite the inside of my cheek. *No. Don't think about it.*

I still haven't fully processed everything that happened, but I don't want to. I shove those thoughts and feelings away into a black box in the corner of my mind and force my thoughts on the future.

We stop, and I realize I missed the entire walk here while lost in my head.

"Ah, there she is. Raegan, it's so nice to see you again! We're all relieved that you're back. How do you feel?" The tall, dark woman standing in front of us smiles warmly. I met her when Aiden brought me around the Guild for some meeting of his. What was her name? Sarah? Serena? Also, we? All? Who is she talking about?

"Oh, uh, thank you. I'm all right."

She nods and focuses back on Aiden, who's sitting behind a simple wooden desk. "I'll come back another time to finish our conversation. I'm sure you have a lot to catch up on."

"Thank you, Cibrina." Aiden nods in return, though his eyes are locked on mine.

The door closes, and it's like all the oxygen has been sucked from the room. There's so much to say. So many things that have happened. I could start with anything, really, but I'm suddenly at a loss for words now that I'm in a room with all of them again.

"Have you eaten?" Aiden prompts, already lifting the phone on his desk and pressing a key. He looks me up and down as if my appearance will somehow answer that question for him, his brow pinched.

"No, but we need to talk—"

"Yes, she's awake," he cuts me off when someone answers the call. "Is the rush there, or is someone able to bring it to my office? Yes. Okay, I appreciate it. Thanks."

He hangs up, and Kellan snorts on my left. "No food for the little people, huh?"

Dane scoffs from his desk in the corner of the small room. "Who the hell has ever called you little?"

"It's an expression, Rapunzel. I'm just saying—"

Aiden and I continue to stare at one another in silence through their bickering. As much as I want to be annoyed with him for ordering me food anyway and not even asking what I want, I can't deny that I'm already beginning to feel a little dizzy. My body might annoyingly need more rest, or maybe I am hungrier than I realize. Either way, I don't immediately chew him out for it.

"I need a map," I blurt out. I have so many things to catch them up on, and it all wants to come out in a rush. Anything to keep the attention on our next steps and not on me.

My knee begins to quiver, and Aiden stands just as Jackson wordlessly takes my hand and nudges me to sit in one of the chairs at the mini round table. I drop into it and expel a breath of relief when I'm no longer standing. Aiden pulls out the seat across from me, and Dane joins us to my right.

Kellan falls unceremoniously into the loveseat sofa, spreading his legs out and leaning over them, while Jack stands behind my chair, hands buried in his hoodie pocket.

"A map of what?" Aiden asks smoothly, his voice strangely void of his usual cynicism.

"The Caribbean and the Gulf. One that shows the islands on it."

Dane leans toward me over the table. "Wait, you want to jump into that? Are *you* okay? Do you need to talk about—"

"No, I don't." That's the last thing I want: to share my trauma with them. There's nothing that happened to me that's going to help us get rid of GE. I gave myself up, thinking I could hold out long enough to take them down from the inside on my own.

But more time with Gordon put a lot of things into perspective for me. He's a master manipulator. I was too young, too inexperienced before, but this time I saw it. There was no choice for me or the guys back then. Gordon made sure to create the division between us. To cut me off from them.

I'm not going to let that happen anymore.

And this time, I may have been his prisoner, but I didn't come back empty-handed.

That's what's going to help me move forward more than anything else.

Dane frowns, his expression filled with questions and concern, but Aiden surprisingly intervenes on my behalf. "I don't have any maps like that here, but I'm not sure it would matter." He taps his fingers on the table. "When Dane tried to look them up online, the imagery conveniently didn't show certain islands."

"I had to use real-time satellite images to find them," Dane adds, though he doesn't seem pleased by the topic shift. "But I kept getting kicked out. Vera probably has some sort of alert set up on that satellite when anyone tries to hack in. So, if I try again, she'll be able to trace back who's looking and from where."

Which means we can't do it from here or else we would lead her and GE right to the Guild.

"If she blocked you last time, how are we supposed to get what we need?" Kellan drawls from the couch.

Dane leans back in his chair and crosses his arms. "She didn't know it was me last time. There's a chance she'll let me in at the opportunity to trace where I am. We would need to be fast enough to get what Rae needs and get out before she and a swarm of GE agents show up."

"I'm assuming these maps are for locations of specific islands for something?" Aiden queries, and I nod.

"I think they're other *training* facilities. We can free a lot of people and take away their source of new agents." I picture Mallory, recalling her story of why she was there. Even if some of them are freed, do they have a home to go back to? And one that wants them?

"Do we have enough room here for them?" Dane directs to Aiden.

There's a knock at the door. "No. Not yet, anyway," Aiden says before he stands. "Come in!"

The door opens, and a cart full of food and drinks rolls in. Aiden thanks the man who delivers it. "We'll take it from here. Thanks,

Jordan." The man smiles and closes the door behind him.

Aiden piles plates in front of me, filling the small round table with more food than I could ever fit in my stomach in a day, let alone one meal. Pancakes, French toast, eggs, bacon, sausage, biscuits with gravy, fruit, muffins, yogurt...

I reach for a strawberry from the dedicated bowl of them. Aiden sets a mug of coffee and a glass of orange juice in front of me, makes himself a coffee, and then returns to his seat.

"You're all going to help me eat this, right?"

"We already ate," is Aiden's answer, though Kellan snorts from behind me.

I turn in my seat. "I'm not going to eat all of this. Eat whatever you want."

He chuckles and shakes his head. "It's all yours, beautiful."

My lips turn down, but a glance at each of them shows me that no one else intends on touching it.

Well, fine. I'll eat what I can, and maybe once they see how much is left, they'll dig in for themselves.

"So, where were we again?" I ask, proceeding to stuff myself silly.

"I'll need time to make room for whomever we rescue. We have a dozen of the quarantine rooms, but that won't be nearly enough." Aiden types something out on his phone and pockets it again.

I pause my chewing as what he says sinks in. It'll take forever to construct more room underground. How did they even build this underground fortress in the first place? Did the bunker get built before the Tower?

Aiden catches my gaze. "Let me worry about it. That aside, we'll need to go somewhere with computers in a public space. They'll be less likely to cause a big scene if that place has too many others around."

Easy. "The University library," I offer between mouthfuls. "I doubt they'll attack us freely with all the students and faculty around. A fight there would make headlines." I wash the food down with hot coffee.

Dane's face pinches again with concern as he watches me eat. I'd reassure him that I *did* eat on the island but my mouth's occupied.

"Slow down before you give yourself an upset stomach," Aiden chastises.

Kellan laughs and shifts toward the table, his hand out like he's preparing to pinch some food. "Are you going to bite my hand off if I steal a piece of bacon, beautiful? You're making it look irresistible."

I chomp my teeth teasingly at him. He grins and snags himself the nearest piece between his teeth, ripping it in two.

Wiping my hands on a napkin, I push my seat back.

All eyes are on me in that instant. Even if I can't see them all in my field of view, I can feel it. "What?"

"Where do you think you're going?" Aiden asks, his voice smooth and dangerous. "And the answer better be your room to rest."

I scoff. "I've rested plenty. I thought we were going to the library."

Dane and Kellan both speak at once.

"The hell you have, beautiful."

"You've only been awake a couple days!"

I check in with Jackson behind me to see if I have at least one person on my side. He lifts his eyebrows when our eyes connect, but he stays silent.

Traitor.

I stand anyway. Kell and Dane jump up while Aiden's eyes narrow. "I need to show you the islands before I forget where they were.

And I can't stay cooped up in that room anymore."

"Are we supposed to pretend like we didn't see you almost collapse when you walked in here?" Dane demands, his finger jabbing at where my knee gave out.

"That wasn't because I'm tired!"

"Right. It was your knee hurting, though, wasn't it?" he counters. I snap my mouth closed before admitting anything, but he doesn't stop. "What did he do to it?!" His fist slams down on the table, and all the dishes jump with a clatter. "What happened?!"

I recoil from his anger. I know it's not directed at me, but my body reacts involuntarily anyway.

"Don't yell at her!" Kellan snarls at Dane.

I feel Jackson hovering closer behind me, offering me his strength and support.

"Enough. Both of you," Aiden orders before Dane has a chance to respond to Kell. His dark gaze pins me beneath his stare, and my breathing suspends itself to wait for what he'll demand from me.

He's always been the one to push me for my secrets. The one who doesn't trust me because I won't share this part of me. What will he do to find out what happened between Gordon and me this time? Will he lock me up again? Does he think it was some ruse for me to work with Gordon or something horrible like that?

"Dane has a point about your knee. It's not safe for you to leave the bunker if it's still in too much pain. We can go in a week after you've had more time to rest."

That's...not at all what I expected.

It's also not the answer I'm looking for.

My knee won't get better with time. It's permanently damaged, and it was healed wrong, so too much physical activity will always aggravate it. One week won't make a difference.

But I can't admit that to them.

"One day," I argue, hoping he'll agree to a compromise. I'll just pretend it's better tomorrow and work on masking the pain and weakness.

"A week," Aiden responds, and I frown.

"That's not how a negotiation works. You have to at least lower yours."

Aiden's stoic expression doesn't budge. "This isn't a negotiation. One. Week."

Our eyes lock in a stand-off. I debate leaving on my own before his timeline, but there are two problems with that. One, I swore I would do better at working *with* them this time around. I can't hack into the satellite by myself anyway, and Dane will side with Aiden. Two, it might take me the week to learn the layout of the bunker. I have no idea where the exit is, even if I wanted to leave.

I break the staring contest with a huff and plop down. Kellan reclines back on the sofa, but Dane doesn't move. His arms pulse with tension as he glares at the table. It's as if he's taking my injury personally. But he had nothing to do with it. Or my being there. It was my choice. He never asked me to give myself up to get Vera back. This is all on me.

No. This is all on Gordon.

My hand idly swipes over my injured knee.

"Dane," Aiden prods when he still hasn't moved.

The muscle in Dane's jaw ticks. Finally, he closes his eyes and inhales deeply, then sits.

"He shot it." The words fall from my lips before I even realize I've decided to give him something. I know I don't owe any of them an explanation for what happened to me, but I can't stand to see him so upset on my behalf.

He jerks his head up to look at me with surprise.

"That's all I'm going to say about it, okay?" I pick up another strawberry to nibble on as a distraction.

Dane nods and leans an elbow on the table, his hand burying itself in his hair. "Sorry. I didn't mean...I shouldn't have..."

"It's fine." I reach over and touch my hand to his arm. He releases his hair to take my hand, pressing it to his forehead with his eyes closed and expels a breath.

"I'm so sorry, Rae. It's my fault. I don't fucking deserve you in my life," he whispers so low that I'm not even sure I heard it right.

I pull my hand from his. "That's not true." My thoughts immediately bring up Vera, and I gasp when I remember something. "Oh! I almost forgot. Thorne's back." I twist around to gaze at Jack. "He's looking more like one of the zombies in Kellan's video game now, but his head is reattached."

Jackson pushes his hood back. "We need to get the person bringing him back, then."

"Just get me a flamethrower. I'll turn him to ash," Kellan jokes.

"Did you say his head was *reattached*? When was it...not...attached?" Dane looks over my head to Jack and pales. "Never mind. Don't answer that."

"His name is Royce," I continue, my attention still on Jack before I swing it around to Aiden. "And the guy sounds like he's close to GE's president. He could be our way in to the people in charge. His gift is controlling souls."

"Of course, GE has someone who can raise a zombie army. Why the hell not?" Kellan mutters.

"Thorne wants Jack to help him capture Royce, so that his soul can get moved to a board member's body. That gives him power, and his current body is...well, last I saw him it was falling apart. But Royce said something about using other souls to fix him up, so that may have changed things. He's sent Thorne back here to find the Guild," I add.

"Damn, he can do that?" Kellan asks in disbelief.

"Wait," Dane cuts in. "Is that...is Vera like Thorne?"

I move slowly in my seat to look at him. "I don't know for sure, but that's the only thing that makes sense."

"So, does he bring people back to life, or are they still dead? Does he control what they do or how they act? Is he the reason she's working for GE?" he asks, and I can see his thoughts beginning to spiral from the look in his eyes.

"I don't know. Thorne didn't really go into that much detail." The hope in his expression feels like a stab to the chest. We have no idea what any of this means yet. Would killing Royce kill Vera? Or is his work done once he's locked her soul back in her body? Does he have any control over her? Or is she acting on her own?

I know Dane is wishing for an excuse to explain why Vera's been acting the way she has since she came back, but what if it has nothing to do with Royce?

"Jack! Go pretend to help Thorne again so we can get to that guy," Dane exclaims.

"What? No!" I balk.

Jackson angles his head to the side while regarding Dane. "It won't be that simple."

"Why not? It didn't seem that hard for you last time," Dane snarks.

"Dane!" I scold, then look back at Jackson, who smirks coldly.

Aiden's mug taps against the table as he sets it down, drawing all our attention to him. "We're not trusting Thorne to get us to Royce. Or even pretending to trust him." His gaze meets Jackson's. "Do you think you could follow him without him knowing?"

Jack holds his stare for a few beats and then nods.

"Good," Aiden replies. "Then here's what we'll do. Jackson will find and keep an eye on Thorne to get his routine. Where he goes, what he's doing, when he's alone...we'll pick the best chance for us to trap him. Then see what answers we can get out of him about Royce—" Dane opens his mouth. "—and how his gift works."

Dane's mouth closes.

Kellan chuckles in the background. "Right. No problem. We'll just trap the undead wind master and make him tell us all his secrets."

He has some good points.

Oh! "The cuffs in my room—"

Kell shakes his head, but it's Aiden who speaks up. "Taken by Vera."

Damn. Does that mean Vera was at Old Red? Is that why we're here and not there?

"We have time to figure it out. Jack still has to find and follow him long enough that we know his routines," Aiden remarks, unperturbed by the obstacles Kellan mentioned.

I've already moved on from that conversation, though. It's a problem for future me. The me right now is stuck on if I'm living underground for the foreseeable future. "Are we going back to Old Red or..."

"No, we'll be here from now on," Aiden replies, and my heart sinks.

Kellan's eyes slide to mine. To read my reaction, I think. I try to force a look of indifference, even though I'm disappointed not to have our own space anymore. Old Red was really growing on me. It started to feel like a place I could call home.

I'd even accumulated *stuff* while living there.

Wait.

Portia's butterfly hair clip. It's still at Old Red, and it was her *favorite*.

Ugh. This better not be a fight.

I point my finger at Aiden. "Don't get mad," I start, and his eyebrows raise. "But I need to go back there. I left something important. I can be quick, I swear, I just need someone to show me the way out of the bunker."

Three of the four begin to protest or give reasons why that's not a good idea, and I sigh.

A fight it is.

Chapter Sixteen

RAEGAN

One heated conversation later, I find myself in the passenger seat of Aiden's Aston Martin at a bar parking lot. He finally caved under the condition that he and Jackson would accompany me while Kellan stayed back with Dane. We would be in and out, I promised. It might take me a second to find it, considering its size and the mess I heard Vera left behind, but hopefully, it isn't too far from where I'd left it.

I caution a brief glance at Aiden in the driver's seat. His face is pensive as he stares through the windshield at something in his mind. We've been quiet since splitting from the others. Aiden sent Jack on some task before joining us, so it was only me and him walking together from the bunker through one of the tunnels to this bar.

I'm grateful for the break while we wait for Jack, so my knee has more time to recover before we get to the firehouse.

But now that we're no longer walking, I begin to fidget.

I can't stop thinking about the last time we'd been alone together.

Maybe it's been long enough for Aiden to forget what happened between us and move on, but it's the *only* thing occupying my thoughts now.

The spanking. The sex. Then the blowout where I finally told him how I felt.

Did what I said mean anything to him?

He hasn't brought it up, which leads me to believe that it didn't make a difference. He still doesn't trust me.

Then why did he come to save you?

That has to count for something, right?

The questions are piling up at a dizzying speed, circling my mind on repeat as I try and guess where he stands with me.

It doesn't matter. You can't trust him.

Even if I want to. Even if he *did* save me, that doesn't mean anything has changed.

I close my eyes and draw a calming breath.

"What's wrong?"

Aiden's watching me when my eyes open. His dark brown eyes are as guarded as they always are, like he's intentionally blocking everyone out. To put on a brave face for everyone else or to protect himself?

Taking one more breath, I answer, "I want to thank you."

"For what?"

"For coming after me."

He frowns. "You should be thanking the others, too, then."

"I know. And I will, but I understand why the others came for me. I know you don't trust me and…I'm not your favorite person, but you rescued me anyway." *You didn't abandon me this time.* "So, yeah. Thanks," I finish awkwardly.

Aiden's gaze darkens. His hand reaches for mine, but I jerk it away before we can touch. I don't want his comfort. Not when I know that he doesn't mean it in the way I would want. Because he can't care for me like that if he doesn't trust me. It's a hollow offering that would tear me up inside if I accepted it.

His hand hovers where my hand had been, then closes.

"Raegan, I—"

The door opens, and I visibly jump in surprise. Jackson cocks his head with a small smile. "Ready?" His blue gaze shimmers with amusement, and I get the distinct feeling he interrupted Aiden intentionally. The only question is how long he had been watching from outside.

I nod while Aiden gives him a look that only incites a more wicked smile on Jack's face.

Yup. Definitely on purpose.

"She sacrificed herself to get me to Grams and away from them. I don't know how they found me, but that's how I was born on the island and then lived in Alaska. I was too young to remember my mom or any of that," I finish breathlessly. I needed something to fill the silence of the car ride, and it hit me that I could finally give Aiden an answer about my birth that he's been questioning.

Aiden's eyes haven't strayed from the road, and Jack's been quiet in the backseat.

"So...that explains my birth certificate," I fill in just in case he didn't make the connection. Because if he had, he would have said something by now, right? "And the picture you have."

Jackson straightens slowly, his stare snapping to Aiden's in the rearview mirror. "What picture?"

What does he mean, what picture? I thought all the guys had seen it.

My head swivels back to Aiden, and I open my mouth to ask him, but he speaks before I get the chance.

"Did you find anything on your father?"

"Ah, no. Just his name one time and that was it. Charles Whitmore."

The car slows to a stop, and he puts it in park. "Hm. I'll see what I can find." Aiden turns, his eyes intense as he finally looks at me. "Raegan Laivins."

My face heats at the way he says it. Like we're meeting again for the first time, and he's testing my name on his tongue. I shouldn't let anything he says or does get this type of reaction from me, but my body refuses to get the memo.

I grab the door handle and push it open, almost falling onto the ground in my rush to add some distance between us. Air catches and pushes me back inside.

"Wait," Jack murmurs softly at the back of my neck, and warm tingles spread across my skin. "I'll sweep inside first to make sure no one's there."

Aiden lets him out through his door and then sits. "Now that we're here, what are we looking for?"

Ha! Hard pass.

I can already imagine the flaying look he'd give me if he learns we're here for a *hair clip*. He wouldn't understand its importance to Portia, and therefore, to me.

"Something of Portia's that I need to return to her," I reply casually.

He watches me expectantly as if I'll crack under the pressure of that stare and tell him more. When I do nothing of the sort, he tries again, "I can't help you look for it if I don't know what it is I'm looking for."

"That's okay. I'll find it." No one would look twice at a hair accessory, so I'm sure it's still in my room somewhere. My only concern is that it's intact from whatever destruction happened there. From how Kellan made it sound, it was like they let a bull loose inside the building.

His eyes narrow, but thankfully, Jackson has returned.

"No one's in there. I'll check the woods and surrounding area and then join you inside," he tells us.

"I'll be fast," I promise him with a smile, hurrying to the door without waiting for Aiden. I freeze in the open doorway.

I mean, I knew what to expect from Kellan's description. But imagining it and *seeing* it...

Wow.

This is more than just looking for the cuffs.

This is anger. Fury.

Because Dane left to save me?

"It's only surface damage," Aiden's voice appears right behind me. I doubt this matters to him. As soon as GE is taken care of, he'll be moving back to their fancy Loft in the Tower. This place didn't mean anything to him. Maybe not to the others, either.

I bite my lip to break through the storm of emotions gathering in my chest. Rather than give him a response that might give away how this place has affected me, I move inside. Every step is a crunch beneath my feet, and I fight back a cringe.

Old Red is broken.

And just like that, it's been abandoned again.

Fuck, stop it. It's just a building.

"Speaking of Portia," Aiden muses slowly. "I got a call from Elias the night before we brought you back. They found her."

My footing slips on the next pile of debris in my rush to spin around, and I fall face-first into his chest in an ungraceful *oof*. His hands steady me at my elbows, but I push off him and grab the lapels of his jacket in each hand. "What?! That is the *first* piece of information you should have shared when you saw me. Fuck eating! Where's your phone? I need to call her."

I start running my hands all over his jacket to hunt for his phone, moving them down lower to his pants to check his pockets next. I see him with the damn thing all the time, so where the hell does he keep it?

"Raegan. What are you—Wait!" He grabs my wrists and drags me up against him. "Stop."

My heart pounds erratically as I gasp in his grip. I tell myself it's out of excitement to hear from Portia again. I'm sure it's that.

It's not because of his firm grip tucking me into him.

It's not because I inhaled the delicious combination of cinnamon and bourbon when I slid back up to his chest.

Or because he's been holding me here without speaking for at least thirty seconds.

"Do I have your attention?" His voice is low and smooth, like warm chocolate.

My lips suddenly feel parched, and I lick them self-consciously. "Yes."

"Good girl." Oh, fuck me. My thighs clench at the responding ache between my legs at those words coming from *him*. "Elias said he found her, but they aren't able to come back for a while still. It sounds like they're dealing with something else."

My heart drops like a rock. I straighten and pull away from him. "What? I need to call her. Now. Where's your phone?" I demand, trying not to panic. Elias said she got her memories back. Is that it? Is she upset that Elias found her?

I wish I had my phone so I could call her directly, but Aiden's will have to do if I can at least talk to Elias.

Aiden sighs and hands me his phone—from wherever the hell he was keeping it—and I snatch it when I hear it ringing already. The screen reads *Thorton*, and I cling to it while waiting for him to answer.

After the tenth ring, there's a click, and then Elias's voicemail answers.

"Elias? It's Rae. How's Portia? Can you have her call me? I lost my phone, so call Aiden's number until I get a new one. I hope you guys are doing okay." Fuck, I'm terrible at this. "Bye."

I end the call and glance at Aiden.

"Was that your first voicemail?" he asks dryly.

I smack the phone into his chest and whirl around, stalking through the wreckage to my room. "Shut up, Aiden!"

Because, yes. Yes, it was.

I dig my arm into the back of the drawer, scrambling along the seams and then the middle until my fingers roll over something small and hard. Pinching the item, I bring it out and smile. "Found you!"

"Please tell me we didn't come all the way here for that." Aiden's arms are crossed as he leans casually against the doorframe.

My hand closes over it to block the butterfly clip from view. "We did. I'm not going to bother explaining why this is so important because you wouldn't understand." I slip it into my pocket. "We can go now. I told you—What?"

Aiden stiffens as he looks down the hallway. His arms snap to his sides, and blades drop into his grasp. "GE." He checks the other side of the hallway and curses.

I peek around him, and there are GE goons pouring out of a portal on either end of the hallway. "Shit!"

"Get back in the room," he orders, then something catches his eye. "Go out the window and call for Jack."

"What about you?"

"I'll be right behind you." Aiden changes one sword into a shield before the first attack strikes.

I run to the window and throw it open with a gasp. "There are more of them outside!"

Fuck! We're surrounded!

How did they know we were here?

Vera was here. Did she plant cameras or sensors before she left?

"Get Jack!" Aiden shouts. He's fighting off three of them in front of the doorway, his whip sword sailing down the hallway and leaving pain-filled cries in its wake.

I grip the windowsill, leaning my head out, and then take a deep breath to yell. "Ja—AHHH!" I scream when fingers dig into my scalp and yank me back into the room by my hair.

"Raegan!" The sound of metal on metal and yelling intensifies, but something else steals all my attention before I can wonder if Aiden is okay.

A voice I'd hoped to never hear again whispers harshly against my ear. "Did you really think I'd let you go again, *pet*?"

Chapter Seventeen

RAEGAN

Fear grabs me in a chokehold.

I can't breathe. I can't move. My body begins to shake uncontrollably.

No. I can't go back.

Gordon drags me across the floor, and knocking into the debris is enough to snap me out of my stupor. I'm able to twist to see that there's another portal in my room that he's bringing me to.

NO!

I kick and scream, flailing in his grip.

I'm not going back!

I claw at his arm over my head and fall through it where he's made himself intangible. Gritting my teeth, I seek out his hand at my scalp and have the disorienting feeling of my hand passing through my own head. He's spread his gift onto me from his touch.

Knives fly through him above me. Jackson climbs through the window and holds out his hand, then fists it.

Gordon chokes, and his hand loosens in my hair. I tear free, ignoring the pain of hair snapping, as I rush toward Jack.

"Not so fast!" Gordon bellows.

Another cry rips from my throat as I'm wrenched backward by a section of hair and pulled to the floor. *How?* My hands fly instinctively to the hair that's being pulled to try to win it back. I search for Jackson.

Jack straightens from a crouch to standing on the windowsill, his blue eyes burning into Gordon behind me. He's holding knives in each hand like a spread of cards, and just as he looks ready to leap at Gordon, something small bursts through his thigh. The end of it snaps out like a diamond blade and then jerks back just as quickly as it appeared.

"Jack!"

Glass sprays the room as he crashes rearward through the window.

My arms fly up to cover my face. "Jack!"

"Time to go, pet."

"Fuck you!" Yanking a shard of glass from my leg, I throw it at him for whatever time that distraction will give me. I call on my gift, and it answers me without hesitation. The burning heat doesn't even hurt while it consumes my hand, and I slam it to the ground.

I clench my teeth together and focus on it, steering my gift through the debris to aim it at Gordon and nothing else. A crack of destruction snakes in his direction.

It stops under him.

"You know you can't hurt me," Gordon taunts.

No. There has to be a way.

I push up on my feet to run at him, and he releases my hair and jumps out of the way.

Gordon's face darkens. "I understand now." His voice is threateningly calm. "Your friends gave you false hope. You think you can fight me now, but you can't." His lips peel back in a sickening smile. "I'll use this as another lesson for you. I already promised you that I would kill your friends if you left me. It's time I followed through on it."

My breathing shallows.

"I will send hunters to kill every last one of them. And only when they're gone, and you've realized your mistake, will I come for you."

He laughs and steps back into the open portal until it begins to swallow him. A blade flies at him, and the portal consumes the rest of Gordon and the blade before disappearing.

Arms wrap around me from behind, tugging me back into the smell of leaves and crisp autumn air. "You're safe, little one. I'm here."

I turn in his arms, my hands sliding up to his shoulders and around his neck. "Jackson! Thank fuck you're okay. We need to get Aiden and get out of here." Pulling back, I turn to the door to search for him.

Jack swings the door back and steps in front of me to check the hallway first.

"Where is she?!" Aiden demands when he sees Jackson. I push under Jack's arm to see where he is, but he doesn't let me squeeze any further than that.

"I'm here! Jack, move out of the way so we can help him!"

Aiden dodges an attack and swings his whip sword at three of the opponents trying to sneak up behind him. He's surrounded on all sides by gifted GE agents. "Get her out of here," he calls to Jack.

"What? No! We're not leaving without—Wait! Jack, put me down!"

Two short leaps and we're on the broken window in my room, and then we're airborne before I get a chance to do more than gasp and cling to his neck.

The agents who'd been outside are all lying on the ground, dead most likely, so there's no one to slow us down as Jackson takes us into the woods.

"We're not leaving him! Gordon just told me he's planning to kill all of you. We can't leave him alone with them!" I bang a fist against his chest. A flash of red makes me pause and stare at my hand. "Jack? Are you shot again?" I rub both of my hands over his black hoodie until I find what I'm looking for. He's bleeding below his left shoulder.

"It's nothing," he murmurs.

"It's not nothing. And I know your thigh is injured, too. We need to go back for Aiden so we can all go back to the bunker. Where are you taking us?"

We land on a wide branch high in a tree. Jack carefully sets me on my feet, where the limb meets with the trunk. "Stay here. Don't move or let them see you if they search this far."

"Are you going back for him? Take me with you. I can help."

He brushes my hair aside and presses a chaste kiss to my forehead. "It's you I'm worried about. I'll be back."

"Jack, wait—" He's gone before I can stop him.

"Son of a..." I gripe, my nails digging into the hard grooves of bark as my body trembles at this height.

This is fine.

I'm only thirty feet off the ground, clinging to a tree with a bad knee.

Maybe sitting would be better.

I sink into a squat—that my knee *hates* with a fiery passion—and lean into the trunk of the tree to give myself greater balance. I'm not *thrilled* that I'm stuck in a tree, but as far as hiding places go without being too far from Old Red, I can see why he picked it.

Shifting one foot out to straddle the branch, it slips and sends me backward. I throw my weight forward, yanking my other foot out for counterbalance and slapping my hands around the trunk in a bear hug with a string of curses. I glance to the ground, and the world spins. Ohhhh fuck. Fuck, fuck, fuck.

I squeeze my eyes shut and take a deep breath.

I'm okay. I didn't fall.

There's no way I'm getting down from here with my knee, which means I'm stuck waiting and hoping Jack and Aiden are okay.

Dammit, Jackson.

"I heard something over there!"

Panic clutches my chest, and I slow my breathing to listen. There's no way...

Two GE agents search the woods.

Why are they all the way out here?

"I found her!" one of them yells, pointing directly at me.

Fuck me.

The two agents surround the base of the tree.

"Get her down."

"You got her when she falls?"

"Yeah, as long as you make sure she's asleep when you hit her. I'm not touching her while she's awake."

"Don't worry. She'll be out for a long time with a single shot."

"Good."

Not good.

I'm a sitting duck in a fucking tree with a bum knee.

One of them aims a gun at me and fires. I duck and swing to the side. When I look up, there's a tranquilizer dart stuck in the bark where I'd been.

"Don't move!" the one with the gun actually shouts. As if anyone in their right mind would willingly wait to be hit by a tranquilizer while they're thirty feet up in a tree.

"Don't shoot!" I counter with an equally ridiculous request, hoping it's enough of a distraction that I can delay his next attempt. Turning awkwardly to one side, I lie forward on the branch where I'm sitting and cling to it like a sloth. I hear another round fire, and breathe a short sigh of relief when there's no answering sting.

I move quickly, but in short adjustments, until I'm upside-down on the branch, and then release my legs to dangle to the branch below.

Another shot.

"How are you missing? Give me that!"

I have to loosen my arms a bit to gain a few more inches until my toes dance over my goal. Once the pads of my feet reach, I let go and lean toward the trunk again.

One down. A bunch to go.

The next few branches are closer, so I'm able to drop more easily to them. The last one snaps beneath my weight. I jump to another one and pray it's strong enough, but it bows and then cracks. My back and sides knock into more branches as I fall. I reach for a branch. Then another.

I finally catch one, and it bounces and sinks. *Don't break. Don't break.*

"There. She's close enough now without other branches in the way that you shouldn't miss."

I'm maybe ten feet from the ground but there aren't any branches left between me and it.

One of the goons aims the gun at me, and I have no choice.

I let go.

I don't even feel the pain in my normal knee because it's completely eclipsed by the searing pain in my injured one. I'm on my feet for a split second before the pain takes over and I collapse to the ground, clutching my knee and locking my jaw to keep my screams contained.

No, no. Get up!

I can yell at myself all I want, but the wave of pain hasn't subsided enough for me to move.

The crunch of boots on sticks and leaves gets closer, and I curse my fucking luck. I'm able to turn on my side in the direction of the sound and see the two goons walking toward me.

The tranquilizer gun is pointed at me again, and I thrust my gift into the dirt. I've used my gift through the haze of pain before, so I'm able to control it even though my knee hasn't improved. It's almost like an out-of-body experience. I know I'm in pain, I know I'm paralyzed by it, but as long as my hand is touching the ground, my mind can will my gift to do what I want.

I shove at it, pushing it to reach them faster and splitting it once I do.

I take them both in seconds.

They drop to the ground in hard thuds that I hope no one else is close enough to hear. My body rises and falls as I catch my breath and the wild burning in my knee slowly subsides. I close my eyes, panting and trying not to fall into the pit of despair that's waiting for me in the back of my mind. If I let it, it would suck me down like quicksand.

Gordon's threat to the guys.

The idea of being taken back by him. Of killing for him again.

The severe disadvantage I'm in now with my knee.

My thoughts flirt along the line of giving in, bringing me too close. Its pull is like a magnet drawing me in whether I want to go there or not.

"Raegan!"

My eyes snap open at Aiden's voice.

He breaks into a run when he looks from the dead guys on the ground to me. I hurry to push myself upright before he makes it here.

Aiden kneels in front of me. I open my mouth to tell him I'm fine, but he wraps me in his arms and pulls me into his chest. His heart thunders in my ear at a frightening pace as he works to catch his breath.

I don't move.

This is the first time Aiden's held me like this.

Like someone important to him.

I'm afraid to bring any attention to myself that'll snap him out of whatever headspace he's in that caused him to give me this unlucharacteristic sign of affection, so I freeze like a rabbit pretending to be invisible.

His hand slides up my back into my hair, clutching me closer to him as the rapid beat of his heart finally eases.

He eventually releases me to inspect my face. "Are you hurt?" His dark gaze slides to my hand on my knee, and I quickly move it away. The pain there is reduced to a resounding ache, but it's manageable now.

"I'm fine," I answer softly. I'm still not fully recovered from his reaction to seeing me, so there's no strength in my voice. He scoops me into his arms anyway, and I gasp, clutching at his suit. "What are you doing? I can walk!"

"You were holding your knee." He walks us a few steps in the opposite direction of the firehouse before I realize he's not taking us back.

"Wait, where are we going? Where's Jackson?"

"He's finishing the last of them."

I flail in his grip, fighting to get free of him even if it means falling to the ground.

"What are you doing?"

"I'm not leaving without Jack. Without either one of you." Why didn't Jack come back with him? They were both supposed to escape. Did Jackson really think I would leave without him?

"I'm not giving Gordon the opportunity to grab you if we're all fighting. I'm getting you out of here, and I'll go back for Jackson if he doesn't meet up with us before then."

My chaotic thrashing finally does the trick, and rather than let me fall, he sighs and helps me back to my feet. It's only after I'm standing that I notice the trail of blood running down the side of his face. The vibrant red splattered over his suit like a wild paint night.

"Are you—"

"Don't leave my side," Aiden interrupts. He takes my hand in his, tugging me close before he lifts his sword arm in front of us. "If you're going to walk, then stay with me."

I try to jerk my hand from his, but he doesn't let go. "I'm not some damsel in distress for you to rescue," I snap angrily. "Gordon didn't kidnap me last time, and he didn't this time either. Give me some credit and let me fight with you. You're giving Gordon what he wants by splitting us up. He's going after all of you now because you broke the deal. I need to get *you* to safety."

His expression darkens. "Your safety is the only one that—"

Twigs snap, and we both swing around to search for the source. Jackson's strolling toward us, his hands tucked in his hoodie pocket and his hood down. He's smirking at us, obviously listening in on our argument that's over him, no less.

"You could have said something, Jack," Aiden remarks, annoyance coloring his tone.

I unfortunately agree with him, but I keep that to myself.

"Did they give you any trouble?" Aiden continues.

"No. We're clear."

Aiden nods. "Good. Let's get back to the car and leave before they realize that and send more."

Jackson walks right up to us, stopping in front of me. His eyes flick to Aiden behind me for a beat and then he cups the side of my face and kisses me.

Right here.

In front of Aiden.

While Aiden still has my hand in his.

I panic for all of three seconds before I'm so consumed by Jack's kiss that I don't care about anything else.

His kiss melts away my fears, my inhibitions. Every negative thought vanishes until I'm cocooned in his warmth. I moan, my free hand instinctively clutching at his hoodie as I lean into it.

Aiden's hand tightens on mine, and reality floods back in a rush.

Jackson must sense the change in me because he draws back with a smile. He takes my hand from his hoodie, weaving our fingers together, and then turns to lead us back to the firehouse and the Aston Martin.

I'm waiting for Aiden to drop my other hand, but he merely scowls at Jack over my head and meets his stride until I'm centered between them.

It's confusing and unexpected, but having them on either side of me brings a wave of warmth and fluttering to my chest.

I risk a glance in Aiden's direction. Our eyes connect for seconds that stalls the air in my lungs before he turns his head to stare at the woods around us instead.

"You're so easy to please, little one," Jackson whispers. He's bent over to keep his words between us, his heated breath tickling my ear. "The others just can't get out of their own way to see it."

His gaze darts to Aiden and then back to me, and my face burns.

CHAPTER EIGHTEEN

RAEGAN

"WHY ARE YOU IN her bed? You were supposed to keep an eye on her overnight. It was your shift."

"I did. No one's going to touch her if I'm wrapped around her," Kellan drawls groggily and yawns.

There's a long pause, and I'm tempted to crack an eye open to witness whatever expression is on Aiden's face, but decide against it. I doubt I'll be able to read it anyway, and my eyelids are heavy with sleep.

"Get up. It's already past noon and you're still in bed," he demands, switching tactics.

"I'm just continuing my shift. She and Jack are still sleeping, so I may as well, too." Kellan curls around my back. I can feel his grin spread against my head. "Don't be jealous."

"Why would I be jealous? You've wasted half of your day in bed."

"Jealous that she would let me, no, *invite me* into her bed."

Aiden's voice softens to a deadly croon. "Don't mistake your wants with mine."

My chest tightens. I don't know why I thought him holding me yesterday meant anything.

I should know better by now than to believe I mean anything like that to Aiden.

Even if it did mean something, it doesn't change what he did to me. That he locked me up, threatened me, told me repeatedly that he doesn't trust me while demanding personal information in return.

Kellan snorts, then nuzzles into my hair. My heart somehow aches and burns simultaneously.

"Out. Now."

"Why are you up?" Kellan grumbles. "Cassandra healed you yesterday, too. Shouldn't you be sleeping like them?"

"I don't have time for that. Now that we're making room for more gifted, I need to stay on top of the progress to make sure it doesn't fall behind schedule. There's also the upcoming Guild event to prepare for, adding more safety precautions for job requests which are still coming in, handling food orders, and obtaining more medical supplies for the additional people—"

"Alright, I got it. Geez. You're making me tired just listening to all of that. Did you even sleep last night?" Silence. Kellan sighs heavily. "Go get some sleep, Aiden. I'm getting up. What do you need me to do?"

"I need you to get back to your training."

Kellan rolls away from me. "I'm not sure how that helps you to sleep, but who am I to question what you want," he teases with a chuckle.

The door clicks shut, and I'm once again surrounded by Kellan's warmth.

"Time to get up, beautiful," he murmurs. "I know you're awake."

Oops. Caught me.

I turn on my back with my arms raised over my head, stretching from my arms down to my toes. Kellan straddles me on all fours while I'm occupied, burying his face in my neck. "I know exactly what I'm having for breakfast," he rumbles, and the sound vibrates from my skin to between my thighs.

"Nngh," I groan, finishing my stretch and shivering from the kisses he's peppering me with. "Kell, no. Ahh—" A moan slips out unbidden. "Stop!" I smack his side, but it's like hitting a wall. "Jackson could wake up."

My shadow is sleeping on the air mattress in the corner, but I have no idea how long he'll stay that way. I didn't have much to heal, but both he and Aiden had a significant number of injuries that Cassandra fixed before prescribing them sleep.

"And?"

"*And* we're not doing this again while he's asleep in the room."

"Then, go wake him up. He can finish sleeping in the other room, or he can join us."

My hands push at his chest. "Join us?! You'd...do that?"

Kellan grips my wrists in one hand and pins them above me. "Don't get me wrong, beautiful. I'll pummel the life out of any other man who dares touch you. I told you you're mine, and I meant it." His free hand seeks down my front, his rough, calloused hand slipping beneath my shirt and grasping my waist.

"But I'm not blind, and I know how you feel about the others. I know I'd lose you if I forced you to choose me. So, I won't. Whether the others agree or not is on them. But don't worry or stress over trying to hide what you do with the others around me. Sharing you with them is the price I'm willing to pay for not protecting you when you needed it most."

When I needed it most? "Kellan, what—"

He cuts me off with his lips on mine, his tongue sinking in deep as he claims my mouth in hot demand. I wriggle in his grip, desperate to touch him, but he doesn't let go. His kiss melts me down to my core, filling my limbs with warm molasses until I'm putty beneath him. It's long and slow, like he's taking his time to devour me.

Kellan chuckles when he withdraws, and my body instinctively chases after him. "Now, now, beautiful. What were you saying about not doing this again while Jack's sleeping?"

I groan. Prick.

His grin sharpens as if he can read my mind. "Dress in something comfortable. You're coming with me for training."

My face falls while his back is turned to gather clothes from his bag. I try not to let the thought of *training* trigger memories with Gordon.

It's just Kellan. I'll be fine.

After a light breakfast, Kellan leads me through the bunker to a set of double doors. He doesn't hesitate—why would he?—and shoves them both open to waltz inside.

Me? I falter at the threshold.

The training room is eerily similar to the one on the island.

"...you're going to prove to me that you can follow orders..."

It's a massive space with solid black walls and a lacquered wood floor.

"...kill the three of them simply because I am telling you to..."

A pile of mats is stacked against a wall with other training equipment lined up beside it.

I can picture the three chairs in the center of the room as clearly as I had that day. The three people I killed at his command. For Mallory. For...nothing.

My knee throbs at the memory, and I clutch the doorframe.

"What's wrong?" Kellan asks from the center of the room, breaking me from my thoughts. He's partially turned, like he stopped walking when he realized I was no longer behind him. His dark brows furrow the longer he looks at me.

I push off the doorframe and tuck my hands behind me so he won't see them shaking. "Nothing. I...I think I'm still a bit wiped from yesterday. Do you mind if I head back?"

He jogs to me. "I'll walk you back."

I nudge him playfully, hoping to ease his worry enough that he'll let me go. "We just got here and I don't want to hold up your training. I'll be fine getting back to my room. I'm a big girl."

Kellan frowns, but he must see something in my expression that begs him not to follow, because he relents with a sigh. "Alright, get some rest. I'll come check on you in a bit."

"Sounds good," I agree with a small smile.

Before he can change his mind, I spin away and make a beeline for the elevator. My steps waver at the sight of Aiden striding toward me.

I keep my gaze on the elevator, hoping he'll pass me to get to Kellan, but he grabs my arm and stops me in my tracks. "What happened?"

"Nothing happened," I evade, looking away from him. He's the last person I want to talk to about what's going on in my head. "I'm just going back to my room to rest."

There's a stretch of silence before he states firmly, "You're lying."

I yank my arm from him. "Are we really doing this again? I thought I made it clear last time; I'm not sharing just because you want me to."

"I know. If you're not willing to tell me, then...I'll let it go."

"I'm not telling—Wait. What did you say?"

"I asked out of concern, but if you don't want to tell me what happened in your past, then I won't push you. Not anymore."

Who is this and what did he do with Aiden?

I stare at him incredulously. There's no way he's just...dropping it. Unless...*did* what I say make a difference? We haven't really had this sort of confrontation since then.

No, there's no way...

"I don't believe you," I argue softly. "You must have found another angle to get what you want. Because I can't believe that you suddenly decided you don't want to know anymore."

"I never said I stopped wanting to know everything," he replies smoothly. "Just that I'll stop trying to force it from you. I'll wait until you're ready to tell me."

"And if I'm never ready?"

His lips flatten, clearly not pleased with that possible future. "Then I'll accept it," he manages slowly.

That's hard to believe.

But it's not something I feel like arguing over now. I don't want to keep talking about...whatever this is. I want distance from that room. I want a distraction.

"We'll see," I tell him and walk away.

Aiden follows. "You'll get lost if you go alone. I'll escort you."

And give him the opportunity to try and sneak information I don't want to share out of me?

No, thanks.

"I'm good. I paid attention on the way down, so I can make it back without a babysitter."

I push the button to go up, and the elevator doors open instantly. I step inside, spinning and hitting the doors close button while standing in the way of Aiden trying to join me. He could get past me if he pushed by, but he just stands in front of me as the doors begin to close between us.

We stare at one another in silence until the doors shut and the elevator ascends.

I close my eyes and angle my head back, taking a calming breath to settle my frazzled nerves from the last fifteen minutes.

And then the elevator jerks to a halt.

My eyes fly open. I'm already running through the possibilities of what's happening. The lights are still on, so it's not a power outage. Are we under attack? Did Aiden stop the elevator?

"You should clear any room you enter before lowering your guard," a husky voice murmurs into my neck.

I'm pretty sure my heart skyrockets to the ceiling and thuds back into my chest in that half-second moment I realize I'm not alone in the elevator.

"Holy fuck, Jackson!" I gasp, clutching at my chest and whirling around.

He steps into my space, and the adrenaline rush I'm still riding out of surprise has me backing up. He doesn't stop, though, and I wind up hitting the wall.

"What are you doing here?" I ask breathlessly.

Jackson leans his forearm on the wall above me. His hand slides up my front to wrap around the side of my neck. "I was looking for you."

"No, I mean...hanging out in the elevator."

He smirks. "I came with Aiden. It looked like you were heading here anyway, so I waited."

He could have *said something* when I walked in. I was under the impression we were safe here. But the challenge in his gaze tells me that shouldn't matter.

Right.

Jack pushes his hood back, revealing his messy black hair. He lowers to one knee and bends his face over my forearm, pressing his full lips to the *memento vivere* tattoo.

My heart skips a beat. He looks like a dark prince swearing his allegiance. Only, he's a prince who stalks me and kills people with a smile.

"Jack?"

"I'm sorry, little one. I failed you." His voice gravels. "I let my pride shadow the reality of what we're up against. I put you in danger."

"Hey, none of that is your fault. You wanted to send me home. I was the one who pushed you to bring me along."

"If I had stayed awake—"

"What?! No. You can't blame yourself for passing out after that fight with Thorne. Stand up." He does it without hesitation. My eyes follow his as he rises, and I reach out to trace his face. Sometimes, he seems so untouchable. It's moments like these where I need to feel him to remind myself that my shadow is real.

"You're human. I'm just relieved that you're okay."

His smirk returns. "Then I'll shed the trappings of humanity to become the monster you deserve."

My breath catches in my throat.

"Now it's your turn, little one." He takes my hand from his face and crowds over me. "Tell your monster you're sorry."

"Sorry?" I repeat, confused.

"You ordered me not to do anything sacrificial, and that's exactly what you did."

Ah, right. Why did I think he had let me off the hook when he hadn't mentioned it earlier? But now that I'm reminded of it, I *technically* never said I couldn't do anything like that. "I never promised—"

His thumb strokes across my lips to stop me, and he chuckles. "That request applies both ways. But I'll let your punishment slide. *This* time. An apology will do."

"Punishment?!"

He hums. His blue eyes are locked on mine, staring deep into my soul while he waits for me to give him what he wants. Can I apologize for doing what I thought was the only way to save them? I'd do it again if it would guarantee their safety.

"Jack, I'm sorry, but—"

He kisses me before I can finish.

His kiss is demanding, revealing more about his current temperament than the cool demeanor he portrays on the outside. I'm forced to bend to his will as he directs the kiss with a mixture of passion and fury. I don't try to fight him. It's a glimpse into Jack's mind that no one else sees, and as the cause of the anger and pain there, I know I should bear it all.

I sink my fingers into his longer locks at the top of his head, sliding them between my fingers and then latching on tight. Jack makes a noise in the back of his throat in response, and my core throbs. Fuck, it's a heady feeling to be able to make him react. To know that I'm the only one who can draw this side of him out.

He's mine.

My monster. My shadow in the night.

He's proven to me the lengths he's willing to go. And what have I ever done for him? How have I earned that loyalty? Or his devotion?

I push him back, and he lets me, so our lips smack apart. "Jack," I exhale in a rush. "I'm sorry. Let me try and make it up to you." He's still leaning over me, his hands braced against the wall on either side as he catches his breath. I start working on his pants, getting them undone before he circles my wrist to stop me.

"That's not what I meant—"

"I know. I want this." The very idea of Jackson, this untouchable god of death, falling apart for me makes my mouth water, and I wonder why I hadn't done this sooner.

I know the reason...I thought Gordon had ruined this for me a long time ago. I'd taken control over my body and sex a long time ago, but I'd never pushed through this act. I never wanted to do it again after my past.

But now, it's different. I want to do this.

Jackson's cold, hard eyes search mine.

I sink to my knees at his nod, but instead of the hard floor of the elevator, they're greeted by a cushion of air. Jack pulls weapons from his pants, tossing them behind us in a symphony of clinks and clangs that I'd probably laugh at if the mood was different. Instead, our eyes are locked on each other, and the world grows quiet.

There is nothing and no one outside of us in this moment.

Once he's done, I drag his pants and boxers down. His cock springs free before me, and I swallow at the sight of it. I line my face up with it, then pause and crane my neck back to look at him.

Jack's watching me as he always does.

Waiting. Reading my every move and expression as if my body can be interpreted in a language made just for him.

Nerves jitter beneath my skin. I'm sure he can sense how important this is to me. I've never willingly taken this step with another before.

But he's not Aiden. Even if he sees something, he won't push me for answers. And that certainty is what allows me to continue before I can psyche myself out of it.

I wrap my hand around the base of him and poise my lips at his crown. Jackson gently strokes my hair behind my ear, sending a rush of warmth through me. His touch is so real and comforting; it's like he lights me up from the inside until I'm glowing from his affection, and it makes me stronger. Braver.

My tongue flicks out before I can overthink anything. I lick from base to tip along the underside of his shaft. Jackson's fist pounds against the wall. The heated intensity of his dark blue eyes while staring at me gives me another thrill.

I open my mouth and take him inside. My tongue dances around him, making sure his length is good and wet before my lips slide further down.

Jackson groans long and low. My core aches at the sound, but I consciously ignore it. This is about him right now, and I'm going to enjoy every second of trying to make him fall apart like he does to me.

His sound of pleasure is all the encouragement I need to continue.

I take my time with him, moving forward and back in measured strokes as my tongue teases him in slow circles. I'm not here to rush this. I want to learn every inch of him. Test every spot, every pressure, every movement that pulls a reaction from him that even he can't contain.

Jack's hand curls into my hair, wrapping it around his fist.

My mouth falters, but when he doesn't try to take control, my confidence returns, and I continue.

He's breathing heavily above me, and I can feel the quiver of his muscles as he holds himself back.

I pick up my pace, gripping him tighter at the base as my head bobs, and I hum my own excitement.

Jackson hisses, and his hold on my hair tightens. "Yes, little one. Just like that," he praises huskily. "You're doing so well."

My internal glow brightens at his words, and I work faster at the opportunity to gain more of his approval. I think he's realized I apparently respond well to encouragement, so he continues, "Mm...yes. Keep going. Harder. Yes. You're so perfect."

I'm working him in a frenzy now, eager to please him and do

anything he asks. My tongue swirls around his head before I sink his shaft as far in as I can, taking him until he hits the back of my throat, and I have to consciously breathe through my nose to avoid the gagging reflex. Every time it hits there, it draws another moan, another sharp inhale, another reaction from Jack that drives me to do it again and again.

My clit pulses with need, and I'm tempted to touch myself, but I busy my free hand on his balls instead. It almost doesn't matter, though. It feels as if I'll detonate without any touch the more I hear his voice, thick and heavy with lust, as he rains praise down on me, and it soaks deep into my skin.

"I'm going to come," he warns me, and I take him deeper. Jackson breathes in sharply. His dick pulses as it spurts ropes of cum against the back of my throat, and I swallow it down. I suck him clean when he's done, and Jackson's body shivers in response.

He grabs me by the nape pulls me upright, crushing me in a kiss. I wrap my arms around his neck as I lean back into the wall, dragging him down against me. I haven't even gotten myself off, and my body feels hot and languid.

Jackson draws back, but his breath is still scorching over my lips when his gaze sticks to mine. "I would bring the world to its knees before you. Burn your enemies to ash beneath your feet."

I'm dizzy with pleasure. Faint with breathlessness. His words make my heart beat faster, and the limited air in this elevator thins to dangerous levels. I don't question him or brush his words off as an exaggeration. I know he means every bit of it.

"So, tell me. What do you want most, and you'll have it."

What do I want most?

I draw in a long breath, using whatever oxygen I get to soothe my racing heart and bring my wits back. "I want Gifted Enterprise destroyed to nothing. So not a single piece of it is left for anyone to try and run it again."

Jack nods. He fixes his pants and then turns to leave, as if he's ready to take off just like that to fulfill my request without hesitation. I grab his arm, and he looks back over his shoulder at me.

"I'm not finished." He turns around, fixing me with his undivided attention that I've come to love and crave. "I want Gordon on his knees, begging me for mercy while he gets what he deserves for everything he's done. But, most of all, I want the five of us to stick together. No more solo missions. And I want all of us to make it through this."

I'm asking for a lot, but I don't care. He asked me what I want, and so I told him. I don't want him trying to take down GE on his own and getting killed for it. I want us to work together to take them down. And I want all of us to survive this. I didn't think I would before, but I'd been on my own then. I didn't trust that they would have my back.

Now, I know that we need each other. Not one of us can do this alone without the others. And I need to know that Jack won't run off to try to do this on his own again, just like I've made my own promise not to do the same.

Jackson doesn't argue with me or try to tell me that it's highly unlikely for me to get everything I'm asking for. He doesn't try to hit me with probabilities or what's realistic. He takes in every word, every feeling behind my wishes, and he holds on to them like something precious. He closes the distance between us, his hand finding my face before he sweeps me up in another kiss.

When it ends, his forehead presses to mine and he breathes, "As you wish."

Chapter Nineteen

RAEGAN

A GIRL A FEW tables over laughs out loud, and I grip the cup of coffee in my hand to keep myself from standing and interrupting them. Kellan grins at her, his white teeth flashing brightly against his golden-brown skin. He's wearing a tight shirt beneath his leather jacket, his dark tattoos scrawling up the side of his neck. His hair is half up in a knot, with the rest of the brown locks covering the back of his neck.

Kellan has his hands tucked into his jean pockets, thumbs out, as he visibly flirts with the university student in an attempt to convince her to let him borrow her ID badge.

Apparently, that badge is required to access the library. I hadn't needed one for the coffee shop or bookstore before, so this was news to me. Aiden knew, though, and had already planned on this pit stop.

He and Dane are seated at the table with me, our overpriced drinks in hand, as we are supposed to blend in with the others. Jackson is keeping an eye on things from outside and overhead until we get the badge, and then he'll join us in the library.

"Relax," Aiden remarks coolly. "You're going to draw attention if you keep glaring at her like that."

"Like what?" I reply distractedly. The girl's leaning on her hand and giving Kellan a dreamy look. It doesn't pass my notice that this girl is pretty. She's wearing some sort of sports uniform, too, which makes her an athlete. I don't know why that matters to me when it comes to Kellan, but it does.

Of all the girls in this shop that he could have spoken to, why this one?

"Like you're going to rip that poor girl's throat out if she laughs at one of Kell's jokes again," he answers in a low croon.

I shiver involuntarily in response to his tone, then blink when the words sink in. I finally drag my stare away from them to look between Aiden and Dane. Aiden dares me to challenge him with a raised brow while he sips from his coffee cup. Dane looks...annoyed? Or upset about something. His jaw is sharp and tight like he's holding himself back from saying anything. Does he think I'll cause a scene with the girl to ruin the plan?

"I wasn't," I snap at Aiden, annoyed he would put that thought in Dane's head. "I'm just watching his back."

Aiden stares at me. I'm clearly not fooling him here, but I'm more annoyed with myself for getting jealous over a random girl. He's told me several times that he's not going anywhere, but my abandonment issues like to pop up at times like these to remind me that being physically free is not the same as being free mentally and emotionally from the shit Gordon put me through.

"No one needs you. It would be better for you to be alone."

"Hey..."

Something touches me, and I startle back to the present. Dane squeezes my hand. "Are you okay? We can come back another time if you're not up for this so soon." His face is shadowed by the hoodie he's wearing, but I'm close enough to see it when he looks directly at me. His annoyance is long gone and replaced with worry while he waits for my answer.

I glance at Aiden, who's watching me with similar attention, his eyes dark and chilling.

"I'm fine," I mumble, tugging my hand free and shoving both under the table. I didn't think they would notice me getting lost in my head for a second, but now they're both on high alert as they inspect my every move and word. It's been a week since I woke up. Almost two since they rescued me.

In some ways, a lot of time has passed, and in others, none at all.

It took me two years to redefine what normal meant to me and how to get there after getting off the island. I'm already doing a million times better this time around, but it still creeps up on me in moments of weakness.

"Beautiful, come here."

I snap my head over to Kellan. His hand beckons me over to him and the girl. This isn't part of the plan. What is he...?

"Stop acting like you're shy and get your sexy ass over here."

Oh.

Warmth floods my chest at his public claim. I stand without thinking, joining him at his side wordlessly while his arm wraps possessively around my waist.

"Here she is. Michelle, this is my girl, Raegan. Raegan, this is Michelle. She's offered to let us borrow her ID badge so we can"—he bends down to murmur suggestively in my ear, though it's still loud enough for anyone around us to hear—"do what we wanted in the library."

The heat creeps up my neck to my face. Wait. *What?*

Kellan chuckles and nips my ear with his teeth.

The girl, Michelle, grins and waves her badge between her fingers. "Good luck with your bet. The librarians are sticklers for that, so your buddies will need to be good at distracting them. You're too tall to hide," she adds while looking Kell up and down.

His fingers scissor closed over her badge. "Sounds like a good challenge."

I point to the last island I can remember on the screen. "...and that one."

Dane zooms in close enough to see the general landscape of the island and its buildings, then hits a bunch of keys until I hear the printer along the wall starting up again. He zooms in and out, getting whatever pre-planned shots he needs up close and from a distance so we can see the other islands nearby.

Kellan shifts behind me, yanking my hips back against him as his beard scratches across the line between my neck and shoulder. "Now that's done, how about you and I take up that challenge between the shelves?" he drawls seductively.

Fuck, I love how resonant his voice is. It's so low that hearing it feels like he's stroking some deep part of me. If I were a feline, I'd be purring.

I lean my head to the side, granting him more access as I shudder with pleasure. "Kell...we can't..." I whisper, though it doesn't sound convincing at all. But I *do* mean it. Aiden and Jackson are patrolling the library so we can get the information and leave as soon as possible. The longer we're here, the more in danger we are.

Dane's chair whips back, somehow managing to roll over Kellan's foot before it thuds back to the floor. Kellan doesn't flinch, but he does stop what he's doing to aim his taunting chuckle at Dane. "We won't be long, Rapunzel."

"Vera's probably on her way here now with a squad of GE agents. Unless you want to be caught with your pants down, we need to get Aiden and Jack and get out of here," Dane bites out.

I pull away from Kellan. "He's right. Now's not the time." He tries to grab me as I keep stepping back from him. "I'll go find the other two and bring them back here. You guys collect the papers off the printer and stay put."

I hurry out of the computer room before Kellan can try to stop me. He'll have to stay behind to make sure no one sneaks up on Dane. If I had my phone on me, I could have tried calling them, but that's been lower on my priority list. Maybe I should bump it up if we'll be doing outings like this again.

When jogging gets me yelled at by a librarian, I drop it down to a fast walk as I peer down each of the aisles to look for them. The first set of aisles doesn't have either one of them, so I move upstairs to the next few sections. "Jack! Aiden!" I call out in a harsh whisper that still garnishes glares from others.

I huff when I reach the back corner with no sign of them. Why is this library so big?

I'm turning back the way I came when I'm suddenly shoved forward. My hands catch me before I land face-first on the rough carpet. I push to flip myself onto my back and face my attacker. My gift sparks instantly, shooting to my hands like an activated line of electricity as I prepare to eliminate the enemy.

Vera lands over me, straddling me with a knife aimed at my abdomen. "Touch me, and I'll gut you before you can finish."

Fuck.

Of all the people, it's the *one person* I can't use my gift on.

I raise my hands up and to the side, and she watches as the reddish glow of my gift dissipates.

Instead of lowering her weapon in response, she just smirks and moves the blade up to my neck.

Great.

"I forgot you made that promise to Dane. But he's not here right now. You can't be so stupid that you wouldn't try to fight to save your life. Because I'm taking it now. You *owe me* your life."

My mouth flattens as I realize that this could very well be the end of it. But she's just as much a fool if she thinks I can only fight with violence. I stare at her, taking in her amber eyes that look back at me with a sense of desperation. I remain completely still under her, which is how I notice the fine tremble of her body. There's a manic energy about her, and it reminds me of the time Dane had held a gun to my head.

"I'm not breaking my promise to him," I reply slowly, as one would a cornered and dangerous animal.

She applies more pressure to the knife, and a sharp sting echoes back. "No, you will. Your life is more important to you, just like anyone else. But if you tell me where the Guild is, I'll make this less painful than I want it to be. I'll make it quick."

A bead of liquid slides down my neck, warning me that she's broken skin.

I'm too afraid that talking loud or fast will result in a sliced neck before either of us gets what we want, so I keep my voice low and calm. "Vera. I know about Royce. Tell me about him. Is he controlling you? Is he why you're with GE? We want to save you, Vera. Just tell me how, and we'll do it."

She bares her teeth at me. "Shut up! Why would you try to save me now? It's too late! I already know how you feel about me. You want me dead."

More liquid runs down my neck.

"No, I don't. Killing you was an accident, I swear. I never meant to hurt you. I would never wish for you to be gone." My voice thickens with emotion, but I'm too scared to swallow it down and risk a deeper cut. "You were like a big sister to me, Vera. Losing you...was one of the hardest things."

Vera's eyes widen. I concentrate on keeping my breaths shallow as she processes what I've said. Her face blurs as I struggle with the limited oxygen. If she doesn't decide what she's going to do soon, I'm going to pass out and be completely defenseless. I can't let that happen. Should I buck her off? Does that count as hurting her?

Sorry, Dane, but that can't count against me.

She leans back, bringing the knife with her. I gasp, heaving a deep breath to fill my lungs.

Vera narrows her gaze and then stands. "Get up. Either tell me where the Guild is or fight me, Rae."

I stand, keeping my hands open and to my sides, and shake my head. "I'm not going to fight you. Tell me how we can help."

She scowls and slashes at me with the knife. It cuts across my chest, drawing blood, but it's shallow. Her face darkens more when I don't retaliate. "Give me Dane, or give me the Guild!"

"I can't do either of those. How can I save *you*, Vera? Is Royce the answer?"

Vera cuts me again, this time on my left cheek before she snarls and shoves at me. "Why won't you fight back?! Dane isn't here! He wouldn't even know. Fight me!"

Another cut on my forearm. Stomach. She pushes me back against the bookcase, holding the knife back to my throat. Her eyes are wild as she glares at me, the V-shaped scar over her eye looking longer and darker now that she's so close. A foul smell wafts by, but then it's gone before I can look around to see where it came from.

The knife at my throat again also steals my attention from anything else.

"How can you say you want to save me if you won't give me anything?" she spits at me.

"But—" I stop. Has she been telling me how to save her? Is she in danger if she doesn't get one of those things? "Are you—"

"Raegan!" Aiden's voice commands nearby. Others shush him, but when he calls my name again with the same tone and volume, he makes it clear that he doesn't give a shit about their silence policy.

Vera and I stare at each other. Aiden's coming. She could kill me before he gets here. Her knife is already flirting dangerously into my skin, so I can feel the sharpness of the blade. I haven't given her anything she wants, and she should know by now that I won't give her any of those things even with more time. What reason would she have to keep me alive, then?

Killing me, getting revenge, it's something else she needs, isn't it?

She presses the knife a bit further in, and her gaze flickers with some emotion. Then she hesitates, freezing when we can hear Aiden's footsteps scuffing across the carpet and getting closer.

Vera drops her hand and runs, disappearing around the corner.

I don't breathe until she's gone, and then I'm hauling deep breaths as the world spins. My heart is jackhammering in my chest, but I hadn't even realized it until now. My fight instinct kept me focused on Vera, on doing whatever it took to keep her from killing me without actually fighting back.

I glance at my hands and find the fading glow of my gift.

Shit.

When had I turned that on? Or did my body do it on instinct?

If Vera had tried to kill me, then would I have killed her first?

"Raegan!" Aiden shouts. He takes one look at me from the end of the aisle and then, in his imposing tone, shouts, "Jackson!" He runs down the aisle to me, and Jack appears on my other side at the same time. "What happened? Is Gordon here?"

Jackson pulls a strip of fabric from somewhere and wraps it gently around my neck.

"What? Oh, no. It was Vera." They both freeze. Jackson turns first like he's about to take off after her, but I grab the fabric of his hoodie. "Let her go. Have you seen any goons? Are Dane and Kellan safe?"

"We'll get them and head out now. They said you were looking for us, so we came to find you, and I'm glad we did," Aiden replies while inspecting the other wounds on my face and body. "I'll have Cassandra meet us in your room, and you can tell us what happened on the way."

CHAPTER TWENTY

RAEGAN

AIDEN OPENS THE DOOR after a few short knocks, and Cassandra bursts inside with her hands thrown up. "Where is she?" Her red curls bounce as she swivels her head to seek me out. It doesn't take her long to find me seated in one of the sofa chairs next to the bed, and her nose sprinkled with freckles twitches as she takes me in.

Her eyes switch between the guys, who are all positioned throughout the room, and she frowns. "Why is she the only one injured? Why is she *always* the one who gets hurt?"

Is she...angry *for* me? Or complaining about needing to heal me again instead of getting to touch one of the guys?

"It's not a big deal. I told Aiden he didn't need to call you," I respond defensively.

She strides over to me and perches herself on the arm of the chair—which is a bit closer than I would have liked—before she presses a palm against my chest. Cassandra shakes her head. "You've been awake a *week* and this is now the second time I'm healing you. Is trouble drawn to you, or do you seek it out?"

Before I can answer, she pins Aiden beneath a stare. "There are four strong and fully capable men around you who shouldn't let you get hurt anymore. We all know you've been through enough."

Oh.

Since when does she care about how hurt I am? But I don't care for her attacking the guys, either. The attack at Old Red and the fight with Vera are both my fault, not theirs. If I hadn't pushed Aiden to go back for Portia's hair clip or gone off on my own in the library, neither would have happened.

"Don't blame them for my actions. I'm responsible for them."

Warmth fills my chest from her hand. Her eyes glow, appearing sightless as she searches for every wound to heal. Cassandra makes a clucking sound.

"We ordered a doctor, not a lecture," Dane snipes from the loveseat sofa in the middle of the room.

Kellan chuckles and adds, "If you think it's so easy to keep my girl from getting into trouble, you're welcome to join us tomorrow to see for yourself."

"Don't jinx us!" Dane snaps at him. "And stop calling her that. It's like you're pissing on her to make a point."

Kell's grin widens. "And what if I am? She doesn't mind me calling her that. Do you, beautiful?"

Nope. "Don't drag me into that."

Cassandra smiles, even as her eyes stay simultaneously focused and far away. The warmth has spread throughout my body, easing the ache and pain from the various shallow cuts. Before long, she retracts her hand, and her eyes return to their green-gold color. "I know it doesn't seem like a lot, but your body will need rest from the healing. If you're planning on joining the mission tomorrow, then I recommend staying in this room to rest for the remainder of today."

"Thank you, Cassandra," Aiden speaks up.

"Of course," she says with a nod. "I'll be around today and tomorrow if you need anything else. But try not to need anything else," she adds with a soft laugh while standing.

"Thank you," I say earnestly. "For this and for healing me when they got me back."

Cassandra's smile falls a little. "I'm sorry I couldn't heal everything. They told you about your knee?"

"I already knew."

She gives a curt nod. "Well, I should get going. Call me if you need anything." Cassandra waves to the rest of the room as Aiden escorts her to the door and closes it behind her.

"I thought she hated me," I muse aloud. She healed me after Old Red, but she had been in such a rush that we didn't get a chance to talk. And, well, I had assumed she still didn't like me, so I hadn't tried to start up a conversation.

Before the last island, we'd put up with one another, but she had seemed to resent me being around Aiden and the guys.

Kellan laughs and plops himself down on the bed across from me. "She respects you as do a lot of others here at the Guild. I wouldn't go wandering around alone unless you're ready to meet everyone."

"What? Why? I don't know anyone at the Guild other than her and Cibrina. Why would they know about me?"

Aiden sighs and moves closer to us. "Things happened behind the scenes here while you were gone. Aside from Jack, I had a few Guild members helping search for you. Now that you're here, some of them have been waiting to meet you." He sees a look on my face—horror? Fear? Confusion?—and continues, "Don't worry about that now. Like Kellan said. Don't go wandering around yet, or make sure one of us is with you."

Right.

"Get some rest. Kell and I will be working on preparations for the first island tomorrow. Jack should be back from spying on Thorne by midnight tonight." Aiden waves Kell after him, but he stops to kiss me. It's not a quick kiss either, his body pressing me back into the sofa chair while he kisses me long and deep. "Kellan!" Aiden commands sharply.

Kellan grins into my lips, leaning back and shooting me a wink before he strolls after Aiden out of the room.

What the hell is he up to?

My fingers brush against my swollen lips. I'd be embarrassed if I wasn't so confused by what his intention is. Aiden doesn't trust or like me. Dane has only recently come to terms with us trying to be friends again. And Jack wasn't here to try and instigate him.

"Hey," Dane calls from the loveseat. "Do you want to watch a movie?"

"Sure." That counts as resting, right? I don't feel the need to take a nap from the healing, so I'm not sure what else to do while I'm restricted to this room. I am not up for meeting all of the Guild yet, so I won't argue with having to stay here another day.

I make my way behind the sofa. The chairs are both positioned on either side of the bed, leaving only this double-seated sofa in the living area section of the room across from the television. Should I drag one of the chairs back over?

"Rae." Dane's expression has shifted from relaxed to serious since I walked over. "About Vera..."

"Don't worry. I didn't hurt her," I jump in before he can ask.

He winces and shakes his head. "That's what I was afraid of. Look." Dane's face turns upward until his eyes meet mine. "What I asked from you before was selfish. I didn't trust you then, but I do now. So, I take it all back."

"What do you mean?"

"I mean, the promise you made about not hurting Vera."

"You want me to hurt her now?" I ask, confused.

"No, of course not." He scrubs his hand back and forth through the hair on top of his head. "I don't want you getting hurt, either. So, if she's attacking you...fight back. Just...try not to kill her?" Dane drags his hand down his face. "Shit, is that still asking too much? I don't want either of you to get hurt, but I know I can't have both right now while she's with them."

He's looking more stressed the longer he tries to explain himself. I take a seat next to him and touch his knee to stop him. "Okay. I get it." I told them about the attack by Vera and her wanting information on the Guild. But I didn't explain that I'd asked her how to save her. Or that she *chose* not to kill me. She could have. There was plenty of time for her to finish the job before Aiden got there, but she didn't.

Why?

That's all I've been asking myself since then. I don't want to give Dane false hope if it doesn't mean what I hope it does. That maybe I got through to her, even just a little bit, and she's now second-guessing her options.

I didn't get an answer from her on what role Royce plays in all this, but I'm not giving up. If she left me alive, then there must be a reason.

His hand closes over mine. "Rae, I'm sorry—"

"It's okay," I interrupt. "Let's just chill and watch a movie, okay?"

His face pinches, then relaxes, and he nods. "Alright."

He grabs a blanket from the air mattress and brings it to the couch, settling it over both of us before he turns on a romantic comedy. It's sweet and simple, which makes it an easy distraction long enough for my eyelids to grow heavy.

I shift to find a more comfortable position if I do fall asleep, and Dane lifts his arm when he notices. "Here."

I have a few seconds of hesitation, staring at his side and then his face. He doesn't seem annoyed or put out by his offer. He looks...like Dane. Like I'd remembered him on the island. Giving in, I settle into his side, and his arm and the blanket cocoon me.

The change in position gives me a new burst of energy, so I focus on the screen again and try not to think about the solid warmth from his body. Or the way he didn't shy away from holding me against him. There's nothing hesitant about his touch as there had been a few months ago.

His thumb grazes over my skin, brushing against the exposed area where my shirt has ridden up above my pants. I fight back a shiver at the light touch and try to keep my attention on the movie.

Eventually, sleep beckons me again, and my eyes close. The sound of the movie is like white noise in the background as Dane's touch continues to lull me to sleep. We haven't done this in years, and yet the second his arm wrapped around me, it felt like coming home.

Safe.

Warm.

Cared for.

A loud noise in the movie startles me from deep sleep, but fingers stroke continuously over my scalp and keep me from waking completely. My eyes stay closed, and I shift my head against what feels like a pillow before I sink into slumber under words softly spoken above me.

"Shh...go back to sleep. You're safe. I'm here."

Chapter Twenty-One

DANE

The movie credits scroll up on the television screen, and I realize it ended. I didn't watch a single minute of it while Rae was pressed into my side.

I can't focus on anything but her when her warm, soft frame is leaning into mine. When the smell of vanilla fills my nose and draws out a feral side in me that I never knew existed. The need to touch her is overwhelming. My body is practically vibrating with the need for *more*. To wrap her in my arms. *Kiss* her. To breathe her in as I trace her skin with my lips.

Fuck.

Stop thinking like that.

It's that line of thinking that forced me to slide a pillow between my lap and Raegan's head.

Even that amount of separation isn't enough to calm the demanding desire to do more than stroke my fingers through her hair like I'm doing now. I tuck the blanket back in where it popped free and exposed her shoulder to me.

I was tempted to kiss it.

A bare shoulder.

I'm so fucked.

I return to her hair, slipping my fingertips between her blonde strands at her scalp and dragging through to the base of her neck before starting again. It's not much, but at least the action keeps my hand busy and I *am* touching her in some way, even if it's far friendlier than what I wish it was.

I restart the movie. I'm afraid she'll wake up if it's too quiet.

And I'm not ready for this moment to end.

I know I'm an idiot for pretending like this means anything. I hadn't expected her to agree to lean on me when I offered. After all I've said to her...all I've done and she's been through because of me...I don't understand how she doesn't hate me. How she can smile at me. Comfort *me*.

I should be the one comforting *her*.

I'm the reason she was put in the position that killed Vera.

I'm the reason she was stuck with Gordon for a year and had to endure his abuse.

The reason she went *back* to Gordon for two months and got tortured.

And she still tried to keep her promise to me to not hurt my sister, even if it might have gotten her killed.

Lifting my hand from her head, I fist it to hold myself back from the impulsive need to draw her tight in my arms. I close my eyes and drop my head back against the couch, breathing in deep through my nose.

I owe her everything.

It makes the time I hated her seem like a faraway dream because now, looking back, I can see how much of that hate stemmed from a part of me still wanting her, even then. I never stopped. I'd worn my anger like armor, more pissed at myself for still harboring these feelings when I thought she betrayed us, and now that it's gone...

Now, there's nothing holding back that longing.

Now, I want her so fucking badly that it hurts.

It's not a light ache or the classic butterflies in the chest feeling.

It's an all-consuming, bone-deep ache that crushes my chest and leaves me breathless.

I want the girl who gave up everything for me, and I want to spend the rest of my life doing the same for her.

The girl who will put her life on the line to help those she loves.

The girl who fights for what she believes in.

And I'll do anything it takes to become worthy of her.

Even if it means putting my sister's rescue on hold.

I want my sister back, but not at Raegan's expense. For now, it's enough to know that she's alive. I'll keep my focus on taking down GE and Gordon, like the others moving forward.

All that's left is telling her how I feel and figuring out what the fuck to do about her with Kellan and Jackson. And trying not to lose my cool every time I see them doing couple things together. Or when she was clearly jealous of Kellan giving another girl attention in the coffee shop.

"Your movie still on?"

I startle at Kellan's voice, and Raegan stirs in my lap. I hurriedly return to pulling my fingers through her hair and wait for her breathing to even out again before looking over my shoulder at him. "Yeah," I lie, not ready to admit how I'd purposefully restarted it to keep Raegan snuggled on me. "What's up?"

"The plan for tomorrow is all set. Aiden wants you to come with us on any of these island missions. Since we haven't been able to confirm or dispel the possibility of a spy in the Guild, it's safer for you to stick with us."

"Alright. What time is the mission?"

Kellan's gaze slides past me to Raegan. He lifts a brow in question, and I try to appear nonchalant as I shrug one shoulder. "I can move her to the bed," he offers, walking closer to the couch.

I stiffen instinctively, stopping my reflex to lean over and block him from taking her. "She's fine. Just leave her," I bite out too sharply because Kellan's eyebrows ratchet up his forehead, and a grin slides onto his face.

"Oh, really?" he drawls, then snatches the remote from me while I'm distracted. "Same movie, huh? Or did you start a new one?" He smacks the controller back in my hand after a quick pause revealed the movie was only twenty minutes in.

Scowling, I grip the remote. "Does it matter? It's helping her sleep. Are you going to answer my question about the time tomorrow, or should I ask Aiden for the details later?"

His grin sharpens with an edge of challenge, but I refuse to rise to the bait and wait for his answer. "We're heading out from the training room at midnight. We'll be bringing some Guild members along with us, too, to make sure everything runs smoothly."

"Who?"

"Evie, Silas, Fabian, and Harvey. Then Reid and Tinsley."

Makes sense. The four members already know about GE and have *some* fighting experience. Most of the other members didn't know Gifted Enterprise existed until the attack on the Tower. They're here for the community of other gifted people and the extra work that's suited to their gifts.

As for Reid and Tinsley, the former is a given since he'll be needed to get us there and back. But this will be the first time Tinsley will be involved with anything. Did Reid request that she join the mission?

"That's a lot of people for Reid to transport if we're bringing people back, too," I muse.

"We'll be using Evie's gift of mass manipulation to shrink everyone. That'll be a lot less stress on Reid's gift, since he'll only be teleporting himself, Evie, and a tub full of three-inch-tall people."

I frown at the picture of being carried around in a plastic tub coupled with the off-putting feeling of being teleported.

"Don't worry, Rapunzel. It'll be fine. Just make sure you're ready to go on time. And let Raegan know when she wakes up."

"I will," I reply with a nod.

He smirks and turns to leave. "I'll let you guys finish your movie, then."

Prick.

Chapter Twenty-Two

RAEGAN

"Kell," I whisper roughly. "Who are these people?"

Kellan tugs and pulls on the Kevlar vest he's strapped me in until he's satisfied. He pats it and grins. "Just some of the Guild members who wanted to help. They're the ones whose gifts will be useful, and Aiden trusts enough to follow directions."

I smack his hands away and twist to get a feel for the weight. "Isn't this overkill?"

"With you?" He laughs. "We should have wrapped you in one of these from the start." Kellan waves at the rest of the room while others don their protective gear. "Everyone's getting it, so no complaining, beautiful. This will make a few of us more at ease to know you're in this."

"Everyone except you and Jack?" I nod toward my shadow, who smirks at me while leaning against a wall. As if summoned, he stalks toward us.

"Well, we both know there's no point in me having that. It would only get in my way. And Jack's already wearing his." Kellan turns to look at him once he's stopped in our space.

Jackson taps a finger to his chest to indicate his is beneath the hoodie.

Damn. I see the point of it, but it's so *heavy* that I'll be much slower in a fight.

Glancing around at the others, I catch more than a few stares before they hurriedly look away.

Dane walks up from behind and nudges my arm with his. "Don't worry about them. They won't bite. But as long as Jackson is near you, I doubt any of them will try and talk to you."

Anger pulses in my chest, and I frown. "They don't like Jack?"

Kellan and Dane laugh. "Easy, beautiful. Don't go planning any murders on his behalf before you know the whole story."

"They do like him," Dane answers my question once he's gotten over his laugh at my expense. "He saved the Guild from Thorne once he learned what he was up to, and he's the one who brought Aiden in."

"Then why...?"

Dane shrugs. "Just because they're grateful for what he did doesn't mean they're not still scared of him."

Jackson smirks and raises my hand in his. He kisses the edge of my matching tattoo that's peeking out of my long sleeve. "As they should be," he remarks coolly, his eyes locked on mine. My blood heats beneath his look, which holds me hostage until Aiden's raised voice announces his arrival in the training room.

"Everyone, gather around for the mission plan."

My breath catches when I see him. He reminds me of the soldiers in one of Kellan's video games. All black, long sleeves and pants, wearing a vest and black baseball cap to shadow his already dark eyes. The stubble on his face looks darker as well, and I might not have placed him immediately if not for his voice and the iconic cross of swords strapped to his back.

What skin should be exposed between his sleeves and hands is covered in metal gauntlets, not to mention the metal around his neck and likely strapped somewhere under his clothes. His greatest weakness is the lack of metal he's touching, so he's making sure that won't be an issue. The whip sword is retracted, and the diamonds that usually spread out are pressed tightly together to resemble a jagged sword on his hip.

Cibrina stands to his right, her hands tapping the air in front of her as golden light fades in.

We all move to a half-circle formation around them before Aiden begins. "This is a rescue mission. A trial one at that. We're testing their response time, the setup of these islands, and how well our plan works to save the trapped gifted with minimal casualties. They'll be brought to the quarantine floor that we roughly carved out last week." He nods at someone like that instruction was meant for them.

Following his gaze, I see Reid geared up with arms crossed over his chest. Tinsley's bouncing on her feet beside him with a grin stretched from car to car.

"Once we're on the island, we'll split into two groups. Kellan will lead the rescue team, and my team will be the distraction. You are not to seek out or engage in a fight unless you have to, and only if it is to incapacitate them so you can escape.

"Raegan, Jack, Reid, Tinsley, and Evie will be on the rescue team. Silas, Fabian, and Harvey, you're with me and Dane." Aiden continues to go over the plan, pointing to the map Cibrina has in front of us in shimmering, golden lines that outline the island and the buildings on it. The specific areas he speaks to glow brighter when he mentions them as he discusses the highest probability buildings where the prisoners are likely to be.

I try to stay focused on the plan, but after he lists out specific gifts of a few of the members in this circle, I'm too stunned to keep listening.

I cast a glance to Kellan, who shoots me a grin and bends down to murmur, "You have no idea."

A familiar blond-haired member raises his hand. "Uh, Master? Can I switch to the rescue team? I think my ability is better served there, don't you think?" He grins and shifts his blue gaze toward Kellan.

"No, Harvey, I'm keeping you with me. If you've got a problem with that, you can stay behind. I'm only taking members who can follow orders," Aiden states matter-of-factly.

Harvey laughs and raises both hands, palms out. "Nope. My bad. Whatever you say, Master."

A guy with styled black hair and dark eyes scoffs. He jabs the large, broad-shouldered guy with short curly hair standing next to him, who's been binging on a plastic container of food the entire time Aiden's been talking. "I've got money on him disappearing the second there's trouble."

The guy eating shakes his head. "I'm not taking that bet, Silas," he mumbles with food still in his mouth.

"Damn," the betting one—Silas—mutters. Then he leans forward to look at the only other female Guild member here, aside from Cibrina. "Hey, Evie! Care to make a wager?"

A tall woman with light brown skin and dark brown hair folds her arms but doesn't look his way. Her focus doesn't falter from Aiden, who is now whispering something to Cibrina. "If it's about me hitting you for getting distracted, then sure."

I lean around Jack on my other side to whisper to Dane. "These are the dependable members Aiden chose?"

Dane smirks. "Don't let their laid-back attitudes fool you."

Hm. "Last question, and please don't take this the wrong way. I heard you were always being held back to stay out of danger and GE's hands. Why are you coming on this mission?"

"Thorne warned me there's a spy in the Guild," Jackson answers between us, his voice low.

"What?!" I gasp, and Dane sends me a look to stay quiet.

"It could have been a lie since GE doesn't know where we are, but rather than leave it to chance, Aiden wants us to stick together. So, where you guys go, I go."

Fuck me. A spy?

If there was one, they would have given away where the Guild has been hiding the last few months already, right?

Or else, what are they waiting for?

Chapter Twenty-Three

RAEGAN

Cibrina's gift dissipates before her. "Good luck, everyone. Claudia and her staff, as well as Cassandra, will be ready and waiting on the quarantine floor for your arrival. Be safe, and don't cause Aiden too much trouble."

Aiden steps forward. "Evie, if you would."

The dark-haired woman picks up a small clear tub from the floor and walks it to the center of the deformed circle we've made. She sets it back down and then taps it with a finger. One second, it's the size of a shoe box. The next, it's a translucent wall blocking my view of the people on the other side of the circle.

I reach out, knocking my hand against the firm plastic. Aiden had mentioned Evie's gift in the plan, and seeing it in action did not disappoint.

"What the fuck are you doing?" Dane snaps. Kellan lifts him up at the knees so he's higher than the edge of the massive tub.

"Climb in, Rapunzel. How else were you going to get inside?"

"A fucking ladder!"

The others are already inside the tub or climbing their way in. The wall is at least ten feet high. How…?

There's a low chuckle beside me. "I've got you, little one." And then I'm airborne, shooting almost to the ceiling before gliding down to the tub in a controlled descent.

I wrap one arm around Jackson while watching the scene below. Kellan finishes dumping Dane over the side and offers his hands to Aiden so he can step on. The betting guy, Silas, is being placed in the tub by a set of vines coming out of something on the floor. The rest, aside from Evie and Reid, are already inside.

I remove my arm from Jack once we've landed, but I keep close. How do you prepare for something you know is going to happen but have no reference for?

Kellan and Dane move to stand with us. Kell rubs the back of his head while his other hand rests on his hip. "Don't worry about the shrinking. She's done that to me a few times. You won't even notice it. It's the teleportation that sucks."

Great.

The tub jolts beneath us, and I stumble. Jackson tucks me against him as everything moves back and forth, up and down, like we're on a ship on the rough seas. Dane and Kellan are falling this way and that, catching themselves before they wind up on their hands and knees, but nowhere near stable like Jack's been keeping me.

I look up, and Evie's face fills my view as she peers down at us like a giant with her box of toys. What's most disconcerting is the fact that she's keeping us relatively stable, but the slightest movement she makes has a massive impact on us in the tub.

"Ready?" Reid's stoic voice booms.

Silas is lying down like a starfish. I can't tell if that's in preparation for the teleport or to avoid falling from the tub's movement. Harvey looks like a newborn foal on his shaking hands and knees, while the guy that's *still* eating is sitting in one of the corners with his legs crossed. Aiden's leaning a hand against one wall, looking like he's got the hang of balance, and Tinsley—with her gift of speed—is making a mockery of everyone else with her quick adjustments.

"Ready," Evie replies, her voice just as loud.

My stomach drops as the world tilts, but then I blink and the training room has disappeared. Seagulls screech piercingly overhead. The smell of salt is thick, coating my tongue and clogging my lungs.

"That wasn't so bad at this size," Kellan remarks almost excitedly.

Dane coughs, covering his nose and grumbling, "Traveling in the tub probably helped, too. But being small makes everything else suck."

I grit my teeth, slapping my hand over my mouth as my stomach roils from the overwhelming smell and motion sickness combined. That, and the nauseating reminders of where I'd been not long ago.

The beach.

Another island.

Panic jolts through my muscles like electricity, seizing my body with fear.

Fuck. Keep it together. If I mess this up now, Aiden won't let me come again.

Jackson pulls my face into him, his arms wrapping around me tight. I can't see anything but the black of his hoodie. The smell of dead leaves and crisp air battles for space in my lungs. My hands cling to the fabric. I take another breath of him. And another. Each one pushing the ocean air out and letting him in.

Then it's gone completely, and I sigh in relief.

"You alright, beautiful?"

"Rae! Was it the teleporting?"

Jack releases me, and I turn to face Kellan and Dane while keeping one arm linked to him like a lifeline. "I'm fine." I realize my senses are no longer being overwhelmed, and when I scan the tub, we're the only ones still in it. Well, us and Aiden who's walking over.

"What happened?" he asks.

"Nothing. Just a bit woozy from the trip," I lie, not wanting to ruin the plan.

Aiden's eyes narrow.

Please don't call me out on it, for once.

"We need to hurry out of here and start the mission before we're seen. I can have Evie shrink you back down, and you can ride in my pocket if you're not up for this." Aiden holds his hand out to me, and I stare at it.

What?!

"If anyone's going to carry a miniature Raegan around, it should be me," Kellan argues. "You're on team offense, Aiden. And same goes for Dane. She'll be safer with me."

"What?! No miniature Raegan. I'm not riding in *anyone's* pocket!" I shout, turning to Jackson. He tilts his head to the side, and a small smile curls on his lips as he considers that idea as well. "No." I point my finger at him to make sure he's just as clear as the others. "Just get us out of this tub before we all get caught because of *us*."

Wouldn't that be dumb? I asked for these missions, Aiden planned them, and then it all falls apart because of us?

Thankfully, the others agree because Jackson takes Aiden and me out while Kellan gets Dane and then himself over the edge.

Evie taps the side of the tub, and it immediately reverts to its smaller size.

We've been free from our island for five years.

For five years, GE continued to grow and kidnap and brainwash.

Now, at last, we're really fighting back.

We're going to save people like us.

It's the beginning of the end of GE.

Whether it's luck or good guessing, the building Aiden directs us to check first holds all the imprisoned gifted. Dane hacks into their system from wherever Aiden's group is, and all the locked doors spring open at once.

"Evie and Tinsley, get them out and direct them to the lobby. Jack and Raegan, load them in the tub there. Reid, you and I are going to clear the building," Kellan directs like a born leader. I'm used to him goofing around or breaking rules. Seeing him take charge like this...

He catches me staring and waggles his eyebrows.

Nope. Same old Kell.

I roll my eyes and follow Jackson down the stairs to the lobby. Once we confirm the kids are here, Evie sets up the tub, so all we have to do is wait. Jack stands next to the tub while I position myself at the stairwell.

It isn't long before a flurry of steps pound down the stairs. The first one to see me as they turn the corner for the last flight falters. She looks to be in her young teens, with a black bob haircut and glasses.

"It's okay. This way. We're going to get you guys out of here. You're safe now." My voice is calm and soft. Between that and my words, she doesn't hesitate any longer and barrels through the open doorway. Once she passes through, the rest follow without question. I continue to encourage them down the stairs, pointing to Jackson. "Everyone's going in that giant container, and it'll take us home. He'll help you get in it; just listen to him."

Jackson uses his gift to send two to three kids in at a time, lifting them by air and setting them down on the other side. I wonder if it feels like lifting weights. Up. And down. Up. And down.

The last of the crowd of kids and teens piles through the door, but one hangs back in the stairwell. I peek inside, trying to get a good look at them. "It's okay. We're going to take everyone somewhere safe," I repeat again, in case they didn't hear me over the noise of the others before.

The young girl shyly steps forward into the dim lighting. She has medium-length brown hair and dark eyes, and she's dressed in a frilly princess nightdress. She stares at me with big, round eyes.

"It's okay," I try again. "We're not going to hurt you. You're safe now."

Calm, soothing voice. Nice smile. I'm sure I'm doing this right, but there's something about the way she's looking at me that sets my teeth on edge. I've never met this girl before, so why...?

"Are you taking us home? I'm...I'm not better yet."

Her voice makes my heart skip a beat.

I know that voice.

Squinting past the poor lighting, I get a better look at her face and see the fear in her eyes. She's not afraid of us being caught. She's afraid of *me*.

"Mallory?"

The girl tenses, squeezing her hands together against her chest and then takes a step backward. "N-no." She lifts some of her hair in front of her, and then tears erupt from her eyes. Her hair shifts back to blonde the moment she releases a wail that echoes through the stairwell.

I lunge forward in an attempt to cover her mouth. She must take it as an attack because she screams louder and runs away, but she runs into a corner of the stairwell and traps herself instead.

"Mallory! Mallory!" I whisper sharply to get her attention. I creep forward, palms outstretched so she can see them. "I'm not going to hurt you. Please, stop screaming and crying. You'll wake the bad people." Hopefully, Kellan and Reid have taken care of everyone else in this building, but the fact that they aren't here yet says otherwise.

Mallory curls into a ball in the concrete corner. Her tears are streaming down her face as she sniffles and hiccups, biting her lip to keep quiet, but the fear is still there as she looks at me.

Boots thump behind me. Jackson stops next to me, his head cocked to the side as he regards the girl. "Do you know her?"

Shame burns in my chest with the memory of what I'd done for her. And then in front of her. It wants to put the blame on her. Tell everyone that all the bad things I did for Gordon this time around were her fault. I thought I'd been saving her, but I was the fool being played.

It would be so easy to tell Jackson that version of the story. It might absolve me of the guilt that's been eating me up inside.

So easy.

No.

I don't make choices based on whether they're easy or not. I can't shift the blame to her. She's *six*. A child. I'm the adult. It was my gift. My training with Gordon. My choice.

Jack looks my way, and I realize I haven't answered him yet.

"Yes."

"She's scared of you," he comments mildly. It's not a question. He's not asking if that's the case because he can see it clearly. The reason she's crying and trembling in that corner is because of me.

"She is," I agree anyway.

He nods and squats within reach of her. I tense, afraid that she'll scream at the scary man, and prepare to intervene to give her some space.

But she doesn't cry.

She...smiles?

Jackson must be whispering something to her because she nods and wipes snot from her nose with the back of her hand. He holds his hand out, and there's a piece of candy sitting in the center of his palm.

Where did that come from? Does he carry candy on him all the time, or did he bring it specifically for this mission?

Mallory takes the candy and gives him another short nod. Jackson turns his back to her, still squatting, and she wraps her arms around his neck. Jack's arms loop around her legs, and then he stands.

What in the actual fuck?

Jackson smirks at me and motions with his head to follow.

I do, only because I want to know what the hell is happening and how he made that terrified girl smile at him.

Fully grown Guild members? Terrified of him.

But children? Apparently, not a problem.

Jack jumps at the tub, and they fly over the edge before he touches inside. He kneels for her to dismount, but I can't hear anything they're saying this time because all the other kids are chiming in about that being unfair or cool.

Another batch of kids clamor down the stairs, and I hurry back to my post to guide them to Jack. It's a smaller group this time. After a dozen or so kids, Tinsley and Evie follow behind them.

"That's everyone," Evie announces, stopping with me at the door. Her gaze slides past me to Jackson, then jumps back to me. "Have Reid and Kellan come back yet?"

"I'll go find him!" Tinsley shouts. My mouth opens to stop her, but she's gone in a flash with her super speed.

Evie sighs, but her smile returns by the time she faces me again. "Everything go smoothly down here? It looks like they're all in."

I follow her stare to the tub. There aren't any other kids milling about, and Jackson's leaning against a nearby wall with one foot kicked back and his hands in his hoodie pocket.

"Yeah, we're good," I answer.

"—waste…dammit!" Kellan's voice appears mid-sentence, then pauses and shifts to a curse when he drops to a knee to catch himself. He glares at Reid, who's standing next to him while Tinsley's arms are wrapped around his neck. "We weren't that far away and could have walked."

"Don't get mad, big grumpy dragon," Tinsley teases with a smile. "This was faster." She turns her face to Reid's. "Is it time now? Are we going back? If it is, can you put me in that big plastic box?"

Reid nods, completely unfazed by her excitable energy, and teleports them both inside the tub. She squeezes him in a hug and lets go. Reid reappears in front of us.

Kellan growls, "Aiden's going to kill you if you waste your gift and can't get us back."

Reid's blue eyes slash to Kellan. "I know my limits," he states indifferently. His stare lands on me next, holding my gaze long enough that I'm positive he's going to say something, and then breaks away at the last second to Evie. "Ready?"

"Yes. Let's get them back." Evie shrinks the tub full of children and Tinsley, lifting them in one arm and holding Reid with the other.

Reid faces me. "We'll be right back." Then they disappear.

"The fuck was that all about?" Kellan mutters. "Jack, call Aiden. If they're all done, they should meet us here before they get back so we can get out of here."

The lobby doors fly open. I jump and call on my gift, then diffuse it when I see who it is. Silas's arm is draped over Aiden for support as they come through first. The food guy, who is covered in blood, hobbles inside, then drops to his hands and knees once he's far enough in. Dane comes in after him, with Harvey on his back, eyes closed.

Kellan rushes over to Aiden. "Is everyone alright? Reid and Evie just left with the kids and should be back soon."

"They'll need Cassandra when we get back, but they'll live. We'll talk training after we're back," Aiden answers. He lifts his head to scan the room, finding only Jack and I after Kellan, before he reassesses his own group. He looks as if he's about to say something else, but Reid and Evie pop back to the center of the room, and it's time for the rest of us to get back to the bunker.

RAEGAN

KELLAN ROARS, THE SOUND echoing through the training room like thunder. His fists fly at a punching bag in the corner of the room, pummeling it at an angry pace. He yells again and pulls one fist back, throwing his back into the next punch, and the bag snaps off its hanger and slams into the wall.

He stays like that, his exposed and tattooed chest rising and falling as he catches his breath. There's the faintest sheen of sweat glossing over his bronze skin, catching the overhead lights so every muscle is highlighted and shadowed in greater definition.

It reminds me of the times on the island when I'd caught him working out before, how I couldn't take my eyes off him. It's the same, if not worse, now.

But I'm here for a purpose, and this seems like my chance to interrupt.

I push the door open to the training room. I'd been watching him through the window in the door when I first arrived. Too scared to try entering again at first, and then all those thoughts fell away when I heard him.

Kellan's head snaps up when he hears me enter, his focus melting into a shit-eating grin. "There you are. Ready to train again?" His eyes drop to the brace that Aiden gave me, but he doesn't change his mind and turn me away at the reminder of my bum knee.

My steps clomp across the lacquered floor, and the normally quiet sound now makes me feel like I'm wearing wooden shoes on a stage. My heart beats faster with every step as I move further into the room. Bad memories are clawing at the edges of my mind, trying to slip through the preparation I'd put in place to keep them out.

Ready or not, I'm here.

"Yeah. Put me to work."

Kell grabs a small towel from the bench along the back wall, patting the sweat from his skin and throwing his head back to guzzle water. His throat works, drawing my attention there and then trailing down his chest.

"See something you like? We could do another sort of exercise to warm up if you want, beautiful," he drawls thickly.

Focus. I've been awake for over a week, and it's time to get off my ass and keep preparing for the fight with GE. "Nope, just looking for your weak spots," I shoot back with a saccharine smile.

He laughs and tosses bandages at me. "Wrap up, then. We both know you won't find any, but I dare you to try."

I start weaving the fabric around the first hand, and my smile increases another notch. "Oh, I think you'll find I'm a bit different from the last time we trained."

"Oh?" Kellan slaps a mat down on the floor, then pauses with his hands on his hips to look at me from head to toe. "And how's that?"

"You'll see," I answer cryptically.

He shrugs, unbothered, and waits patiently for me to finish getting ready. "Start on the mat. We'll try to keep our fighting there to warm up. Then feel free to use the rest of the room."

Considering the training room is the size of a football stadium, that's a lot of room for two people. But would it be any different fighting on an island? If someone is chasing me or I'm chasing them, I need to figure out how to close the distance as quickly as possible to use my gift.

I scan the rest of the room to see what we'll be working with, taking a long breath to settle the nerves still lurking beneath the surface.

This is fine. I'm fine. Just concentrate on Kellan.

I step onto one end of the mat.

"I'm going to set a timer for ten minutes. Whoever has the advantage at that time or gets the other person to yield before then wins the match," Kellan explains. His thumb compresses the button on the side of the timer as he shouts, "Go!" before he tosses it to the side.

I run at him, ignoring the initial twinge of discomfort from my knee while keeping close attention to Kellan's hands and arms to try and read what his first move will be. He pulls his right arm back, and I drop under it before it swings out, then pop up in front of him to throw my own punch. It nails him in the jaw.

But aside from turning his face away, his body doesn't move.

Kellan smirks and rubs his jaw, raising a taunting brow. "Is that all you've got?"

I smirk in return, and this time, while his guard is down, I fill my fist with my gift and knock it into his stomach.

He falls backward, his hands automatically moving to his abdomen as he hunches over it. In seconds, his thick, golden skin takes its place over where I'd hit him. Kellan's grin when he looks at me is wild. "Oh, I see how it is. If that's how we're going to play…"

He rushes forward, and I dive to the side, curling up to lessen his chances of landing a strike against me. He keeps coming, and I keep dodging, all while I struggle to find another opening to hit him again.

"You can't win if all you're doing is running away!" Kellan challenges, pushing me around the mat. "If you can't find an opening, then you need to *make* one!" he bellows, his fists swinging harder.

I plant my feet this time, throwing my arms up like a wall in front of me, and lighting them up with my gift. His fist slams into them, but then he roars and pulls it back. I felt the impact from his punch, but my gift took the brunt of it and allowed me to keep my balance. My knee is screaming from so much activity, but I refuse to miss this opportunity and clench my teeth through the pain.

Now!

I jump forward, my gift already active, as I start fighting him with everything I've got. For a second, I think I have him on the run as he tries to fend off my blows.

His leg kicks out, and I fall forward. The mat dusts when I touch it and push myself up.

Kellan laughs. "No mats for your training anymore, beautiful."

With the mat gone, our fight spreads through the rest of the room. I clench my teeth when he easily evades me with all the room we have now. It's harder to strike him when he's no longer within jumping reach, and I don't have speed anywhere in my gift. I could send it to him through the ground, but then I'd ruin the training room.

"I see the wheels in your head turning. What are you going to do now?" he taunts, suddenly behind me.

I whirl around, throwing my punch before I can even see him and hitting golden scales. Again! I keep attacking him now that he's close, but their impact is like a regular punch now that his gift is active. *At least it can still affect him. Without my gift, he wouldn't even feel anything.*

He doesn't run away anymore, letting me get my shots in before he flips me up and drops me to the ground. He straddles me, his golden hand with sharp scales along the back of it wrapping around my fragile neck. His hand twitches around it, and it's enough to cut off my airflow.

Kellan's blue-green eyes are dark, glowing in their ferocity as he leans over me. His voice comes out in a deep rumble that I can feel straight to my core. "You've learned some fun new tricks but forgotten all the fighting techniques I taught you."

The timer goes off. Cheers erupt around us. Kellan grins, releasing me and stepping back so I can look around. A crowd has gathered at the doors, which have been propped open so more people can watch without entering the room.

"That was amazing!"

"I want to learn how to fight like that!"

"Did you see what she did to that mat?"

"Can you believe she kept up with Kellan?"

"Kellan, you look so cool!"

"Raegan's so strong!"

My face burns, and I throw my hands up to cover it. "How long have they been here?" I whisper roughly to Kell.

Kellan helps me to my feet. My knee throbs, the pain sharp like broken glass, but I draw a slow breath to keep my expression clear. Kell drags my arms down while laughing and walking us away from the peeping Guild members to the bench. "Around the time you got your first punch in." He knocks the back of his knuckle atop my head. "They shouldn't have surprised you like that. Don't lose your focus in the fight, but still stay aware of your surroundings," he chastises.

He hands me water that I guzzle down, then work to unwrap my hands. The Guild members at the door stream inside.

"Kellan, can you train me next?"

"If I go change, can you train me too?"

While he's surrounded by eager Guild members, I hurry to put my things away and sneak out when a girl stands in my way. "You were so cool! I'm Trinity. How did you learn to fight like that? Do you think you could help me? Kellan's going to be so busy with the others..."

"Uh, I'm not really that great at fighting yet. I think he'd still be a better teacher..." I skirt around her until she's no longer between me and the door. A couple others catch my eye and start walking over.

Nope. This is too much.

"Sorry, I uh, I have somewhere I need to be." I hurry from the room, keeping my pace *just* under running but fast enough to avoid anyone else. Even after I pass the doors, another group of members exit the elevator. I switch to the stairwell instead, hobbling up a few flights and picking a random floor when my knee can't take anymore stairs.

The floor seems calm at first, but five minutes in brings a new group who notices me and tries to wave me down.

This is why they told me not to wander on my own.

I curse my knee for slowing me down, turning down a hallway and then another in my attempt to lose them. I pause after the third hallway, listening for following footsteps.

"—gan! Wait!"

Ahh. *Why?*

Just as I rush back into a fast walk, something grabs me and yanks me into another room.

The door closes after me, cutting off any source of light. I struggle against whoever grabbed me. "Hey—!" I shout before a hand slaps over my mouth.

"Shh!" a voice hisses in my ear.

The pounding footsteps of the others who followed me get closer. They call my name again.

Is it GE? The spy? Were they just waiting for me to be alone out of my room?

My gift heats in my gut. "Let me go, or I'll kill you," I speak into the hand, but it comes out garbled and far less threatening than I'd like.

"It's me, Rae. Just stay quiet until they're gone," Dane whispers. I pull my gift back in and scrunch my nose. His citrusy scent is more noticeable now that my heart rate is slowing, but *what is he doing*?

Oh, fuck. Is he trying to get us away to find Vera again? This is just like those times when he'd pulled me aside to keep his promise of bringing me with him.

The Guild members run by whatever room we're in, their steps getting farther away until we can't hear them anymore.

Dane sighs with relief. There's a soft click, and a dim light fills the room in a haunting glow. His hand falls from my face.

"Please tell me we aren't sneaking away to meet with Vera again," I rush out first.

"What? No. I saw you were running from them and thought I could keep you hidden until they were gone."

"Oh." That's a relief. I look around the room—closet, I amend—and the organized shelves of cleaning supplies as well as a floor covered with buckets, mops, brooms, vacuums, and...

I shift back to get a clearer picture of the room with what little light the small bulb is giving us, and Dane reaches for me. "Wait, don't—!"

Whatever I step on rolls, and I fall back. Dane throws himself at me, his hands cradling under my head as we topple to the floor, and the mess of cleaning supplies crashes down on top of him.

His amber eyes are locked with mine while we both catch our breath. There's a look in them that sends a rush of heat through me. It's a look he hasn't given me in a long time. One that had always been there on the island. I thought it was just what his eyes looked like back then. Hot as fire. Like melted gold with burnt edges and flecks of green.

The look that causes me to melt in return when it's pinned on me, raising my body's temperature until I think I'm also turning to liquid from the inside.

Those eyes flick to my mouth, so close to his, before they return.

He licks his lips, and it's like he's imagining what I taste like.

My heart skips.

"Rae, I…" He pauses, his face lined with concentration as if all the things he wants to say are firing rapidly through his head, and he's struggling to pick one at a time. "Thank you."

Even though my head's fuzzy with his proximity, the words shock me enough that I immediately fight them on reflex. "What? No, you shouldn't—"

His palm covers my mouth again. "Let me get this out. I've been meaning to say this to you since we got you back, but you're either recovering or not alone."

I offer him a short nod, but he doesn't remove his hand.

"I never thanked you for saving me that time in the lab. I know…the result of saving me messed everything up between us, but you were doing it for me. And then…when you were with Gordon…all of that was because you chose to save me. You had to go through everything because of me. You gave yourself back to *him* to save me and the others and to give me a chance with Vera."

I try to argue into his hand, but his fingers press more firmly to keep me quiet.

He's making me sound like more than I am.

It was simpler than that.

"You're amazing, Rae. The strongest person I know. You've been through hell and come out stronger. Only you could turn everything on its head and stand taller because of it."

His hand slides away, but his fingertips linger along my jaw. My cheek.

"I've said this before, but I'll say it again. I don't deserve you in my life, but I'm a selfish fuck and I want you anyway."

I stop breathing.

His fingers slide under my ear, weaving into my hair at the nape of my neck.

His face draws closer.

"Rae..." he breathes.

My lips part on instinct. Maybe in the hopes of him resuscitating me, because I've gone numb with shock.

Did he say...he wants me?

But what about Vera? What about everything *bad* I've done? Those couple of things can't possibly outweigh everything else. I must've misheard him.

My chest tightens. "You...want me?"

My words don't stop the measured crawl of him closing the distance between us. He moves in slow motion, his lips edging closer to mine while all I can do is fall into his molten gaze.

"I—" he starts to answer, and then the door whips open. Bright light pours over us, eclipsing the warm glow of the room. Fresh air sweeps in, inducing a cool shiver to run through me.

"Oh, dear. I thought I heard someone in here," a female muses.

Dane jerks back. He climbs to his feet and snaps at the woman, "And that gave you permission to barge in? There's no lock on the door. We were fine." He helps me to my feet next, and I'm careful to put some space between us.

My heart is still jumping around my chest, but the fresh air is clearing my mind. I don't know what was happening in there. He thanked me. And then...he was going to kiss me.

And I would have let him in that moment. I wasn't going to stop him.

But now that I can think again, I remember the reasons why I shouldn't. He may see some glorified version of me right now, but I know he's only looking at one side of me. And I can't forget what I did to his sister.

He knows I've been with Kellan, too, but that wasn't stopping him.

"Rae?" I jerk my head up to find the woman gone and Dane watching me worriedly. "Is it what I said? I'm not taking it back. I meant every word in there."

He reaches toward me, and I step back. His face falls.

"Sorry, I just need a minute to process everything. Do you mind if we...finished this later?"

Dane runs his outstretched hand through his hair. "Yeah. Sure."

I nod awkwardly. "Thanks. I'm going to head back to my room for a shower. I'll, uh, see you in a bit?"

He nods, and I take that as my cue to walk—the normal speed—to the elevator so I can be alone and figure out what the fuck just happened.

Chapter Twenty-Five

RAEGAN

I step out of the bathroom and pull on my hair to tighten the ponytail. I'm dressed in my training leggings and sports bra, ready to meet Kellan for our regular morning practice. It's been a week since we started training again. A week since Dane confessed to me.

He hasn't brought that conversation up again, giving me the time I need to figure out what I want to say and how. He's showing uncharacteristic patience that I'm grateful for because I'm too afraid I'll say something to fuck this up.

Do I want him like that? Of course I do. I had a crush on all the guys on the island, and that's intensified to dizzying levels since seeing them here. Even when he hated me, that didn't mean I had stopped caring about him.

But can I let anything happen between us when I can't fully believe that he's moved on from what happened between me and

Vera?

Can I act on it when I'm already selfishly with Kellan and Jackson while neither of them is making me choose?

I don't date. I don't do relationships. I expected to lose my life in my fight with GE.

But now? Now, there's a chance for a future.

Now, I'm in too deep with Jack and Kellan to question it, but I don't know what to do about my feelings for Dane. Or Aiden. It isn't fair to them.

"What are you thinking about?" a husky voice fans across my exposed nape.

I jump out of my skin, my soul ricocheting like a pinball in my body.

Jackson circles me from behind and stops when he can see my face. He cocks his head to the side as a slow smile stretches his lips.

"Fucking hell, Jack! You're going to kill me if you keep doing this to me."

Then I see the specks of blood on his face. "Are you hurt?" I demand, trying to check his face and then pull his sleeves up to look for any injuries. "Whose blood is this?"

"Not mine," he replies coolly.

I step back to look at his face. "Thorne's?"

"Mm...no." He pauses as if trying to think of the right word before returning his attention to me. "Hunters."

The kill force Gordon sent out for the guys.

Damn it.

We're so isolated in this bubble down here that I forgot what waited for the guys above ground. If any of them were to go out into the city...

"We should rethink our plan with Thorne. You shouldn't be alone out there."

"Why?" he asks calmly. Not in a condescending way, but like he's genuinely curious.

"What if he sends too many and you're outnumbered? What if he makes a trap for you? I don't know, Jack, I don't want you to get hurt and have no one there to back you up."

Jackson smiles. His fingers circle around my ear as if to push hair away, even though it's tied back. "We almost have what we need. I'll keep my promise to you, little one."

I want all of us to make it through this.

I take a calming breath.

Right.

I trust Jackson. He'll help me make my dreams a reality.

His smile sharpens, and his hand wraps around my ponytail. He jerks it back, then kisses my throat. "Let's play a game." His voice is soft. Dangerous.

"A game?" I repeat in a breathless whisper.

"I'm going to count to sixty, and you're going to run. If you make it out of the bunker before I catch you, then you can demand anything you want from me."

I open my mouth, but he presses a finger to my lips.

"It can be something fun, silly, and I can't refuse."

Oh. I see. He would already do anything I asked of him for fighting GE or things more serious, but he's looking to keep this more relaxed. What can I ask him to do that he wouldn't do already?

"And if you catch me?"

He licks my pulse. "Then I get to do whatever I want with you."

A shiver snakes around my spine and settles in my core.

"Five minutes," I counter.

Jackson draws back. "Two."

"Four and a half."

"Two and a half."

"Jack! You move twice as fast as me. Five minutes."

He smirks. "As you wish. Five minutes. Go."

"Wait, right now? I'm supposed to meet Kellan to train—"

"Four fifty-four," he counts aloud. "Four fifty-three."

Shit.

Sorry, Kellan. I'll be a few minutes late.

I take off, running to the door and down the hall. Thankfully, Aiden gave me a tour a few days ago for the major areas. Including how to get to the security room that leads to the tunnels to exit the bunker at different points around the city.

The stairs to get there slow me down. I curse them and my fucking knee, knowing full well Jackson will likely fly past them.

I should have asked for ten minutes.

I shove the door open to the security room and everyone turns to look at me. I wave, having just met them a few days ago. "Everything's fine. Which door leads to the Tower?" At least that building is secure if I make it there, rather than winding up at a random public building in the city.

One of the guards grins and points to the left. I'm not sure what she thinks is so funny, but I don't have time to hang around and ask. As I'm leaving the room to get to the room full of doors, another guard calls out, "Does Aiden know you're leaving?"

I let the door closing behind me act as my answer, then take the first door to the left. I remember this tunnel. It's long as *fuck* and dark.

He may not see me, but he'll definitely hear me with the hollow echo of carved dirt and stone blended with steel reinforcements. At least Aiden had his phone flashlight when we'd walked this path before.

I run for so long that I think I must be near the thousands of stairs I'll have to take to get above ground. My knee aches, pain sharpening with every step. All I can hear is my harsh breathing and feet crunching the dirt. If this game winds up being more of a marathon than a sprint, then it's only a matter of time before Jackson catches up to me.

That asshole knew I was never making it out of here.

"Woah there," a baritone voice drawls just before I crash into something. Arms wrap around me, steadying me, as I'm surrounded by the smell of musk.

"Kellan? What are you doing here?" Wait. I don't have time for that. I can ask him later. Right now, he's just slowing me down. I push back from him, but his arms tighten, locking me against him. "Let me go! I'm running out of time!"

I struggle in his arms, trying to wriggle my way free. If I can find the sensitive spot on his elbow…

His beard tickles my shoulder. It's the only warning before he bites down.

"Ahhh! What the—*nngh*! Kell!"

Kellan's tongue and lips melt the pain away as his hand wanders to grip my ass. His other hand slides into my sports bra, scooping a breast free that he immediately proceeds to tease with his mouth.

My thighs grow damp as he continues, my struggle only adding to the pleasure when I'm trying to break free. "Kell, please, ahh!"

"You got her?" another voice, dripping in darkness and danger, calls out coolly from where I came.

Kellan's teeth pull harder on my nipple when I jerk with surprise at Jackson's voice. My cunt pulses and I moan before I can stop it. He chuckles. "She ran right into my arms, just like you thought she would."

Wait. What? My lust-addled mind fumbles through this information, but he's making it damn difficult as his tongue circles my nipple before drawing it back into his mouth.

Kellan. Here. Waiting. Jackson planned this?

Jackson comes up behind me, his hands finding my hips, and then he whispers, "Caught you." His lips trail down my neck. "Do you want us both?"

Oh, fuck. I must be dreaming.

Who am I to ruin the dream?

I nod vigorously.

"Say it," Kellan growls. His tongue flicks my stiff, elongated nipple that's feeding on his attention like a fucking weed as he fists the other breast. I writhe from his touch, my ass inadvertently grinding against Jackson and finding his stiff cock. *Fuck. Yes.* A thrill of desire shudders through me, pooling at my center. I'm pinned between them, unable to escape the pleasure he's arousing.

"Tell us what you want us to do to you, beautiful."

I lick my dry, thirsty lips. "I want...both of you. Together."

My leggings are dragged down with my underwear. My shoes are tugged off, and then the rest of my clothes are removed and tossed to the darkness.

"Keep going," Kellan rumbles, his thumb and forefinger pinching and rolling the nipple not in his mouth and drawing another moan past my lips when a shot of pure pleasure strikes my core.

"Fuck. Jackson inside me, and your dick in my mouth." Fuck, why does saying it aloud make me feel like some newbie at sex? I've lost count of how many times I've had sex, but never like this. I've never been made to ask for it, either.

"Good girl," Kellan praises. Then he and Jack are gone. I'm alone in the pitch black, no clothes left on me, while these two can do anything they please with me.

My heart races like it's on steroids, and energy sings through my veins with the anticipation.

Hands push me down by my shoulders. My knees land on a pillow of air, and I could cry with relief that my knee won't be interfering with this.

Heat radiates in front of my face, and I can hear a faint rubbing of skin on skin. My tongue flicks out to wet my lips, and strikes something warm and soft.

"Open up, beautiful. Show me that sharp tongue of yours."

I do as he says, spreading my mouth wide and laying my tongue out like a red carpet. My hot breath acts as a guide in the dark, and his cock finds my tongue without any trouble, weighing heavily as Kellan releases it.

My lips suction around his crown, and my cheeks hollow as I suck more of him inside.

"Oh, *fuck* yeah!" Kellan groans, his voice a guttural, cavernous sound. "You're a goddamn queen, beautiful. Sucking my dick down like that."

Hearing that is as big of a compliment as I could ask for, and I try not to smile. Time to turn the tables on these two and show them I can control their pleasure just as much as they do mine.

Or so I planned.

Until Jackson shifts my legs apart and spears me with his tongue.

I almost choke on Kellan in my surprise, lurching forward to grab his thighs.

Jack chuckles, and the sound sends a pleasurable shudder through me that ends between my thighs. His tongue drags up to my clit, moving in maddening circles around it and everywhere other than that one spot.

My thighs tremble as he draws my pleasure out, one lick, one suckle, one circle at a time.

Even though I can't see a fucking thing, my eyes are closed with bliss as I focus on how good everything feels. On Jackson, playing me like I'm an instrument, and he, its master. On Kellan, as my lips and tongue glide over the warm ridges of his cock and he serenades me with sounds of his pleasure.

Jackson strokes his tongue over my clit, and my moan reverberates from my mouth through Kellan.

"Fuck yes, that feels so good. Whatever you're doing to her, don't stop," Kellan demands. He fists my hair, encouraging me deeper but not taking over.

I swallow more of him. Even as my jaw aches and drool spills from the corner of my lips, I moan and suck him down like I've never tasted anything better.

"For the love of—" he cuts himself off and hisses, his fist clenching and pulling my hair. "You're a fucking goddess. So perfect. You take me so well."

Jackson hits all the right places, and Kellan's words have me feeling weightless and buzzing. I shift one hand to the base of Kellan to give myself more leverage, using it in tandem with my mouth to stroke and suck until not a single inch of him is spared.

Fingers sink into my heat without warning, and my entire body convulses at the stimulation. Two thrusts later, and I'm crying out around Kellan, my body tightening and exploding in a rush. My thighs quiver and almost fall, but hands on my hips guide them back up.

Jackson's hard length rubs into the mess I made, coating himself, and then he drives inside, shoving me deeper on Kellan's dick until it hits my throat.

It all feels so good. Too good to think clearly and keep myself moving in any sort of rhythm on Kellan. He picks up on this, and his hand in my hair works in sync with Jackson's thrusts. I give in to the bliss, to the headiness that's taken over.

"We're not doing this in the dark again. I want to see her face when we're taking her like this," Kellan growls.

My cunt clenches, and Jackson chuckles.

"She likes the sound of that."

Kellan strokes the side of my face, where he's probably trying to imagine my expression. "Good girl." He gasps, then grits out, "Are you going to swallow my cum, too?"

I try to nod, barely shifting my face before it slides over him again.

"Here it comes," he warns, and Jackson slows so I can focus on swallowing the hot cum that slides down my throat. Kellan steps back, and the hand in my hair finds my chin. His thumb rubs over my lips, and he kisses me just as Jackson picks up his pace.

Cool fingers tease and flick my clit. I cling to Kellan, drawing strength from him as another orgasm crawls up my spine. It locks around me, stealing the breath from my lungs and throwing me over a cliff. I scream as it wrings me dry, and then Jackson shudders and curls over my back. He kisses my spine as Kellan steals a kiss of his own from my lips.

Kell withdraws slowly like it's an internal struggle to convince himself that I still need air to breathe. We're all panting and breathless, but he gets his voice back first to ask, "Who's up for a shower?"

Chapter Twenty-Six

AIDEN

The phone rings endlessly in my ear. If it clicks over to voice-mail, I'm quick to end the call and redial.

There's no avoiding me. Just answer your phone so we can be done with it.

Sleep nags at me like an unrepentant pest. It sits in the recesses of my mind, waiting for a moment of weakness to sweep in and drag me down.

Moments like this, where the droll ringing threatens to lull me into its sweet surrender, are the most dangerous. I've been able to avoid it for a few days now, slipping in a twenty-minute nap here or there when absolutely necessary, and otherwise, I've been here. Losing myself to achieve my goals.

Because nothing else matters to me anymore aside from taking down GE and fixing what I ruined.

The mission to the first island had been a test. We rescued the kids there, as Raegan had wanted, but that wasn't my primary goal.

We tested the skill and mettle of the Guild members who have been asking to join the fight. They passed the test for their bravery, but skills-wise left a lot to be desired. They aren't practiced enough to fight, so we've had to put a hold on any further trips until Kellan can train them on how to fight against people who want to kill you. It's not the same as their friendly squabbles here.

I also had Dane pull more data from their computers. Because I'm looking for proof of someone that I'm now convinced is still on one of these islands or is working for GE.

Raegan's father.

The ringing stops. I almost miss it; the echo of its sound continuing in my head. But a deep drawl, one I've never heard before, sounds in my ear. "What the fuck do you want?"

For a second, I think I've fallen asleep. I shift forward to lean over my desk, making sure I'm awake and can feel the hard wood of my desk. "Who is this?" I demand.

There's noise on the other end that I can't place, and then I hear Elias's voice further away. "Don't answer my phone." More shuffling, like the phone is being moved around, and then Thorton's voice is loud and clear. "Adams. You don't seem to understand the notion that someone not answering their phone means they're busy."

I smirk, and the sentiment carries through to my voice. "Well, you've answered now. I'll keep this quick." When he doesn't hang up or argue, I continue, "I need your network again. Anyone taken by GE who has seen or heard of a man called Charles Whitmore."

It's unfortunate that I have to resort to asking Elias for this information. While I have my own resources here, they're limited to the people in my Guild and this city.

Elias's network is worldwide. He has a far greater reach and more gifted contacts than I'll ever have or want.

"How urgent is this request? I've just finished your last one, and I have my hands full with other priorities."

"It's for Raegan."

Silence. Then Elias sighs. It almost makes me wonder what the hell he's working on that has him sounding so tired. Is it still because of Portia?

"I'll get the word out and let you know what I hear back."

"Raegan is also waiting for a phone call from Portia," I remind him again.

"I haven't forgotten. She will call. When she's ready."

The door to my office opens. Dane and Kellan stroll inside, closing it behind them quietly when they see I'm on the phone.

"You should worry more about your requests stacking up, Adams," he continues.

Like I care.

"I'll pay you whatever you want."

"I don't want money."

I frown, my hand pinching the phone a little harder. "Then, what do you want?"

"Favors. I'm doing quite a bit for you right now. I hope you'll remember that when my time comes and I call you with my own request. And, no questions asked, you'll do it for me."

"Fine. Just get me closer to Mr. Whitmore as soon as possible."

Elias chuckles, and the call ends.

"What the fuck was that about?" Dane asks, moving to stand in front of my desk. Kellan hangs back against one of the bookshelves, arms crossed.

"Where's Raegan?" I ask first. While the bunker should be secure, the threat of a potential spy and the gifted with the ability to portal makes me cautious. I'd rather one of us have an eye on her at all times to ensure she's safe.

Kellan answers, "With Jack. He's getting ready to leave for Thorne duty, so he's spending time with her first."

Relief eases a pinch of the tension coursing through me. It's not nearly as much as I'd get by seeing her safe for myself, but I settle with what I can get for now. With that worry resolved, I return to Dane's original question. "That was Elias. I've added his assistance in trying to find Raegan's father. Have you found anything on him from the data you pulled at the last island?"

He shakes his head. "Nothing. It looks like they keep all their data siloed to each island, so unless he was on that particular island, there's no mention of him."

The only island we're fairly certain he was on was the one we'd escaped, and where Raegan had been born, before it crumbled to the bottom of the ocean. There's nothing left of it.

"You really think this is what she wants? To meet a father she doesn't even remember?" Kellan questions, and it's clear in his tone he thinks she doesn't.

That isn't up to me to decide. I'm going to give her the option, and she can choose what she wants to do. This is the only family member she has left. If he's still alive, she could have part of her family back. Someone to talk to about her mother, who knew her when she was alive. Questions answered.

I've already done every record search for him in the States and come across nothing. He's like a ghost.

Just like Raegan.

Which now has me looking to GE and the islands for answers.

"When was the last time you slept?" Dane prompts, his face drawn with concern. "You criticized Jackson for doing this, and here you are, working yourself to death."

My standards of care for my brothers are not the same as for myself.

"We aren't leaving on another mission for some time yet, but there's still the impending Guild event that we need to prepare for. My sleep patterns don't adversely affect anyone while we're staying put."

Dane drops into one of the chairs and leans on my desk with a long sigh. "Just tell her you're sorry."

It's not that simple.

"She'll barely look at me," I admit sharply.

Kellan pokes at something on one of the shelves and mutters, "Shouldn't have been a dumbass, then."

I pin him with an annoyed look. "If I want your opinion on this, I'll ask for it."

He laughs.

Prick.

"She doesn't even know what you're doing for her. Are you planning on telling her it was you?" Dane keeps going.

"No, I'm not looking for credit. I know I've messed things up too much to gain her forgiveness. I'm not doing this for me."

I'm doing it for her.

Whatever I can do to make things better. For her.

I've broken whatever we once had between us, and I'm not trying to fix that. It's better for her to not see me the way she used to. All that matters is that I spend my time righting whatever wrongs are in her life as a result of the mistakes I made.

Her injuries.

Her parents.

Her future.

Her happiness.

"Is there anything else?" I ask.

The worry on Dane's face deepens. "No. Just...get some rest."

My door crashes open. I grab my whip sword at my side, ready to swing it at whoever or whatever entered the room, and freeze at who I see.

Raegan stumbles forward, and I jump from my seat to catch her before she falls to the floor. The sweet smell of vanilla is overpowered by the whiskey on her breath.

Where the fuck are Dane and Kellan? Did they let her walk around the bunker drunk? Or did they pass out first? Either scenario is unacceptable.

The clock on the wall shows it's after two in the morning.

Had I fallen asleep?

"There you are!" she shouts, jabbing a finger into my chest. Her finger slides down my tie a few inches, and then she grabs it and pulls it to rub against her cheek. "So silky," she whispers to herself.

She's trashed.

Anything I say to her now will only disappear into oblivion, so

I don't bother reprimanding her for wandering around alone and drunk in the middle of the night.

I'll save that for the morning when she's hungover.

Raegan's head plops against my chest, her face nuzzling into my shirt and tie. "Mm...so soft and warm."

My heart attempts to leap from my chest at the easy way she's touching me now. My blood heats, perking my cock to attention with this slightest affection.

Fuck's sake.

She's done this before. It doesn't mean what I want it to. Drunk Raegan likes me far more than sober Raegan. I can't take anything she says or does while under the influence as truth.

The tease is torture, though.

"Why are you always hitting on me when you're drunk?" I mutter, trying to help her back to her feet while she leans all her weight on me. "Any other man might get the wrong idea."

Her face falls to a pout. A fucking kicked puppy, sad-face pout. "But not you?"

Deep breath.

Draw the line.

"You've been clear you want nothing to do with me like that," I answer slowly, still trying to help her walk to the door. I need to get her to bed before I do or say something I'll regret. She won't remember it come morning, but I will.

Raegan plants her feet and would have toppled backward if not for me already holding her. "You don't like me, then?"

I click my teeth together, grinding them with the effort not to lose my temper with her. Everyone else, and I can keep my head and my wits without much difficulty. It's easy to remain objective and keep my focus on the bigger picture. Easy to remove myself and any emotions from the equation.

But her?

It's like I store up all the rage and passion I have exclusively for this woman.

I'm a hollow man without her.

The moment I'm near her, every emotion floods through my veins until I'm fit to burst, and it's a struggle to control anything I do or say. She brings out the best and the worst in me. I only wish I had some say in it before it ruins everything.

I snap and push her back against the wall.

She gasps, her blue eyes lighting with excitement.

"No. I don't *like* you. I fucking love you. Even though it makes me say and do crazy things. It feels like my chest is on fire whenever I'm near you. Because I want you so much that it burns me alive to know I'll never have you. To know that you're going to choose Jackson or Kellan, and I'm not even in the running. Even though you've had my heart since the moment I stepped on that godforsaken island. I watched you gather the others around you like you're their goddamn sun, but I had you first."

There's a moment of silence as she stares at me, and then she breathes in a soft command, "Then kiss me."

I don't think; I hardly ever do around her, so I shouldn't be surprised with myself.

I kiss her before her demand has completely fallen from her lips. I steal the breath from our lungs, kissing her like it's the only thing giving us life. I hate that I'm a slave to this burning passion inside me. That I give in without a second's hesitation.

She owns me, body and soul, and that loss of control is infuriating.

My body presses her back against the wall, my hands scrambling into her hair and locking our mouths together as if they were made to be one. I need her kiss more than I need anything else in this world. Her hands grab at my clothes, pulling and yanking me closer like she's just as desperate to close any distance between us.

Our kiss is like a volcanic eruption. Sudden and hot, the lava filling my chest to the brim with its blistering heat and clouding my lungs with ash. Her kiss is the life support I need as it spreads through my limbs and saturates me with uncontrollable desire. My dick is harder than steel against my leg.

Raegan's hand moves down my chest like it's being drawn by some invisible force until it cups my hard length and squeezes.

The jolt of pleasure that rips through me makes me groan. Fresh oxygen fills my lungs, and sanity slips a harsh reminder into my mind.

She's still wasted.

Fuck.

I step back, but I can't put the distance between us that I really need because she pitches forward when I'm no longer there to hold her up. I catch her in my arms, cursing at my fucking luck and then chalking this up to karma.

"Aiden?" she whispers huskily. Her voice is thick and sensual, which makes me even crazier.

It's a lie. She hates you.

If she wanted me like this, she would kiss me when she's sober.

If I do anything now, I'm taking advantage of her.

The image of Gordon comes to mind, and all lust-filled thoughts come to a crashing halt. Rage replaces desire. Fury for lust.

I'm going to find him, and I'm going to make that man wish for death.

I lift Raegan in my arms, cradling her against my chest. It would take far too long to return her to her room if I let her try to walk. I need her as far away from me as possible, as soon as possible.

I make too many mistakes when I'm with her.

I don't know if it's the motion of walking or that I've stopped responding, but she curls into my chest and closes her eyes for the walk back. She mumbles a few things to me, but I've got one hand on the wheel again and keep myself from saying anything back. I've already said too much. But I take comfort in knowing she won't remember any of it when she wakes up.

Dane and Kellan are both passed out in her room. Dane is on the mattress, and Kellan in her bed. Did she wake up still drunk to find me? And what happened to make her think to come to me?

This is the first time she hasn't been angry and yelling at me while drunk.

I get her in bed, tucking the sheets around her and resisting the urge to stab Kellan for being in there, too. I might've if it were a few weeks ago. But now, if she hasn't kicked him out, then I have to assume she wants him there. So, unfortunately, he stays hole-free.

I stroke her blonde tendrils from her face, watching her peaceful expression and finding it difficult to walk away. Time disappears when I'm with her like this. When I can watch her without restraint, without worry that she'll notice how long and often my gaze tracks to her. Like I'm irrevocably drawn to her.

"Aiden?" a voice whispers at the partially open door I left behind me.

It's Cibrina, still dressed like she hasn't gone to sleep yet either.

Probably sought me out here when she found my office empty. Which begs the question, how long have I been standing here?

"What's wrong?" I gather the strength needed to pull myself away from her and walk to the door.

"He's arrived."

Chapter Twenty-Seven

RAEGAN

"Wake up, beautiful."

A pounding headache and a pinch of nausea remind me that I drank too much last night.

I reach for the nearest blanket to yank over my head.

What happened last night? I can usually hold my liquor, at least in terms of avoiding getting sick or being too far gone, but when I try to recall specifics after our drinking game...nothing.

Kellan had challenged me and Dane to a drinking game he'd picked up on the streets, and like idiots, we accepted.

I haven't been blackout drunk, where complete chunks of time are missing, in a long time.

Or...maybe I wasn't? Didn't we all just go to sleep?

The thought of Aiden springs to mind. I reach for it, trying not to panic on the reason why, but the only thing that comes back to me is Dane trying to convince me to talk to Aiden about something.

The blanket is pulled away from my face, and the strong smell of coffee fills my nose.

My eyes pop open.

Kellan grins at me while wafting the steam from the coffee mug at my face. "Morning. I'd planned to wake you in other ways, but food just got delivered."

I groan and push myself upright. "Why did you order food so early?" I grumble, reaching for the coffee, then gasp when he moves it out of reach.

The man formerly known as Kellan breathing his last seconds of oxygen *drinks my coffee*. To my face. With a roguish grin and dancing blue-green eyes that says he knows exactly what he's doing.

"It's almost afternoon. And we didn't order it," Dane says from somewhere in the room. But I don't take my eyes off the dead man.

I lunge at him like a lioness going in for the kill. He has one second of wide-eyed surprise-turned-laughter before I tackle him to the ground. My hands go for his throat, but he grabs my hips and flips us around.

Doesn't matter.

I try to strangle him with my bare hands even while his massive body engulfs mine, and he could squish me without trying.

The bastard's still grinning at me, and it makes me wild.

"How dare you, you motherfucking prick! You. Don't. Tease. Me. With. Coffee!"

Kellan laughs and takes my wrists, tugging them from his throat and slamming them back on the floor above me. He leans down, his facial hair teasing up my neck to my face. "I think I still have some on my lips if you want it," he mocks, and I snarl at him.

He licks his lips.

"You asshole! Get off me! You'll be lucky if I ever kiss your lips again," I rage, twisting and struggling in his hold.

Kell rolls away, and I rush to my feet. I jump onto the bed and then leap at him to land on his back. My arm wraps around his neck, the other arm holding it tight as I fight to get some advantage over him.

He grabs my arm and stalks to the bed, then jerks forward and throws me over his head so I thump onto the mattress.

And then the motherfucker steals an upside-down kiss from me while I'm too stunned to stop him.

"I love it when you're all riled up." He points a finger to my chest and the sprinting heart beneath it. "Now save this for training later, and you can try to kick my ass all you want there." Kellan gives me another kiss and then squeezes a breast just to drive another nail in his coffin.

Oh, I'm going to *destroy* him during training.

He sits at the portable table that's set up in the middle of the room and gives me a knowing smirk.

Dane's sitting next to him, his fork shaking in his grip as he stares at his plate.

All the anger pops like a balloon and leaves me in a rush.

He catches me looking and loosens his hold on the fork before giving me a small smile of reassurance. Which only makes me feel twice as shitty.

The coffee mug—*the* coffee mug—appears in my peripheral vision. I sit up. I thought Kellan had dropped it when I attacked him, but there it is. Uncracked and still full. Looking around, I spot Jackson by the door. He sends the coffee to me now that I've noticed it and then strolls over.

I take the coffee floating before me and bring it to my lips, swallowing the bitter warmth and trying to contain my addict groan of satisfaction.

Jackson bends so we're eye level and kisses me. I kiss him back, because I did miss him last night and I'm glad he's back safe and without any blood this time—from what I can see. But I do cut it shorter than I normally would because I don't want to upset Dane any more than I already have.

Jack smiles in that perceptive way of his that tells me he knows every little thing I'm thinking and then asks, "Did you have fun last night?"

Oh yeah.

Alcohol breath.

"I think so," I reply honestly. I still feel like I'm missing something incredibly important, but the more I try to remember, the further away it seems. "When did you get back?"

"Now." Ah. So, right in time to witness my moment of insanity with Kellan. At least he made it in time to save the coffee. Fuck, this man takes care of me more than I deserve.

I grab his hoodie and pull him down for one more kiss.

"All right, come eat. Both of you, since I doubt you've eaten anything in the last twelve hours either, Jack," Kellan interrupts from his seat.

I give Jackson a full smile of appreciation, then take his hand for the brief walk to the table. There's already a plate made and ready for me, as well as a glass of water and ibuprofen beside it.

"Oh, thanks, Dane." I take a guess, since Jackson just arrived and Kellan was busy harassing me.

Dane finishes the bite he's eating and shrugs. "The plate was me, but I didn't order the food or the medicine."

Kellan snorts. "I love how there's only enough medicine for one of us. Is he saying we have to accept whatever hangover we might have? Because joke's on him. I'm clear."

Him.

Aiden?

Wait. How would he know I need medicine?

Realization sinks in my gut like a lead weight.

Fuck. Did I go see him last night?

If I did, it can't be too bad considering he ordered food and medicine for me, right?

I hope I didn't do anything embarrassing.

Jackson picks up a whole pancake and takes a bite out of it. He's hardly sitting, just perched on the edge of his seat like he's ready to move at a second's notice. He catches me watching him and smiles. "Eat up, little one. There's a guest waiting to meet you when you're done, and you'll need your strength."

What does that mean?

After the food's taken away and we take our turns in the bathroom getting ready for the day, Aiden joins us in the room. The light stubble he usually sports is a bit thicker than usual, and his face has lost some of its color. But the rest of him, his perfect suit, his firm stance, his controlled tone...all of that is the same.

When he looks at me, my heart trips beneath his stare, and it feels like he wants to say something.

Is he going to chew me out for last night? Because I'm sure, whatever I did, pissed him off.

His eyes take in my tight jeans and shirt before snapping back to my face. "Are you comfortable?"

What the fuck kind of question is that?

"In my clothes? Yes. With this conversation? Debatable."

Aiden smirks. "Good enough. Come sit, and I'll fill you in before he arrives to meet you."

"He, who?"

"Sit," he repeats tersely, and I sigh but do as he asked.

Aiden takes the seat opposite me, Dane between us and Kellan and Jackson in their own spots in the room. "His name is Gabriel. He's here to see if he can fix your knee," he explains, his voice smooth and nonchalant.

A sting of pain pierces my chest at the reminder. "No one can fix my knee." I've accepted that. I won't let false hope ruin what I worked hard to accept after it happened.

Aiden responds just as calmly as before, "He has a special gift that says otherwise. Are you willing to meet him and find out?"

"Are you saying I have a choice?" It's Aiden. I'm sure he's made up his mind about what's best for me. Do I want to put myself through false hope?

"If you want to think about it, he can stay here for a bit until you decide. If you're adamant this isn't what you want, then I'll send him home right now."

We hold eye contact as I consider what he's saying. Would he really send him home if I asked him to? After whatever work was put into finding this guy?

A part of me wants to do that. Just to see if he'll follow through on it.

"Don't you want to at least hear what he has to say?" Dane chimes in softly. "This isn't another healer like Cassandra. And it took Aiden—"

Aiden slashes him a look, and he stops.

It took Aiden what?

"What would you like me to do?" Aiden prompts.

I glance at the others in the room. Kellan and Jackson both stay quiet, letting me decide what I want. It's clear that Dane wants me to give this a try.

The piece of information that's prodding at me is how Aiden found this guy. If he's a guest, then he's not part of the Guild. Where did he come from? And how did he happen to find someone who may or may not be able to fix an already-healed injury?

"I'll meet him." I won't get my hopes up. I'm just going to meet this person that Aiden apparently found and treat it like that. Nothing at stake.

Aiden nods and calls someone on his phone. "Yes, she would like to meet him. I'll unlock the door for when you get here." He taps more on his phone and the door clicks open.

They must have been waiting nearby because it's only a few minutes before Cibrina walks in with two strangers.

The first one is as tall as Kellan but smaller in size. He's not bulky or a fighter from what I can tell. He's wearing dark pants, a checkered shirt with a black dress vest on top, and he has multiple piercings. One in his nose, on his lip, two beads over an eyebrow, and then his ears are lined with them. His hair is buzzed on one side and long on top, flipped and hanging to one side and red at the tips before it fades to black midway up.

He peers around the room, looking at each of us and then checking out the rest of it with a bored expression.

The second one is average height with short brown hair sticking up in all directions. He's wearing skinny-jeans and what looks like a woman's cardigan. It has a plush interior and feathers running along either side of the opening in the front and along the edge of the sleeves.

This guy beams at us the moment he enters the room. "Well, hello!" he greets cheerfully. His gaze flips through everyone and then lands on me. He beelines it to me, and both Kellan and Jack are on either side of my chair in an instant. Dane and Aiden stand at once. "Oh! Did I get too close to the queen bee?"

He takes a polite step back, bumping into the first guest who had followed him like his own personal guard. Then he bows at the waist and slaps his hands together like he's praying, bending his head behind them. "Sorry, sorry. Introductions first." He straightens with another smile. "I'm Gabriel. Or Gabe. Or Gabby. Or Gabe-ey. Or whatever else you'd like to call me," he adds with a chuckle.

The man behind him manages to frown harder.

Gabriel whips his hand over his shoulder to hit his statuesque friend in the chest. "And this is Zedd. He's a bit of a grump, but he's my grump, so don't be too hard on him."

"Wait." Dane stares incredulously at the grump. "Zedd, the singer?"

"I don't do autographs," Zedd replies in a bored tone.

Dane slams his fist onto the table. "I wasn't asking!"

"Right!" Gabriel claps his hands together. "Now that's out of the way, is it correct of me to assume you're Raegan?"

"Uh, yes, that's me."

"Wonderful." He pulls out the open seat next to me. "Can I have a seat? Standing is *incredibly* exhausting."

I don't know why I bother, but I reply, "Sure," after he's already plopped himself in it.

Gabriel sets his elbow on the table and leans into his hand as he settles in, making himself comfortable. "So, tell me what you need, dear."

Kellan growls at the endearment, and Gabriel rolls his eyes at me with a smile. I can't help but smile back. His energy is infectious. Already, I feel more relaxed in his presence.

I glance to Aiden, having assumed he'd already filled him in, and he shrugs. So, he did, but Gabriel wants to hear it from me?

"I guess to see if you can fix my knee?"

He nods and waves me on. "Yes, but give me the whole story. How did you get it, what happened to it, and you know...all that jazz." He waggles his fingers at me.

My eyes immediately move between my guys nervously.

"Don't worry about them," Gabriel says with a flippant wave of his hand. "It's just you and me right now. Or, do you want me to have Zedd kick them out? He can do that, you know."

I can feel the sudden tension radiating at my back and side from the others.

There would be an all-out war right here in my room if he tried that.

No, thank you.

"It's fine. They can stay." They already know the gist of it anyway, right? "Someone shot me in the knee. And he had the healer make sure to heal it wrong."

Gabriel hums softly, the humor gone from his expression as he listens intently. "Why did he do that? Shoot you and then have that done?"

"Does it matter?"

"It matters," he answers solemnly.

"He shot me because I didn't do what he asked the first time. And he had it healed wrong so that I would remember that moment. Remember him."

Gabriel leans back in his seat and clasps his hands together behind his head. "Is he still alive?" I nod, and he blows a breath out and shifts forward again with an encouraging smile. It's like he can't keep still for more than a few seconds at a time. "Well, let's fuck up his plans then, shall we? Which knee is it?"

I point automatically to the messed up one. Wait. "Are you saying you can fix that? How?"

"I have the *unfortunate* privilege of the gift of *memento dolor*." He says the last two words with a heavy lilt. "Or, as they say, remember the pain."

I twist around to Jackson, who looks as surprised as I am. What are the chances someone else has some attachment to a similar phrase?

"Does that mean something to you?" he asks, and I turn back in my seat.

"It's...it's nothing. Sorry. You were saying?"

Gabriel blinks but thankfully continues without pushing it. I doubt it's more than a coincidence, and I don't want to share with others what Jack and I have with the similar Latin phrases. "My gift replays the memory of when you received that injury. You'll live through it again as your body rewinds that injury back to the state of the memory. So, your hack healing job will go in reverse, and then we can have a healer here fix your knee properly."

"I'll call Cassandra," Aiden says, his phone in hand again.

"I'll bring her in," Cibrina—who I completely forgot was still in here—says to him before leaving the room.

My stomach drops. "I have to re-live that?"

He smiles and pats my knee. "Yes, but I'll be there with you, so you won't be alone."

"If you can do that, why don't you bring her knee back to before the injury? Without making her go through that again?" Dane demands angrily.

Zedd shifts his stance to square off with Dane. "Don't speak to him like that."

"I'm just saying—"

"If it worked like that, he would do it. Gabe lives through the memories with them. He feels every injury he's brought back. Don't think this is easy on him, either."

I stare at him in shock. He's going to feel like his knee is shot, too? Why would he go out of his way to help me if he has to go through it?

Gabriel chuckles and strokes Zedd's arm. "It's fine. There's no need to worry." He searches around in his cardigan and pulls out a clear plastic bag filled with multi-colored pills. "That's why I brought these!"

"Are those...drugs?" Is he joking, or...nope. He's serious. His hand roots around in the bag, picking one out with a frown, dropping it back in, and digging for another one. "I don't do drugs," I tell him when it's clear that's exactly what they are.

Gabriel's head pops up. "Oh. Good, good. *Nasty* habit." He pinches another pill and smiles when he sees it, then pops it in his mouth without hesitation. "Don't mind me. I'd go crazy if it weren't for these. Too many re-lived torturous memories and all that."

Fucking hell.

"Maybe this isn't a good idea. I don't want you to have to go through this—"

"Nope." He grabs my hand, pulling me up and leading me to my bed. "We're doing this. I've got you. We're going to stick it to whoever this guy is, and then you can use that leg to kick his ass." We stop at the bed. "You're going to want to lie down and close your eyes."

Gabriel kicks off his shoes and hops on my bed, scooting to the other side and lying down. "If it didn't hurt so bad, I would stand, but if I have a preference—and I do—then I'd rather feel it lying down on a comfortable bed, wouldn't you?"

He has a point.

I sit on the bed and lie back as the others gather around us. Gabriel puts his hand on my messed-up knee. Then someone takes my hand. Craning my face, I find Jackson with his hand over mine.

"I wouldn't touch her if I were you, good sir," Gabriel tells him when he spots it. "You'll feel and see everything, too."

Jackson smiles. "Good."

"Jack, no." I try to tug my hand free, and the next thing I know, the other three have pulled chairs over and have their hands on my leg. "What are you doing? Absolutely not. I don't want you guys to see—"

"What you went through for us?" Dane snaps. "If you didn't have to go through it too, I'd ask him to make me feel every second of pain you went through on that island."

"That's not what I want," I grit out.

"Sorry, beautiful, but let us do this," Kellan speaks up.

Aiden's thumb circles my ankle, his gaze intense on my knee. "None of us are leaving, Gabriel. Let's get started."

Gabriel chuckles. "You're all crazy. I like you." He closes his eyes. "Now, picture the moment right before he shot you. I need at least thirty seconds to a minute before it happens. Tell me when you have it in your mind. Once it's there, I'll trigger my gift."

A minute before.

Great.

I was murdering people a minute earlier.

I picture the indoor training room. The wood lacquer floor and boring gray walls. Mallory passed out at Holt's feet. And Gordon watching me with crazed eyes as I use my gift to kill three people at once, tied to chairs in the middle of the room.

"Now."

Heat flares in my knee, and I think I might have rushed too far in my memories, but I'm still picturing the three innocents in my mind. It must be his gift.

My memories begin to play out from there without my doing anything. Finishing the kill. The gunshot. White-hot, excruciating pain as I cry out and then collapse to darkness.

Chapter Twenty-Eight

RAEGAN

I scream, grabbing for my knee and finding firm resistance. Something squeezes my hand, but the other one is free and swings toward my knee. It's stopped before I can reach it, and my arm is pulled back over my head.

The pain needles into my knee, stabbing and blinding me with pain. I struggle against whatever's holding me down, fighting back and then going rigid when the pain becomes too much.

"Let her heal you, beautiful. It's almost over," Kellan's voice cuts through the pain, reminding me that I'm not back with Gordon.

Warmth spreads through my knee, and the pain recedes.

I open my eyes to find the guys at my side, Cassandra between them as she concentrates over my knee. Gabriel thrashes on the bed next to me.

"Gabriel?!"

"I've got him," Zedd states stoically, turning Gabriel to his side until he settles and then lifting him in his arms.

"I can heal him after Raegan," Cassandra offers distractedly, her glowing eyes still pinned on my knee.

Zedd strides from the bed toward the door. "There's nothing physical to heal. I'm taking him to our room to rest."

Cibrina steps forward. "I'll walk you there and get whatever you need for him."

He nods, leaving the room with Cibrina close behind.

I hope he's okay. I know he said he felt the pain, but was that a seizure? He didn't say there would be more to it for him.

A sharp pinch stings my knee, and I clench my teeth and squeeze my hands to get through it.

And then the pain is gone, replaced by a dull ache. Weariness sweeps through me. My eyelids grow heavy, but I force them to stay open.

"There. Your knee is good as new again." Cassandra smiles at me and stands. "After some rest, I expect you'll be fully recovered tomorrow."

"Thanks," I say with a smile in return.

She looks apprehensively at the line of men at my bedside, like she's considering saying more but thinks better of it. "Let me know if you need anything else," she offers instead, waving and exiting my room.

Leaving me with them.

Aiden. Kellan. Jackson. Dane.

How much of my memory did they witness?

I tug on my hands, and this time, Jackson releases them. I push myself upright to lean on the headboard. Jack helps me up and shifts my pillow at my back.

I'm too scared to look at them. Too scared to see their faces. Would it be disappointment? Anger? Fear?

I killed three people at Gordon's command in that memory.

Aiden speaks up first. I expect this. He would be the one to flay me for giving in. For proving that no matter what I say or what I intend, I'm a villain when I'm with them.

"How does your knee feel?" he asks instead. There's nothing angry or accusatory in his tone.

"It's fine. I mean, it aches, but I can already tell the difference." He nods like he's satisfied with that answer, but I'm still confused as heck. "Did you...see?"

His dark brown eyes bore into mine. "Did I see what Gordon made you do before he shot you? Yes. We all did."

Uneasiness swirls in my gut. I feel lightheaded and woozy now. From the healing? Or knowing that they saw all of that? My face falls into my hand, hiding half of my expression from view. I close my eyes. *Don't freak out. Don't lose it right here when they're all watching.*

Aiden stands. "Get some rest. There's nothing else you need to do right now aside from that."

Kell stands abruptly. "I need to go train," he mutters roughly.

"I'll go with you," Dane says, getting up to follow him.

All three of them leave without further comment.

I'm not sure how to take it. Are they upset with me? Did that just screw up everything I've worked for?

"Don't misunderstand," Jackson says, shifting to stand where I can see him. His hood is down, revealing his haphazardly sexy black hair and bringing more light to his deeper blue eyes. He smiles knowingly. "It's not you. They need to let some anger out, and your room isn't the place."

If it were anyone else telling me *it's not you*, I wouldn't believe them.

But coming from Jack, I try to accept it as the truth.

"And you?" I quietly ask.

"Mm...I can be patient. Save it for when it'll be used better."

Oh. I wish I had his level of control, but I'm sure my impulsivity falls somewhere between Dane and Kellan.

"Right now, all I need is you, little one."

He heels his boots off, then pulls his hoodie over his head and drops it to the floor. Pulling back the covers, he encourages me under them first before he joins me.

Jackson tucks me into his side, my head on his chest and his arm wrapped around my back. He strokes my hair, staring at the ceiling like he's viewing and processing all the information in his head.

"That was the girl on the island," he observes calmly.

"Mm," I confirm softly, even though he hadn't posed it as a question.

"He used her against you." Again, he's stating it as a fact. I don't say anything this time, not trusting my voice or mental state to attempt to elaborate any further.

He kisses my hair. "Sleep. I'll stay with you until you wake."

"Catch." Dane tosses a fresh water bottle at me after I finish off my first one. "I know you're gung-ho with training now that your knee is better, but can we stop for a lunch break? I'm starving."

I take one more mouthful and screw the cap back on to prevent myself from drinking too much, too fast after the workout we've put in. It's been a few days since Gabriel fixed my knee. When I went to check on him after getting sleep from the healing, he was bright and chipper. No sign of what he'd gone through for me. No visible one, at least.

I can't imagine what memories he's been left with from others. What horrors and tortures has he seen—*experienced*—to help them?

And, of all people, why did he help me when he didn't know me?

He brushed off my concern with some off-handed comment about fighting for love that I didn't understand and sent me on my way to test out my new knee while he enjoyed himself a bath.

Since then, I've spent most of my time training with Kellan and Dane. More Guild members have been steadily joining these sessions as well, so Kellan has partnered me with Dane when he needs to help other teams decide what to work on.

"Good idea," Kellan cuts in, stealing the bottle from my hand and drinking the rest of it. I smack him, and he grins. "Let's hit the showers and meet out here in fifteen."

I wrinkle my nose. "Wait. Here? I was going to go back to my room—"

"Today, we're going to the mess hall for lunch." He turns his gaze to mine. "To sit. At a table." His grin progressively widens as he tacks on more expectations. "With people."

I snatch the empty water bottle from him and take the opportunity to move away and toss it in the bin. "Is there a point to all this?"

"Well, I'm glad you asked, beautiful. You've been here now, what, a few weeks? And you've somehow avoided all interaction with the members here. I know you're not shy. So, I figured I'd help you out."

I haven't been *avoiding* them. Have I?

I guess I do spend all my time when we're not out of the bunker either in my room, Aiden's office, or this training room. I'm not avoiding anyone. I'm just...not going out of my way to meet them, either.

Am I putting them in danger by knowing me? Look what's happening between the guys and Gordon. And poor Reid got mixed in by association.

Could I really risk these people, who Aiden and the others fought to save?

"I'm trying to reduce her casualties by association."

My gaze clashes with Dane as his words ring in my ears. He catches my stare and holds it as if waiting to see what I need from him. It's such a different look from when I'd first arrived in this city. The vitriol he'd slung at me during that time burned deeper than I'd ever admit.

His eyes shutter, and he inhales sharply. "Fuck." He storms over to me and crushes me in a hug. "I didn't mean that. I was just angry and trying to say anything that could hurt you. I'm sorry, Rae."

I breathe him in, my hands gripping his shirt.

"What the hell did you say?" Kellan growls, yanking Dane back and looking like he's ready to swing at him.

"Kell, it's fine. He wasn't wrong." Portia was taken because of me. The guys are being hunted down because of me.

"Of course I was," Dane snaps. "If you're guilty of that, then so are we. So am I. They've been looking for me, too."

"And you were staying hidden until I came along."

"Will someone tell me what the fuck you're talking about?" Kellan snarls.

"I made a stupid comment about people getting hurt around her," Dane grumbles at him before turning back to me. "Everyone associated with GE has that risk, Rae. Especially the members who are starting to help us when we go to the islands. That's why Kellan's been training them and why you should get to know them. So, we can reduce that risk by being better prepared and working as a team."

Kellan smacks the back of Dane's head.

"Gah! What the fuck, man?" he shouts, grabbing and then rubbing that spot.

"Dane's an idiot. But also, yes to what he just said. I'm not letting you hide in the shadows anymore, beautiful. So, get that fine ass in the shower and meet me here, or I'll drag you, sweaty and sexy as you are, to meet them right now."

"You wouldn't..." I start, but the words barely leave my lips before I know he fucking would.

He bends, a wolfish grin on his face as he fingers a strand of hair hanging free from my tie. "I'll even throw you over my shoulder and make you greet them like that if you test me."

Prick.

After a shower and picking out our lunches in the mess hall, Kellan leads us to one of the many tables in this two-story space. I still can't get over how large of a room this is and the fact that it's underground. The greenery in this area makes it feel like the room was built into a forest rather than the other way around.

Kellan sets our tray down in an open spot with room for three. I recognize the small group around us as the ones who joined us on the last island, and wonder if he picked this table because of them.

"Kellan! Hey, is that her?" someone further down the table asks excitedly.

"Welcome." Evie smiles across from me.

There's more hushed whispering at the other end of the table, but thankfully, the ones we're closest to are content to let me settle in and eat. "It's...Evie, right?" I ask, giving her a return smile.

She nods, her brown hair falling over her shoulder in the movement. "I'm glad you've joined us for lunch. I've been told by new members that things can be overwhelming, so feel free to ask any of us if you have questions or need something." The voices at the other end continue to heighten, eclipsing her last words.

Evie slams her fist down on the table, and everything on it rattles. "Quiet down there!"

"Aw, come on, Eves. Either ask the good questions or trade places with me!" one of them calls back.

Someone else leans to the middle of the table, craning around the line of others on this side until they can see me. "Is it true you've escaped GE twice?"

"Are you Aiden's girl?" another jumps in.

"Of course, she is!" a third person answers. "He had a whole manhunt for her. The entire Guild was out looking. He's never asked us to do anything for him before."

"I'll bet you five hundred, she's not!" Silas, the one who'd tried setting up a wager before the rescue mission, stomps his feet down and leans forward. He grins wildly down the table at the others, waiting to see who'll take his bet this time.

Evie's hand pushes the side of Silas's face, forcing his head to the side. "Stop trying to take everyone's money. No one's going to bet against you anymore."

"Leggo my face," he mumbles, his cheek smushed behind her hand. A vine wraps around her wrist, and her hand gets pulled back.

Dane leans to whisper in my ear, "Eat, Rae. They'll keep going like this until someone stops them."

Right. Eating. I take another bite of my meal, but it's hard to focus on it when the two across from me are going at it.

Evie yanks against the vine, then grabs the knife by her plate and cuts herself free.

Kellan chuckles on my other side as he eats and watches the show.

"Just say the word, and I'll get you out of here, sweetling," a voice whispers behind me.

I jolt and spin around, but no one's there.

The invisible guy.

Kell fists the air and jerks his arm like he's shoving something back. Dane's out of his seat and takes a half-step in front of me.

"You got something to say, Harvey?" Kellan challenges.

The invisible man chuckles as his body slowly appears. His face is split with a grin, his blue eyes twinkling, and his hands shoved casually in his pockets. Harvey shrugs, his gaze flipping between the two at my side before landing on me. "Just offering an escape from the table before another fight broke out."

"And you had to hide yourself to do that?" Dane crosses his arms over his chest, looking unamused.

The Guild member laughs again. "You know me," he answers

flippantly. "It's too much fun surprising others. It's one of the few talents I have," he adds, holding a hand to his chest.

Kellan snorts and shakes his head, readying to say something else, but it's my turn. "I'm all set right here, thanks."

"Is that you, Reggie?"

Gabriel saunters over from another table, wearing tight pants, tall boots, and a colorful poncho. His hazel eyes sweep over Harvey as he passes. "Mm, hello." He hip-bumps Kellan to nudge him over so he can squeeze onto the bench next to me. Kellan frowns, but does it while I make as much room for him as possible on my side.

"Gabriel," I greet him with a smile. "How are you feeling?"

"Oh, I'm just swell," he says, smiling warmly. "Really enjoying this jungle of fun. Have you seen the waterfalls here? Fascinating!"

"I've seen that one." I point to the raised stream that spills over this floor to the one below.

He makes a sharp noise with his lips. "That one has nothing over the one by the koi pond. You must explore more, dear! Or is your knee still giving you trouble?"

"No, my knee's been amazing. I still need to make that up to you. Is there anything I can do to repay you?"

"Oh, Aiden-dear's already taken care of that." His head angles back to take in the view of this two-story eating and common area. "This is everything I've wanted."

"You're joining the Guild?"

"Yup! Me and Zedd." He flicks his hand back to the table from where he came, and I realize that Harvey is nowhere to be seen. It's probably for the best. I don't mind his carefree nature, but he's playing a dangerous game sneaking up on me.

Zedd's sitting on the opposite side of the table, girls swarming around him while he ignores them for his lunch.

"Unbelievable," Dane gripes when he sees the musician.

"What?" Kellan prompts with a shit-eating grin. "Still salty he refused to give you an autograph?"

Dane turns his glare on him. "Shut it, Kell. I just can't believe this is the same guy they show on TV and in concerts."

Gabriel snickers. "My Zedd is a different person on a stage or with a mic in his hand. It's one of the reasons we usually try to keep a low profile." He waves his hand. "In any case, I'm looking forward to the party Aiden said will be hosted here soon. Can you imagine what that'll look like in a jungle like this?"

I frown, confused. "What party?"

"Oh. You're here," a low, steady voice interrupts from behind Evie. I turn in my seat, as most of the rest of the table does while they whisper and gossip amongst themselves about everything they're hearing and watching. The voice belongs to Reid, who's holding a tray with both hands as Tinsley hangs on one of his arms with barely contained energy. "How are you feeling?" he asks, his blue eyes pinned to mine as if there isn't a full table of faces staring at him. The whispering pauses, like they're all holding their breath to watch this exchange.

I must be missing something. Why would he care about me? Aside from him helping the guys find me, and that he was also a captive of GE's, I know nothing about this guy.

"I'm good," I reply slowly.

He nods stiffly. His gaze shifts to Kellan and Dane, who are both eyeing him suspiciously. "Don't get the wrong idea," he says to them, then walks away without further explanation.

Dane and Kellan share a look.

I decide to ask them about it later, when we're not surrounded by others who are now returning to their gossip.

"Woah."

"Did you see that?"

"He talked to her!"

Evie's still staring after him with her brows furrowed.

"What's the big deal?" I ask her.

She turns slowly, dragging her gaze from them after they sit at a vacant table. "They've been here for over a month and he hasn't said a word to anyone here. Other than the mission, where I think he spoke two words, some of the members were beginning to think he was mute."

Oh. He talked plenty when we were at the library.

I check in with Dane and Kellan, and the latter shrugs. "He's not chatty, but he does talk."

Gabriel chuckles. "He fits the brooding man role quite well. What's his interest in you?"

I frown, staring across the tables to where he and Tinsley sit. "I have no idea."

"There you are." Aiden strides up to the table, looking from Kellan, to me and Dane. "I've got a fresh lead. Be prepared to leave tomorrow evening for another island."

"Lead on what?" I ask, curious.

His eyes lock on mine. "On your father."

Chapter Twenty-Nine

JACKSON

Thorne stalks down a sidewalk, the collar on his trench coat up and buttoned at the front to hide the scar around his neck. He looks the same as he had after his first death, with the exception of the added scar and crookedness of his ears. The smell of death that followed him before is less potent, but enough for me to follow with assistance from my gift.

It had taken me a few nights to find him, but good timing and an aerial view helped me catch him prowling the streets. I'd followed him that night until he ended up in a penthouse apartment, which appears to be where he stays during the day. I set up motion sensors on the door to alert me anytime he leaves, so I can find and follow him from there.

He turns beneath a neon sign, throwing a door open and moving inside.

I smirk from my perch. I know exactly where he's going now.

The Pits, the gifted fight club Kellan started over a year ago, runs in the basement of this dive bar.

Any of the others might rush to get the people out now that he's found them.

Me? I learned a long time ago to wait and see. A predator doesn't jump the second it finds its prey. It waits. It watches. And then it attacks when it knows it's already won.

I hop from roof to roof, dropping in the alleyway behind the bar with the staff entrance. The bouncer standing guard shouts in alarm.

My heels don't get a chance to touch the ground before I'm flying at the bouncer, my fingerless-gloved hand slapping over his mouth as I shove him back against the brick wall.

"Shhh..."

His eyes widen in a panic, and he tries to reach for something.

I pull one of my larger knives and jab it against his thigh, pointed to his dick to make sure I have his attention.

He freezes.

My head tips to the side as I get a better look at him. Tall. Burly. Mustache and a goatee with earrings in one ear. He doesn't look familiar, but then, I'd only been here that one time when Kellan convinced me to fight for him so he could win a big bet. The only name and face that comes to mind from that night is York's, and he runs the Pits for Kellan now.

A slow smile curls my lips, and a full-blown shudder rocks through him.

I probably shouldn't enjoy that reaction as much as I do.

"Call York. Let him know Kellan's brother is here so he can

inform your coworkers. I'd hate to be forced to kill anyone over a misunderstanding."

I drop my hand from his mouth, but keep my knife secure where it is. No need for him to think he has any other option.

The man reaches slowly for the microphone dangling in front of his chest. "What's your name?"

I don't answer him.

He brings the microphone to his face, and the pinhole red light switches to green. "York. York!" He raises his voice the second time when he doesn't get an immediate response.

"What's the matter? We're in the middle of a match, Gregor!" York's voice crackles from the earpiece.

"There's a guy here. He said to let you know he's here so you can tell everyone else."

"A guy? Is this some kind of joke? I don't have time—"

"He said he's Kellan's brother," he cuts him off. I'm sure that information means nothing to Gregor. As far as the people here, other than York, Kellan goes by Dragon. They wouldn't know a Kellan. "He's wearing all black and is freaky as fuck, York."

That last part makes me chuckle, and Gregor startles at the sound like he thinks I'll attack him for saying it.

York curses on the other end. "Yes. Let him in. Just stay out of his way. I'll let the others know."

I draw my hand back, flipping the blade and grabbing it again. Gregor rushes to open the door, and I offer him another smile. "Thanks, Gregor."

His face pales when he realizes I now know his name, but I save him the heart attack and step inside to relieve him of my presence, pulling my gaiter back over my mouth and nose. The back hallway is primarily filled with storage rooms and back offices for the bar, but one door leads to the basement, where I'm confident Thorne is now.

Gregor slowed me down from following him but it was a necessary step to ensure the rest of my time here would be unbothered. The guard posted at the door for the Pits spots me and hurries to open the door without a word. When I look at him, his eyes drop to avoid mine.

I move quickly down the stairs. The last thing I'd need is Thorne leaving as I'm arriving and having us bump into one another. Once I'm at the bottom, I slip into the crowd. Just another head, another body here for the show. The mass of people makes it easier for me to hide, but it also gives Thorne the same advantage.

Looking up, I observe heavy lighting and catwalks hanging from the ceiling.

Always take the higher vantage point whenever possible.

I move to the back corner of the room, away from the cage that has captured everyone's attention, and then use my gift to rise onto the nearest catwalk. The metal walkway is painted black to blend in with the ceiling, just like the hardware attached to the massive lights, which means my attire helps me to do the same. I'm invisible up here, and now I have a view of the entire room.

It only takes a few seconds for me to spot Thorne.

His smell no longer helps me when he's indoors because it gets lost among the others, but he's the only one wearing a trench coat with greased back hair. He's talking to two people at one of the raised bar tables to one side.

I move across the room until I'm on the catwalk directly above them. The din from the fight and cheering below covers any noise I would make, but I use my gift to contain it regardless.

Crouching down, I concentrate on drawing the sound of their voices through the air to me.

"—my son. He has black hair and blue eyes. Usually wears all black. Last I heard, he was staying at a place called the Guild. Do you know where that is?"

I'm not interested in the fact that he's been calling me his son while looking for me. It means nothing. Either he's a shitty parent who abandoned me to the foster care system, or he's lying to garner sympathy to get what he wants.

If I had to bet on one, it would be the latter.

"Sorry, I don't," one of the patrons at the table replies.

The second one shakes his head. "Never heard of it."

"Ah, well. Please call me if you hear anything. I'm offering a hefty reward to anyone who helps me find him." Thorne slides a business card to the center of the table. Both patrons agree vehemently that they'll be sure to call if they see or hear anything now that there's a reward on the table.

My old mentor turns away from them and moves on to the next table.

It's the same story. Most take his card after he mentions the reward, but a few wait for him to leave before ditching it to the floor.

I pick one of those to bring to my hand.

It's all black, with only a phone number and *Reward for any information* listed in metallic gold.

The flashiness of the cards is supposed to help convince people that he has the cash needed for a large reward. A simple yet effective trick.

Thorne works his way through the large room in a circle. Once he's back to the start, he casts a final sweep over the room and then leaves.

My phone vibrates in my pocket as I wait to give him a head start.

"We've got a lead on her father," Aiden says when I answer. "It's on another island, so we'll be bringing Guild members again to help us get in and out like last time. How are you making out on your end?"

I tuck the gaiter beneath my chin. "He was at the Pits."

"What did he do?"

"Asked around about me. And the Guild."

He pauses, considering. "Do we need to shut it down?"

"No." I flip the card in my hand. "I have a plan."

"We're going to the island tomorrow night. Will you be back for that?"

"I'll be back tonight. The plan can wait." It needs time to sit anyway.

"We can talk about the plan tomorrow, then. See you soon."

The call ends, and I slip the phone back into my pocket. I tug the gaiter back in place and sneak to the floor before exiting the bar the way I came. The bouncer at the back door startles when I leave, and I can't help myself.

"Good night, Gregor." Then I jump into the air, climbing higher until I reach the rooftops, and then follow the rotting scent that will lead me back to Thorne.

He returns to his penthouse without any additional stops. I watch him for another hour, prowling around his living area and talking to himself for too long to be considered sane before I decide to call it a night. If he leaves his apartment again tonight, my motion sensor will alert me. For now, I've no interest in watching a man who's clearly losing his mind.

It's a good hour between the penthouse and the long length of tunnel to the bunker from the nearest Guild-owned business, but it's still early in the night. When I enter the bunker past the security room, I pivot to the elevators instead of my usual route.

There's someone I've been needing to speak with, and now's as good a time as any.

Especially as we're about to potentially add another person to the mix.

I'm not thrilled with the idea of Raegan's father. She hasn't mentioned him, and I haven't seen any sign that she's looking to find him. Her hunt for her mother's information had merely been a method of proving to Aiden that she was innocent of his accusations after finding her birth certificate. Not out of some need to find or learn about her parents.

And I have no interest in sharing her attention with one more person. I've compromised plenty with my brothers and Raegan. And I've only done so because it's them. If anyone else tried to win her affection, another Guild member perhaps, they'd disappear before getting the chance.

It doesn't matter that a family member's attention is different than the kind my brothers and I have with her. I want all of it.

This latest lead is merely Aiden overcompensating for his mistakes. I'm only going to go along with it in the small chance that Racgan's now become invested in it. I won't take away her hope, even if it's new and unplanned.

The elevator jolts to a stop. I step out, strolling through the corridor until I reach the locked double doors at the end. Pulling out my phone, I tap through the app for all the Bunker locks until I see the one for the new quarantine area for island rescues.

There's an audible *click* when it unlocks, giving me fifteen seconds to open the doors and walk inside before they automatically lock again. Claudia looks up from a table at the entrance, her laptop and a notepad in front of her.

"Oh, Jack. I didn't know you were coming. Can I help you?" she asks politely.

Claudia joined the Guild after Aiden took it over. They'd met some time before, and he brought her in when we'd needed someone with medical training to assist with brainwashed or traumatized gifted.

I slip the gaiter down and remove my hood as well. "I'm looking for a young girl. Five or six years old, and who can change her appearance."

"That sounds like Mallory. Is everything alright?"

I nod, slipping my hands into my hoodie pocket. "I have a few questions."

Claudia's brow knits. "Oh. Well, she's been through a lot. I'm not sure—"

"I won't push her," I remind her, and her face clears. Claudia's seen me with kids before. I may have no qualms about hurting other people, but when it comes to children, I won't harm them. Aiden thinks I have a soft spot in my jet-black heart for kids because I was once an ignored or feared foster child, but that's not it.

Children are innocent of the crimes and immorality of adults. That's worth protecting for as long as they have it.

"Right. I'll take you to her now. She's had a difficult time sleeping, so she'll most likely be awake. If she is asleep, however, you'll have to come back."

I give her a curt nod of understanding. She smiles and leads the way through a long hallway. This area has a kid section that the Tower and bunker didn't have before to help us accommodate younger children we've rescued. The FBI agent Elias put us in contact with for protective services has limited us to only one child a week that they can handle, so Aiden and Cibrina put this together for the children waiting their turn.

Claudia pauses in front of a door. "Just wait here. I'll bring her out if she's awake." She goes inside and returns with Mallory a minute later. "Mallory, this is Jackson. He just has a few questions for you."

Round blue eyes peer up at me. I can see the moment she recognizes me as some of the fear fades from her gaze, and she offers me a small smile. "Hi."

I squat, as I had on the island where we rescued her, and this time, pull out a lollipop with a smile. "Hello, Mallory."

CHAPTER THIRTY

RAEGAN

THE LEAD AIDEN RECEIVED on my father brings us to another island. We split into two teams again, following the same protocol as the last mission, but this time the gifted kids aren't sleeping soundly in bedrooms.

The prisoners here are cuffed to beds and hooked to various medical bags and machines in an open room. There are no curtains. No privacy between them as their lives are slowly sucked away from them.

I look on in horror at what Gordon had once threatened me with. At what others have had to endure for however long they've been here. The ages range from preteen to adult. The ones who couldn't be controlled or brainwashed were sentenced to spend the remainder of their life experimented on for GE's pleasure.

It's sickening.

Tinsley releases another sob into Reid's chest, clinging to his shirt and hiding away from where he probably would have ended up if they hadn't escaped.

Reid lifts his gaze to mine over her head, our eyes connecting with knowledge and understanding. Somehow, he must have found out about this because while we're horrified by what we see, we're also not surprised like the others.

"What the hell is this?" Kellan growls at my side.

He and Reid were supposed to have moved on to seek out threats in the building, but we've all been frozen in the doorway of this room.

"It's where the non-compliant wind up," I murmur, my voice fighting to remain stable.

"Is it safe to move them?" Evie asks solemnly.

"Safer than leaving them here," I reply. I walk to the nearest bed, eyeing the IVs and machines and then the girl asleep on it. None of them have stirred since we entered. Are they tired from what they're going through or in some sort of coma?

The girl looks like she's in her early teens. Her dark hair is cut short below her ears in ragged and uneven lengths. Like someone took a pair of scissors to her hair while she was lying here.

Jackson inspects one of the bags on the other side of the girl's bed. "Propofol," he reads aloud.

I frown. "What is that?"

"It's a general anesthetic," Reid answers instead. "It puts them to sleep."

"Bring the tub in here, Evie." Kellan surveys the room. "Shrink them and put them in the tub as they are. Cassandra and Claudia can figure out what they need from there." He turns and puts his hand on my arm. "We'll figure out who everyone is once we're back at the bunker."

Right.

My father might be one of the people in this room.

I scan the room of unfamiliar faces. I wouldn't recognize him even if I saw him. They'll have to be identified or wait until they're awake to ask if there's a Charles Whitmore here.

If Aiden's lead is right and he is here, then how long has he been trapped like this? How long can someone survive it?

"Reid, let's go. Jack, make sure this floor is clear." Reid follows Kellan out the door to the hallway as Evie and Tinsley get to work. Evie shrinks a bed, and Tinsley uses her speed to pick them up and put them in the tub.

Jackson stops next to me. "I'll be right back," he promises, and I nod once before he leaves.

There's a high likelihood that there are others in this building aside from the guards we'd taken care of outside, but I'm not worried. If any goon tries to enter this room, I'll take care of them. Evie and Tinsley already have the evacuation under control between the two of them, so I decide I'll be their guard and keep this room secure.

I stroll the perimeter to keep out of their way and to get a clearer idea of the exit and entry points. Aside from the door we came through, there are three long exterior windows and two more doors.

I pause in front of the window on its own wall. This wasn't a corner room. How can there be a window here? My fingertips press against the coolness of the glass that overlooks sand and palm trees on a dark night. The fronds sway in the sea breeze as waves roll and crash upon the shore.

I knock my knuckles against it, but it sounds like any other window. There's no echo or hollowness to it.

Still...

Stepping outside of the room, I check both directions of the hall and walk down the side to where that window is positioned. The wall continues beyond it to another door.

I settle one hand on the grip of my gun in its holster, then reach for the knob and turn it, swinging the door open wide.

Wheels squeak and roll over laminate flooring and a chair crashes into a high counter. My gun is in my hands in an instant, pointing at the room as I search for who is inside. One wall looks into the room where Evie and Tinsley are still busy at work. A one-way glass.

I step into the room, swinging my gun to the left and freezing when something hard and small taps my back.

"Are you seriously wearing a bulletproof vest?"

I peek over my shoulder, and Vera draws her gun up to point at my head instead.

"Where's Dane?" she demands.

I'm really getting tired of her threatening me. The only reason she's so confident against me is because of my promise to Dane. The promise that I no longer have to abide by, according to him.

"Not here," I snap out.

It's not a complete lie. He's not here. He's somewhere else on the island with Aiden and the others.

I lower my gun so my hands are hidden in front of me, releasing one hand and calling on my gift. It settles like a warm tingle of nerves beneath my skin.

"Liar," she snarls and presses the gun harder into my skull.

I spin and throw my gift-filled hand at the gun, grabbing and pushing it away from me. A gunshot fires, and my muscles tense.

The gun disintegrates in my hand.

Holy fuck. She was really going to shoot me! My heart hammers in my chest as the sound of gunfire continues to ring in my ears.

That was too fucking close.

Vera gasps and stares at the gun I'm now aiming at her. Her eyes slide to mine. "I knew you weren't serious about that promise."

I cock my head at her. "I haven't broken it. Are you hurt? Or am I the one who almost got shot just now?"

"That was your fault for surprising me!"

"Maybe I wouldn't have had to surprise you if you weren't holding a gun to my head!"

"And what is this?" She gestures wildly at my gun. "Don't act like you're any better than me. I thought you said you wanted to save me."

"I do. This is called self-defense because I'm not an idiot. You were ready to blow my head off just like that. If anyone in this room can't be trusted right now, it's you."

She raises her hands and shakes them with a frustrated yell. "God, I hate you so much! Stop acting like you're so innocent and better than me. *You* killed *me*. You've killed more people than I have! You were the one who strung my brother along with his friends for years because you were too greedy to pick one! And I don't know what lies you fed them this time that they're *still* drooling over you. Apparently, your pussy's laced with drugs because even my own brother cares more about his sister's murderer than me. He was more worried about you being gone than having me back! Do you know what that was like?!"

Her words are like knives, slicing me with invisible cuts.

Vera's voice cracks, and hearing it breaks something in me, too. But she doesn't cry. I don't know if she can. It sounds like she would if she could, but her face remains dry through her choked words.

"I hate you more than anyone. If I put a bullet in your brain, I'd be doing the world a fucking favor. Then you could stop haunting me. Stop showing up and interfering with my brother. You ruined what I had with Gordon and Dane. With the only people I really cared about. Even Gordon is obsessed with you. He liked me first, and now all he wants is you!"

The gun shakes in my hands.

Don't let her get to you.

Easier said than done.

I have killed a lot of people.

And I had no idea about what Dane was like with her when I was gone. I assumed he'd been working hard to rebuild their sibling bond.

Was he that worried about me?

As for Gordon...

"You're better off without Gordon. He's a manipulative and abusive piece of shit. Stay away from him."

Her face tightens. "He was different with me."

"Oh, really? Is that why I heard him hitting you that night I found you two?"

Vera looks away. "That was...it was my fault. Things got out of hand, but that was the only time."

Or it was only the beginning, considering she'd died that week.

"It doesn't matter," she snaps, though it sounds like it's more to herself than me. "The point is that you took them from me. I even tried to warn Dane away from you by telling him what Gordon did to you.”

I stop breathing.

She did...what?

“He knows what happened on the last island. He knows that Gordon was trying to make you into his personal pet. So, why? Why did he leave me for you?”

Shame and self-disgust twists in my chest. I never wanted any of them to find out. What does he think of me?

But...if she told him before they rescued me...

“I don’t deserve you in my life, but I’m a selfish fuck, and I want you anyway.”

Why would he say that if he knew?

“I don’t know,” I reply honestly, my throat thick with emotion. Why would he leave his sister behind, the person he’s been desperate to have back in his life again, after hearing that I was used and broken by Gordon? Trained to be his pet and do his bidding, just like the guys all thought I’d been doing for so long.

Vera scowls, clearly pissed with my answer.

“Why didn’t you kill me at the library?” I ask, switching topics to something that might get us somewhere.

She hesitates, then shrugs. “I didn’t feel like it.”

I narrow my eyes. “Bullshit.”

We stare at one another, challenging the other to break first.

Her eyes dart to the side and then widen. “Get in the closet.”

“What?”

Vera sprints to another door in the room and throws it open. “If you want the answer to your question, you’ll get in here and shut the fuck up. He’s coming.”

"Who—?" I start, but she storms past the gun and pushes me from behind toward the closet.

"Hide these." She shoves something in my hands, but I'm distracted by the air shimmering to my right.

Fuck. A portal? Is it Gordon?

I run the last two steps to the closet and close the door, leaving a crack of space open for me to peek through. Whatever she handed me isn't sharp from what I can feel, so I tuck it up my back between my shirt and the Kevlar vest to hide it.

A man steps from nowhere into the middle of the room. He's tall and angular, his joints sharp and narrow like he's devoid of muscle. His clothing is dark and covers nearly every inch of him. From his turtleneck and gloves down to his slacks and shiny black shoes, I wonder if there's nothing but bone underneath. His profile reveals a pointed nose and chin beneath an old-style cap.

He stares through the window to the patients being evacuated and clicks his tongue, but ignores them in favor of Vera.

"I thought I told you to leave already," the man says, his voice chilling and bleak. *I've heard him before.* "Or did you think you could run off with them again?"

Vera scoffs and turns away from him. "I was trying to pack up the last of the samples. Or do you not care about saving all my hard work here?"

She stiffens. Her body jerks forward awkwardly, and she grabs something, lifting it and then slamming it on the counter. Whatever it was shatters. Vera lifts a piece of it and holds it to her eye. "Wait! Don't—"

Her words cut off, even though I don't see anything blocking her mouth. Her lips just...close.

The man—Royce, I realize from his voice and Vera's strange be-havior—raises a single finger to his lips. "Shh, shh. No excuses. I'm growing tired of your rebellious streak. I call, you answer. I tell you what needs to be done, and you do it. It's quite simple." He moves slowly around the room, his gloved fingers raking over items on the counter and knocking them down. "I never asked you to return here. You're to find the location of the Guild. That's the one—*and only*—task you have. If you can't manage that, then it's my turn."

"Mmmy b-bruh—" she forces out until her lips press shut again.

"You had your chance with him, and you failed. He's to be killed like the rest of them and brought back to me." He stops in front of her and pinches the hollows of her cheeks. "You should thank me. I'll be reuniting you with your brother." Royce pats her face mockingly. "Don't look so upset by my gift. It won't be today, but I'll bring him to you soon. The president has a specific timeline for these things now."

The necromancer might be the key to getting to the top if he's so close to the person in charge of GE.

What should I do?

They're still busy talking, so I draw my gift to one hand in prepa-ration. My hand heats and tingles, and I leave it hanging at my side while I consider my options.

Royce's head snaps my way, and I jump back from the opening.

Did he hear or see something?

No, I was quiet. I'm sure of it. What made him look this way, then? I take slow, calming breaths in the dark, waiting for what feels like long enough for him to convince himself that there's nothing going on over here. I shift forward again, moving back to the light, and freeze when it goes dark.

CHAPTER THIRTY-ONE

RAEGAN

Royce stands there, his dark eyes on me and a frown on thin lips.

"What is this?" He whips the door open, and it slams against the wall.

I launch at him. My gift is already active, and I don't know if I can hurt him just enough without killing him, but it's better than standing and doing nothing.

He snaps his fingers.

Invisible hooks pierce my limbs, my chest, my neck. My body pauses mid-attack, then pulls back to stand still in front of him. I try to move. My head. My hand. A fucking *finger*.

Nothing.

My heart pounds rapidly as it realizes the cage it's now in.

I knew he would be tough if he was higher up in GE, but I

also thought he was limited to controlling dead people. What had Thorne told me?

He controls souls.

Fuck.

"None of that," he chides, waving a hand at mine glowing red with my gift. It flickers, then dissipates. My other hand with the gun drops to my side. "That's better." Royce steps back, so he has both Vera and I in his view. "The question is, did you know she was there?" he directs to her. "Either you willfully allowed her to spy on you or you were too dumb to realize you were being watched."

Neither Vera nor I say anything.

We can't.

This man could do anything he wanted with us right now.

I struggle against his hold, trying to move something. Trying to call my gift back out. Maybe my gift can trip whatever control he has over me. But nothing works.

I fight back the terror that's clawing up my chest.

Royce sighs, and his attention flicks back to me. "You can't fight it. Or, you can try and waste your energy in the process, I suppose." He shrugs. "It does not matter to me."

He turns his back on Vera to move closer to me, his brows pinched as he studies me. "Oh, I see." His face relaxes. "This is the girl Gordon's making a fuss over. I don't see the appeal but to each his own. Should I return you to him?"

I want to scream at him. Shoot him. Anything to get him away from me. I'm not going back.

The portal shimmers mockingly in the air a few paces back from him.

It would only take a few forced steps, and I would disappear again.

Vera makes a noise. Royce looks over his shoulder at her. "What's that? You disagree?" There's a long pause, and then he's focused back on me. "Oh, right. Gordon's teaching his pet a lesson first. I'll leave you be, then." His smile is dark and threatening. "If you don't fall in line with Gordon after this, I'll dispose of you myself."

He walks to the portal. "Come now, Vera. We have some things to discuss, you and I." Her legs jerk forward on his command, and they both disappear in the portal.

The moment he's gone, I can feel it. My body becomes heavier again, the weight of its control falling back to me where before I'd felt like a hollow doll on strings.

I move my arm to make sure, then close my hand in a fist.

Now that I've seen his gift in action, we need a plan on how to fight him. If he can control anyone with the snap of his fingers, then throwing more people at him isn't going to help us.

Which reminds me that I was supposed to be keeping an eye on Evie and Tinsley. A quick glance through the one-way mirror shows that they're already finished. All the beds are gone, leaving a large empty room and the two of them.

I still jog back to the room. They both look up when I enter.

"Where were you?" Tinsley asks, hopping forward on one foot.

There's no sign that either of them heard what was happening on the other side of the wall. Was it soundproof? "Looking at the room next door," I answer casually. "Everything okay in here?"

Evie nods. "We're all set here. Just waiting on the others to get back."

Should I see if the others need help?

You're supposed to be keeping these two safe. I already slacked on that responsibility and I'm lucky nothing happened.

Jackson returns first.

I smile at him when he enters and strides directly toward me. His cool blue eyes sweep over me. He stops just in front of me, so I'm forced to angle my head back to see his face. A smirk catches the corner of his mouth. "Couldn't sit still?"

"Who? Me?" I ask innocently.

He leans forward, the side of his face nearly brushing against mine. "I know you went next door," he whispers.

My mouth falls open, but I know better than to lie to him. How does he know that?

Jack chuckles and pulls me into his arms. His hands move down my back as he props his face on my head and inhales deeply. Something clinks behind me, and he draws back, dangling something in one hand.

"What—" I gasp when I see what it is.

The cuffs that block gifts.

"Where did you get those?"

"They were on you."

On me? Wait. Are these what Vera told me to hide? But...why? Why steal them and then give them back?

He holds them out to me, and I take them.

"You have some explaining to do, little one."

Aiden's giving orders as soon as we return to the bunker. Evie, Tinsley, and Reid are tasked with getting the people we rescued to Claudia and Cassandra for their next steps. I know I won't get answers anytime soon even if my father is part of the group, so instead of sticking around, I walk behind the other Guild members so I can return to my room for sleep.

Jackson steps in front of me. I halt before I crash into him.

He angles his head to the side, and a small smirk twitches the corner of his lips. "Where are you going?"

"To sleep."

His gaze flicks over my head, and when I turn to follow it, I see Aiden, Kellan, and Dane approaching us to listen in. "You were going to share what happened back there," he reminds me.

Ah. Right. Leave it to Jack to hold me accountable. It's my default to keep things to myself and work through them. But I told him I wanted us all to work together now, which means filling them in on what I learned about Royce and on the cuffs.

"Something happened?" Dane asks, concern lacing his voice.

"Vera was there," I answer, stepping to the side so I can see him and the others. My eyes pause on Dane.

Was she lying about what she told him?

He would have said something about it if she had, right?

"Did she see you?" Aiden asks, his eyes raking over me.

Dane runs his hand through his hair, halting partway through to grip it. It's a sign that he's stressed, even though he tries to play it off like it's nothing. "Did she attack you?"

Kellan pushes past Dane. "Are you hurt? Aiden, call Cassandra. The others can wait."

I hold my hands up before he grabs me to look me over himself. "I'm fine. Yes, she saw me, but..." My gaze slides to Dane. A few months ago, I would have kept this to myself. I don't want to give him hope about Vera. Even though she gave me the cuffs and hid me in the closet from Royce, she also almost shot me in the head and told me how much she hates me.

But the way Royce was treating her…

Is she fighting back in her own way? Was it against GE or just him?

I don't know enough yet, and I'm too worried Dane will take any positive interaction as a sign that he'll get his sixteen-year-old sister he remembers back.

"We were interrupted by Royce," I finish.

Dane tenses, his jaw sharpening. "The guy who brought Thorne and Vera back?"

"Yeah. I can confirm his ability to control souls—or bodies, at least. He snapped his fingers, and he had complete control of my body. Like I was trapped inside a puppet." I rub subconsciously at my arms, remembering the feeling of hooks sinking in. "He only let me go because he recognized me and knows what Gordon is up to. He left through a portal with Vera."

Kellan curses, and I nod. "I don't know what his limitations are or if he has any, but he's going to be hard to fight. He was controlling Vera and I at the same time, and it didn't seem like it bothered him at all. Who knows how many people he can do that to at once."

Aiden watches Dane, waiting to see if he'll say something, before he asks, "He controlled Vera's body like yours?"

"Yeah. He…made her stop gathering her things there. Threatened to have her hurt herself for not leaving already and then made her follow him through the portal."

Silence fills the training room.

I think we're all waiting for Dane to jump on that to try to defend

Vera.

He doesn't.

Aiden rips a Velcro strap on his vest, breaking the quiet, then re-secures the metal there. "They're up to something. If Royce is as powerful as you say, then it doesn't make sense that they would abandon the island rather than fight for it. Or else he has a limitation based on quantity, or perhaps a particular gift on the island that put him at a disadvantage."

I shrug because that's all I have.

"We'll have Thorne soon," Jackson calmly adds. His gaze switches to Kellan. "I need you to make a call to set it up."

"We can go in two nights," Aiden speaks directly to Jack. "As long as we have a way to hold him once we have him."

"Oh." I reach under my vest and pull the cuffs out. "And I got these back."

Kellan throws his head back in laughter. "Good work, beautiful. That'll make this a *breeze*."

I roll my eyes at the dumb pun but smile anyway.

Aiden holds his hand out expectantly to see them.

Ha. Ha.

"You're joking," I say, holding the cuffs close to my chest.

He frowns. "No. I'll keep them safe until we go after Thorne."

This asshole really is serious.

"Do you not remember what you did with these the last time you had them?" His frown deepens, but he doesn't respond. "You locked *me* up with them. So, no. I think *I'll* hold on to them so you don't try to use them against me again."

Aiden's eyes narrow. "You're leaving out some important details."

"Am I?" I demand, my voice rising.

Dane steps between us, hands raised. "It's fine. Raegan's not going to lose them. We aren't even leaving the bunker again until we capture Thorne."

Aiden concedes with a terse nod. "All right. Everyone, get some sleep." He strides from the room without looking back, and I stare broodingly at his back.

A kiss on my temple startles me. Jackson smirks knowingly at me.

"I'm going to check on Thorne," he murmurs.

"Okay." I'm looking forward to catching the zombie. Then, Jackson won't be out most nights keeping an eye on him.

Kellan stretches his arms and groans loud enough to echo. "Gaaaargh! Ahhh! Nothing like sleeping after a successful mission of kicking ass."

We start walking to the door, him on one side and Dane on the other.

"You should go see Aiden," Dane says, knocking my mood back to where it had been with the cuffs.

"Why?"

"He hardly eats. He's not sleeping. He told all of us to get some rest, but I can guarantee he went straight to his office and will be up all night."

My chest tightens. I've been noticing small signs of it, but I haven't wanted to acknowledge it. It's not my problem. *He's* not my problem.

"He's a big boy. He knows how to take care of himself," I answer, trying to keep my voice calm.

"He's become obsessed with doing whatever it takes to make things up to you. Even if that means skipping sleep and forgetting to eat. He found Gabe for your knee, now possibly your father; what do you think he's going to do next? It's not going to stop. *He's* not going to stop."

"What are you asking of me, Dane? To tell him that everything's all better? It's not my responsibility to make him feel better over what he did," I snap, heat gathering in my chest.

Dane takes my arm, and we stop walking. Kellan does the same, crossing his arms but staying quiet. "He made some mistakes, Rae. Haven't you ever made those before? What matters is that he's trying to fix it now."

What else is he trying to do? How far is he planning to take this?

Why do I care?

Because I still care about him.

I press my lips together, and Dane sighs. "Just...think about it. Okay? I've already tried to talk sense into him, and I don't think anything will change unless it's coming from you."

Chapter Thirty-Two

RAEGAN

I toss and turn long after Kellan and Dane fall asleep. It doesn't matter that my body is tired or that we've been awake for over twenty-four hours. My mind is spinning from one thought to the next. The second I try to push something from my mind, another item pops up to take its place.

Vera.

Royce.

Why did she give me the cuffs?

Dane maybe knowing my secret.

And if he does, did he tell the others?

The possibility of having a father.

The plan to capture Thorne.

Dane's worry for Aiden.

Sighing, I rub my face. None of these thoughts are getting me anywhere. I need to get up and move around.

I'm dressed in a simple pajama shirt and shorts, but throw on slippers and a satin robe that came with the set before leaving the room.

It's still the early hours of the morning, and most of the bunker is fast asleep. The lights in the hallway cast a soft, muted glow as if walking in the moonlight. It's enough to see by, but also casts shadows and adds to the silent eeriness of a sleeping underground fortress.

I don't know where I'm going at first. I think I'm wandering just to move, but when I find myself standing in the open doorway of Aiden's office, I realize a part of me knew I was seeking him out.

Picking a fight with him is an easy distraction.

But I don't like that I immediately ran to *him* when I needed one. Jack's out watching Thorne, but why didn't I wake up Kell? Or even Dane? Why did I go to Aiden?

I shouldn't need him.

I shouldn't want him around.

He tolerates me for the others, but that's as much a concession as I think he'll ever give.

Why can't I let him go?

Aiden sets his pen down as he watches me watch him in silence. He gives me an assessing once-over, dragging his gaze over my night clothes and bare legs in slow measurement.

I resist the urge to pull my robe tighter and hide the flush that his stare incites. Just one look and my skin warms with an ache that can't be satisfied. I hate to admit that I miss his chastisements. The way he'd cage me in his shadow. His words were meant to warn, but the way he looked at me offered dark promises instead.

"What are you doing?" I finally ask, teetering on the edge of if I'm going to start a fight or walk away.

"Looking at you? Or what was I doing before you appeared in my doorway to stare at me?"

A spark ignites in my chest.

"Why aren't you asleep like everyone else?" I challenge, feeding that flame a little bit more.

"I'm working."

"At four in the morning?"

"If that's what time it is."

"I didn't ask you to stop sleeping," I snap defensively. The anger swells in my chest, and I let it grow and take hold of me. "I didn't ask for anything from you but a little trust. Or is that still too difficult for you?"

Aiden stands abruptly and stalks over to me. "You're here for a fight. Why?" he demands, backing me into his desk. My thighs hit the edge, and I half-fall, half-sit on it.

My heart races furiously, trapped between anger and desire now that he's invaded my space.

"I can't sleep," I admit. "And rumor has it that you don't do that anymore, either. That you're too busy trying to fix all my problems, which I would find hard to believe, but somehow you found someone to fix my knee, and now I might have a father. Why are you doing this?"

"I didn't think a simple apology would mean anything to you."

"It sure as hell wouldn't hurt to try."

I'm expecting hesitation. Side-stepping the apology in some way. But he doesn't even stutter.

"I'm sorry."

I freeze, stunned by his admission while my heart is hammering like it's trying to break free of my chest.

"I'm sorry for what I did on the island. For not taking you with us on the boat. For not trusting you. For failing you as miserably as I have when I should have been the one protecting you. I know I've broken your trust, so these words may not mean anything to you. That's why I'm going to fight to earn it back. I'm going to do whatever I can to fix my mistakes. To make it up to you."

His words—words I never thought he'd say to me—make my eyes burn with emotion. Make my throat tight and my chest ache.

"I don't understand. What changed your mind so suddenly?"

Aiden plants his hands on the desk on either side of me. "So suddenly?" he croons. "You risked your life for us. Went willingly back to hell and torture. You also didn't give me a chance to respond when you finally talked to me in the locker room. I've had a lot of time to think of nothing else. And..." he hesitates.

"And?"

His eyes find mine. "I know what Gordon did."

The fire that was stoking through my veins instantly chills.

"You...what?"

"We all know," he tells me like he isn't dropping a bombshell of catastrophic proportions in my lap.

Not just Dane. Aiden. Kellan. Jackson.

When Vera said she told Dane...how much? And he told the others?

Aiden's finger and thumb gently pinch my chin, drawing my gaze back to his. "We've known since before we got you back. I don't know what you've been telling yourself, but none of us are going anywhere. Nothing's changed aside from what we have planned for

Gordon. Slow and painful doesn't begin to describe it."

He's still talking, but I'm frozen in my head.

They know.

They *know*.

How can they look at me?

How could they say the things they did?

Was that why they didn't say anything when they witnessed my memory of killing innocents for Gordon? Did they already know?

I can't stay here. How can I look them in the eyes, knowing that they know?

Murderer.

Whore.

"Raegan," he calls my name, sounding faint and far away as I begin to spiral.

A stinging pain on my ass cheek breaks me free.

I gasp more with surprise than pain and find myself lying chest down on his desk.

"Since you don't seem to listen well with your ears, I'll just have to impress it on your body." Another smack rains down on me, and I inhale sharply.

This time, I notice it's somewhat dulled by the barrier of my panties still in place. I can't see or tell where my shorts went. His hand pins me to the desk between my shoulder blades, even when I struggle fruitlessly against him.

"Aiden," I breathe out in an attempted reprimand, but it comes out as more of a desperate plea.

His hand rubs the pain away, and the chill in my blood thaws a little.

Another smack.

More stroking over the inflamed area.

Over and over again.

Each impact stokes the flames, and every following caress spreads the heat through my veins until I feel heavy. Languid. Warm.

At some point, my cries changed to moans of pleasure.

I can't think. My mind is too consumed with anticipation for the next one. Too absorbed in the way my body feels and that growing ache between my thighs.

The next slap of his hand lands close to my core, and I shudder with pleasure. "Oh, please."

I need more.

I need him to touch me.

I don't want this to end. I don't want him to turn me away after whatever lesson he's supposedly giving me.

"Aiden," I beg, my voice heady with lust.

His fingers push my panties aside and glide through my arousal. He hums his approval. "Such a good girl, soaking your panties for me," he praises on a purr, my pussy clenching in response.

"Don't stop," I pant, my hips twitching to encourage his hand to continue.

He drags my arousal to my clit and works it at a dizzying pace. My hands grip the edge of the desk as I lean my weight into him, grinding against his touch as pressure builds at the base of my spine.

I'm so close. So close.

Aiden gives one last flick, and I scream his name as it pushes me over the edge. I collapse against the desk, fighting to catch my breath.

Oxygen filters back into my lungs. My brain.

What were we talking about that led to this?

I blink and raise my head to rediscover my surroundings. Aiden's office. In the bunker.

What he's been up to and...

He spanks me again before I can finish the thought. "You're in your head again," he chides firmly. There's a soft click and then a buzzing noise. "Was that not enough to make you understand? Should we go again?"

Something presses between my thighs in a firm vibration, and I jolt with surprise.

"Is that a vibrator?!"

He drags it over my underwear, pulling another guttural note from me. "Was...was that..." I huff with frustration as he continues to move the toy, and it's becoming more difficult to remember the words I'm trying to say. I try to reach for it, and him, with one hand so I can focus long enough to finish my question, but he shifts it out of reach. "...in...your drawer?" I finally manage with the brief reprieve.

"It was," he answers unashamedly. "Now, no more interference."

I'm pulled up off the desk for his jacket to slide down my front, and then he pushes me down and brings both of my arms behind my back. The jacket tightens around me, locking my arms in place. "What—?"

He covers my eyes with something soft, then kicks my feet further apart.

Whatever he used blocks out any chance for light, and I'm now trapped and blinded. I struggle against his jacket. The last time I trusted him with anything, I wound up gift-less and locked away for the night. "What are you doing?" I demand, anxiety spiking my heart rate.

Aiden presses down between my shoulder blades, and my cheek finds the cool wood of his desk. He leans over me, his velvety tone caressing my ear.

"You're going to stop thinking. Focus on me and *only* me. Let yourself feel it all. Because if I catch you getting distracted"—his hand meets my ass— "I'll punish you for it and delay your release that much longer."

Holy shit.

It's everything I'd always wanted from him. Every dark promise. Every threat for punishment and reward. We'd always flirted with the idea of this, but he'd never followed through.

Why now? Why is he doing this?

The buzzing starts up again, and my muscles tense.

Is it ironic that the one guy I think I can trust the least is the one I'm trusting now to do whatever he pleases with me?

He lands another slap on my backside and then brushes over it.

"You're failing already," he reprimands sharply. Then his tone flips back to a croon whispered in my ear. "I'm going to make you come so hard, you won't have any room in that head of yours to think."

I shudder at his words.

Fuck, that's hot.

The vibrator trails from my clit to my cunt, moving over the fabric of my underwear in a torturous tease. I move my hips and try to sink onto it, to take in more of it as it pulses and plays with me. "Aiden," I mewl. "My underwear."

The toy disappears, and I whimper at the loss.

He spanks me again. And again.

"That sounds like thinking."

Oh, fucking hell.

I press my lips together and struggle to keep from wriggling in my impatience for him to touch me again. When it comes back, he picks up exactly where he left off.

And he doesn't remove my panties.

The asshole is probably going to make it a point to leave them on now just because I tried to tell him what to do.

Smack!

He doesn't bother saying anything this time, but it does the trick.

Even though my eyes are covered, I close them. I take a deep breath and try to focus only on what he's doing to me. On the way my legs twitch and quiver from the fast vibrations. On the aching pulse of need from my clit for *more*.

Once I let go, there is nothing but the pleasure he's feeding me. I don't monitor the noises escaping my lips as he builds me higher than I thought I could go without breaking. When I think I must be at the top, he orders me, "Not yet," and encourages me further.

I'm shaking with the need to come. "Please, please…" Words fall mindlessly, begging for release. The vibrator slowly pushes into me, but the fabric blocks it from entering me more than the barest amount. I push and grind onto it, desperate to fulfill the need that's clawing at me from the inside.

His other hand strums over my swollen clit just as he commands, "Come for me, Raegan. Let go."

I'm not in control of my body anymore.

He is.

It reacts to his words without hesitation, and finally, *finally*, I'm free-falling through my orgasm. My pussy clenches in rhythmic waves, seeking out more but taking whatever it can as it wrings me dry.

My knees give out, and I slide back to his desk, but Aiden catches me. He pulls my hips back until it feels like I'm sitting in his lap but leaning forward on the desk.

I have maybe thirty seconds to catch my breath before he speaks.

"Again."

I'm floating on a cloud.

Or that's how it feels because I'm too exhausted to so much as crack my eyes open to see where Aiden's taking me. My body is nothing but a bliss-filled leaden weight.

Something squeaks, and then there's the sound of rushing water. A bath?

I drift back to sleep to the sound of running water and don't wake until my bare backside touches the heated water. It feels nice, cocooning me in its warmth until I'm submerged up to the mounds of my breasts.

But it doesn't hold me enough on its own, and I start leaning to the side. I open my eyes in a panic, the fear of drowning enough to give me that control back to find Aiden undressed to boxers.

"You're awake?" he questions, drawing his leg back and foot to the floor as if he'd been about to join me.

"I..." My eyes catch on his toned body, and words fail me. His chest and torso are smooth and firm...but his *arms*. He clearly works out, or uses his gift frequently, because there is more definition with the muscles in his arms than anywhere else. The urge to run my hands over them is almost all-consuming, and I'm grateful that I can't move right now, even if I wanted to.

I drag my gaze down his legs as far as I can see from my seated position and where he's standing.

Aiden clears his throat, then inquires dryly, "I take it you like what you see?"

Blinking to break my stare, I force my eyes back to his face. "Oh, uh, um...sorry?"

I'm not sorry.

"If you're finished staring, can you wash yourself?"

I want to say yes. He gave me orgasm after orgasm, and I don't think I could handle another without putting my health at risk, but having him looking like *that* reminds me that while he got me off, we didn't have sex.

I try to lift my arm, but everything aches.

He should've let me stretch before tying me up and keeping his word.

I shake my head. "Can you help me get out? I can shower after some sleep."

"You should wash before going to sleep," he murmurs, shifting forward again and kneeling onto the folded towel. He picks up soap from the floor and lathers it in his hands.

I watch him, entranced. And then it clicks that he isn't getting in the tub with me. "You needed to take your clothes off to help me?"

"You were asleep at the time, and it would be easier if I was in with you," he explains evenly.

Oh.

Well, I'll pretend to not be disappointed that he caught me awake.

His hands work a soaped-up washcloth over my back. I close my eyes and hum with pleasure.

The soap smells like cinnamon. Like him.

"You know," I muse dreamily. "If your plan all along is to drown me, then you've done a good job," I tease, only half kidding because seriously. I can't move.

"Don't joke about that," he admonishes, and my lips curl to a small smile.

I can joke about it because I know he would never hurt me. Spanking or rough sex aside. Tie me up? Yes. Lock me up? Without question.

But even when he said he didn't trust me, he let me in more than anyone else. He looked out for me. After Portia was taken and Vera surprised us all, he brought me back into their inner circle. He could say whatever he wanted, but that didn't stop him from doing what he always did, what he's still doing now.

Taking care of others.

Like he's doing for me. How he's been protecting Dane. Running the Guild.

He may be controlling and demanding or make me do things I don't want to do, but it usually winds up being what's best for me, even if I can't see it at the time.

Not that I'll *ever* admit any of this to his face.

"Here." I open my eyes. He holds a washcloth in front of me. "Wash between your legs."

His ebony gaze is intense on mine. I still can't read anything from his expression, but his eyes...

They're so dark that they appear endless, like two black holes that would suck me in if I let them. I feel drawn to them when I have his full attention, their gravity drawing me closer.

My breathing shallows. "I can't move," I repeat, knowing full well that I'm asking him to touch there again.

"Brat."

The nickname brings me back to our days of push and pull between us, and I smile.

He shakes his head, then raises himself off his heels to position himself better.

Aiden shifts against the side of the tub, his hand and the washcloth disappearing beneath the water. The next thing I know, his face is hovering close to mine as he rubs the cloth along my inner thigh. The side of his nose brushes against mine, and the air between us heats to scorching levels.

I can't breathe.

His eyes are focused downward on his task, but I can't see past how close his lips are to mine.

The washcloth moves to my other thigh and up. Up. It grazes over my core, and a shiver of pleasure curls down my spine. My muscles clench eagerly, even as weary as they are.

I pop my mouth open to drag in more oxygen.

Aiden's stare pierces mine. "Is this what you wanted?" he purrs. "I thought I'd worn you out." The washcloth runs along the hollow of my thigh.

I grip the edge of the bathtub on either side to keep myself from grabbing and directing his arm. "If I'm going to go out, then I choose death by orgasm."

His head drops, and I catch his shoulders shaking for a second.

"What? Do you have something better?"

The washcloth and his hand disappear. I almost make a noise of disappointment, but I really do think another one might kill me, so I let it go. Aiden pulls back and moves to sit on a step stool behind me. "Lean your head back. I'm going to wash your hair."

I realize he never answered my question, but take his non-answer for one.

There isn't anything better.

I bend far enough to dip my hair underwater; then he has to help me back upright before he starts the wonderful task of scrubbing shampoo into my hair.

I'm feeling good.

Even though I know what upset me earlier is still lingering in the back of my thoughts, I'm unwilling to give it any room to breathe right now. I'm practically glowing with the way Aiden made me feel, and being pampered right after is the cherry on top.

I won't let that be ruined.

And because I'm feeling so good, I choose to talk. Aiden's behind me, so I can almost pretend I'm just purging all the bad things from my mind during a bath without any consequence behind it. At this point, he knows the worst there is already. This is all just...filler.

"After you knocked me out on the island, my roommate Tara found me. She got others to help bring me into a boat, and we left."

His fingers slow when the story flows out of me, and I know I have his attention. But he doesn't interrupt, and I'm able to continue as I feel comfortable.

"Everyone split once we made it back to the States. I only had Grams to look for, but I didn't know anything about how the world worked. I was homeless and stole food to survive. I stole a couple of wallets and purses, too, to get enough money for a bus to bring me North. It landed me in a big city, and I tried to find a job to earn money to get to Alaska."

I pull my knees up and fold my arms over them, resting my chin on top as Aiden pulls the soap through the ends of my hair.

"A guy found me on the streets and offered me a place to stay. Long story short, he became my boyfriend and my boss. I worked his bar for him as anything he wanted. I can see now that I leaned on him for too much. I believed everything he said. He just used me for free work and sex. I'd forgotten what my purpose was or if I even had one. I was just...lost...for a long time."

Clearing my throat and swallowing the lump there, I continue, "I was with him for almost two years when he brought his buddies over one night. They cornered me in the shower and raped me."

His fingers freeze in my hair. "What was his name?"

"James. But it doesn't matter."

"It—"

"He's dead. I killed him and his friends that night using my gift. I hadn't used it up until then. I'd been afraid of it since leaving the island. And using it reminded me of GE and what I was running from. I was tired of running. I found my new purpose in taking them down. I started hunting them after that. And once they knew I was alive and out there, they began looking for me, too."

I breathe in deep and exhale. "Anything else you want to know?"

He proceeds to rinse the soap from my hair in silence, but I know he's considering my offer seriously. I almost fall back asleep in the quiet as he tugs my hair and massages my scalp before he finally speaks.

"What happened this last time that Gordon had you?"

"Training, mostly. Would not recommend his method," I add with a slight giggle. I think I'm becoming overtired because things are just feeling silly now when I know they shouldn't be. "Five out of ten. And it's only that high because he did get results. I'm stronger. I can control it better. It doesn't hurt anymore. So, joke's on him." I chuckle again at the irony.

"Did he touch you?"

"No, thank fuck. Not like that. My progress and mind control meant more to him this time, I guess. Even put me in a crazy water tank to fuck with my head. Used a little girl against me." The next thoughts sober my mood. "I killed people again."

"No. He killed people. I'm sure if you weren't there, he would have found someone else to kill them for him." Aiden kneels by the side of the bathtub, where I can see him. His eyes search my half-lidded ones, and I think he was going to say something else, but he reaches behind him for a towel instead. "Come on. Let's get you to bed."

Chapter Thirty-Three

RAEGAN

Everything except for the one place Aiden never touched.

Now that the rest of my body is thrumming with the delicious ache of being used so thoroughly, the lack of feeling at my core is blatant. My pussy throbs with need, demanding the attention it missed out on.

I roll onto my side and slide a hand between my thighs.

The sound of breathing snaps my eyes open.

Aiden's face is inches from mine, his eyes closed. I scan the room quickly and confirm that we're alone before returning my gaze to his sleeping face. I've never seen his expression so relaxed before. So...unguarded.

I reach a hand out to him, compelled to feel it for myself, but he snatches my wrist as soon as my fingertips graze his cheekbone.

Gasping, I find his eyes wide open and pinned on me.

"What are you doing?"

"I thought you were asleep." Was he just pretending?

"I was. I'm a light sleeper, and you moved."

Seriously? I could probably jump on the bed, and it still wouldn't wake Kellan up.

Aiden moves my hand away from his face like he's giving it back to me but halts without warning. His nostrils flare, and it's in that second I remember I'd started touching myself with that hand. I rip my hand back from him and hold it to my chest.

His eyes are dark as he regards me, and rather than wait for that commentary, I change the subject.

"What time is it?"

Aiden reaches under his pillow and pulls out his phone.

"Really? You sleep with it, too?"

A tiny smirk tugs at his lips. "If I didn't know any better, I'd think you were jealous," he remarks dryly.

"Nope. Just a concerned friend," I counter.

"It's after six."

Oh. So, I guess I didn't sleep as long as I thought. It feels like I got plenty of rest, though.

"In the evening," he adds. "You've been asleep for almost twelve hours."

Twelve hours?! Did Kellan and Dane not notice I was gone in the morning? Is Jackson back from following Thorne?

"I told them all you were here and to find something else to occupy their time with while you got some rest," he answers like he could read the worry on my face. "Jackson still came in a couple of times to check in."

Oh. "Did you sleep at all?"

He's the one who needs sleep more than anyone else. And somehow, I ended up almost orgasmed to death, bathed, and rested.

"Some," he replies simply, pushing himself upright. The sheets fall from his chest, revealing nothing down to the hem of his boxers.

I remember that I'm still naked.

He slept with me last night. He did all those things, but it hits me again that he didn't fuck me. He could have. I begged him to, and he didn't.

I squeeze my thighs at the resounding throb of emptiness there.

What was last night? Or...this morning? Whenever the fuck that was. Was he just trying to "help" me out of some obligation? Giving me a distraction and helping me go to sleep? Was that it?

My heart sinks into a pit in my stomach.

This is better. I should still be angry with the way he treated me before...right?

He's done nothing but look out for me since I came back, though. And he apologized...but is that enough?

Why can't I get over him? We would never work out anyway. All we do is fight and butt heads.

It shouldn't bother me.

This is fine.

It's okay that he doesn't think of me like that. I should just be grateful he doesn't hate me anymore.

Aiden lightly pinches the sides of my face, drawing it up until I look at him. "Stop. Whatever it is you're thinking, stop."

Right.

I'm not upset.

I'm not...

"What is it?" he demands, and my falling gaze snaps back to his.

"It's nothing," I lie. His eyes narrow, and I know he's not going to let me get away with only that, so I add, "I'm just feeling a little guilty. I came to tell you to get some sleep, and then you ended up...taking care of me. Which...I'm guessing was all that was. Because I know you don't think of me that way. But...I don't think we should do that again, as...hot as that was," I finish with a hollow chuckle.

He grabs me, slamming our lips together so fast and hard that I taste blood. It doesn't stop him from thrusting his tongue against mine. Or devouring me from the inside. His kiss is bold and controlling as he holds me by the back of my head. I couldn't escape if I wanted to. He takes what he wants like he's been waiting for this and knows exactly what he wants.

I'm too stunned to do anything but reciprocate, following his lead and sinking into the kiss as wings flutter and fill my chest. I'm brought back to the library on the island where I had my first kiss.

Where his kiss was just as all-consuming then as it is now, and it sends a hot wire of desire straight to my cunt.

His fingers dig into my hair and grip tight. My head is tugged back, our kiss breaking just as quickly as it started, and I'm left gasping for air.

"You're maddening," he murmurs with a husky edge to his silky voice. I try to move my head, but his hold keeps me exactly where I am. "You can't make up your damn mind. Do you want me, or do you hate me? I can't figure it out anymore."

I open my mouth to answer, but the tightening hold in my hair warns me he's not finished.

"Because for as long as we've known one another, I've wanted you. I've *loved* you."

I struggle to shake my head. "That's not true. You abandoned me on the island—"

"I didn't."

I freeze, oxygen stilling in my lungs.

"*I* brought you to Tara's boat. I made her promise me that she would bring you home to your Grams, and then I saw your boat driving away from shore. I see now that trusting her was a mistake, but I didn't leave you with GE. You were supposed to be safe."

"Then why...why did you fight me so hard when you saw me again?" I demand, my chest twisting itself in knots.

"To get the truth! If you were with your Grams, I shouldn't have seen you again. I had to assume you chose to leave home and safety to get back to GE. I couldn't trust you because you told us that you killed Vera and were with GE. From what I knew, you betrayed us. And it was my fault for being too busy falling for you to notice." He draws a slow breath, his voice quieting. "Then you came back into our lives, and I knew. If I let you back in, there would be no turning back. Even if you were bad...even if you worshipped the Devil himself, I would follow you to the depths of hell."

"And...where do you stand now?" I ask, my voice faint and breathless. But I have to know. Did he let me back in? Or is he still keeping his distance? Will he push me away again?

Aiden pulls me into him, answering me with a kiss.

It's all the response I need.

We don't do well with words between us. But this kiss.

It's everything.

I lean into it, my hands running over his chest. He flips us over, his body covering mine so he can deepen the kiss and free his hand to outline my body.

Our kiss ends, but he doesn't give much room for oxygen between us as his lips brush over mine. "Does that answer your question?"

I give him a small smile. "I don't think I heard it well enough."

His mouth crashes back onto mine. There's nothing sweet about his kiss. It's filled with hot demand for me to give him everything and more. Like he can't get enough, but he's determined to try anyway.

Aiden slips his hand between my legs, and he withdraws to look at me. "Was this from before I woke up or now?"

"What?" Oh. I'd hardly touched myself before I realized he was in the bed with me, and I stopped. But I won't lie that my thirsty cunt woke up preheated. "Both." He frowns, and I switch my answer. "Now. It doesn't matter as long as we can fuck right now."

He removes his boxers and then guides my leg up against his shoulder, positioning the head of his cock at my entrance.

Immediately, I attempt to wiggle down the bed to encourage him inside, but he collars my throat and pins me. I gasp, foolishly expelling air in my surprise.

Aiden grabs the base of his dick and teases along my folds, spreading my arousal over himself while driving me crazy when I can't rub against him. Then he holds himself at my core, pushing just enough that my desire skyrockets.

I release a whimper, pinned as I am, while he holds me at the precipice of something I've been primed for since last night.

He, on the other hand, is in complete control as he watches me from above. Or so it appears at first glance. But when I look into his eyes, they're simmering with heat.

"There's no need for you to touch yourself like that anymore. This pussy? It's mine. You wanted me; this is what it means to have me. If I find out you've gotten yourself off or even played with my pretty little cunt, I'll punish you."

Before I can react, he slowly...*gradually* pushes himself inside. It's so deliberate, so controlled, that I swear I can feel every ridge, every inch of his hard cock.

The moan he draws out of me is obscene.

"Good girl. You're going to take every inch of me, aren't you?"

I don't have much freedom of movement in the position he has me in, but I shift my hips as much as I'm able to encourage him deeper, even though I'm pretty sure my cunt's running out of room.

He hilts himself, and I breathe a sigh of relief. And tell myself that it's deeper at this angle.

"Your body fits me so well. So perfect," he praises. And coming from *him*, I feel lighter than air.

Aiden begins to move, but he's not rushed. He takes his time to draw himself to his tip before sinking back into me. Like he's just as obsessed with feeling every bit of me as I am with him.

He palms my breast with his other hand, then licks his fingers and teases the nipple. He strums and circles it, and when he pinches and tugs on it, I gasp at the current of need that ripples through me.

His pace intensifies, and all I can do is hold on when he drives into me again and again. He fucks me at a furious speed. All the leisurely sex is out the window as if something in him has snapped. I cling to the bedding. To his arm. But through his intention or because of the increased haste, his hand has closed tighter over my neck, and all my oxygen has been cut off.

Aiden barely touches my clit, and it's over.

My pussy clamps down on him over and over, and my back bows as pleasure rips through me. He slams inside one last time, his body shuddering above me before he releases my neck, and air fills my lungs. My orgasm leaves me with a warm buzz under my skin. I drop my hands to the bed and stare at him with a contented smile.

He helps my leg back to the bed, keeping himself sheathed when he leans down to kiss me one more time. "I don't know if I have it in me to share you," he murmurs, leaving me speechless as I realize what he's saying.

Is he just talking about me masturbating, or the others? Kellan. Jackson. Maybe even Dane.

Aiden eases back and leaves, giving me another few seconds to go over what the fuck I'm supposed to say to that before he returns with a warm washcloth. He wipes me down first and then moves on to himself.

I know he's not wrong. I shouldn't ask them to share. That's not fair of me.

I guess I'd been spoiled by Kellan and Jackson just...being okay with it. More than okay. When the three of us had sex in the tunnel...it was amazing.

It made me believe that this fantasy of mine might actually work out.

"When you said share me," I begin when he returns from cleaning himself up. He lies back in bed, tugging the covers over both of us and then pulling me to lean on his chest.

"We'll talk about it another time. Right now, I'd still like to try to get more sleep."

"It'll probably wind up as a fight," I mutter.

He kisses the top of my head. "I would rather spend all my time fighting with you than be with anyone else."

"I don't need all of you with me," I try again, looking at all four of the guys at my back before we enter the medical wing.

Cassandra informed Aiden that Charles Whitmore was up and rested enough for a visit. When asked about any family members that could be contacted about his rescue, he told her he had none.

It's not a great start.

"As the leader of the Guild, it's not out of place for me to introduce myself," Aiden states mildly while sliding his phone into his pocket. "The others can wait out here."

Kellan barks out a laugh. "Like you do that for every rescued person?"

"It is weird that you'd meet him while she's there," Dane adds.

"How about you all stay out here?" I growl, reaching for the door and walking inside. I have no idea what I'm expecting out of this. If this guy doesn't even know who I am, and I've lived this long without a father, is it right of me to drop this on him? He just escaped from being a lab rat. Having a daughter is the last thing he'll want to think about.

It's not like you're a child he'll have to look after. You're just letting him know you exist. If he wants a relationship with you, then great. And if not...then that's fine, too.

The door swings open behind me, and I sigh. I didn't really believe they would sit patiently waiting in the hall for me. A small part of me appreciates the support. But the bigger part? Is terrified they'll barge in and do something embarrassing when Charles and I are still trying to feel each other out.

"Ah, you're here." Cassandra smiles warmly at me, then frowns at my entourage. "Nuh-uh. No. He isn't ready for all of you. Just Raegan." She winds an arm around the back of my shoulders. "You'll scare the man away before he even knows what he's running from."

She leads me away despite the noise of protest behind us, and I grin. "Thanks for that."

Cassandra returns my grin. "Anyone would be nervous getting approached by one of them, let alone the whole group. I'm only partly jealous and mostly in awe of how you've managed to hold all of their attention."

Partly jealous. It reminds me that she'd tried to get Aiden to go out with her that first night I met her. And she'd been shamelessly rubbing up on Kellan.

A faint burning sensation fills my chest, and I fist my hands. *They're mine.*

She glances at my hands and back to my face, dropping her arm from around me but keeping her smile in place. When her head shakes, her mass of tight red curls sways behind her. "Don't worry. I know they're all yours. Aiden made that perfectly clear a few months ago." She sighs dramatically. "I've been looking for new candidates since then, but there hasn't been much time to get out. Maybe after all this GE nonsense is over with, I'll have better luck."

Aiden did what? A few months ago would have been before I was taken. And before he learned my secrets.

Even when we'd been fighting, and he didn't trust me, he knew. Just like he'd said last night. If there was any remaining doubt in my mind about how he feels, it melts away.

I loosen my hands and smile. "Let me know what you're looking for and I can see if I know anyone who fits." Not that I know a ton of people, but there are some of the workers I'd met and worked with at Hype.

She waves me off. "Don't worry about me. I know you have enough going on." Cassandra stops us in the aisle and points to a curtain, her voice lowering. "He's there. Everything checked out normal this morning, so he'll be released to the floor with the others after lunch."

I nod, nerves circling in my gut as I stare at the curtain. "Did any of the paperwork at his bed mention his gift?"

"Yup. It said he has telekinesis."

"Did it show what sort of testing was being done on him or the others?" What samples was Vera referring to when she'd been talking to Royce? What does her gift have to do with the prisoners? Is she trying to steal gifts, like she'd attempted with Dane when it almost killed him?

Cassandra shakes her head. "No, the paperwork was only a simple patient face sheet. Unless Dane gathered more information from their servers, we don't have anything else."

The servers had already been wiped clean by the time he got to them. Probably Vera's doing. I smile at her in thanks and she walks away, leaving me to it.

I force myself forward before I can change my mind. "Excuse me," I call out at the curtain. "Can I come in?"

"Please do," he replies, and I slip the curtain to the side enough for me to step into the semi-private area and let it fall closed behind me.

For a second, I wonder if Cassandra led me to the wrong bed because I look nothing like the man sitting up in bed. His hair is black, and the lines in his face are sharp and angular. The five o'clock shadow peppers his jawline and around his mouth. But when his eyes find mine, it's like looking in the mirror. They're the same ocean blue, the same thick and dark lashes.

"Hi."

He smiles politely. There's no recognition in his gaze when he sees me. "Hello." Like he's greeting a stranger.

"I'm Raegan."

"Are you my next nurse?"

"No, I'm...your daughter," I finish lamely. There's no good way to announce that, right? Seems better to just rip the Band-Aid off.

His smile falters. "I'm sorry, but I don't have a daughter."

"Did you know a Merina Laivins?"

Charles blinks several times, then peers cautiously at me. "Yes. A long time ago."

"She was my mother. And she listed your name on my birth certificate as my father," I explain.

"I...have a daughter?" He stares at me with disbelief, and I shift uncomfortably.

"I mean...that's what the paper says. If you and Merina didn't have a relationship, then—"

"We did. I just didn't consider that she might've gotten pregnant. We were separated soon after."

I nod, wishing I had a wall or counter or *something* to lean or sit on. "Well, I just wanted you to know that I exist. I'm...here."

He looks me over, his eyes assessing as he takes me in again with new perspective. "You look like her. Like Merina," he observes with a fresh smile. "She was quite the fighter. You have that same look in your eye, even if they're colored like mine."

Hearing about her eases some of my nerves, and I smile, curling some hair behind my ear. "Oh, yeah?"

"I'll bet you're giving Gifted Enterprise hell, just as she did at the end."

My eyebrows draw together. "You know what happened to her?"

Charles sighs and nods. "Word got around about what happened, and I overheard it. But they never mentioned a child at the time. Only that she took out around two dozen agents."

"Will you tell me more about her some time?"

"Of course, though I'm sorry to admit that it may not be as much as you'd like. We were a bit of a whirlwind romance in a short period of time together."

"That's okay. It's still more than what I know."

"Now that I know I have a daughter, I'd love to learn everything I can about you. Are you staying here, wherever that is?" He casts his gaze above us and the fluorescent lighting. "I haven't seen anything yet outside of these curtains. Maybe you could give me a tour."

"I'm the last person to ask for a tour," I say with a light laugh to avoid answering all his questions. He may be my father, but that doesn't grant him immediate trust from me. "I'll come find you once you've finished settling in and we can talk some more."

Something flickers in his eyes, and I wonder if he's disappointed that I'm not jumping at the idea of spending more time with him right away. Or maybe I'm overthinking things because this already has been a bit much for me. He knows I exist, and I now know he's my father. But now? What do I want to do with that?

"Of course," he finally responds with a small, reassuring smile. "Thank you for coming to see me and telling me about you. You're already an adult and seem to be doing just fine on your own, but now that I know I have a daughter, I'm hoping we can get to know one another. I wasn't there for you when you grew up, but maybe I can be there for you now in whatever way you want."

My chest tightens at his words. At the easy way he's already accepted me.

Rather than chance my voice, I give him a firm nod and a terse, "Sure." I part the curtains and slip out. My face crashes into someone who catches me when I bounce back.

Kellan offers me a grin, but Aiden speaks up behind him in a hushed tone. "Hallway."

We walk quietly down the aisle, the five of us moving as one until we're standing outside of the medical wing.

Dane slides his hands into his pockets and asks me, "How did it go?"

I shrug. I'm not sure what I expected, so how do I say if I think it went well or not? Considering he wants to know more about me, that should be a good thing, but I feel...uncertain. Why? "It went okay. He is my dad from the sounds of it. How long were you guys standing there?"

"The entire time," Aiden answers.

Kellan grins. "And you thought we couldn't be quiet."

Jackson turns his face in the direction of Charles, though we can't see him from here, but it's clear something is on his mind.

"You don't trust him," Aiden surmises aloud, his eyes pinned on Jack.

He looks back to us, but Jack's stare settles on mine when he answers. "No."

That uneasiness grows. "Why not?"

"It's just a feeling."

Aiden looks at his phone. "It's almost lunch. We'll let him eat, and then I'll introduce myself and see what more I can learn about him. He'll be staying on the quarantine floor with the others for the time being, and that's secure and separate from the rest of the bunker. That gives us time to keep an eye on him until we know more." He looks at me like he's checking in, and I give him a small nod.

Knowing that he's not wandering freely around the bunker gives me a small piece of comfort until I can wrap my head around everything. I'll keep my promise to visit him and getting to know him a bit more might clear up our concerns. We all have some trust issues, so hopefully, that's all this is before we let him into our lives.

CHAPTER THIRTY-FOUR

DANE

"WHAT'S TAKING HIM SO long? He's twenty fucking feet away," I snap, jumping to my feet in preparation to storm over there and drag him out. I'd say do the plan without Reid, but he plays a key role. Particularly with me.

Kellan steps between me and the door with a stupid grin. "Relax, Rapunzel. We've got time."

I don't get what he's so excited about. He's fought with Thorne twice before, but since finding out his *zombie* status, it's like he's been itching for a rematch.

I'm the opposite.

I'm secretly dreading the fight with the undead wind master. I know it needs to be done, though. I just want to get it over with already.

"What time did your buddy agree to meet with him? Isn't it in five minutes?" I argue back.

If we miss this window, what are the chances Thorne will take the bait again? This is our chance to make a bigger move on GE. I've been waiting for this moment since Raegan told us about Royce and Jackson started following the wind psycho again.

Kell shrugs, smirking.

"It's all right, Dane," Aiden intervenes, as he always does. Normally, his involvement would mollify me enough to keep my mouth shut. He's done more for me than anyone—aside from Rae, now that I know about it.

She's sitting in one of the sofa chairs, practicing twirling and catching her knives. Jackson pinches a blade mid-spin between his finger and thumb, and she cranes her head back to look at him. He's sitting on the back of her chair with his boots perched on the arms, his head leaning into one fist as he smiles at her. They exchange words in a hushed conversation, completely oblivious to the rest of the room.

It's fine.

This burning in my chest won't kill me.

Drama king.

Fucking Kellan.

"Thorne isn't going to leave just because this guy he's meeting is a few minutes late. It works in our favor to be late so he drops his guard," Aiden continues, and I force my stare away from Raegan and back to him. "He's the one who bumped the meeting time up with short notice, so he can't expect punctuality."

I'm not looking for reasoning or logic right now.

I want action.

I glare at Kellan, debating throwing a fist at that smirk, but the asshole would take it like a brick wall and wind up grinning more.

Even if I muted his gift first.

Prick.

Turning away from him to fight that temptation seems like the best option, so that's what I do. I stalk over to the wall and press my head and forearm against it to cool down.

I know I'm getting too worked up. If I let my emotions run wild, I'll fuck this up, and the only person I can blame will be myself. I take a long, slow breath.

This is going to work.

Another breath.

We're going to capture him and get answers on Royce. On GE's president.

Another breath.

We're going to end this war once and for all.

"Hey. You, okay?" Raegan pokes her head under mine at an angle, her blonde hair tumbling behind her to expose every line, every soft curve of her face. Her vibrant blue eyes swim with concern, and my gut reaction is to reassure her.

"Yeah." I lift my head and turn to her, scratching the back of my head out of nerves to keep my hands occupied. "But I'll be better once we've got the cuffs on him."

She reaches tentatively for my hand. I don't move it. As much as I want to reach out and take it, I'm still doing my best not to push anything between us. I've already admitted what I want. What happens next is up to her.

And she wound up sleeping with Aiden instead, a dark part of me snarks.

She takes my hand, and I squeeze it gently. She smiles, and it takes all my willpower to keep from tugging her into my chest, from wrapping her in my arms and holding tight. I want to feel her strength, and I want to share mine.

There's knocking at the door, and her hand drops. Aiden opens it to let Reid inside.

"Sorry I'm late," he speaks evenly, without an ounce of actual apology in his tone. He scans the room, stops on Raegan, and then shifts to me right beside her. It hasn't passed my notice, or the others', how he seems to watch her.

"Here's your comm. Make sure you get somewhere close but out of sight until one of us gives the signal." Aiden hands Reid the earpiece. He looks to me, and I offer him a short nod.

I'm ready.

Reid brings us to a rooftop in the heart of the city. We're a couple blocks away from the meeting location in case Thorne plans to scope out the area first. Jackson does just that as soon as we arrive to make sure Thorne doesn't have backup of his own hanging around.

The rest, aside from Reid and I, head out to meet Thorne first.

Waiting is the worst.

I'd rather be walking with them or doing any-fucking-thing else than pacing this rooftop and trying to be patient. Reid's settled himself against something, his eyes closed and arms crossed as if this isn't the worst time to fall asleep. We have to be ready to move at a moment's notice because, with Thorne, every second matters.

"Hey!" I shout at him. "You can sleep when we get back."

His eyes open and lock on me, but he doesn't say anything.

As usual, the guy's harder to read than anyone I've ever met.

"What's this?" Thorne's voice echoes through the earpiece, and I stop moving. He gives a sinister laugh. "I'd asked for information, but having you appear instead is a surprise."

"I heard you've been asking around about me," Jackson replies.

I move to Reid's side and grip the open bracelet, which is more like a handcuff, in one hand, and hold his shoulder with the other.

"Oh, I have. There're orders to kill you on sight, but I think you and I can work something out."

"I think we've proven neither of us can be trusted."

"Now!" Aiden orders.

I barely have time to bend my knees before Reid transports us to the meeting location. He does a double jump. Once to assess everyone's positions and then again to put us at Thorne's back. My fingers dig into his shoulder to hold on as I fight the wave of nausea at the extreme disorientation.

We land behind him while he's focused on the others who've now joined Jack to act as a distraction. My body threatens to fall forward, but I take a step and use it to launch myself at him. I grab the arm he's raised to attack and choke when his stench hits me.

"Ah, fuck!"

My already uneasy stomach clenches.

"Get off!" Thorne growls, jerking his arm and moving me with it.

My hand clings to his arm as tight as I can. I hold my breath, for whatever good it'll do now, and scramble to reach the open bracelet. The psycho apparently has the same idea because he cuts off my oxygen.

That's fine. I didn't want to breathe near him anyway.

I snap the bracelet around his wrist so we're now linked together with the other ring around me. The others are fighting him at his front, forcing him to defend himself rather than attack me, and it gives me the time to concentrate on my gift. A soft white glow encompasses my hand as my gift activates and I press my power over his, smothering it like a lid over a fire to cut off its oxygen.

Air rushes back into my lungs, and I curse at the foul smell. I keep pushing my gift until his is completely muted, then hold it there. "It's done!" I yell.

The others rush at him, but I'm too preoccupied keeping my grip on him as he fights to get me off to pay them any attention.

"Let go, you little shit!" Thorne bellows.

I plant my feet and lean back as he tries to pull his arm free from me. Even if it does slip, the bracelet won't let me get far, and I'll just grab him again.

"It's on. Get his other wrist," Aiden directs.

Thorne curses and fights against us, but his strength lies in his gift, not his rotting body. With six of us against him, it doesn't take long for us to restrain him.

Kellan grabs the arm I'm holding and brings it forward to click the other cuff to his wrist. I undo the bracelet on him as soon as that's done, ready to put some distance between me and this fucking corpse.

I'm going to need a scalding hot shower after I get back just to cleanse the odor from my lungs.

Thorne's voice raises to a higher pitch just before Reid teleports us to the butcher shop Jackson and Aiden had prepared. "—die!" He stops and licks his bloodless lips, hunched over and heaving deep breaths as he acclimatizes from the jump. His one good eye seeks out Jackson and he grabs him by the front of his hoodie.

"You have to let me go. If I don't check in, if he thinks I've been compromised—"

Jack holds a blade to his wrist. "Let go, or I'll cut off your hands."

Thorne's lips stretch to a creepy smirk. "Do it."

Fucker.

I grab his upper arm and cover his gift with mine. I hate that I have to touch him again, but if we have to move the cuff to his ankle just so Jackson can make a point, then let's get it over with. "You asked for it."

Thorne grabs for the knife, but Jackson flips it just out of reach. The zombie curses and glares at me. I raise my eyebrows at him. I'm not fucking excited to have any contact with him, either.

"Oh, shit!" Raegan exclaims.

My attention snaps to her to see what I missed. She's staring at Thorne's chest. Where Jackson's embedded his knife in to its hilt.

"Fuck! What did you do?!" We haven't asked him *anything* yet! I shove Jack back, and he takes the knife with him with a smirk.

"Dane, wait," Aiden says, placing a hand on my arm. I pause and look back at where Thorne had been stabbed. "There's hardly any blood."

Thorne sneers and I realize he hadn't even noticed being stabbed. He looks more annoyed that Jackson did it than by the hole in his chest.

Jack holds the knife up before him, canting his head as he studies the thin streaks of red. His gaze falls back on Thorne. "Do you feel pain?"

Raegan's eyes widen.

Kellan gives a dark chuckle. "Well, that's damn inconvenient."

How are we supposed to get information out of him if that's the case? Ask nicely?

Thorne smirks at Jackson. "You can't hurt me. You can't kill me. And there's no reason for me to share anything with you. This was a daring move, but a foolish one."

Fuck.

Aiden steps forward, drawing his attention. "Was it?" Thorne frowns, his brows pinching as he turns his attention to Aiden. "Or are you doing exactly what we want?" he mocks in a slow croon. "Because the second you realized you were being taken hostage, you freaked out. You're more scared of being here, held captive, than of anything else we might do to you."

Thorne's lips thin.

"So, that's exactly what we'll do. We'll keep you here. So long as you refuse to share any information, we'll let you sit here another few hours. Another day. A week. It doesn't matter to us. How long do you think your master will let you sit here without reporting in before he comes to retrieve his lost puppet?"

"You're using me as *bait*?" Thorne spits out.

"Or..." Aiden leans forward, ignoring Thorne and dropping his voice to a threatening tone. "You could answer our questions, and we may let you be on your way. You're not the one we're after. You're just an annoying pebble caught in our shoe." He smiles at Thorne and straightens. "We'll let you think it over." A loud *clank* echoes through the freezer—that's no longer cold—and a heavy chain rattles from the cuffs on Thorne to the metal loop bolted to the floor at his feet. Aiden walks out, and we all take that as our cue to leave and follow him.

CHAPTER THIRTY-FIVE

DANE

THE KNIFE TAPS ON the cutting board as I slice it through the strawberry. I cut the stem free, then cut it in half before tossing it on the mound that rises above the bowl. I should get another one, but I'm too zoned in on the repetitive tasks to break the process.

I've prepared dozens of loaves of bread, multiple stacks of crepes just waiting to cool before I put them in the fridge, a few batches of cookies, and now I'm finishing fruit preparation to be used with the crepes for tomorrow's breakfast.

The kitchen is a mess.

Rather than cleaning up as I go like usual, I've hyper-fixated on each food idea and jumped to the next one without giving myself a break. My back aches from standing for however many hours I've been here. The massive stainless-steel table in the center of the kitchen has a layer of powdered sugar coating it from when I prepared some dough for sugar cookies. There are bowls, discarded egg shells, flour mixed with baking soda, and now empty fruit containers littering the table.

After we left Thorne, I needed an outlet for my frustration. I've been trying to put it to better use than arguing with the first person I see. Now, I'll either put in an extra training session with Kellan or come here.

I toss another halved strawberry to the pile and frown when I notice there are only a few remaining.

What's next?

I didn't get the answers I wanted tonight.

We got nothing.

Abso-fucking-lutely nothing.

I know it's a win that we have Thorne and he's powerless.

But I thought we would have our next step to taking GE down. I thought...we'd have *something* for all that planning. Anything.

I see Aiden's plan, and if I could think of a better one, I'd tell him.

But I don't.

So here I am.

"Dane?"

I whip my head over my shoulder at the sound of her voice. Raegan looks around at the chaos of the kitchen and then to me. "What are you doing?"

Finishing the last strawberry, I set the knife down and turn to give her my full attention. "Making some things for tomorrow. Were you looking for me?"

Hope swells in my chest like a balloon. I try to squeeze and deflate it, but controlling my emotions has never been a strength of mine. It sits there no matter what I tell myself, waiting to jumpstart my heart or explode at her whim.

"You weren't in the room still when I woke up. Aiden thought you might be here, so I came to check."

I try to hide my disappointment.

At least she thinks about me when I'm not there.

But she isn't here to give me her response, either.

If it's taken this long for her to tell me how she feels, then is there any point pretending I don't have my answer?

"Do you help make things here a lot?" she asks, moving closer to look at the food I've already prepared.

My body instinctively shifts to follow her. Like she's my sun, and I'm just the lucky idiot caught in her orbit.

"Not as often as I'd like," I admit. When it was up to me to do all the cooking at the Loft, I realized how much I enjoyed trying new recipes and making good, tasty food. We tried taking turns at first, but Aiden is awful with everything on the stove. His phone distracts him, and he winds up burning it every time. He's only useful at assistance with baked goods and prep work.

Kellan can manage grilled cheese sandwiches, bacon for BLTs, and pasta from a box.

Jackson...he'll eat anything put in front of him, but he'll never cook. He just hangs out near someone until his growling stomach pisses them off enough to get up and make it for him. Me being that someone ninety-nine percent of the time.

"Is there anything I can help with?" She traces a finger through the powdered sugar on the table and lifts it to her nose for a sniff. Her tongue darts out to taste it, and she hums appreciatively.

My dick springs to attention in my own show of appreciation, but that is the *last* thing I want her to see right now. I lean a bit into the table to hide it from view. "Sure. Grab that bowl over there." I point to the bowl of cookie dough I'd taken a break from.

She strides over to it with her back to me, and I quickly rearrange myself so my hard-on isn't so fucking obvious.

Rae sets the bowl down in front of her. "What do I need to do?"

"Have you made sugar cookies before?"

Her cheek indents from biting it on the inside, and I remember her bare apartment. She said she was always on the move. "No."

What else has she missed out on?

And how can I help her experience everything while we're hiding in the bunker?

After we take down GE, we can do whatever we want. Go wherever she wants to go.

I realize I'm not the best travel guide, considering my own limited experience, but then we'll both get to try and see things for the first time.

Stop planning a fucking trip like you're going on a honeymoon.

I grab the empty containers where the fruit had been to busy my hands. "Grab the sifter and put more powdered sugar down on the table. It'll help keep the dough from sticking." It was a happy accident when I used powdered sugar instead of flour one time, and the results were so good that I always use it for baked desserts now.

She searches the table. "Sifter?"

Right. Zero baking knowledge.

Rather than make her get it, I walk around the table to pick it up and bring it to her. Then, I slide the bag of powdered sugar next to it. "Add some in the top here, and then squeeze the handle like this over the table to spread it out."

I toss the fruit containers away and cover the heaping bowls of fruit with plastic wrap before putting them in the fridge. When I check back on her, she's smiling as powdered sugar falls like snow over her workspace.

Fuck, I miss that smile.

I miss it being directed at me most of all, but I'll take this.

I wish I could freeze this moment because I've learned to be grateful for what you have when you have it. Happiness? Fun? Those were like a pipe dream to me not long ago.

But since she's come back into my life, I've experienced both more times than I can count.

It doesn't matter if she rejects me.

Because I choose her.

I'll be there for her in whatever way she'll let me. I won't be picky.

I remember my phone in my pocket and sneak a quick picture. She's wearing the navy shirt and short pajama set that Aiden bought for her, which means her legs are bare from her thighs down to her slippers. Her hair is bunched over the front of one shoulder with rebel strands sticking in different directions from the short amount of sleep she had.

She's fucking gorgeous.

Her face lifts, and I shove my phone back into my pocket before she catches me. "What's next?"

I reach for the roller and hand it to her. "Put the dough on the table and then roll it out with this. You want it to be a quarter inch thick."

Rae dumps the dough, and a plume of sugar flies into the air and her face. "Oh, shit." She coughs into her arm, and I can't help but laugh. She grumbles something under her breath and grabs the rolling pin. She tests a short and light roll on top, then frowns at it.

"Here." I step up beside her and hold out my hand for the pin. "I'll show you."

She gives it to me, taking a step to the side to give me more room in front of the dough. I shift over, fully aware that she's chosen to stay close while she watches me push and knead the roller into the dough. I get the dough from a round blob to a more flattened shape before handing the tool back.

Raegan's forehead bunches with concentration as she adds more weight to her task, spreading the dough out further and further. I'm so entranced watching her that I don't realize until too late how thin she's made it. The dough thickness is completely uneven, with lumps and mounds in some spots and then areas so thin that the table is visible.

"Did I do it right?" she asks hopefully, and I'm fucking tempted to tell her yes. If we were at the Loft and these were just for us, I would. But supplies are limited in the bunker.

"It's close," I say, giving her a smile to soften the answer.

She huffs, and I move closer. "We'll do it together." I roll the dough back into a ball and press it into the table. Picking up the rolling pin, I settle my hands on the outside of hers and shift myself behind her with my head over her shoulder. I only have a few inches over her in height, so my lips and jaw are even with her hairline, and the smell of her shampoo fills my nose.

Focus!

Roll the dough.

Don't think about how my arms are wrapped around hers.

Quarter-inch thickness.

Or how my heart is thundering in my ears.

Make sure the dough is even.

Or how my body's caging hers.

"Dane?"

Hm? "What?" I ask, snapping to attention.

"You're poking me."

What?

Oh.

"Fuck!" I shout, jumping back and spinning to adjust myself again. It's hard as fucking granite. That's how crazy she makes me. I curse at myself for letting my thoughts go in that direction. And then prodding her with it like a fucking stickup robbery.

When I chance a look over my shoulder to see how upset she is, she's biting her bottom lip with a barely restrained smile.

"You thought that was funny?" My voice comes out sharp in my embarrassment, but I'm more confused by her reaction and still angry with myself.

Raegan's smile slips free from her teeth, and she tries to cover it up by clearing her throat. "No?" She cringes when she hears the amount of amusement still in her tone. She turns and leans her back into the table. "Actually, I've been meaning to talk to you. I know this isn't the *best* segue into that conversation, but we should talk about the elephant in the room."

More like elephant *trunk* in the room.

Ha.

I make sure I've better contained my dick to avoid any future potential for stabbing or knocking into anything else before I face her fully.

She hesitates, her eyes focused on mine. "Right. I think…I mean, what I can't stop thinking about is…your sister."

Not really what a guy wants to hear, but I know what she means.

"This isn't about her."

Rae shifts off the table. "Isn't it? How can it not be when it comes to us? How can I know that there's no more lingering resentment that'll affect us? And what if…" She wavers, then pushes through. "What if she doesn't make it by the end of this? Can you still look at me if that happens? This…what we've been building back, I'm scared to lose it, Dane. I'm scared to lose you again. And it'll hurt that much worse if we start something together." She exhales sharply with a shake of her head. "And that doesn't even include how I shouldn't consider this while I've been with the others. That's not fair to you. To any of you. But if you asked me to leave them, I can't. I…won't."

Her fierce blue eyes are drawn up to mine again. They're so blue, so bright. Like the hottest fire when it turns blue. That's what they look like. And she is fire. She's stronger than she knows.

But I can see her walls going up behind that fire. The way she's trying to shield herself from me.

I won't let her.

I want to be let in. I won't ruin this. No matter what happens after this, after GE, there is no going back to the way I was when she was out of my life.

It takes two steps to bring her back in reach. Two steps to close the distance between us and cradle her face. She holds my wrists with both hands and watches me.

"You won't lose me again. Whatever the outcome is with Vera, I won't let it come between us. Everything to do with her is because of Gifted Enterprise. And we aren't going to stop until they're destroyed." My thumb strokes her cheek. "But you and me? This is *only* about us. And you'll have me for as long as you want me. With those other assholes, too, if that's the deal."

Her grip on me tightens. "But, Dane—"

"I know I've said and done some fucked up things. I know I'm impulsive, and maybe Kellan isn't completely bullshitting to say I can be dramatic. But I want this with you more than I can put into words. I want to get to know you again, inside and out. What you think, feel, want, need. I want all of you, Rae. Let me in, and I swear, I won't mess this up."

Her eyes are glossy as they search mine. I hold my breath. This answer means more to me than air, and I won't miss it.

"You're really okay with the others...?"

"Yes," I respond quickly on an exhale. "I can't promise I'll...participate...with them. Not unless that's something you really want. But I like seeing how happy they make you, and I don't want to take that away. I just want to be a part of what makes you happy, too."

She grabs my face and kisses me.

My chest explodes in a series of fireworks that knocks my heart completely out of rhythm. I'm lightheaded and dizzy, but I've never felt better.

The surprise of her kiss gives her the advantage while I gather my bearings, but now that I know she wants me too, I don't have to hold back anymore. I lean into the kiss, pressing her back into the table as I take over.

I'd dreamed about this moment before I even realized what my feelings for Raegan were. What it would be like to kiss her. To taste her. To hold her in my arms, not as a friend but as someone more.

She moans into the kiss when I deepen it, and my cock swells back to its full, rigid length. I move my hands down her sides, over the small curve of her ass, then break our kiss to grip and lift her thighs and plant her on the table. Raegan opens her legs and pulls me between them to restart our kiss where we left off.

My hands slide under the back of her shirt. They graze over the scars there that only further remind me of how fucking strong she is. I'm suddenly obsessed with the feel of her bare skin beneath my fingertips. Like a contact drug that's slipped into my veins and demands *more*. She's braless beneath the shirt, and my heart thrashes wildly at that discovery. The extra blood flow rushes in my ears, and my dick throbs almost painfully with the need for friction.

I palm a breast in one hand, feeling the weight of it with a male giddiness that I'll never admit to.

Fuck me.

Raegan releases another wanton sound when my thumb flicks over her nipple.

Yes! That sound. That's all I want to hear right now. It's fucking music to my ears. I test her shorts, and they're gaping holes with more accessibility than I think Aiden realized, but it works out well for me now. I graze my fingers over her underwear and she inhales sharply.

"Tell me how you like it." I drop to my knees, yanking a nearby box over as a stool to get my height right, then peel her panties to the side. I draw a line with my tongue from her opening to her clit. Her thighs quiver over my shoulders and she groans.

Then her fingers bury at the top of my head. Raegan grips my hair tight, and *holy fuck,* I almost come then and there.

I grab my dick with one hand as it pulses with need while I return my attention to her. She guides me with her hand, her voice cooing and *ahhing* between instructions that tell me what she likes.

"Yessss. Like that. Right there. A little to the left. Ahhh, yeah!

Yeah! Fuuuuck!"

Her words and moans spur me on, my hand squeezing and stroking my cock as I feast on her pussy. The pitch of her voice shifts seconds before she comes, but I don't stop. Her thighs clamp my head between them, her fingers and nails pulling my hair with all her might like she's trying to kill me with her orgasm.

I'm enjoying every filthy second of it.

She doesn't release me until her body falls slack. I crawl up her legs, see her lying awkwardly on the table to avoid the mound of dough, and shove the food to the side. "Rae…" I breathe, her name passing my lips with all my years of longing.

Her dark lashes flick up to take me in as I hover between standing and joining her on the table. I grip my dick through my sweats, and she drops her gaze to it. Her lips part, and I'm hoping that's a good fucking sign of what's coming next.

"Tell me you want this." I stroke my cock.

She licks her lips. "I want this," she answers huskily. Her eyes find mine. "I want you, Dane."

Before I'm lost in the heat of the moment, I quickly ask, "Condom?"

Her head shakes. "Birth control."

Thank fuck.

I don't usually carry those around on me with all the sex I'm *not* having.

I groan, pumping myself two more times and then shoving everything off. I yank her shorts and underwear free, flinging them wherever-the-fuck and climbing onto the table. I slide my dick into her welcoming cunt, and let out a long, low groan.

Holyyy fuckkk, she feels amazing.

Her voice joins mine in a chorus of *fucks* and *yeahs* as I drag my cock out and then push it back in.

I'm going to need a distraction so I don't lose it with a few strokes. I'm already worked up and primed for a release, but I can't let her first experience with me look like I'm some fresh schoolboy.

I grab the sifter near her head and tuck her shirt up to her underarms so her torso is exposed. It only takes a few clicks to give me what I need.

Raegan gasps. "What are you—" Her words cut off and her back arches as my tongue absorbs and sucks the powdered sugar from her nipple.

"Don't worry. I'll clean you up," I tease, then grind my hips into her as I work to lick and clean the sweet substance from her skin. Fuck, this is hot. I'm tempted to get the chocolate sauce and other ingredients, but there's no way I'm leaving her pussy yet.

Maybe next time.

She's panting by the time I've cleared the sugar, and I take that as my cue to pick up the pace again. I drive into her, keeping track of the sounds and faces she makes until I find the right one. Her nails find my arms and dig in with a draw- out moan, and I know I've found it. I don't leave that spot, thrusting my hard length over it again and again. Watching her with rapt attention as she curls and tightens, her body trembling.

She screams, and her pussy grabs my dick in a vise that triggers my own release. Absolute euphoria floods me in a rush, and I moan without a single fuck given about how loud I am. It's over much too soon, but my body is wrecked from lack of sleep and working in the kitchen that I don't think I could try again soon if I wanted to.

Raegan's eyes are closed as she catches her breath.

I kiss her eyelids. Her nose. The corner of her mouth.

Her lips curve to a lazy smile, and she opens her eyes. Even though her face and body appear content, her eyes seem guarded. She shifts her gaze beyond me, but fuck that.

I take her chin and bring her back to me. "Look at me, Rae. This wasn't just some random fuck. When I told you I wanted all of you, I meant it." I brush some powdered sugar from her temple. "So tell me why you look like you're going to bolt the second I give you an inch of space."

She worries her lip. "It's…it's not you. I just don't know how to do…this part. If we get up and start working on something else, I'll be fine. But…"

I frown at her. "No."

"No?"

"I'm going to stay right here, and we're going to talk."

"What?!" she sputters. "I just said—"

"I know what you said. But you're not running away from me after that. If I want to kiss you, or tickle you, or cuddle with you, then we're going to do that. If you want to tell me what's on your mind or just share something—doesn't matter if you think it's nothing—then share it."

I shift onto my side so I don't crush her but wrap my legs around hers to keep my satisfied dick housed in her warmth. She still doesn't look convinced, so I start pulling my fingers through the top of her hair down to her scalp. It always worked to soothe her or put her to sleep back on the island.

Raegan takes a deep breath, closing her eyes for a moment. When she opens them, she's looking at me. "Okay."

I smirk, pleased with myself, but my fingers continue their work.

"What time do people show up in the kitchen to start breakfast?"

I pause. I did tell her anything, but...this is what's on her mind? "Uh, around five."

"So, it was just after three-thirty when I came down. Should we check the time?"

My head snaps around to look at the clock on the wall. Fifteen minutes until five. *Shit.* Raegan's wearing a smirk of her own when I turn back to her. "You win this one," I concede, untangling myself from her and hopping off the table.

I rush to find where I'd thrown her clothes, grabbing and tossing them at her. "Hurry up. Miranda's going to run screeching to the whole Guild if she catches us."

"Miranda?"

"The head cook." I roughly dress myself and attempt to fix my clothes and hair without a mirror. Then I go to Raegan and help tidy her hair before guiding her back to the floor.

"Ah. I'll help you clean up, then."

Chapter Thirty-Six

RAEGAN

A VINE DIVES IN my direction, its end sharp and lethal. I jump to the side, my arm swinging in an arc to cut it with my knife. Another one flies from the other side, but my gift is running hot through that arm, and I dash out of the way and grab it. The entire vine dusts to fine particles on the training room floor.

Silas runs at me. I reel in my gift, storing it somewhere safe and away from contact but readily accessible, and meet him halfway across the mat. I dodge his first attack, ducking and slamming my fist to his gut, then spinning up and kicking him back.

He coughs and holds up a hand. "Wait," he wheezes.

Oops. I'm wound up from fighting Kellan earlier and forgot that's not who I'm fighting now. But I *still* haven't bested Kell in any of our sparring. I'm not expecting to suddenly be better than him. But just *once*, I'd like to get a win. Some sign that I'm making progress. "Sorry!" I call out while jogging over to him. "Are you all right?"

He laughs and rubs his gut. "Yeah, I'm good. They weren't lying when they said you're a fierce fighter. I'm not sure how to get a hit in with your defense."

"You're not thinking outside of the box enough, Si." Kellan strolls up to our mat with a wide grin. "That was good work, beautiful," he murmurs, bending in my direction and sending a quick wink. "Here's how you beat her." He whispers to Silas, and the other man's eyes widen like a lightbulb turned on.

"I got it. Okay. One more time?" Silas asks, a mischievous smile on his face.

Kellan takes a few steps back and folds his arms over his chest to watch. His smirk is already set deep behind his facial hair as if he's confident whatever plan of his will work.

I'd really like to mess that plan up, but I have no idea what it could be. It would be smarter to take the time to figure it out, but I'm more a girl of action. I learn better by experience.

Taking my place at the other end of the mat again, I nod and raise fisted hands before me. I keep my grip on the knife firm in one hand and shift my gift to the other in a reddish glow. "Ready."

He sends four vines at once from his outstretched hand. I move to cut and destroy them from the middle, just like I had the last two. They're gone without much effort, so I keep moving to get to him. If I land a hit on him, it'll be another win.

Silas throws a thicker, stronger vine to intercept me, but it hardly slows me down.

Something tickles around my ankle. And then I'm jerked upside down and into the air. "Woah! What the hell?!" A vine is holding me high enough up that I don't try cutting it. I'm not sure of my flipping and landing skills from this height.

Where did it come from? I'm sure I took care of everything he had.

I follow the vine to the ground, watching it wrap tightly around the edge of the mat to blend in, then to the seed it sprung from at his feet.

I'd been so focused on what was right in front of me that I didn't even realize he'd snuck that one behind me.

Silas *whoops* excitedly as his vine gently carries me back to the mat. Kellan bellows with laughter and applauds.

I push back to my feet and circle stray hairs behind my ear. "That was a neat trick, but don't think I'll be fooled by it again."

"We'll see about that. For now, let's call it a day. Everyone else has already wrapped up." Kellan pulls out two water bottles which he passes to me and Silas.

We walk to the benches to catch our breath. Jackson's leaning against the wall, one foot up and his arms crossed, his piercing blue gaze staring out from the shadow of his hood.

"Why don't you ever help Kellan train the others? I heard you're pretty badass," Silas directs to him.

"The only way I know how to train is the way I was trained," Jack replies coolly.

"How's that?"

"He told me *don't die*. And then he tried to kill me."

Silas's throat bobs. "Oh. Yeah, I'll pass on that."

"You ready to go?" Another Guild member walks over, eating what looks like a barbecue skewer. Fabian? "The party starts in a couple hours, and I want to eat before we get ready."

Silas stretches his arms over his head. "You know there will be food there, right?"

I stare between them. *Or the fact that he's eating right now?*

Fabian shrugs. "Party food."

I look over my shoulder at Kellan. "Explain to me again why the Guild is having a party in the middle of us attacking GE's bases while they're actively trying to kill or kidnap everyone here. *And* after we kidnapped and locked up one of their zombies?"

Kellan chuckles. "Because we don't let GE control our lives, and if we want to have a good time, then we'll have it."

"Because it's a tradition!" Fabian cheers.

Silas caps his water and stands. "These parties were started to bring us all together. It's a celebration of the Guild and its members."

"Wasn't that the party around Christmas?" I ask.

"That's the biggest one that we combine with the holidays. But it's similar," Kellan answers. "You'll love it. It has the big three." I give him a questioning look, and he drawls, "Music, alcohol, and dancing. Your favorite."

Ha!

He's not wrong.

Fabian and Silas wave goodbye as they leave first. I pause while gathering my things when I realize something. "I don't have anything to wear."

"Aiden already has something for you lying on your bed."

Of course, he has.

I chew on my cheek to bite back a smile.

"You guys go ahead. I want to stop by to see Charles first."

I can *feel* Jackson behind me before I hear him. "I'll go with you."

"He's not going to talk to me if you're staring him down in that way you do, Jack," I say as I turn to face him. I reach up to slide my hand over his cheek, and he leans into it. "I need to learn more about him. Whether he's just a good guy caught by GE or something else, I have to earn his trust enough that he'll talk."

"I'll go, then." Kellan steps up.

I angle myself to look at him. "That's still—"

Jack tucks my hair behind my ear. "He can't be alone with you."

Sighing, I drop my hand. "Fine. But let me do the talking, Kell."

He grins and leads us from the training room to the elevator. I push the button to bring us to the floor where the rescues from the island are living temporarily, then look to Jack when he doesn't choose a floor for himself. "Which floor?" I prompt, and his lips curl to a smirk.

"I'm visiting someone else," he answers cryptically.

"Who—?" But the doors open, and he strides out before us. Jackson has the locked doors open when Kellan and I catch up. They nod to whoever's standing at the door and proceed further in.

It's my first time here, so my head is swiveling left and right as I take it all in. Medical area, bunk rooms, and at the end of the hall is a large open area full of tables, chairs, and couches...it's like a mini, single floor version of the Guild Hall. Except this one has a kid-friendly area with a jungle gym and toys off to one side.

Jackson keeps moving beyond the open area to more rooms in the back, but Kellan takes my arm to stop me when I automatically begin to follow. "He's visiting someone else, beautiful. The one you want to see is over there." He points to the man sitting at one of the long tables reading a book.

As if sensing that others are looking at him, Charles raises his head. He smiles when he sees me.

I smile back. Awkwardly.

I'm still not sure how to do this family thing. He's a stranger to me, but this is why I'm here. To see if there's more here that we can work with, to find out more about him and my mother, and go from there.

"Raegan!" He slides a bookmark between the pages of his novel and sets it on the table, then moves his gaze to Kellan. "And who is this?"

"Hi. He's Kellan. My fr—"

"Boyfriend. Lover. *Soulmate,*" Kellan interjects with a sharp grin.

I spin and jab a finger into his chest, whispering angrily, "What are you doing?!"

"Making sure he knows you're being taken care of. And have someone like me on your side. And also"—his teeth flash— "getting my claim in before the others."

Ahh! Prick!

"Go stand over there," I snap, pointing away from the table. He can still see and potentially hear everything, but then I don't have to worry about him saying something else to either embarrass me or derail the conversation.

Kellan laughs. "Are you putting me in a timeout?"

"Call it whatever you want. But you're banned from joining this conversation."

"All right, all right. I'll go stand over there and look pretty for you."

He winks and saunters to where I'd pointed out. I didn't realize that I'd directed him to the kid area, but he doesn't hesitate to greet them as he stands at the soft block wall that separates that area from the rest of the room.

Charles's brow is furrowed while looking from Kellan back to me.

Great.

Relax. You don't owe him any explanation.

Clearing my throat, I ask, "Do you mind if I sit?"

"Please." He gestures to the seat across from him, and I take it.

"How are you feeling?"

"Good," he replies. "I'm fully recovered. I guess now they're trying to decide what to do with me."

Aiden told me a little bit about the plan for the rescues. They'd try to find any surviving family members they could go home to and enter witness protection if needed, thanks to Elias's FBI contact. Those who had no one else were stuck in limbo here. They aren't members of the Guild to join the rest, but it's too dangerous to let them back on the streets where GE could pick them up again. Aiden also wants to make sure none of the rescues have already been brainwashed to follow GE before releasing them.

"Do you...have a home somewhere? Some place to go back to?"

Charles chuckles. "Can't say that I do. I've been missing for a long while."

He looks like he's in his late forties or early fifties. And if he was with my mom, even for a short time, on the island twenty years ago...

I'm amazed he seems...normal. Not a brainwashed soldier or a zoned-out lab rat.

A child cries loud enough to draw my attention back to Kellan and the kid's area. Kellan's kneeling down to comfort the little boy. He raises his arm. It's bright red like he'd been cut with something, but golden scales slowly fill in over it. The little boy stops crying to stare at it, wide-eyed.

"What's on his arm?" Charles inquires, and I realize he'd also stopped to watch the scene.

"It's his gift," is all I say because I'm still not trusting enough of this man to tell him everything.

He smiles with a look of understanding and doesn't ask for more. "So. Are you here for stories about Merina?"

I nod and smile back. "Yes. If you don't mind."

"Not at all. I'll start at the beginning, then. When we first met."

I frown over my shoulder at the mirror. The dress Aiden bought me is the perfect party dress. Long sleeves, a V-neckline, and a short, swishy skirt. It's a black skater dress that shows off my legs, especially in the matching pair of heels that I doubt I'll last more than an hour in. But the back…it's open in a larger V than the front, exposing my scars for everyone to see.

I left my hair down, styling loose curls in the hopes that it would hide the worst of it, but even with the top third of it covered, there's no mistaking them.

There's a knock at the bathroom door. "How's it going in there?" Dane calls out.

I can't wear this.

According to Kellan, *everyone* in the Guild will be at the party tonight. The members who may spend more of their time out on jobs or living in their own space will be coming. Aiden's been working tirelessly on security measures and the best way to discreetly get the arrivals in, so I haven't been able to see him since I found out about it.

"I'm coming in," Dane announces when I haven't answered, and the door opens before I can tell him I'm fine. He stops in the doorway, his hand frozen on the knob as his eyes trail up my legs. His amber gaze turns molten the more he sees, until he finally stops on my face. "You look…" He swallows hard. "You're beautiful, Rae."

Warmth floods my face. "Thanks." I shift to hide my back from being visible in the mirror. "I need to find something else to wear, though."

"Why? It's perfect."

I reach for my shoulder subconsciously. "It's not the dress."

Dane steps closer, his face drawn with concern. "Well, it definitely isn't you, so what is it?"

I know he's seen them. They all have. But when I wear my usual clothes, it's easy to forget about the crisscross of ugly scars that run the length of my back.

My other hand reaches around, fingering the rough patch where it ends at the small of my back. No, I can't…

His stare follows that hand, and realization has him clenching his jaw.

Dane turns my back to the mirror again, so we're both looking at my scars. "These? You don't need to hide them."

"They're ugly. They tell everyone what GE did to me."

"They're not ugly." He pulls my face to his. "They show the world that you can't be beaten. Wear them like a badge of honor. GE had you twice, and not only did you survive, but you came out stronger. You're unstoppable. I've never met anyone as fierce as you."

My heart flip-flops at his words, and butterflies gather in my gut with nerves. I scrutinize my back in the mirror one more time.

Deep breath.

"Okay. I'm ready."

He smiles and kisses my cheek. "Let's go have some fun." His hand finds mine and squeezes before he leads us out of the bathroom to my room.

Kellan pops off the chair arm he'd been leaning against. His face lights up when he sees me, his smile growing until he sees my hand in Dane's. "How the hell did you manage that?" His long stride brings him to my other side in two steps. "I was sure your asshole drama ways would give me another few months," he teases.

Dane scoffs. "It's none of your damn business."

Kell's eyebrows jump up. "No? I'd say it's all our business now. Or didn't she fill you in on the rules of the club?"

"Club?" I jump in. "What do you think you're calling a *club*, Kellan?"

He gives me a roguish grin. "Just something Jackson and I chatted about."

Right. Because Jackson *chats* about things like this.

I give him a look to express that very sentiment and he rolls his eyes.

"Fine. I did all the chatting. But he didn't disagree, so it's all the same." He leans down to my ear. "You look ravishing, by the way. If I can get Dane on board, should we pause to pregame the party with me devouring your pussy?"

"Fuck's sake," Dane grumbles from my other side, clearly having overheard.

I smack Kell in the chest. "Knock it off. Where are Jackson and Aiden?"

Kellan isn't deterred in the least and slides a hand around my back. "Jack's on guard duty somewhere, and Aiden is at the party. He had to give the opening speech or whatever boring announcement, and now he's gotta mingle. Dane and I will be your dates for the evening."

I smile through the tiny sting of disappointment. It would have been nice to have all of us together for the party, but I get why the other two have other responsibilities. The three of us had a few good times together at Old Red, so I know tonight will be even better.

We make our way to the main area of the bunker, where members usually lounge or eat. The top area still has tables for people to sit at, but there are food and alcohol stations throughout. We pause at the railing to look over the lower level.

All the tables and lounge areas have been cleared to make room for the mass of people dancing in front of a stage. The lighting is dim, giving way to floating colored lights that bob and drift overhead. The music carries easily through this open, two-story room, so even though we're upstairs, it sounds like we're right there.

Kellan hands me a drink. "I see Aiden," he shouts over the music and points downward.

I squint, but it's still dark, and too many people that I can't find him. I should thank him for the dress. And maybe ask him why he picked this one. Did he pick it intentionally with my scars? Or maybe he forgot I had them?

It's Aiden. He doesn't forget.

I jerk my head to indicate I want to go to him, and Kellan leads the way with Dane at my back. We get down the stairs, and Kell wraps an arm around my shoulders to pull me in close. Dane keeps a grip on my hand as we move through the throng of people. It finally clears, revealing Aiden standing beneath a large tree.

His eyes are already on me.

And where Kellan and Dane are touching me.

Great.

When Kell doesn't loosen his hold now that we're free from the crowd, I crane my head back and find him baring his teeth in a grin at Aiden like a damn challenge.

"Stop trying to start shit," I growl at him, ducking and twisting free. All without spilling my drink, I internally cheer. The movement breaks my hand away from Dane as well. I'm not here for a pissing contest or club rules or any of that crap. We're here for the party, and I've finally given in to having a good time and forgetting life for a few hours.

It feels weird to let my guard down after everything going on, but Kellan made it sound like the bunker is the most secure location in the country tonight. That Aiden has spent months working out the details and putting the necessary measures in place so that this event wouldn't be canceled. And so members would feel safe enough to lower their inhibitions and have a good time.

Who am I to argue with that?

I toss the rest of the whiskey down my throat, swallowing in burning gulps as if I'm downing shot after shot.

"Fuck, beautiful. Let me catch up." Kellan downs his glass just as fast, and we grin at each other. He takes my empty drink with his and sets them down on the tray of a passing waiter. Then grabs the shots there and passes them to me and Dane.

"Don't drink too much," Aiden warns, reminding me of the time he'd caught the three of us drinking at Old Red. I'll never forget how he made us work out and train the next morning as punishment.

I move nearer to him so I don't have to shout. "I thought you were going to be nicer to me," I tease, smiling wickedly with the shot in my hand.

Aiden pinches either side of my jaw and pulls me in close. "I never promised nice," he purrs. "Only punishment."

A thrill of desire shoots through me in a rush of heat.

Oh.

Fuck.

Yes.

I take a step back, my eyes locked on him, and suck down the shot. His eyes narrow, but I smirk and walk away into the mob of dancers. There's nothing he can do right now with the entire Guild present. But later?

The people around me are jumping and grinding to the music. I stop at a small opening and begin to move to the beat, swaying and hitting the rhythm in a way I haven't felt since Hype. There are girls squealing closer to the stage that cuts through the song. I try to ignore them, but when I hear the name they're shouting, I look up.

Zedd, the serious guy with Gabriel, is the one singing on stage. My brain glitches at the sight of him grinding into the microphone stand and pouring so much emotion into the song. He screams sex, from the way he moves to the sound of his voice ear-fucking the crowd. It can't be the same guy. A twin, maybe. But then I spot Gabe dancing and yelling for Zedd at the base of the stage.

A hand slaps over my eyes, and I'm tugged back into a lean chest. "Don't look," Kellan drawls. "I accepted my brothers because I knew how you felt about them, but there is fuck-all chances of any other man touching you. If you think you can handle more dick, then *I'll* give it to you. I'll tell the others, and we'll fill every pretty hole of yours until you're dicked out of your mind."

Holy shit.

If I hadn't already been turned on by Aiden, I'm well past that point now. I clench my thighs as arousal pools between them.

Am I going to make it through this night?

"You hear me, beautiful? That's not a threat; it's a promise."

He waits for my nod before he traps my hips against his and we start dancing to the music. Dane joins us a minute later, and then the three of us keep dancing song after song. We switch places; sometimes, it's just me and one of the guys, and sometimes, it's me with both. Most often, it's me on my own while the other two create a barrier around me that keeps anyone else from trying to join.

I have no idea how many hours it's been before I decide it's time for a pee break. Dane left a short while ago to check on Aiden and Kell is getting us more drinks. I ask someone for directions, then head that way, quickly taking care of my business. I'll be back before Kellan knows it.

Yessiree.

Giggling, I glance up and see a waterfall among the foliage, and a dark, rock tunnel beneath it. Wait. Where am I? Did I make the right turn? I don't remember passing this on the way to the restroom. The music is gone, replaced with the rush of water that echoes against the stone while my ears still thunder with the beat.

I look behind me and find more greenery and stone trails.

Shit biscuit. How did I get here?

I move to the tunnel behind the waterfall, fascinated by the roaring surge of water. It smells like rain. Or that earthy smell of water on stone.

No way I passed this earlier without pissing myself. I made a wrong turn.

Something moves in the shadows.

I yelp, but it disappears behind a hand as I'm pressed chest-first into the damp wall.

"Where are you going all alone, little one?" a familiar, husky voice whispers.

Jackson.

One of these days, I'm going to surprise and grab each of them out of nowhere to see how they like it.

"You should be more careful. You never know who might be wandering in the dark."

There's half a second for me to relax before his fingers find my swollen, needy cunt. My filter's currently garbage with the amount of alcohol swimming in my veins, so my moan is loud and long into his palm.

He moves my underwear to the side, and then his dick fills me in one quick thrust. I cry out in surprise, the sound once again muffled by his hand. Even though I'm wet enough, the sudden *stretch* has me seeing stars. My hands slap against the cool, stone wall as he drives into me like he's on a mission. He's relentless, taking me like a prize found in the shadows.

And I'm *loving* it.

This is wild. It's raw.

My body clenches at the pleasure building fast and hard.

"What the—Goddammit, Jack!"

I turn my face as much as I can in his grip to see Kellan sauntering toward us. "What about the rules? Where was my invite?" He bends to my eye level and smirks. "You like that, beautiful? How about I take your fine ass and start on that promise of mine?" He blinks, then curses. "I need to start carrying lube on me from now on."

Jackson doesn't let me stay distracted for long.

He fucks me rough and frenzied, showing me how desperate he's been to have me again. My nails scratch and claw at the rock as he builds me up higher. Faster. Stronger.

I'm a whimpering mess behind his hand, just as needy for this as he is.

He slams into me one last time and it sends both of us breaking apart at once.

"My turn," Kellan snarls before I've had a chance to catch my breath. He reaches for me.

"Did you hear something?" an unfamiliar voice asks from deeper in the tunnel.

"Dammit, Jack!"

Jackson extracts himself from me with a small chuckle. I wobble on my feet, and then my world flips upside down and I faceplant with Kell's back. "We're going back to the room to finish this," Kellan rumbles against my face.

I punch his back with the side of my fist. "Put me down!"

"Keep warming me up, beautiful." He doesn't run, but he takes full advantage of his long strides to get us to the nearest elevator. Jackson stays with us, and I get the giddy feeling that he plans to join in.

We make it to the room in record time. Kellan, thank fuck, sets me on the bed instead of dumping me while my stomach is still filled with alcohol. I sit up to unbuckle my shoes, but Kell grabs my wrist. "Leave them on."

I lean back on my elbows, looking up at him seductively through my lashes. "Where do you want me?"

Kellan's grin sharpens. "Oh, I know just where to—"

"Wait." Jack angles his head at the door like he's listening for something.

"I don't care what anyone's doing in the hallway," Kell growls, shoving his pants and boxers down, his erect dick springing free, just as Dane bursts through the door.

"Thorne's dead!"

CHAPTER THIRTY-SEVEN

RAEGAN

REALITY DOUSES MY WARM buzz like a bucket of cold water. I'm not even sure what Dane means, but hearing that man's name and seeing the panic on his face is enough to derail any mood I'd been in.

Kellan looks away from Dane, the initial concern on his face gone once the words register. "We know," he drawls. He kicks his pants to the side, completely unbothered that the door is open and his cock is bobbing with every move.

"Fuck's sake! Put your dick away." Dane tears his gaze to the opposite side of the room.

"Get over it, Rapunzel. You're gonna see my dick a lot from now on, I'll bet."

"Your dick is the last thing I'll be looking at!"

Jack helps me off the bed while the other two bicker back and forth.

Kellan snorts and shakes his head. "Sure. Now, shut the door if you're joining, or get out."

"You're coming with me. All of you," Dane argues, though he closes the door enough that any passerby can't peek in the room. "Thorne's not moving. There's no heartbeat, no sign of breathing—"

"—so what? He dies all the time, and he comes back. It's what zombies do." Dane frowns and doesn't budge. Kell sighs. "Look, if he doesn't respawn in an hour, then maybe it's a problem, and we can all stare at the dead guy together to figure out our next step."

I finish cleaning myself up in the bathroom, change into more comfortable shoes, and walk to Dane. Turning, I give Kellan a look. "Are you coming?"

He blinks. Looks at me. At the empty bed. Then curses viciously and pulls his clothes back on, muttering about cock-blocking dead people.

Aiden's waiting for us in his office, where the security footage of the freezer at the butcher shop fills his laptop screen. The wind master is lying on the floor in a crumpled heap, like a puppet whose strings have been cut. The cuffs are still on and linked to the chain and metal ring Aiden stuck to the floor to keep him there.

Kellan rests a hand on the desk and leans closer, his eyes narrowing as he studies the body. "Are we sure he isn't faking it? It could be a trap."

"He's dead," Aiden confirms, hitting a key that brings up a side panel of various monitors. "There's no sign of breathing or heartbeat, which he did have before. But I agree that it could be a trap, which is why we're standing here instead of rushing there."

I chew on my lower lip in thought, my eyes glued to the screen. Aiden and Dane had that room decked out with every possible monitor and scanner to alert them the second anything was detected. *Anything.* We were prepared for Royce showing up and containing him to that freezer with his zombie puppet.

If the only thing going off is Thorne's heartbeat and breathing missing, then that means Royce was able to manipulate him remotely.

"So, we have nothing?" Dane is the one to ask aloud.

We didn't get any information from Thorne in the week we've had him, and Royce didn't show to collect him.

That can't be right.

It had sounded like Thorne was Royce's favorite—or at least most useful—puppet when he'd been talking with Gordon. Is this just a temporary termination to fool us?

"We have Thorne," Jackson chimes in, unfazed by this turn of events.

A set of knocks at the door grabs our attention.

"Come in," Aiden calls.

Cibrina and Reid walk in, closing the door behind them. The tall, dark woman takes one look at us, and her expression sets to one of fierce determination. "What do you need, Aiden?"

"Have there been any reports from those on security detail at the bunker entrances?"

"No incidents have been reported, and they've all met their check-in times and provided the appropriate codes. We're still secure."

Aiden nods. "Good. We're—" He freezes.

I follow his stare to the laptop screen.

A beeping alarm goes off from his computer seconds before the shimmering air near Thorne materializes to a portal.

Where Gordon walks through.

Not Royce.

Gordon.

Vines spring free of the seeds positioned around the room by Silas, whipping out and latching around anything they touch. Flower buds bloom along the vines, and bursts of sleeping powder explode at once.

All measures put in place to capture and sedate Royce.

Gordon steps toward Thorne, passing through a cross of vines like they're not even there, and bends with his back blocking our view.

"What the fuck is he doing?" Dane demands, leaning closer to the screen as if he might be able to see around Gordon.

"I'll go," a low, deadly voice says from behind me. I turn to Jackson. He smiles at me, but it's a cruel, sharp pull of his lips that triggers a chill to run down my spine and warmth to pool at my core. There's a strange light in his eyes; a gleam that promises pain and bloodshed. He carves his fingers around my ear, then grips my nape and murmurs against my lips, "Let me bring him to you."

My heart thunders at his request.

"We'll both go," Aiden adds before I can respond, and I draw back to look at him.

Kellan steps up to us, his hands clenched so tight that the veins in his arm muscles pulse. "I'm going, too."

"If I can get ahold of him somehow, I can block his gift," Dane inserts.

"No, we can't all go. Kell, stay here and keep Raegan, Dane, and the Guild safe. Cibrina, wrap up the party without causing a panic. I want the bunker's lockdown to continue through the night, so find space for the visiting members who weren't planning to stay, and add more security to each of the shifts. I'm not convinced there isn't some plan to strike here while drawing us out, so stay vigilant," Aiden instructs.

"I understand," Cibrina says with a terse nod.

"And Reid?" he continues.

The teleporter looks between the group of us, his eyes lingering on mine, before he pins Kellan with his stare. "Keep an eye out for Tinsley while I'm gone." He turns to Aiden and nods to indicate he's ready.

Aiden and Jackson put a hand on each of his arms.

"Stay safe," Aiden orders before they disappear with Reid.

It isn't until they're gone that my gut twists with unease.

Are they walking into a trap?

Chapter Thirty-Eight

AIDEN

We land outside the door to the butcher shop. With all the trips to rescue gifted from various islands, the teleportation doesn't affect me as it once had, and my feet remain firmly planted on the ground.

I close my eyes for the seconds of concentration I need to feel what metal I'm in contact with. My whip sword hidden beneath my jacket and strapped to my back. Forearm and shin gauntlets. Thick, chain necklaces hanging beneath my shirt.

It's not as much as I'd like, heading into a fight with both Gordon and probably Thorne, but it'll have to do.

Reaching over my shoulder, I grasp the handle on my sword and draw it out. "Jack, your knives have hit him before. How?"

He slides a few more blades free of his hoodie, releasing them into the air to join the others that hover around him. "Luck."

I was afraid of that.

Using my free hand to release the top buttons on my collared shirt and my jacket, I remind the other two, "He doesn't leave through that portal."

Jack and Reid nod in unison, and the former replies, "I'm bringing him back to her."

I check in with Reid, making sure he's ready with his two needle-point, twin blades in hand and then grab the door, unlocking it with my gift. Once it's cracked open, the sleeping spores drift out into the night. Jackson waves his hand in long, sweeping motions that drag the mist free of the building and sends it away from us.

He jerks his head and drops his hands when it's all clear, and I take point leading us inside.

"—did what you asked, Royce! Your puppet is free, and our debt is squared. Now, bring him back because I'm not carrying this corpse through the portal," Gordon snaps.

We creep through the storefront, making our way to the open and thawed freezer room in the back.

He continues, oblivious to our presence. "Waiting for what, exactly? What game are you playing at?"

Reid appears between Gordon and the portal, blocking his exit while swinging his long daggers through him.

"Send me some agents." Gordon pockets his phone and turns on Reid, giving Jack and I the opening we need to strike from behind.

Jackson sends a host of blades in all shapes and sizes hurtling at Gordon. They fly through him, stopping short of Reid, before he flips them and tries again.

I release the hold on my whip sword so it separates to a bladed whip, swinging my arm and yanking it out and down to slice through him. As it falls, I send more metal through the sword to spike out at the end where Gordon is in the hopes of finding a solid point.

Reid shifts back, keeping out of the way of our attacks and guarding the portal so Jack and I can attack from a distance without striking him.

Gordon laughs and holds his arms out in a mocking gesture. "You can't hit me, you fools!"

We ignore him, continuing to attack persistently. *There must be a weakness somewhere. Something we're missing.*

My sword slashes down on the floor by his foot, and he shifts it out of the way.

There!

I whip it back and strike at it again. The sharp edge cracks into the concrete floor where his foot is.

Damn.

"You've slept long enough, Thorne." Gordon sneers, his mood shifting from smug to angry too fast to be a coincidence.

I was close.

Gordon reaches for the gun on his hip and fires at me before I can gather my metal into a shield.

The bullets slow seconds before they hit, then zip back at Gordon as Jackson lands by my side.

"Thanks. I almost had him."

Jack angles his head, his eyes locked on Gordon. "How?"

"He moved his foot before my sword touched it. But when I went for it again, it passed right through. If his body is intangible, why move it at all?"

He hums thoughtfully. "He has a vulnerable spot, then. And he's moving it."

I nod in agreement. "We just have to find it before he moves it again."

Jackson's lips curl up to a menacing smile, and he chuckles. "Leave it to me." He holds his hand out. "Give me the rest of your metal. As many throwing knives as you can make with it."

I do as he asks without question. After Gordon's attempt at shooting Reid fails, he doesn't waste his remaining bullets and focuses on trying to wake Thorne. We have the advantage so long as Thorne stays dead. If he wakes up before we've incapacitated Gordon, I'm not sure if we'll be able to stop them from leaving through the portal together.

"That's all I have," I tell Jackson as he gathers the last few knives from me other than my whip sword.

Thorne groans.

Damn it.

"Get up! UP, you lazy puppet!" Gordon shouts, kicking Thorne with his foot.

Thorne tries to grab his leg, but the scientist has already made it intangible again. That's the problem with Gordon. His gift coupled with quick reflexes. He has so much control over his gift, that he can turn it on and off wherever he likes as easily as breathing.

The wind master looks at his hand. "What did you do?!" he bellows, his face darkening with rage. "Where are my thumbs?"

"Watch how you speak to me! Your hands are free and you have your power back. Be grateful, you undead wretch. Now, hurry up and kill them or I'll drop your thumbs down a garbage disposal."

Thorne stands. His eyes flick upward, a smirk spreading on his face when he looks at Gordon.

Knives rain down on Gordon like a swarm of bees. Blades from

Jack, from me, even knives from the butcher shop he must have collected, are all packed together as they fly down in an instant.

"What—" Reid exclaims a second before Gordon releases a garbled grunt.

Thorne cackles wildly. His thumbless hands are holding one of Reid's daggers between them where it's driven through Gordon to the hilt. "Your entire body becomes solid for a second after your weak spot is struck, isn't that right?"

Blood dribbles from the corner of Gordon's lips, his eyes wide with shock. A couple of the knives are buried in his thigh and both of his feet. The rest litter the floor beneath and around him, points down.

"This is a gift from the president." Thorne slowly twists the blade. The scientist screams in pain, dropping to his knees and crashing into more knives. "Who's going to be the undead wretch now?"

That was...unexpected.

A gust of wind throws Thorne away from Gordon. Jackson stands between the two, his attention on his former mentor.

"What are you doing?" Reid demands of him.

"His death belongs to Raegan," Jackson answers coolly.

"—there," Gordon mumbles, then chokes on blood.

I step to his side, grabbing his hair in a fist and holding my sword to his throat. "Don't you dare die," I warn him in a low croon. "I have too much planned for you to let you go that easily."

"President...your Guild..." he mutters between coughs.

I tighten my grip on his hair, pulling it back so he's facing me when he talks. "What was that?" Wind whips through the freezer from Jack and Thorne's fight, and I'm forced to stab my sword into the floor to help keep myself steady.

"He's there...been there...with your Guild..."

My heart rate doubles, stealing my breath away.

I must have misheard him.

"Who is with our Guild? You don't even know where we are," I press, trying to mask the urgency in my tone. I swing around to Reid. "Get the cuffs on him so we can get him to Cassandra. She can heal him enough that he doesn't die before we get answers." And he can suffer for all he did to Raegan.

Reid doesn't move. His eyes are wide with fear, his body rigid.

"Reid!" I snap.

He startles, looking at me and back to Gordon. He storms over to us and grabs Gordon by the shirt. "Did you say the president is there?"

Gordon coughs more blood from the rough shake. His head lulls forward.

Fuck!

"Reid, the cuffs!"

Reid steps away from Gordon, fear hanging like a dark cloud over his face when he looks at me and shakes his head. "I have to go back. Tinsley—"

He cries out and falls forward, hitting the ground. A long, bloody cut scores across his back, and Thorne laughs maniacally. "Can't have you ruining the president's fun, can we?"

The wind master flies at Gordon, wrapping his arms around him and lifting him into the air. Jackson makes like he's slapping his hand down, and both Thorne and Gordon slam to the ground.

Thorne grabs at the scientist again. He snarls his frustration when he can't get a good grip with his thumbless hands before Jackson's attacking again. He rolls out of the way, then flies back to his feet and sends his own counterattacks at Jack. Thorne's clearly trying to get to the portal, but Jackson blocks him each time, landing more attacks on the zombie so the wind master is forced to focus on defense.

Grabbing Reid's blade still pierced through Gordon, I extend the blade and shove it into the concrete to keep him from being moved, then rip my jacket off to press into the bleeding wound on Reid's back that's starting to pool on the floor.

I yank out my phone and call Cibrina.

It rings.

And rings.

And rings.

Her voicemail picks up.

I call Kellan.

Dane.

My office.

The security desk.

Nothing.

"Jack! Let him go! We have to get back to the Guild. No one's answering."

"You really have gotten stronger, Jack," Thorne says in an admiring tone, a dark smile stretched on his face like he's trying to egg Jackson on.

Fuck.

He's stalling us.

It was a planned attack, going after Reid when his guard was down so we can't teleport back.

Heaviness like a pile of bricks weighs on my chest at the thought of what might be happening at the bunker.

Raegan.

CHAPTER THIRTY-NINE

RAEGAN

FIVE MINUTES EARLIER...

My heart pounds hard and fast, blood rushing in my ears and deafening the sounds of the fight through Aiden's laptop. I'm glued to the screen, too scared to blink and miss anything.

Thorne steals a knife from Jackson's horde above Gordon, using it to cut Reid and grab his larger dagger. The rest happens in slow motion.

Instead of attacking Reid or the guys, I see Thorne turn that blade on Gordon.

I watch it go in Gordon's side from behind, and come out the front.

All the way through.

I stop breathing.

"What the fuck?!" Dane shouts from Aiden's chair.

My legs wobble and shake, and the room spins.

"Rae!"

"Raegan!"

Dane jumps up and Kellan is suddenly behind me, his hands steadying my hips. Cibrina left as soon as the others disappeared, so it's only the three of us in Aiden's office.

I grab the desk, leaning on it for strength to keep myself upright and gasp for air. "Is...is he...?"

"Here. Sit down." Dane swings the chair to face me and Kellan guides me into it.

"Not yet, beautiful," Kell answers me. "What do you need?"

What do I need?

I...don't know. It doesn't feel real, seeing Gordon hurt. Can he recover from something like that? Is it over?

You thought he was dead last time, and he wasn't.

That's right.

"This is a gift from the president." Thorne's voice sounds through the speakers.

"What deranged bastard kills his own men?" Kellan growls.

It was a rhetorical question, but Dane replies anyway. "Clearly the sick fuck in charge of GE."

I keep watching the screen as everything plays out. Jackson fighting Thorne back. Aiden grabbing Gordon.

See? He's still alive.

"What did he say? Turn up the volume," Kellan barks suddenly.

Dane reaches over the laptop and taps a key several times. "There. It's all the way up."

"He's there...been there...with your Guild..."

Dane stiffens next to me.

"He's lying." Kellan snatches the phone on Aiden's desk and hits two keys. "Yeah, I want a full security update. I'll wait."

"You think he snuck in during the party?" Dane asks.

"No. This place is locked up tighter than a frog's ass hole. There's absolutely no way he could have gotten in." Kellan brings the phone back to his mouth. "Yeah? She did? Good. No, that's the order. Everything locked down, no one in or out. Call me if you see anything." A pause. "*Anything*. You see a speck on your screen where it shouldn't be, I want to know about it." He hangs up. "Cibrina already has the bunker entry points secured, and the guards all checked in again that nothing has happened."

Gordon's head drops, his body going limp.

I grip the armrests on the chair, my knuckles turning white as I stare breathlessly at the screen.

Did he...?

Is he...?

"Wait...didn't he say something about *been* here?" I hear Dane talking, but the words don't register as I'm consumed with the image of Gordon collapsed on the ground.

"The bunker is impenetrable. No one from outside got in," Kellan argues.

"That's not true, though, is it? We've let a lot of outside people into the bunker," Dane pushes. "All of the rescued gifted."

"And they're isolated on their own floor in a locked space."

"Then fucking humor me and call them."

The phone on the desk rings, making us all jump.

Kellan answers. "What do you mean, the door opened on its own? No, there are no ghosts—" He stops, teeth snapping together. "It was probably Harvey. Call Claudia and have her keep an eye on him until I get down there." He slams the phone into the cradle and slaps the laptop closed. I blink from my daze and look up. "I'm going to see what Harvey's up to, but in case it's nothing good, you aren't coming with me. Get to our room, put the steel wall down, and hide under the bed until I come for you. I'm not taking any chances." Kellan shoves the laptop at Dane. "And take this with you."

"Do you think the president is actually—"

Kellan cuts Dane off. "I think you both need to get your asses to that room." He helps me to my feet, then draws my face up to his with a pinch of my chin. "Can you do that for me, beautiful? I know you've got a lot going on right now, but I need to know you're safe. I'll come for you as soon as Harvey's dealt with and I've checked in with Cibrina."

I take a deep breath and exhale, pushing the stress and worry from my mind for later. I can't get lost in a sea of what-ifs when there might be danger here in the bunker. I need to be prepared to fight. To defend and protect the Guild for Aiden while he's not here. "I'm fine," I tell him, my voice coming out strong and clear. No more fear or hesitation. "I can help you if it comes to a fight."

He smirks and slides his hand to cradle the side of my face. "That's my girl. Protect Rapunzel for me until I'm back. He's still their target."

Dane scoffs behind me, muttering under his breath.

I turn to tease him, but Kellan yanks me in for a kiss and I forget all about what I was going to say. The kiss is rough and deep, his beard scratching my face and leaving burning in its wake. His hands pin my body to his, one holding my face and the other gripping my ass. I throw my arms around his neck, dragging him into me as much as possible.

It's feverish and raw with a hint of desperation. I don't like that it feels like a goodbye kiss. Like he wanted to taste me one last time before he steps onto a battlefield.

He moves to pull away, and my nails dig into his neck and shoulder. Kellan growls, biting my lip hard enough to draw blood and then sucking it clean as he sweeps in with another kiss. This time, he breaks away sharply with his hand on my throat.

"What the fuck was that?" I snarl at him and grab his arm. "I'm coming with you if you're going to kiss me like that!"

Kellan laughs, still holding me back as if he knows I'm ready to throw myself at him to keep us together. "I couldn't help myself. I always feel that way when we're about to part ways, beautiful."

I frown, unconvinced.

A hand finds mine, and I turn to Dane.

"He'll be fine. We should go." He squeezes my hand, and I nod.

A sinking feeling fills my gut.

Dane tugs on my hand, prodding me to move. I do as if on autopilot, moving at his behest as Kellan follows behind until we get to the elevator. Kell grins and waves us off, waiting for the doors to close. His face drops and his body turns just before the silver doors block him from sight.

My chest feels tight the moment he disappears.

"Dane..." I whisper.

His thumb strokes the back of my hand. "Yeah?"

"This doesn't feel right."

He looks just as conflicted, but I can tell he's trying to do the right thing. If GE is here, if they try to go after Dane, he'll be a distraction for the others too focused on protecting him than fighting. But I know he wants to fight, too. "Come here," he murmurs, setting the laptop down and drawing me against his chest. He wraps his arms around me, holding me close and resting his head on mine.

I breathe in his citrusy cologne, soaking in his warmth and comfort.

The elevator jerks, bounces, and stops.

The lights cut out.

Fuck a duck.

To Be Continued in Remnants

Raegan of Ruin Book 4

https://www.bklnk.com/B0DVTJDL17

Thank you for reading Ramshackle.
Please consider leaving your review.

BONUS SCENE
THE TOWER - AIDEN POV

Two years before the events of Ravage

"What are you doing?" I demand when the passenger door opens wide and Kellan somehow contorts himself to fit inside.

"Coming with you, of course." He slams the car door shut and lifts a full bottle of liquor to his lips.

He swallows several large gulps, and I press my lips into a tight line to keep from saying what immediately comes to mind. I can't help the feeling of guilt that burns in my chest, tightening my throat so I can't speak. Can't say the words I probably should to a friend—my chosen brother—who's struggling to move forward from our past.

It was for the best. I did what needed to be done.

It doesn't make the betrayal sting any less.

"You should stay here. Keep an eye on Dane."

Kellan gasps when he finally takes a breath, swiping his tattooed arm across his mouth before it widens to expose his teeth in a wild grin. "And who looks after you?"

"I don't need looking after. He's the one being targeted, not me."

"Well, he's busy reading through whatever documents that Thorne guy had on the Guild. If you think I'm going to babysit him reading boring shit when I know you're going out, then you've got a screw loose."

"I'm going to an important meeting. If you come with me, you don't say a word. Is that clear?"

Kellan chuckles. He offers me a salute with his glass bottle, then goes in for another drink like he's planning to finish it before we arrive.

I release a frustrated huff, doubting that's the last I'll hear from him but resigned to proceed before I'm late, and start the engine. The place we're meeting isn't far from the Tower, only a handful of blocks away, but showing up sweating and out of breath on this record-breaking day of heat is not the impression I'm going for.

I need to somehow convince a ruthless real-estate tycoon—who's only a few years old than me, I might add—to sell the Tower to me.

I don't need a landlord meddling in our business or having the potential to kick us out and leave us stranded at his whim. He's done similar things to other tenants he's had based on a brief internet search we did on him. It'll also be easier to make certain changes within the building for security and to adapt to the gifted living and working in it if I don't have to get permission every time.

After parking, I frown as Kellan rises from the car with me, tossing his empty bottle into the backseat.

"Not a word," I remind him.

He pulls his elbows back in a stretch, still grinning. "You don't trust me?"

"To keep your mouth shut?" I slam my door closed and he follows suit. "No. I don't."

Kellan laughs and joins me on the sidewalk. "Such a worrywart." His body sways with every movement.

Oh, yes. I'm certain we'll be making an impression today. Just not the right one. "Stay with the car, Kell. Keep *that* safe."

Kellan snorts and crosses his arms. "I've got *your* back, Aiden. Fuck the car."

Shaking my head, I walk to the entrance of the Hype bar and nightclub where I was directed by the secretary on the phone. It's midday, so the door is locked and everything from the outside is closed off. Even the windows are blacked out to prevent anyone from seeing inside. The neon sign looks pale and tacky in the harsh light of day while they're not on, revealing all the wiring underneath. And the black-painted brick exterior and matching door don't help with its less than inviting atmosphere.

I give the door three sharp knocks, then wait. Kellan's fist appears over my head, hammering the door when no one responds within the first few seconds.

"Kell."

He looks at me, confused. "What? No one was going to hear that."

The door swings open, and a large man with dark buzzed hair glares at us.

When there's almost an awkward silence while we wait for him to say something, I speak up, "Good afternoon. I'm Aiden, and this is Kellan. We have a meeting with Elias Thorton."

The guy grunts, stepping back and jerking his head for us to enter. I walk through first, relieved when Kell follows behind without a word. There's an annoyed look on his face as he stares at the guy like he's trying to incite something, but thankfully the guy ignores him and leads us through the nightclub to an office in a back hallway.

He knocks. There's a muted "Come in" and then our escort opens the door enough to poke his head through. "I've got your guests here. What do you want me to do with them?"

Kellan stiffens behind me, and I mentally will him to stay quiet.

Now that the door's cracked, I can hear the voice on the other side more clearly.

"Hm. They're late."

I check my phone for the time. One minute past the hour. That's hardly late.

"Thank you, Bryant. You can let them in."

Bryant opens the door and steps out of our way. Once we're inside, he closes the door behind us with a short *click*.

The office is smaller than I expected for someone with so much wealth and power. It's an ordinary bar office. Maybe twelve by fourteen feet with a simple wooden desk, bookcases and cabinets behind it, and two upholstered chairs facing it.

The man sitting there is young. He's in his mid-twenties according to articles online about him, so a handful of years over my twenty. He has dirty blond hair kept neat and a clean-shaven face. He's wearing a gray suit of a similar style to my black one, but of much higher quality. Maybe even silk with how it shines under the fluorescent lights.

He smiles politely at us. It's not a warm smile, but one I can still appreciate as a businessman who's taking time out of his busy schedule to meet with us. "Welcome. It's Mr. Adams, is that correct? Please, have a seat." He motions to the two chairs.

My jaw tightens at the fake last name that sounds so dumb with my first. "Thank you. And yes." I sit in the one that's almost directly across from him. "But you can call me Aiden. My...friend is Kellan."

Kellan plops into the open chair and lounges back, his arms dwarfing the back and sides of the chair as his legs spread out wide in front of him. "Woah. These are more comfortable than they look."

I should have kicked him to the curb. Taken off the second he'd opened the car door before he could get in.

Clearing my throat, I try pulling Elias's attention away from Kellan to the actual purpose of this meeting. "Thank you for agreeing to meet with me and on such short notice."

Elias's gaze is stuck on Kellan for a second longer before he finally directs it to me. He steeples his fingers on the desk and nods once. "Of course. I was concerned when I heard the news about Thorne. Any idea where he could have gone? Or why?"

"No," I lie smoothly, continuing the false story that Thorne passed the Guild on to me before leaving without notice. "I had a feeling he was planning something when he asked me to run the Guild for him, but I hadn't expected it to happen so soon or without saying anything."

Elias's eyes are hard as they fixate on me. "Yes. Very odd." He pauses momentarily, as if considering his next words, then continues, "Hopefully he's found or returns soon with an explanation. I may have someone who could help you to track him down, if you'd like."

I'd prepared for this line of questioning from the Tower's landlord with such a swift ownership change, but I hadn't expected the offer to help find him. "I appreciate your offer, but we've already been in contact with private investigators to see what they can find."

The man smiles, leaning back in his seat as the mood in the room seems to shift. As if he's no longer entertaining guests, but adversaries.

Fuck.

"Do you know Thorne well?"

"I can't say I do."

"Why did he choose you to be his successor? Why hand over something he'd built from scratch when it's doing as well as it is?"

"I can't speak to what was going on in his mind when he made that decision. Only speculate. Maybe he was overworked. Maybe he just wants a break to travel the world and do something new. Maybe he has family somewhere who needed him. As for why he chose me, I'm the most business-savvy of the Guild. I'll do my best to look after the Guild in his stead so it continues to grow and prosper."

"I see." Elias runs a finger over his lips as he watches me, clearly going over my answers in his head and looking for something.

"You got anything to drink?" Kellan drawls. He's grinning like he's up to no good while his fingers tap incessantly on the chair arm.

While I'm not thrilled by his antics, I'm also used to them and refuse to react or respond. It only eggs him on more when I do.

But his focus isn't on me.

It's on Elias.

"Of course," the businessman replies politely, still maintaining his calm disposition. He taps on his phone, then speaks, "Ethan. Three glasses of water, please."

"Right away, Boss."

"Forgive me if I sound blunt, but I'm sure you have a busy schedule. I'd like to buy the Tower from you. We could work out a lease to own or pay you upfront."

Elias raises a brow. "I'm not sure you could afford it."

"Let me worry about what I can or can't afford."

"And what do you intend to do with it?"

"I don't see why that would matter to you."

The door opens, and Elias's attention snaps to it like a magnet. He stands without warning and strides to the door, blocking whoever's there from sight.

"Who's in there?" a feminine voice asks. "Let. Me. See!"

Elias shifts himself to completely block us from her and her from us. "You're early today." It's spoken like a statement, but there's an implied question in his tone.

"Yeah, well..."

He pushes her into the hall and closes the door behind them.

Kellan jumps from his seat to the bookcase next to the door and starts moving things. Switching books out of order, turning knick-knacks backwards...

"What are you doing?" I demand softly.

"Checking something."

"Did you not hear what I'm asking him for?"

"Yeah?"

The sound of the doorknob turning has Kellan leaping back to his seat. Elias re-enters the room with a different guy behind him holding the three waters. He retrieves coasters from his drawer and sets them before each of us on his desk, and his worker places the glasses down, then leaves.

"My apologies for the interruption."

Kellan takes his glass and swallows half of it in a single gulp, then sets it down...*next* to the coaster.

For fuck's sake.

Elias sees it. Freezes.

I snatch Kell's glass and set it on the coaster. "I'm sorry about him.

He's still feral and it was my turn to babysit."

As if sensing my rising frustration with him, Kellan cups his hand around the water ring and swipes it to the edge. "There. I fixed it."

Elias blinks—as if coming back from some internal crisis—and locks his stare with mine. "Unfortunately, I'm not looking to sell that building at this time. Respectfully, I decline your request." He stands, and I mirror him, my body tensing as I run through possibilities where this meeting can somehow be saved. "If there's anything you need with regard to building maintenance, feel free to call me directly."

"But—"

He holds out his business card, then presses a button on his desk phone. "Bryant. Please escort our guests to the exit. Our meeting has concluded."

Bryant must have been waiting nearby, because the door opens within seconds while he waits for Kell and I to leave.

"If there's a number—" I try again, but he smiles that annoying, businessman smile while his blue-gray eyes flash with something sharper. He plays polite and kind, but there's something else lurking beneath that facade.

"Mr. Adams," he begins, emphasizing my name and causing me to stiffen involuntarily at being called that again, "Kellan. It truly has been a pleasure. Have a good rest of your day."

Bastard.

We leave, and I make a mental note that we need to learn everything we can about Elias Thorton.

Want to receive a bonus scene?

Or maybe stay up to date on the newest releases?

How about early access to ARC or giveaway opportunities?

Sign up for A. L. Rook's newsletter to stay in the know of all things Rook's books.

Scan or click the QR code below, or go to the website to sign up

@

www.alrookauthor.com

Join the A. L. Rook Reader Group on Facebook

The Rookery

@

www.facebook.com/groups/rookery

Or scan the QR code below

STALKING LINKS

amazon.com/stores/author/B0CYQJ2GWL

facebook.com/groups/rookery

instagram.com/alrookauthor

tiktok.com/@alrookauthor

WEBSITE: https://www.alrookauthor.com

NEWSLETTER: https://subscribepage.io/rooknewsletter

SPOTIFY: https://open.spotify.com/user/31g47djeh3oqclz7y
yaag2hwvtom?si=ca7e308dc7ec4b2c

FB PAGE: https://www.facebook.com/61557109453545/

About the Author

A.L. Rook is an avid reader and has been dreaming of becoming an author since the first grade. She's been thinking up and writing stories ever since. Her favorite stories are dark contemporary or fantasy romance with strong characters that leave a lasting impression. When not drinking exorbitant amounts of coffee while writing, she can be found reading, binge-watching various shows, or traveling.

If you want to stay up to date on release dates, news, or for a chance at extra teasers and giveaways, follow Rook on her socials and join her newsletter.